1 MONTH OF
FREE
READING

at

www.ForgottenBooks.com

By purchasing this book you are eligible for one month membership to ForgottenBooks.com, giving you unlimited access to our entire collection of over 1,000,000 titles via our web site and mobile apps.

To claim your free month visit:

www.forgottenbooks.com/free38121

ISBN 978-0-483-73396-1
PIBN 10038121

This book is a reproduction of an important historical work. Forgotten Books uses
state-of-the-art technology to digitally reconstruct the work, preserving the original format
whilst repairing imperfections present in the aged copy. In rare cases, an imperfection in
the original, such as a blemish or missing page, may be replicated in our edition. We do,
however, repair the vast majority of imperfections successfully; any imperfections that
remain are intentionally left to preserve the state of such historical works.

THE HEART OF LIFE

BY

W. H. MALLOCK

Author of "Is Life Worth Living?" "A Romance of the
Nineteenth Century," "The New
Republic," etc., etc.

G. P. PUTNAM'S SONS

NEW YORK   LONDON
27 WEST TWENTY-THIRD STREET   24 BEDFORD STREET, STRAND

The Knickerbocker Press

1895

The Knickerbocker Press, New Rocbelle, N. Y.

THE HEART OF LIFE.

CHAPTER I.

ENGLAND, in spite of railways, still has a few districts which remain, for various reasons, almost as remote and primitive as they were a hundred or even two hundred years ago. Of such survivals there is no more complete example than that afforded by a part of Devon and Somerset, which consists mainly of bleak and mountainous moorland, and confronts for some thirty miles the waters of the Bristol Channel. It is true that here and there amongst its un-visited valleys lonely populations hide themselves in villages with surrounding hedgerows; and in some of the valleys also, streams, brown with peat, slide and pour and foam through cloisters of sequestered woodland. But of spots like these a stranger sees nothing; and even here, in the green glades, or by the farm or by the village mill, there is a sense in the air of the open surrounding country—of rolling hills, bare to the wind and mist, where the tufted heather lifts itself, soli-tary as a wave at sea.

Geographically, however, civilization is not far off. On the western frontier of this region is the well-known water-ing-place, Lyncombe, its wooded crags and hillsides glitter-ing with hotels and lodging-houses; and on the eastern, a shed at the end of a straggling hamlet forms the terminus of a branch line of railway. But between these two points the progressive world of to-day shows its existence only in a modern road connecting them, and even this looks nearly as wild as the solitudes through which it passes. So at least it may well strike a stranger. The coast, from which it is rarely more than half a mile distant, is the loftiest in all

B

279222

Great Britain, reaching in many places a height of twelve hundred feet; and the timid traveller, as he is driven over these elevations, is apt to feel dizzy at the sight of the monstrous precipices to which he constantly fancies that his wheels will approach too near; whilst inland his eyes meet nothing but a world of gorse and heather, bounded only by clouds brooding on the distant tors.

Along this road, during the summer, daily once each way, a tawdry coach rattles, generally top-heavy with tourists; but these incongruous apparitions pass, leaving no trace behind them, except perhaps some fragments of drifting paper; and by the time the dust raised by their transit has subsided all that stirs in the landscape is the fleece of some moving sheep. A stranger, indeed, might look about him during the whole journey and detect no sign of human occupation anywhere except some stretches of dry stone wall, which at certain places appear, skirting the road, and accentuate rather than relieve the solitary aspect of the scene.

Nowhere do these walls produce this forlorn effect upon the mind more strongly than at a point about eight miles out from Lyncombe, where the road, after a long and rugged climb from the sea-level, reaches at last a high and windswept down, which is bare of everything but boulders and stunted grass. What could be the need of any enclosure here is a question that well might baffle the passing curiosity of the traveller; for the land on one side would hardly attract a donkey; and on the other, after fifty yards or so, it appears to tumble into the sea. But a still more perplexing feature is a gate in the seaward wall, carefully painted white, and giving access to a fragment of open road, which to all appearances leads only to the brink of an adjacent precipice. By this gate also, as if to enhance its mystery, a solitary figure used always to be seen standing every afternoon on which the coach passed from Lyncombe—the figure of a lad, roughly but not ill-dressed, who received daily a leather letter-bag from the driver, and disappeared with it over the brow of the cliff, as unaccountably as if he had been changed there into a sea-gull.

A stranger following him would eventually have encountered a sight almost as unexpected as he would have done had this miracle actually happened. For on gaining what, as viewed from the coach, appears to be a cliff's edge, he would have seen before him an amphitheatre of steep slopes, down which, by a feat of great engineering skill, the road was led in a long succession of zigzags till it reached in the depths below a belt of feathering pine woods. Descending it thus far he would have found what was invisible from above—a pair of gate-posts surmounted by moss-grown griffins, a lodge with latticed windows almost hidden amongst the branches, and an iron gate guarding the entrance to a gravelled drive. Resuming his course within, the intruder would have been surprised to perceive that his way, which now lay in a green and sheltering twilight, and was bordered by slanting carpets of moss and of ground-ivy, still continued to descend, zigzagging much as heretofore; and the sea as it shimmered in occasional vignettes through the trees, would have shown him that still it was hundreds of feet under him. At length, however, after he had walked for a good half-hour, certain signs would have assured him that he was nearing the end of his explorations. His eyes would have been caught by a glimpse of slate roofs; and, the road dividing itself in a thicket of rhododendrons, he would have seen that one branch of it led to some stable buildings, whilst the other would have brought him to an open balus-traded space, with the waves breaking a hundred feet below; and with a house on one side of it, whose stucco turrets and chimneys betrayed the Gothic taste which flourished at the beginning of the century. It was indeed like a Tudor man-sion, as the contemporaries of Beckford conceived of one, reduced in all its details to the scale of a good-sized villa.

The bad taste of a bygone period mellows with years, as associations lay their tints on it; and this sham Gothic architecture, in addition to its picturesque outlines, has for our generation the charm of an historic pathos; speaking as it does of an England which is now completely vanished, but which yet, through the pictures retained by us of the grandparents who were surviving in our childhood, almost seems to touch some nerve in our own memories—the unre-formed England of chariots and post-chaises, and the eyes, the necks, and the guitars painted by Sir Thomas Lawrence. And in the case of the present building, the effect of its own aspect was heightened by the beauty and the singular cha-racter of its situation, as it stood with its drawing-room windows opening on a terrace of garden, where two peacocks were accustomed to sun themselves on the stone parapet, and with the woods rising behind it till they seemed to meet the sky, except where some higher rock came peering over the pine-plumes like a cloud.

But up to a date that is still comparatively recent, the life that was lived in this retreat was more curious than the place itself. For inside the arched and nail-studded front door, and the fantastic multiplicity of windows, what survived till the year 188— was the end of the last century, rather than the beginning of this. No sooner was a visitor admitted to the entrance hall than the spirit of that period was puffed into his nostrils like a scent, breathing from beeswaxed floors, from china bowls and vases, from busts on marble tables, and from old Turkey carpets. The past is often associated with decay and dust; but it was not so here. Everything, on the contrary, was as fresh and sweet as lavender. The oak floors were like glass; the china shone with cleanliness; the flowered and faded chintzes were all newly calendered. Only the chairs and sofas were such as Miss Burney or the Miss Berrys might have sat upon; and of the books which filled, with their glimmer of gilt calf, the many shelves, or loaded the square whatnots, few were more modern than the earliest editions of "Childe Harold."

One broad impression this interior would have at once conveyed to a visitor—that the villa appertained to a family of which it was not the principal seat. In the drawing-room was a beautiful Sir Joshua, and there were two Opies in a breakfast parlour; and these, which were the only large portraits visible, had all the air of having a tribe of companions elsewhere. Again, there were certain articles of furniture, remarkable though not numerous, such as one or two large and fine pieces of buhl, and a rose-strewn Axminster carpet, faded and soft like moss, which seemed as if originally they had belonged to some statelier home. And that such was the case was rendered none the less probable by the different kind of evidence supplied by some smaller pictures—miniatures and oval pastels, which spoke of connections with an obsolete world of fashion; several of the former representing well-known beauties of the Regency, and two of the latter bearing, on their gilt frames, the information that they were gifts of the Prince Regent.

But between these mementoes of royalty hung something

yet more interesting—a pastel also—the portrait of a lady in
a turban, in the full regard of whose melting and melancholy
eyes all the romance floated that troubled the days of Byron.
Small as this picture was, it filled the air with sentiment,
like a faint perfume from some single living flower. There
were traces, too, on all sides, of devotion to art and literature. Art, indeed, was represented chiefly by such fragments
of the antique—bronzes and marble busts—as a hundred
years ago men of taste used to bring from Italy; but the
book-shelves, in addition to their fortuitous multitudes of
"Spectators" and "Elegant Extracts," "Tom Joneses" and
"British Theatres," contained a collection of volumes whose
character and whose sumptuous bindings suggested that they
had been got together by some one remarkable man—a
scholar, a dilettante, and a philosopher, as well as a lover of
luxury.

There were other things, however, fraught with very
different suggestions. Amongst the gilded leather bindings
which filled most of the shelves, and not far from the neighbourhood of a fine copy of the "Decameron," were several
rows of works by the Tractarian divines of Oxford—such as
Pusey, Keble, and Newman—in all the holy poverty of
their original cloth backs. On the walls, moreover, were
mezzotints of several of these divines themselves; and, as
if to explain their presence, some cases containing scissors
and knitting-needles — prim little dainty cases made of
shagreen and tortoise-shell—were carefully arranged, like
relics, on certain small mahogany tables; whilst displayed
symmetrically between two pairs of silver snuffers was a
book of family prayers, with a purple marker hanging from
it. Here were signs of the presence, and also of the will, of
some woman; and a certain formality in the neatness and
disposition of everything bespoke the presiding genius of
an old maid or a widow.

Both these sets of suggestions accorded with actual facts.
The villa, which was known by the romantic appellation of
Glenlynn, had, at the recent date to which reference has
been already made, been occupied for sixty years by a certain
old Miss Pole, who was then on the point of reaching her
hundredth birthday. The Poles had from early times been
a considerable landed family. Pole Park, which they had
enlarged in the reign of George II., enjoyed the reputation

of being the longest house in ——shire; and they had contributed to the world of fashion dandies, sportsmen, and
politicians, whose figures had been familiar at White's, at
Almack's, and at Newmarket. But these fashionable
successes were now things of the past; and the family had,
for more than fifty years, been almost unknown in London,
though it continued to flourish in the country. Such knowledge of it as remained in the mind of the world in general
was due to the fame of one of its bygone members—Tristram
Pole, the wit, the scholar, the exquisite; who was remembered less for the qualities which, when he was seven-and-
twenty, had made the Prince Regent call him the best
bred man in England, than for a tragic and unfortunate
love affair which brought his brilliant youth to a close,
which inspired a beautiful but unpublished poem of Byron's,
and left him to the day of his death a changed and a solitary
man.

He it was who, shutting up Pole Park, had built Glenlynn on a remote fragment of his property; and except for
occasional journeyings in Greece, Italy, and the East, he
had there spent in seclusion the latter part of his life.

On his death, at fifty, his estates passed to a brother, with
the exception of Glenlynn, which he left to his one unmarried
sister. This lady, who at the time was close on the age of
forty, though possessed of a fortune which had commanded
much male affection, had never been tempted to renounce
the single state. Delicate health in her girlhood, and a
religious turn of mind, had combined to keep her at home,
and to prevent her mixing in society. She had, indeed,
lived little out of her own country; but first at Pole Park,
and afterwards at a neighbouring dower-house, she had been
a far greater lady than she ever would have been in London.
She had been the Providence of the cottager, the patroness
of the rector, the confidante of deans and bishops. Her third
brother, who had inherited a good estate from an uncle, was
one of the archdeacons of the diocese, a man of great talents
and accomplishments—a horseman, a magistrate, an artist,
a fellow of All Souls, an incumbent of five livings, and a
believer in Apostolic Succession. Through constant association with this dignified churchman, Miss Pole had found
an opening for her benevolence and her talents for manage-
ment; and had early acquired a taste, which never afterwards

left her, for the respect, the deferent sympathy, and the
conversation of the superior clergy. When she removed
to Glenlynn, at the mature age which has been mentioned,
she not only continued, in that comparative isolation, to
organize the distribution of soup and blankets amongst the
poor, but devout and cultivated divines, whose manners had
been formed at Eton, were her frequent guests, with their
neckcloths and old-world faces, and read prayers for her,
and praised and appreciated her Madeira.

As years went on, however, these passed, with their
generation, and their place as High Churchmen was taken
by the sacerdotal revivalists of Oxford. In one respect, and
in one only, Miss Pole marched with the times; she sympathized with the Oxford Movement. She began to talk of
the Church, oftener than of the Church of England; she
admired Archbishop Laud; she read the "Lives of the
Saints"; she bought silk book-markers with brass crosses
at the end of them; and she opened her doors to a new circle
of clerics—eager and active men who rejoiced in being
described as priests. But except for this exhibition of
spiritual or intellectual progress, Miss Pole's ideas and habits
underwent hardly any change. To the day of her death her
views as to the constitution of Society, the humility incumbent on the poor, the importance of county families, the
ignoble nature of trade, and the wickedness of the French
Revolution, were the views of her class at the end of the
last century; whilst her establishment and the appointments
of her house were survivals of its domestic economy. On
the dining-room sideboard the knives were ranged in their
old knife-boxes, and the bright-patterned cups and saucers,
and sparkling Georgian silver, made her breakfast-table
look like an old picture by Gilray.

But Miss Pole's own personal breakfast-table, at the date
which now concerns us, had been for many years nowhere
but at her own bedside; and she had been visible to her
guests or dependants only at certain hours, when her housekeeper, or an old companion, herself verging on decrepitude,
introduced the visitor to an audience in an upstairs parlour.
On such occasions Miss Pole was invariably found sitting
bolt upright in a comfortless straight-backed chair, her face
framed in a cap, her hands covered by black silk mittens,
and her glass of midday port, and a volume of Keble's

sermons, usually standing on the heavy table close to her.
Her voice came like a tremulous echo from a cavern; but
her intelligence was as clear, and her questions were as
shrewd as ever. Each day's post brought her a large budget
of letters, some containing news, but most of them requests
for charity; and two hours daily were spent by her in
dictating answers to them, except when her doctor, the
primæval practitioner of Lyncombe, forbade her to exert
herself, and wrote her a new prescription.

But one August day, the tourists on the Lyncombe
coach, crossing the high downs with the heathery wind in
their faces, heard blown at intervals up from some unseen
valley, the sound of a tolling bell; and on inquiring of the
driver what this mystical sound was, they learnt, for the
first time, probably, that such a lady as Miss Pole had
existed, by receiving the news that she was dead.

CHAPTER II.

THE exterior of Glenlynn that day bore witness to what had
occurred within. All its windows were masses of down-
drawn blind, whose whiteness made the discoloured stucco
yellower. It was five in the afternoon. The sun was
glittering on the chimneys frilled with their toy battlements,
and was populating the pine-woods behind them with
shadows like inverted arrow-heads. A sent of mignonette
came faintly from the garden; but no sound was heard
except the occasional scream of a peacock; nor was there
any movement except the flash of its blue breast.

Suddenly this silence was broken by hoofs and wheels,
and there drove up to the Gothic front door a good-looking
waggonette and pair, having a large-bearded man in it. He
descended slowly, with the peculiar air of one who feels that
the smallest action is significant when he himself performs
it; and before ringing the bell he stood and contemplated
the house, like a statue of Dignity culminating in a bust of
Beneficence. A square of clerical collar which glimmered
in the shadow of his beard was hardly needed to proclaim
the fact that he was a clergyman. His wide-awake hat
itself was eloquent of Anglican orders, and his waistcoat

was a manifesto of his belief in their sacerdotal virtue; whilst a loose jacket, in place of the long conventional coat, quietly indicated a chastened amity with the world.

"Gibbs, my good man," he said, turning slowly to the coachman, "I fear it is all over." And he laid his hand on the iron knob of the bell-pull as if he were blessing the head of a little child.

Presently the door was opened by an old man in white stockings and faded green knee-breeches—a footman old enough to have been the father of many butlers. The visitor scrutinized him, and in a voice that was like a cathedral echo, he gave utterance to the one word "John!" It was a simple word in itself, but as uttered now, it vibrated with every meaning that was most proper to the occasion. It was inquiry, human sympathy, and religious consolation in one. The old man understood it, and looking gratefully at the speaker, he whispered, "She passed away, sir, at nine o'clock this morning." His withered lips twitched, and pressing his hand to his eyes, he shrank instinctively back into the shadow to hide himself.

Fortunately for him, however, this unconventional retreat was covered by the advent of an odd little squat woman, who at this moment came waddling out to the doorway. Her forehead was crossed by a thin black velvet band, and· her face flanked by bunches of corkscrew curls, like a couple of nosegays tied to a horse's blinkers. This was Miss Drake, the late Miss Pole's companion, who had driven with her, sat with her, read to her, and written her letters; had made tea for her guests at breakfast, and judiciously absented herself from dinner, with hardly the break of a week, for the past forty years.

"Oh, Mr. Godolphin, is that you?" she exclaimed, grief and asthma wheezing amongst her syllables. "We thought you were still in Scotland. Of course you have heard what's 'appened." She was by no means without aspirates, but when she was hurried or agitated she would drop one, now and then, much as she might have dropped her pocket-handkerchief.

"I have heard," Mr. Godolphin answered. His manner was as kind to her as it had been to the old footman; but it was more majestic, as to one who could appreciate majesty; and her left shoulder coming within easy reach of him, he laid his hand on it in a way which made him appear to be wrapping comfort round her, like one of his own great coats. "We must remember," he said, "that our sorrow is only for ourselves, not her. Blessed are the dead that die in the Lord, for they rest from their labours, and their works do follow them."

Mr. Godolphin's voice, which had as many tones in it as an harmonium, seemed to have concentrated into these last words an entire religious service. Then for a moment he was silent; but when he began to speak again, his manner, though still solemn, underwent the same change that it did every Sunday when he emerged from his own church door and exchanged with his parishioners in the churchyard observations about the crops and weather. Having paid a due tribute to the profundity of Miss Drake's grief, he sought to lessen its strain by asking her as to the details connected with it.

In simple cases he was an excellent spiritual doctor; and by putting these questions he produced the relief desired. Miss Drake at once became more or less mistress of herself, and in another moment she was not only coherent but voluble.

"Her end," she cried, "was like a child falling asleep; and Dr. Clitheroe gave her the 'oly sacrament. Canon Bulman, as you of course know, has been called away for a week, and only came back this morning; but we've had the Doctor with us, it must be now for a fortnight; and he's been so good and tender, and prayed by Miss Pole's bedside, and helped her about her business—her earthly business as well as her 'eavenly, as if he'd been born a lawyer. Mrs. William Pole—she's here too, and has been this last month; and her son, Mr. Reginald—you can't have seen him for years—he's been telegraphed for. He was coming back to England anyhow from Berlin, or Russia, or Lisbon—I'm sure I forget which; and dear Miss Pole thought she would like to see him. Telegrams were sent to him at I don't know how many places, so as to catch him on his way; but only the last reached him, and now he'll arrive too late. We expect him to-night. We hoped he'd have been here this morning. But, Mr. Godolphin," said Miss Drake, suddenly wiping her eyes with a wrinkled finger which had three mourning rings on it, "won't you step in and take just a cup of tea? Mrs. Pole is busy; and as for me—I'm so 'elpless, I feel all in a dream. I feel, I assure you, as if I were dead, not Miss Pole. But the Doctor, I'm certain would be very glad to speak to you. I saw him a minute ago pass out into the garden."

"Let me," said Mr. Godolphin, with an obeisance, "go into the garden and find him. I won't detain you. God bless you, Miss Drake, and good-bye. To-morrow I will send over and inquire if I can be of any assistance. My house, my carriage, my horses, are all at Mrs. Pole's disposal." And he waved an apostolic hand in the direction of his prosperous equipage.

The Rev. Sunderland Godolphin was a man happy in the double consciousness of valid priestly orders and three thousand a year. His comparative wealth, however, produced no vulgar pride in him. It was for him merely a sort of mental magnifying glass, through which he saw the sanctity of his own sacerdotal office. He was, and had been, for some twelve years, incumbent of a moorland parish, the living of which was in Miss Pole's gift, and in which his generosity had been new every morning. Having long since rebuilt both the church and schools, he was at last treating himself to a billiard-room for the benefit of his boy who was at Harrow. Whilst this was in progress, he had indulged in a two months' holiday, and his duties meanwhile had been taken by Canon Bulman, whom Miss Pole, for that period, had accommodated at Glenlynn as her guest.

Mr. Godolphin's inner being, when he turned from the front door, was full of a melancholy, yet not unhappy, activity. He heard his own voice reading Miss Pole's funeral service; he saw himself bareheaded, advancing to meet her coffin; and he felt that one among the many fitnesses of her death would be his own resonant accents consigning her to her final rest. His broad chest was expanding and straining his waistcoat buttons, and tears were preparing to mount to his handsome eyes, as he passed through the gate into the small Italian garden, whose carpet of bright flowers glittered before the blinded windows.

His solitary emotions, however, had not time to complete themselves, for he saw at once, in a corner of this enclosure, something black and motionless, which he recognized as Dr. Clitheroe. The Doctor was short, and had just a hint

of portliness.   Mr. Godolphin's waistcoat was expanded
across the chest; the Doctor's emulated it, but a little lower
down.   He wore a long full-skirted coat, and a tall silk hat,
which was badly brushed, and very broad in the brim; and
his general appearance suggested that a mere touch would
transform him into a dean.   He was hardly more than fifty;
there was a quiet alertness in his eyes; and his lips were
elongated into a placid and kindly smile, which lost itself
in cheeks slightly pitted with the small-pox.   In his own
way the Doctor was an eminent man.   He was not beneficed,
but he held an important post under Government, and had
now been deputed to visit various parts of the country, in
order to draw up reports for a Royal Commission on
Education.

"Ah, Doctor!" exclaimed Mr. Godolphin, his voice
running before him, like a courier dressed in mourning.

The little Doctor turned himself round promptly; with
short steps he trotted to meet the visitor, and the two were
presently walking side by side.   A series of remarks were
naturally exchanged between them, respecting the excellence
of the deceased, and her painless and hopeful death.   Dr.
Clitheroe's gentle accents were peculiarly suited to the
theme.   At last, however, with an access of finished briskness, he turned from the death itself to certain matters
connected with it.

"Of course," he said, "you know that for her life Mrs.
William Pole has everything; and that after her death it
goes to Mr. Reginald Pole, her son.   About this, I suppose,
there never was any secret.   His father, I have understood,
was Miss Pole's favourite nephew; and as for the son, Miss
Pole, on the father's death, paid for him at Eton and Oxford,
and made him an allowance since, which his mother will
of course continue.   As for himself——"   The Doctor
smiled and paused.   "Perhaps," he said, "I ought not to
talk of these private matters.   By the way, I suppose they
have told you of Miss Pole's wishes about the funeral.   She
especially desired to be buried in the church at Earlsbury,
in the same vault as Mr. Tristram Pole, her brother."

To Mr. Godolphin this news was a thunderbolt out of a
clear sky.   It made him feel as if Miss Pole had unexpectedly
died again.   For Earlsbury was not his parish; and to add
to this defect in it, its church had never been restored in

accordance with modern ideas; its old clergyman was in a condition analogous to that of his church; and it seemed to Mr. Godolphin that the solemn rites he had been contemplating were suddenly emptied of their choicest and their most comforting elements. Dr. Clitheroe, however, was altogether unconscious of the dreadful desolation he had spread over his companion's mind, and continued talking in the same meditative voice.

"I can't imagine," he said, "what they will do here for accommodation; so many relations most likely will want to attend the funeral."

"My dear Doctor," said Mr. Godolphin, rousing himself, "you and Canon Bulman must come and stay with me. I will send my carriage for you at any moment that suits you. I could take you now, if you like."

"I," the Doctor answered, "am going to the home farm. I sent there this morning, and found I could have a bedroom. I know, however, the Canon intended to ask you for hospitality; but he wishes to remain here for a couple of nights, if possible, so as to see Mr. Reginald Pole, to whom he was once tutor. Look—here the Canon is."

A dark figure, pushing aside a blind, had at this moment emerged from one of the drawing-room windows, and with a rapid directness advanced towards Mr. Godolphin, greeting him from a distance with a smile full of gleaming teeth. Canon Bulman had all the air of a sanguine and strenuous traveller on the road of duty, of hard work, and of preferment. His complexion was fresh; his clothes were of the finest cloth. From his watch-chain there dangled a heavy, though plain, gold cross, a miniature compass, and a pencil-case in the shape of a cricket-bat. He carried his chin high. His large broad lips had, in repose, the appearance of being clenched like a fist, and there was on his face a certain expression of belligerence, like that of a man playing football against the devil. He grasped Mr. Godolphin's hand with a dry, business-like vigour, and the three clergymen began slowly to pace one of the walks together.

"I was sorry, Godolphin," said the Canon, when he had first honoured the occasion by referring to Miss Pole's death in a voice of prosperous sorrow, "I was sorry that I was called away; but I suppose you know the reason. I was called to speak, indeed, take the chair, at two meetings,

convened for the purpose of declaring, at this momentous
crisis, that private purity on the part of public men is, to the
nation, even more important than their politics."

It had lately happened that the leader of a powerful
Parliamentary party had increased his fame by appearing as
co-respondent in a divorce case; and Canon Bulman, who
previously had been one of his chief admirers, was the first
clergyman belonging to the Established Church to demand
that the bestial sensualist—the infamous domestic traitor—
should resign his seat, and be hounded from public life.
Chastity, in fact, was the Canon's favourite virtue; so much
so, that many who respected him for his earnest efforts to
promote it, almost felt that he accorded it an invidious
preference over the others, especially when he ventured to
declare in a well-known pulpit at Oxford that the story of
the woman taken in adultery was spurious, on the ground
that it conflicted with the entire spirit of Christianity.

The two other clergymen, as any observer might have
perceived, were considerably milder in disposition. Indeed,
a shadow of pain passed over Mr. Godolphin's face. He said,
however, taking the Canon's arm—

"I know that the cause of right has no more ardent
soldier than yourself."

"Lord Shropshire and Lord Wakefield," continued the
Canon, "both spoke at my meetings, and admirably, too—
quite admirably. Wakefield was staying with me—one of
the finest fellows I know. By the way, since we happen to
be talking of other things, I confess I can't help regretting
that she, who has just left us, did not desire some other
place of burial."

Mr. Godolphin was delighted at the conversation taking
this turn, and hastened to echo a sentiment with which he
so deeply sympathized.

"I confess," he said, "I regret it, too."

"It seems," the Canon resumed, with dry and trenchant
emphasis, "regrettable that one whose life was so eminently
Christian, should weaken the force of her example by thus
wishing to rejoin a man who caused, in his own day, the
same kind of hateful scandal as that which is shocking the
public conscience now."

This was a very different utterance from what Mr.
Godolphin had expected, and neither he nor Dr. Clitheroe

knew how to receive it. They were, therefore, both of them not a little delighted at a sudden interruption supplied by a startling sound. It was the sound of a steam whistle; and, so far as their ears could inform them, it rose from the waters directly beneath the garden. The three clergymen made their movements accordingly; and before long, when they had reached a lower level, they distinguished against the waves some films of ascending smoke. Canon Bulman, who was a renowned Alpine climber, raised himself on a spike of rock, and looked curiously over.

"A launch!" he exclaimed; "a beautiful little private launch! There is nobody in it except the engineer and a sailor."

"I hope," said Dr. Clitheroe, "that on a day like this the place will not be flooded by any intruding strangers."

They had reached, as he spoke, a spot where the path divided, one limb of it, like a gutter, scrambling down to the sea, the other leading up again in the direction of the house and garden. Here Canon Bulman suddenly started forward. He stooped to the ground and raised from it some light, pale-coloured object. It was a woman's grey glove, delicate and slightly scented.

"It seems," he said, holding it out to his companions, "that strangers of some sort must be in the grounds already, though not — I should judge from this — a party of rough excursionists. Hush—listen! People are there above us." To confirm his observation, a few loosened pebbles, just as his voice ceased, rattled down the upward path, and a second later the nervous form of a woman appeared round a corner, descending on a pair of rickety boots. The woman's dress was black, and *piquante* with French neatness; but her face, though not unpleasant, was very far from distinguished, and a metallic exclamation of "*Oh, mon Dieu!*" occasioned by a sight of the clergymen, and by a simultaneous slip of her heels, would to any experienced ears have explained her as a Parisian maid. Canon Bulman, however, being no discerner of persons—or, to speak more charitably—no respecter of them, with much *empressement* offered her a hand to assist her, and tendering the glove to her, said, "I think this must be yours." But before the young woman was able to return a suitable answer, another presence had come into sight behind her—a woman also, but one of a very different aspect.

About her, too, was a something suggestive of France, not England—a certain simple yet fastidious neatness of dress, which in the present scene looked exotic; but her movements and the poise of her figure di﹒ red from those of the other as the figure of one of Watteau's shepherdesses might differ from a Dutch doll. She was evidently quite young, but too self-possessed to be girlish. Her mouth carried in its curves a certain imperious sadness, and the lights in her eyes were like jewels on dim velvet. Canon Bulman gazed hard at her, wondering why he did so. He noticed a pearl at her throat, and one in each ear also. He raised his wide-awake hat, gripping it by the limp crown.

"Could you," she said, in a voice that was at once soft and crisp, "tell me the way to the house? Ah! my glove. How good of you! I knew I had dropped it." And she took it from him with a hand dainty as Dresden china.

"Do you want to go to Glenlynn?" asked the Canon, with grave deference.

"Yes," she answered, "to inquire after Miss Pole. We heard she was ill. I have come by sea from Lyncombe."

"She died this morning," said the Canon, simply. "If you went to the house, I fear you would see no one. Mrs. Pole is very busy. Would you allow me to leave a message for you?"

"Will you? I should be indeed obliged to you. I have a letter for Mrs. Pole." And she drew, from the pocket of her jacket, an envelope, which she gave the Canon. "I am sorry," she went on, "to hear what you tell me; though I myself never knew Miss Pole, nor saw her."

The Canon cleared his throat. "I," he said, "am only an accidental guest here; but I am sure I shall be doing right if I ask you to have some tea."

"You are too kind," she replied, drawing on her glove as she spoke. "But I could not have waited in any case. It is late. I am much obliged to you. Mrs. Pole will know from the letter who I am. Clarisse—come; we must go back to the boat."

"Allow me," said the Canon, "to assist you down this terribly steep path."

The young lady declined the offer with the prettiest grace imaginable; but the Canon's chivalry was much too vigorous to be repulsed; and a moment later he was disappearing between some rocks and rosemary-bushes, with the hand of the fair stranger supporting itself on his broad shoulder.

"He's a good man," sighed Mr. Godolphin, looking after him; "but not always discreet."

Dr. Clitheroe smiled, as though conscious of a little worldly knowledge. "It's a pity," he said, "that the Canon, who is so alive to a certain kind of evil, should not always detect it, when it is present in his own household. I was told at Windsor, that one of his parlour-maids—a pretty girl of the name of Sophie—is the scandal of the place, owing to the way in which she conducts herself; and that the Canon, when the truth has been represented to him, indignantly refuses to believe it. Men of his eager temperament are frequently taken in by women."

A minute or two later the Canon was visible re-ascending, wearing on his face a consciousness of successful gallantry, and yet, together with this, the irritation of some puzzled thought. "That's curious," he said, "most curious! I mean that young woman's face. It's quite familiar to me. Where —now where can I have seen it? It's not a pleasant face. No, no, no—not pleasant."

"The Pole connection," said Mr. Godolphin, magnificently, "is immense, as you, Canon, who live so much in the world, know. In all probability you will hear she is some relation; and you may perhaps have met her yourself at a State Concert. Did you ever, by the way, see Mr. Pole, the head of the family? The last of the squires they call him. He is sure to attend the funeral. And the Duke"—Mr. Godolphin had much simple reverence for high rank, and he pronounced the name of the Lord Lieutenant of the county as if the mere utterance of it was an honour to himself— "the Duke, who is a relation also, and full of all right feeling, will be present most likely—indeed, I should say, certainly. It will be an impressive gathering, if only the service itself could be performed with more seemliness."

The Canon, whose devotion to democratic principles, was only equalled by his taste for aristocratic persons, listened to this information with much smiling attention; but unfortunately the concluding words touched a different part of him.

"You remind me," he said, "of what I remarked just now. The larger this gathering is to be, the more sincerely

I deplore the fact that Miss Pole should have elected to be buried by the side of her adulterous brother. Had I," continued the Canon, "known that such was her wish, I would have frankly told her what I feel about it. I was, in fact, just before my departure, on the point of remonstrating with her on a very similar subject. You both, perhaps, can guess what I refer to."

Mr. Godolphin shook his head. "I refer," the Canon continued, " to something you must be well acquainted with —the picture of a woman which hangs here in the first drawing-room. I have often looked at it for a quarter of an hour together, disagreeably impressed by it; but it was only last week that, by accident, I learnt whom it represented— the shameless partner of the sin of Miss Pole's own brother. My dear Godolphin, I don't blame Miss Pole herself; but I do blame her family for not having long ago urged her to destroy, or at all events to hide this object; and I shall certainly, at some fitting season, mention it to my old friend Reginald."

"We must all honour you," said Mr. Godolphin, "for the feelings by which you are actuated. But tell me," he went on, eagerly changing the subject, " how is Reginald ? Do you ever come across him now ? I call him by his Christian name, but it is years since I set eyes on him."

"Ah," exclaimed Canon Bulman, "one of a thousand—he is." And his manner as he spoke altered and became fresh and breezy with good fellowship. "I too have not seen him for years—except at a levée, in the distance, and once at the late Prime Minister's. But such a good fellow he was—such a scholar too—so easy to teach and guide ! I sometimes used to fancy he was a little led away by all that nonsense about birth and family, and so forth ; and like many of these young aristocrats he was too apt to think that Society was the world, and that the world was a playground for himself. But all that, I fancy, has now passed away. I always say that it was I who formed his mind ; and that my teaching it was, which, in due time, brought forth fruit. When he went abroad first to stay with his cousin the ambassador, he thought only of amusement—innocent amusement, I grant you ; and, as I often dinned into him, he was apt to be shamefully extravagant. But sound teaching tells ; and he hadn't been in Berlin six months, before he had taken to

tudying the industrial conditions of Germany, and was
ade secretary to our Royal Commission. I gather, too,
hat this fault of his, extravagance, has now quite dis-
ppeared ; and that he lives with extreme frugality. Well,"
ontinued the Canon, " to have been living at all these
apitals, and have been received as he has been in all the
est society—it would have been a dangerous life for some—
ery, very dangerous. But as for him, he morally is one of
he cleanest men I know."

These last words were ominous of a return to his favourite
opic ; but Mr. Godolphin interrupted, by exclaiming, " Ha !
here are my horses—look at them—impatient to be off.
henever you can come to me, Canon, remember, there is
our bedroom waiting for you."

They were by this time approaching the front door of the
ouse. Mr. Godolphin turned to his friends, and solemnly
aid good-bye to them, drawing himself up to his full priestly
ltitude ; and mounting his waggonette, which seemed to
ecome full of him, he vanished to the rapid music of hoofs
nd of crunching gravel.

CHAPTER III.

EGINALD POLE, whose arrival was that evening expected,
d whose character had been described with so much appre-
ation by his tutor, was the son of a promising diplomat,
ho, early in his career, had married a distant cousin, and
ad died in Paris about twelve years afterwards. It proved
hat his affairs were left by him in extreme disorder ; and
he mother and her boy would have been in a position of
onsiderable embarrassment if it had not been for the kind-
ess of a certain celebrated Mrs. Steinberg, the wife of a
orgeous banker, who was flourishing under the then
mperor. This lady, true to a constantly expressed friend-
hip, at once offered the two a home for as long as they
equired one, under the painted ceilings and amongst the
rnate candelabra of her hotel ; and with her they remained,
ntil, through Miss Pole's aid, the various debts left by Mr.
illiam Pole were settled. In due time Miss Pole made
nown those intentions, with regard to her great-nephew

and his mother, which were embodied in her will and testament; and he, as Dr. Clitheroe had said, was educated and subsequently maintained by her.

Miss Pole, though an admirer and practiser of all the virtues as she understood them, did not, so far as young men of position were concerned, include amongst the virtues any definite work. Diplomacy, indeed, and the army, she regarded as channels of temptation; and was inclined to desire for her heir, when he left Oxford, a safe career of leisure, which should end in his being a county member. Little as Miss Pole had lived in the world herself, she had always been accustomed to take the great world solemnly; and she reverenced a duke almost as much as if he were a church. It seemed, therefore, to her that one of her heir's most important duties was thoroughly to familiarize himself with that distinguished society which, next to the Church, was a gentleman's most unerring teacher, and with which God had been pleased to connect him by so many ties. He himself, who was full of social aptitudes, and even more social fastidiousness than he had cared to reveal to Canon Bulman, was not slow to fall in with his great-aunt's views. Such fashionable relations as the Pole family possessed—men and women alike—combined to render his entrance into the society of London easy, and the continuance of this conduct was, in the case of many of them, a personal compliment of which at first he had no suspicion; being really an evidence less of their own affection for him, than of the credit done by him to the family by his various social talents, which did indeed resemble those ascribed to his renowned great-uncle. On the other hand, much of the welcome which he received from fashionable mothers and their daughters, and which was in reality due to an exaggerated rumour as to his prospects, he was at first simple enough to attribute to a judicious appreciation of himself. Thus his self-esteem was maintained despite his modesty, till in due time he came to understand men and women better, and it was placed on a new basis, which he told himself was knowledge of the world. Meanwhile, however, in addition to the pursuit of fashion, he gave his attention to things of a more serious nature. He made the acquaintance of certain celebrated men of science, who cashed their drafts on fame occasionally at polite dinnertables; and he read their books and discussed theology with

them in their laboratories, with results which would have
horrified the eclectic freethonght of Canon Bulman.   He
also turned his attention, as Miss Pole had hoped, to politics;
and indeed became gradually intimate with several well-
known statesmen.

He was, however, possessed by the opinion, in which his
intercourse with these veterans confirmed him, whilst convincing him of its singularity, that accurate knowledge of
the life and conditions of nations, the habits of various races,
and the details of trade and industry, were almost as necessary to make a member of parliament useful, as experience
of the House itself, or a fluency on public platforms.   Influenced therefore by this opinion partly, and partly by an
unwillingness to sacrifice the delights of freedom, he determined to postpone any effort to thrust himself into public
life, until he should have mastered one set of subjects at all
events, in a way which should enable him to treat it with
some authority.   At that time a certain extreme party had
begun to proclaim a number of startling doctrines with
regard to the poverty and misery of the masses of the
British nation, and to demand, on behalf of the poor, who
were described as having been wronged for centuries, reforms
of the most violent and the most impossible kind.   Whilst
the majority of practical politicians treated their demands
with a smile, the question of fact suggested by them, seized
on young Pole's imagination; and he set himself with per-
severance, though without exaggerated avidity, to study the
condition of the masses as it actually was then, and also
as it had been during the past century.   It is true that he
attempted no personal investigations himself; but he collected with remarkable judgment the most instructive records
that were available; and after several years had elapsed,
he was at last beginning to think that the time was come
when he might gratify his aunt's wishes, and represent the
Pole family in Parliament, even if he represented nothing
else.   He found, however, that to wait for a seat was a
very different thing from obtaining one.   Amongst seats
which were safe for a Conservative, or even hopeful, there
were, during eighteen months only five vacancies; and for
these there were other claimants whose claims stood higher
than his own.   Disappointed at this, though not ungene-
rously embittered, he began to think of dismissing his

Parliamentary ambition from his mind; whilst a sense of
public duty, which had been growing in him with the progress of his studies, urged him, on the other hand, not to
shirk his responsibilities.   In this condition his doubts
were unexpectedly solved by a severe illness, which completely undermined his strength, and forced him for many
years to spend much of his time abroad.

    Amongst other things which reconciled him to this fate,
was the fact of an unfortunate connection which he had
formed with a well-known demi-mondaine, or rather which
she—a woman of considerable talents—had contrived to
form with him. It was a connection which soon not only
wearied but humiliated him; and he welcomed the circumstances which brought it rapidly to an end. He took with
him on his travels a portion of his political library, and still
from time to time he continued his former studies; but new
countries, new societies, the passing excitement of one or
two slight romances, and the spectacle of a new religion,
filled his mind with other thoughts and interests. In Italy
he became acquainted with many distinguished ecclesiastics;
he made a long retreat in a celebrated Benedictine monastery;
and his natural revulsion from an amatory episode unworthy
of him, called to life in his mind that passionate sense of
contrition to which all that is deepest in the Catholic Church
appeals. He was far, indeed, from becoming a convert to
the Catholic faith; and, to say the truth, his contrition did
not altogether preserve him from a kind of conduct which
again called for its exercise; but on this occasion his heroine
was a complete woman of the world, who first engaged and
then betrayed his affections, and left him with a wounded
heart, as well as a dejected conscience. Some men by
experiences such as these become hardened or enslaved in
vice; others only learn by them to see it in a clearer light,
and to return with a manlier understanding to the rules of
life which they had violated. Pole was a man who belonged
to this latter class, partly owing to a well-balanced mind and
temperament, but still more to the fact that he had in him,
beneath his passions, a capacity and a need for the affection
which passion so often injures. At all events, the next time
that the personality of a woman appealed to him, which was
not till some years later, the appeal was of a different kind.
He had been staying at Berlin, on a visit to the British

ambassador, who was related to him; and it so happened that just about that time the British Government had undertaken to institute a Royal Commission, to inquire into the working of trades unions and the condition of labour on the Continent. At this, his old interest in these subjects revived; and his strength by that time being very nearly restored, he accompanied one of the English officials on several tours of investigation. On one of these occasions, a slight attack of illness detained him for several days in a little German watering-place; and here, at a table-d'hôte, he accidentally made the acquaintance of a young Englishwoman and a child, who were lodging in a house close by. The mother—or rather, as he presently learnt, the stepmother—attracted him, not only by her grace and her gentle beauty, but also by her forlorn condition, of which he gradually gathered the details. The head of her husband's family was a certain Welsh baronet, who enjoyed an obscure celebrity as the owner of a curious castle. The husband himself, it appeared, was devoted to cards and racing. It was not quite clear to Pole whether he was a jockey or a book-maker. It was evident, however, that he was a great student of economy, for, having heard that this town was the cheapest place in Europe, he had chosen it a month ago as a home for his wife and daughter, till the death of a decrepit relation should enable him, without extravagance, to be as liberal to them as he was to himself.

All this Pole gathered in an indirect way. The wife, he discovered, was also related to a family that was known to him; and this fact, which touched her almost to tears in her loneliness, made her the readier to confide in an unlooked-for friend. A day or two after his first meeting her, his friendly interest in herself was forgotten in concern for her situation The rent of the apartment she occupied, it appeared, was to be paid monthly, and it now was due, together with a fortnight's bills; but a remittance from her husband, promised her a week back, had not arrived, though she had telegraphed several times for it, and the landlord of her house had already taken to threats which alarmed her all the more because she hardly grasped their meaning. Pole was enabled to discover her sad story only because, on coming one day to call on her, he found her crying into her hands, with her head resting on the table. It was only little by little that he learnt the nature of her embarrassment; and the tears, when he knew the whole, were not in her eyes but his. In another moment, however, he made light of the whole matter, and offered to lend her whatever she might require for the moment.

"On second thoughts," he said, "I will pay it in to your bankers; and when your money comes you can send me a cheque to Berlin."

She was overwhelmed with shyness and gratitude, and, without more words, he left her, naming the sum which she would presently find at her disposal. He had not at the moment more than half that sum in his possession; he did, however, possess a favourite watch, which, not without a pang, he disposed of at half its value. But even this was considerable. He thought of his own expenses in the immediate future; he resolved to reduce these to the smallest amount possible; and then, retaining only what he judged would be thus necessary for him, he placed the entire remainder to his friend's credit at her bankers'. It was a sum which would suffice not only to pay her landlord, but to support her for another month should her remittances be delayed further.

In common with most people, Pole often had heard of want, but he had never before had so vivid an example of it close to him. On returning to Berlin he wrote to the authorities at home, offering, without salary, to take part in the work of the commission. His offer was accepted, his talents being not unknown, and by-and-by he was accorded both a salary and the post of secretary. It was observed by his friends that, either as a cause or a consequence of his work, he rapidly grew in many ways a more serious man than formerly; and that though his income was for the time slightly increased, he emulated in his own life the poverty which he was engaged in studying. He was never, indeed, ill-dressed, nor did he affect ostentatious economies; but it could not escape the notice of those who had known him formerly, that in matters of personal self-indulgence he acted like a poor man.

This self-denial was in part, though not wholly, due to the continued embarrassment of the lady whom he had already assisted. His headquarters for a time were in the little town of her exile; and he often contrived, without her entertaining a suspicion of it, to supplement, through her bankers' agency, the irregular remittances of her husband. The rest of his savings, as time went on, he set aside also for a similarly unselfish purpose. His official work, which enlarged itself far beyond its intended limits, afforded him occupation which lasted for several years; and most of each year he spent accordingly on the Continent.

His work of inquiry was now at last complete, and even had he not had news of Miss Pole's illness, he would, for other reasons, have been returning then to England. The friend whose interests he had taken so much to heart, and for whose sake he had made so many concealed sacrifices, had some months previously been liberated from her German prison. Her husband's pious hopes for the speedy release of his relations had been accomplished by Providence on a more liberal scale than he had anticipated; and he found himself not only in possession of enough ready money to turn his head, and to appease his most pressing creditors, but also of a baronetcy, of a castle, and of a property with appropriate mortgages. Under these circumstances his wife had, in his eyes, acquired a utility which he never expected to find in her; and as a preliminary to settling her as his ornamental housekeeper in the country, he begged her, with a view to producing between him and her enough good humour and amity for the purpose of married comfort, to join him on a tour which he meant to make in America, and which he intended should unite the excitements both of pleasure and of business.

After much hesitation his wife had accepted the proposal, and during her travels Pole had had no news of her. He was accordingly delighted to receive from her, just as he was starting for England, a letter which told him that she had returned, and was staying for a week in London. Most of that week was gone before her letter reached him, but he arrived in London in time to see her for half an hour, though not, indeed, under circumstances that were very favourable to conversation. A note from her was awaiting him at his club, telling him that she must start for Wales by a train which left Paddington in the middle of the afternoon; and she begged him to meet her at the railway-station half an hour before. Together with this letter was a telegram from Glenlynn, urging him to come with whatever speed he could;

and as the station for both their trains was the same, the
appointment she suggested was thus easily kept. She was
waiting for him at the door of the booking-office; and, leaving
his luggage with his servant, he slowly strolled with her up
and down an empty end of the platform, asking her hesitating questions about her welfare and her immediate prospects.
Pole's manner was naturally not demonstrative; and as for
her, the various replies she made to him were almost as shy
as they might have been had he been a new and unsym-
pathetic acquaintance. At last, however, when he stood by
her carriage door, and took her hand, just as the train was
moving, her eyes suddenly filled, and looked at his dim with
gratitude; and she said in trembling accents, " I can never
repay your kindness—all that you have done for me—or
forget it."

" Write to me ! " he replied.

"Yes," she said—"yes. Of course I will. But wait till
I write to you."

The carriage was already moving. She kissed her hand
to him, and she was gone.

His own train started a quarter of an hour afterwards,
and, lost in many meditations, he was hardly conscious of
the journey, as he was hurried westwards to the house which
was thenceforward to be his home.

CHAPTER IV.

MEANWHILE at Glenlynn, the two clerical visitors, having
bidden Mr. Godolphin adieu, betook themselves to their
respective chambers, where the one copied out a report on
workhouse schools with a type-writer, and the other wrote
a dozen letters in connection with a forthcoming meeting.
Miss Drake was secluded in her own chamber likewise, idle
with bewildered sorrow; and though a message was sent to
her by Mrs. Pole begging her to be present at dinner, she
clung to the custom, invariable during Miss Pole's lifetime,
of having her evening meal alone in her own parlour, where
a chop and a poached egg proclaimed her loss anew to her,
by making her feel how unable she was to swallow them.
At the same hour Dr. Clitheroe and the Canon, fresh from

their respective labours, were awaiting Mrs. Pole in the drawing-room. Their collars shone in the twilight; their hands were pink with washing; and their lips had the faint cheerfulness that is caused by expectant hunger. Presently Mrs. Pole entered. "Dinner is ready," she said. "Shall we come in? Martin and John have settled that there is to be no bell to-night."

The two old servants stood solemnly by the dining-room door, as the small company passed into a glimmer of light which shadeless candles were casting on silver covers. The dishes were placed on the table as they were a century back; nor, except for such articles as were there for actual use, was there any ornament—not even a single flower. But the plate was fine in its simplicity; the linen was smooth as porcelain; and the ponderous old decanters flashed from a hundred facets.

Mrs. Pole was a woman of charming though faded aspect, which touched those who looked at her like a tranquil day in autumn. In spite of her grey hair, drawn from her forehead artlessly, she seemed to be hardly sixty, although she was really more. A sense of humour was discernible in the play of her features, and there still lived in her eyes the light of some vanished spring-time. The death of those who die at so great an age that their life has long been a yearly increasing wonder, can be hardly expected, except for its accidental results, to break the hearts even of near relations; and Mrs. Pole was the last person in the world to put her voice or her manner into any exaggerated mourning. She wore, indeed, this evening the soft veil of solemnity which falls over most faces in any house of death; but it subdued her natural smile without affecting to hide it, and the two clergymen, for her sake as well as for their own, were relieved to read in her demeanour a tacit licence to be themselves. Dr. Clitheroe said to her cheerfully that he hoped she was not exhausted, and Canon Bulman made appreciative noises with his soup. Mrs. Pole spoke in a matter-of-fact voice of the amount of business that had been forced on her during the day. "I sent," she said, "a dozen telegrams in the morning, and more, I think, have come this afternoon than ever agitated my aunt in the whole course of her life." She then mentioned the people whom she expected at Glenlynn for the funeral, and the Canon, who wrote articles

against the House of Lords in reviews, pricked up his ears
at the name of a well-known peer.

"That reminds me," he said, wiping his mouth hastily,
and plunging his hand into one of his coat-tail pockets, "here
is something that I ought to have delivered sooner." And,
giving her the letter which had been confided to his care in
the garden, he explained the incident, alluded to the young
lady's appearance, and watched Mrs. Pole with interest as
she broke the envelope open.

"I think," she said placidly, when she had read the letter
through, "that I can explain the mystery. Your attractive
friend is the daughter of the person who writes this letter,
and that person is a sort of cousin of ours. I dare say you
know we have certain foreign relations, and this is one of
them—Countess O'Keefe, she calls herself. Years ago I
met her at Pole Park. She was a regular foreigner in her
ways, although she was by birth an Irishwoman. She
smoked cigarettes in her bedroom, and never came downstairs till twelve. I need hardly tell you her visit was not
repeated. Well, it seems she is at Lyncombe now with a
yacht. I suppose if she stays long enough it will be necessary
to ask her over."

At the name of O'Keefe Dr. Clitheroe looked up. It was
a name at that time celebrated throughout Europe, being
born by a continental statesman who had great influence
with his sovereign.

"Has she anything to do," asked the doctor, "with Count
O'Keefe, the minister?"

"She belongs to his family," said Mrs. Pole, indifferently,
"and so did her husband, for she married her first cousin.
She met him at Carlsbad. He was an officer in the Austrian
army, and was very rich. His mother was a Polish princess.
As for the young lady, I know nothing about her; but the
women of that family had all the reputation of being
beautiful—of having beautiful figures——"

"This one's figure was beautiful," interrupted the Canon.

"And Reginald heard about one of them," Mrs. Pole
continued—"I hope it is not this one—who got into some
dreadful trouble. This one's name, as I see by her mother's
letter, is Shimna."

The Canon frowned, and listened with grave attention;
but the subject dropped, nor was it again approached till

Mrs. Pole had departed, and the clergymen drew their chairs together. Then when the Doctor, with a smile like a silent grace, had demurely poured out a glass of old brown sherry, the Canon, who was a total abstainer, helping himself to some French plums, at once went back to the subject of the O'Keefe family, and began to explain a number of facts relating to it, which could not so well have been discussed in Mrs. Pole's presence.

"You did not perhaps know," he said, "that Mrs. Pole was an O'Keefe herself. She was—she was the Dean's daughter: and Count O'Keefe, who is the head of her family, is an Irish peer, a naturalized Austrian subject, and also a Count of the Holy Roman Empire." The Canon, like many a convinced and fierce democrat, was an earnest though secret student of the "Peerage" and "Landed Gentry"; and he proceeded with considerable accuracy to inform the Doctor, how an Irish marquis, Mrs. Pole's great grandfather, having died without leaving any heir to his marquisate, had been succeeded in the barony of O'Keefe by his kinsman, the grandfather of the statesman. "It is curious," he said dryly, when he reached the end of his narrative, "that the class whose special pride is to do nothing for themselves or their fellow-citizens, should be the only class who are privileged to have their histories written. But what I have just been telling you is really odd and interesting."

When they went into the drawing-room, Mrs. Pole was not there; and the Canon, after a variety of aimless and fidgety movements, was finally attracted towards the pastel portrait of the lady, which he had, as he said, so often studied before, and whose presence in that place he regarded with such serious indignation.

"Look, Dr. Clitheroe—look!" he exclaimed at last. "Here is what has been worrying me. That young lady we met in the garden is exactly like this picture—except, of course, that she was exceedingly tight-laced, that instead of a turban she wore one of those abominable fringes, and had, what this woman has not, that meretricious foreign look about her. Unfortunately how well one knows it!"

"Ladies' dresses," began the Doctor, "I'm afraid are lost upon me." But just at this moment Mrs. Pole showed herself in the doorway.

"He's coming," she exclaimed, with a trembling agitation

in her voice, "Martin can hear the wheels. I have," she
continued, "just been with poor Miss Drake, such a forlorn
little object you never saw in your life. Dr. Clitheroe, I
wish you would go up and try to comfort her. She always
says 'the Word,' when you speak it, does her so much good.
And listen—I'm sure you might safely tell her this—that
my aunt, to my knowledge, has left her the large silver tea-
urn, the old Worcester tea-set, and a house for her life at
Lyncombe."

The Doctor mounted the stairs, bound on this work of
mercy, with the busy action of a dormouse in a rotating
cage. A moment later, a bell had been rung loudly, and
Mrs. Pole and her son were exchanging salutations in the
hall, with a quiet which had the semblance of indifference,
though it had the semblance only. Taking his arm she led
him into the dining-room, where supper was awaiting him;
and the Canon forbore to follow them. He retired to the
drawing-room instead, where he attentively contemplated
the portrait, and consulted anew the history of the O'Keefe
family in the peerage. With an unenlightened expression
he at last subsided into a chair; and taking up a weekly
review, and turning to an article of his own in it, which
bore the suggestive title of "The Debt of Dives to Lazarus,"
he solaced his mind with admiring a trenchant train of
reasoning, which would, if acted on, have deprived him of
his whole canonical income. He was before long interrupted
by the return of Dr. Clitheroe, and almost on the heels of
the Doctor appeared Reginald Pole.

The new-comer had a face with clear-cut features, and
hair which just on the temples was growing prematurely
grey. In his look there was a certain melancholy, combined
with activity and decision, and there was in his whole bearing
the self-possession and gravity of a man unconsciously
accustomed either to command or receive attention. His
dress even, careless as it was, had a certain air of distinction,
which the best tailor may fail to convey to his most fashionable cloth.

Whatever sadness his features might have when in
repose, their expression changed, when he spoke, into one of
cordial welcome. "My dear Canon," he said, "it is a real
pleasure to me to find you here; and Doctor, for all your
kindness I hardly know how to thank you. I hope you

have both of you found some place to smoke in. My mother is gone to bed. Will you have a cigar with me in the dining-room ? "

Of the two clergymen the only smoker was the Canon; but they both moved as was suggested, the Canon, with a paternal gesture, pushing Pole by the arm. The Doctor condescended to a little whisky-and-water, and the trio were soon conversing with a pleasant but restrained animation.

"It is, Dr. Clitheroe," said Pole, "an odd coincidence that we both of us should be serving the State in much the same capacity. I represent the world, you represent the Church. Things ought to go well when the State is served . by both."

"And I, Reginald," said the Canon, unwilling to be left out in the cold, "have had the honour—if it can be called such—of forming the mind of a Royal Highness in his teens. You and Dr. Clitheroe have been studying the condition of the people—the great problem. I have had to busy myself with the other end of the stick, a very different and less satisfactory operation."

"Ah, Canon," said Pole, laughing, "I know your republicanism from of old. But you have, at any rate, had the opportunity of serving the great cause by teaching a prince directly his own miserable insignificance."

The Canon was a man, who, on his social side, was extraordinarily thin-skinned. Gratified by deference, a slight stung him like a mosquito; and worse than a slight was anything like a sarcasm. He might not have suspected Pole of meaning either one or the other, if there had not been a something in his late pupil's whole manner, which, though really nothing more than the natural result of experience, seemed meant to announce to him that their former positions were reversed; and now this flippant allusion to his sacred democratic theories, coupled perhaps with a glance at his social practice, made him for a moment fret with surprise and anger.

"Princes, Reginald," he said, "are being taught their miserable insignificance by a greater teacher than either you or I." But then with a strong effort he summoned his temper back again, and, abruptly changing the subject, said in an altered tone, "By the way, there was a question about which I wished to speak to you. Have you ever met, when abroad, any of your O'Keefe relations ? "

"Only the minister," said Pole. "I stayed once for six weeks with him. There are any number of others; but I never happened to meet them. I wish," he added pleasantly, "that I had. Though not very reputable, I heard they were extremely handsome, especially one of them, whose good looks were more than she could manage."

The Canon stared at Pole, full of perplexed horror, which, however, was gradually got the better of by curiosity. "There is a Countess O'Keefe," he said, "who is at Lyncombe now with a yacht; and this very afternoon she sent over to inquire after Miss Pole."

"There are," said Pole, "several O'Keefe families. One had a villa at Baden-Baden, and a mortuary chapel there, with a gold dome among the pine-woods. I knew of them by hearsay only. They were half Russian, or Polish."

"From what your mother tells me," cried the Canon, "these must be the very people. But what was that you said about one of the young ladies connected with them ? "

"It was a story," said Pole, "that I heard only by accident; but it was so well known that there can be no harm in repeating it. The hero of it was half a Frenchman —well-born, very handsome, and rumoured to be immensely rich. The young lady, it appeared, had promised to marry him; and scandal said she forgot that she was not married already. In cases like these, the usual story is, that the man, when the time comes, won't marry the woman. Here, however, this usual story was reversed—and the prudent young lady refused to marry the man. Instead of being rich, he proved to be very poor; and it was, so malice said, on making this tragic discovery, that she broke his heart by refusing to let him make an honest woman of her. But all the O'Keefe young ladies, they told me, were wild as hawks, though this poor Countess Stephanie is the only one that I remember even by name. She has married, I think, since then, a man who might be her father."

"Ah," exclaimed the Canon, "this one is Countess Shimna. I see," he said, laughing, "that you stare at me. I suppose I forgot to tell you that the Countess O'Keefe who is at Lyncombe, sent here a daughter as messenger—a most striking young lady; and it was about her I wished to ask you. The moment I set eyes on her there was something in her that I thought peculiar; and I see this evening"—the Canon here dropped his voice, as if he were nearing a subject almost too delicate to touch upon—"I see this evening that her face bears the most singular resemblance to that unfortunate portrait which has been allowed to hang here in the drawing-room."

"The portrait!" said Pole, reflectively. "Now, which portrait is it that you mean? Do you mean the beautiful Lady Thyrza Brancepeth, my great-uncle's heroine, and the heroine of Byron's poem?"

"I mean," said the Canon, "forgive me for speaking plainly—a shameful woman, no matter how beautiful. The portrait, Reginald, should not hang where it does. It is fit only for a certain species of house which a Christian man never enters, and of which Christian women should not know the existence. Come, let us learn to call things by their right names, and not speak of heroines when we mean—well, I won't say what."

"I confess," began Pole, with the faint dawn of a smile, "I always took the greatest possible interest"—he was going to say "in Lady Thyrza," but, with quick good-feeling, he checked himself, and continued in a changed tone, "an interest in strange likenesses. I confess I am curious to see this mysterious young relation of mine. As for the likeness—well, Lady Thyrza Brancepeth must have been some relation to her too. She was originally Lady Thyrza O'Keefe."

"Indeed!" said the Canon, "indeed! She is not in 'Burke.'"

"No," replied Pole. "For reasons with which I think you will sympathize, her name was intentionally taken out of that book of life, the Peerage."

The Canon once again felt the mosquito's sting. He fancied he detected a sarcasm directed against himself in this allusion to a volume of which he knew himself such a frequent reader; nor was his inflammation soothed by the few words which Pole said next. They constituted a second sting, malignant with a new virus.

"I really," Pole innocently continued, "forget about all those relationships, if indeed I ever knew. To-morrow, if you like, we will speak about Lady Thyrza to my mother."

D

"Speak to your mother," cried the Canon, "about your uncle's adulterous mistress! Reginald, pray be decent. My dear boy, what can have come to you? You and I, about these points, used to agree so well."

His old pupil repressed a slight gesture of impatience, and said gently yet indifferently, "No doubt we agree still. I am glad, Dr. Clitheroe, that my aunt's end was painless."

The doctor looked up with a peaceful and serious smile. "Her last conscious act," he said, "was to receive the Sacrament."

"Yes," added the Canon, in loud and strenuous tones as he beat out the light of his cigar-end by dabbing it against a silver salver, "a death like hers is a really beautiful thing, and should give each one of us a robuster belief in life."

"My poor old aunt!" said Pole, as they all three rose. "She was very kind to me. Well, Canon, good night. What philosophers we should all of us be if we took our own deaths as easily as we do those of our friends!"

"Good night, Reginald," said the Canon, with magisterial coldness; and when he entered his bedroom he shut the door with a bang.

CHAPTER V.

Ir the Canon went to bed indignant with his old pupil, and disappointed by him—brooding over the waste of his own bygone teachings, and still more over the complete evaporation of his own personal influence—Pole was conscious of a certain distress also. Having met the Canon again with a sense of cordial pleasure, he was conscious that almost at once he had jarred his feelings somehow; and he examined his memory in vain to discover exactly how: but he hoped that next day things would easily right themselves; and he rose next morning planning many civilities by which he hoped to conciliate his offended tutor.

The Canon's personality was at all events not far off from him. When he was just completing his toilet, his ears became conscious of a sound which he conceived to be caused by somebody grinding coffee. But on entering the breakfast-parlour he found that he had mistaken its nature, and that it really proceeded from the Canon reading family prayers. As he knelt down before the nearest mahogany chair, and rested his forehead on a surface of French polish, he recognized the familiar phrases of the Right Rev. Bishop Bloomfield, whose "Household Devotions for each Day in the Week" had been used at Glenlynn for more than half a century; and he could not suppress a smile, which was certainly not devotional, when he heard the Canon, obviously much against the grain, constrained to prefer the following petition to Providence. "Make us humble to our superiors, affable to our equals, kind and condescending to the poor and needy." It was a petition, however, of which the Canon need have had no personal fear, for it was plain when he rose from his knees that in his case it had not been answered. He was humble to nobody, and to Pole, instead of being affable, he was distant.

Pole saw this with concern—a concern that was all the greater because with each little attention which he happened to pay the Canon, the Canon's manner appeared to become more frosty. Still this breakfast was not an unpleasant meal; and for Pole there were many things in it which had a peculiar charm. The room, with its faded rep curtains, its faded sage-green walls, its old dumb waiters, and sideboard on whose glossy mahogany Georgian spoons and mustard-pots rested like swans on water, the dangling bell-pulls—one on each side of the chimney-piece—the turreted chimney-piece, Gothic, after the fashion of Strawberry Hill, the bright-coloured, large-patterned service of old Crown Derby, which shone on the table-cloth like roses placed on snowdrops—all these things touched him with many subtle associations. So, too, did Miss Drake, who had risen from dreams of her tea-urn, to find that family prayers still had power to comfort her, and who was so far in possession of her faculties as to be able, with her mittened hands, to unlock her tea-chest, and make tea as usual. Every object and incident reminded him of his earliest days, even the delicate, home-made wafer biscuits, and the butter-pats with the Pole crest on them: but everything now seemed charged with some gentle sense of loss; and once, looking at Miss Drake, who was munching a piece of toast, his eyes grew dim as he noticed how a dilatory tear traversed her cheek unperceived by her, and fell into her heap of salt.

As for Mrs. Pole, she had a pile of letters beside her, most of which, when she had read them, she passed over to her son. The Doctor mentioned that he had secured for himself a bed out of the house; and the Canon, without expressing any instant desire to move, explained how at any moment he could betake himself to Mr. Godolphin's. "I hope," said Mrs Pole, "you will stay here, if we are able to keep you. I will talk with Reginald first, and see you a little later."

She and her son had a busy two hours together; and in the middle of a conference with the bailiff and an undertaker from Lyncombe, the air of the room was agitated by the entrance of Mr. Godolphin. He exhaled a fragrance of the Church, as if he had been a censer; but he brought with him also much practical sagacity, which, as he was not to have the privilege of burying Miss Pole himself, he consecrated to the task of suggesting how the mourners might be conveyed to her funeral. He undertook to engage all the flies in the neighbourhood; he settled with the undertaker that there should be a special train to Lyncombe, which would bring, amongst other people, his Grace the Lord Lieutenant of the County; and many of the necessary arrangements he engaged to superintend himself. "I find that we can keep the Canon till the funeral, if he may come to you that night," said Mrs. Pole to Mr. Godolphin, as he rose to go. "At any moment," said Mr. Godolphin, "my house is yours." And with dignified rapidity he made his way to his carriage, proud to be bearing for his neighbours such congenial and important burdens. "Will you, Reginald," said Mrs. Pole, "go and tell the Canon. He'll be glad to have another couple of days to talk to you."

Pole, however, did not at once execute this commission. He went instead to the room where the dead was lying, and opened the door softly, with a useless, yet instinctive reverence. As he looked at the lifeless face he caught his breath and started, for what he saw was so strange, though it still remained so familiar. Death with the young is physically like mere unconsciousness; with the old it is sometimes a transfiguration. It was so in this case. Most of the wrinkles of a hundred years had disappeared; and there lay on the cheeks and lips a peace that was almost girlish, as if the waxen face had gone back to its own youth again, or the last sleep in its mercy had erased the writing of life. Pole stood for some minutes at the foot of the four-post bed, on whose green curtains he had often gazed with awe in his childhood; and vague thoughts came to him, agitating the petals of memory, and blowing to him the scent of the days when his aunt had been a fairy godmother to him, and Glenlynn and its gardens formed a fairyland filled with holidays. The sound of the stable clock broke in on his meditations; and surprised of the lateness of the hour, he made his way downstairs, to look for the Canon, and convey to him Mrs. Pole's message. His mind was softened and solemnized by this converse with the past and death. He felt a desire to be in charity with every human-being, as a fellow-communicant in the cup of a common destiny; and he was now more bent than ever on regaining an old friend's kindliness.

The Canon meanwhile had been in the library, reading with fierce satisfaction a newspaper paragraph in praise of one of his own speeches. It was a speech which, a few days back, he had delivered in St. James's Hall, and in it he had contrasted what he called "the two moral senses;" the moral sense of the workers, and the moral sense of the idle; "that is to say," he had explained, "of the loafing or the propertied classes." The Canon, in fact, had, during the past two or three years, added to his democratic creed certain new articles, which gave him much agreeable notoriety in the columns of newspapers, and also, as he flattered himself, much influence in the country. One of these articles was that, next to inchastity, the thing which required the most denunciation was capital; and as he boasted that he had never, since the day when he left Cambridge, so much as looked into a book of political economy, no one could have been better qualified for attacking the latter evil. His attacks on wealth in general had, indeed, of late been so uncompromising, that some sermons which he preached to a fashionable congregation in Mayfair, conclusively proved the fashionable luncheon to be stolen, at which he was accustomed to refresh himself after service. One of his great successes had been a collection in behalf of a strike, when a beautiful countess, who was more or less of a Magdalene, had handed the bag round with a grace that was almost irresistible. Some of his critics had been so unfair as to say that he looked on every strike as being, in its very nature, just. But there was one which occurred at a colliery in which he had himself some shares; and he considered that the knowledge and energy with which he denounced this, was a proof of the impartiality with which he supported others.

When Pole entered, he looked up from his paper sharply; but the message brought to him was, in many ways, so agreeable, and Pole's manner in giving it was at once so genial and deferent, that he suddenly thawed, and began to recover his conviction that his pupil was still under his healthy and commanding influence.

"My dear boy," he said, "your mother is, indeed, most hospitable, and I shall be truly glad of a few days' conversation with you. If you've nothing to do, what say you to this—shall we take a turn in the garden, and talk about old times?"

Pole assented, full of pleasant expectation, and the Canon, as they went, took his arm in an almost paternal fashion. He soon found, however, that the event was likely to disappoint him. The Canon found little pleasure in retrospection for its own sake; he was impatient of it, as a sentimental frivolity: and instead of dwelling on any personal memories of the past, he plunged into what he was delighted to call "the burning question" of the present.

"There is one thing about you, Reginald," he said, "which does really rejoice me. I mean the fact that the work which has fallen to you to do is a work which has brought you face to face with realities—with the great problem of our time—that terrible spreading poverty which is a new social portent, and which I said in my speech last week may be called 'the shadow of capital.'"

"But, my dear Canon," began Pole, speaking as deferentially as he could, "is what you say a fact? Is poverty spreading? I have figures in my possession here—and besides, there are published Blue-books———"

The Canon, however, interrupted him. "Pooh!" he said, "a Blue-book will prove anything; and I don't care for figures—I trust to my own eyes. I have seen," he was about to say, "the poverty of the poor myself;" but his respect for veracity checked him, as he had long since settled with his conscience that his vocation with regard to the poor was to give them the benefit of his reasoning powers, rather than of his company. "My dear fellow," he said, "the fact is evident. Ask the people themselves. Not all the fudging of Blue-books will cheat them out of their own experiences."

The Canon was a man with whom to argue was to quarrel; so Pole, who was resolved to preserve not only his own temper, but his companion's, without retracting his own views, made no attempt to insist upon them, and for some time he listened submissively to the Canon's attack on wealth, and his alternating doctrines that it should be possessed by everybody and by nobody. But at last he felt that he hardly could listen longer, and interrupting the Canon with the most careful and respectful gentleness, he said—

"I assure you that my interest in these problems is as deep as yours. But your labour and capital, after all, have to do only with the cup that contains life. The great question still for us is, what is the life that it contains?"

"Naturally," retorted the Canon; "and who, do you suppose, denies that? Not I, at all events. To use your well-worn metaphor of the cup and the wine contained in it, who can insist more strongly than I myself do on the duty of each one of us to see that the wine is pure? You are aware, I suppose, of the particular Cause which I am now myself championing, and that is merely an incident in a larger moral movement."

"I was thinking of things," said Pole, with a slight sigh, "which are beyond the reach of movements, but which also belong to the moral world. I was thinking of the fidelity of a man to a woman, or of a father to his helpless child. I was thinking of those concentrated affections, which are the heart and the light of life, and of which your love for the community is merely the diffused reflection."

The Canon halted and looked Pole in the face. "And do you," he exclaimed, "really mean that the affections, as you call them, need no moral government—no control at the hands of Christian public opinion? What is corruption— what is vileness unutterable, except these same affections in their natural unchristian state?"

"Is there anything vile," said Pole, "in a mother's love for her children—in the eyes, the breast that move to the

small hands calling for her, and to the lips on which
language just begins to bud?"

"You are speaking now," retorted the Canon, "of nature,
not of morals. Animals are good mothers till their young
can walk and feed themselves. Where nature does well, let
us leave her to her own devices. Our business, as Christians,
is to fight against her when she does ill, and to arraign her
before the presence of the God who is at once her creator
and her judge."

"And yet," said Pole, "the conqueror of more than half
of the Christian world was not the Judge and the Creator,
but a mother and a little boy."

The Canon, who had been vaguely displeased by the
whole turn the conversation had been taking, was irritated
by this last observation almost beyond endurance. It irritated him partly as a respectful allusion to a Church which
he tolerated with difficulty unless it happened to be represented by a cardinal; and it irritated him still more from
the feeling with which the words were uttered. He disliked
and distrusted all sentiment on principle, making only one
exception in favour of righteous anger. "If that is so," he
said dryly, "the Apostles might have spared themselves their
trouble. The true Church is, according to your view, in
the nursery."

"And if it were not there," replied Pole, unruffled by
this sarcasm, "there would be little good in its being anywhere else. Look! some one is beckoning to us. That
means luncheon. The two things," he added, absently, as
if following out some train of thought, and as if his companion had expressed no disagreement with him, "the two
things that move me most are these—the child for whom we
must do everything, and the dead for whom we can do
nothing."

This last reflection might have been thought sufficiently
harmless. There was nothing unchaste in it; nor was it an
apology for capital: but, all the same, Pole felt, when he
re-entered the house, that it had clenched his failure, in spite
of his best efforts, to secure anything like a really cordial
understanding between himself and one whose temperament
seemed to have risen in arms against his own.

CHAPTER VI.

AT luncheon the Canon was taciturn; but he ate with a vindictive vigour, as if converting the beggarly elements against their will to the service of Christian righteousness; and he afterwards set out by himself on what he said would be a ten-mile walk, treading heavily on the gravel as he started, like St. Michael trampling on the devil.

"I hope, Dr. Clitheroe," said Pole, when the two men were left sitting together in the dining-room, "I hope you will find your bedroom at the farm comfortable. When we have finished our coffee, shall we go and look at it? And if anything is wanting, we can send it down by this evening."

"I am sure," answered the Doctor, "I shall find everything I require; but I should like the walk. There are certain important reasons why I am anxious to have a little conversation with you."

The Doctor's manner expressed such kind and serious solicitude that Pole was set wondering as to what the conversation would refer to. The farm was about a mile off. It stood half-way up a valley which slanted down to the sea, and was reached from Glenlynn most quickly by a beautiful and wooded path, which ran along the cliff-side and hung over the waves and shingle. Along this they took their way, going slowly so as to enjoy the prospect.

"I suppose you know," began the Doctor, with a little nervousness, and a tremor of feeling in his voice, "I suppose you know the kindness—the exceeding kindness—which your aunt has shown me on very many occasions. Your mother, too——" The Doctor paused to clear his throat. "It is difficult to me now even to speak of all this kindness. What I wished to tell you is that in a small way—in a very small way—I have found myself able to repay it: and the way is one which nearly concerns yourself."

With each word of the Doctor's, Pole became more and more mystified.

"Your aunt," continued the Doctor, after a pause, "in many of her business matters was good enough to confide in my judgment; and during her last illness she laid before me the entire state of her affairs. Of the main provisions in her will she made no secret; and you are probably your-self aware of them. She made no change in them at the last. The bulk of this property, with the house, is your mother's for her life; but a certain sum of money comes at once to you. The amount, roughly speaking, is about twenty thousand pounds, which used to bring your aunt about seven hundred and fifty pounds a year—a sum some-what in excess of what she was accustomed to allow you."

"All this," said Pole, "coincides with what I have understood."

The Doctor stood still in the path, and with quiet eyes looked up at his friend. "You will," he said gently, "be far richer than you expected to be. The income you will receive will be much more like three thousand."

Pole could not help smiling, for the news had a pleasant sound. None the less, he stared at the Doctor incredulously. The Doctor was known to be a valuable public servant, but he was not reputed to possess much business ability; and the natural conclusion in this case was that he had some-what muddled himself. He proceeded, however, like a person who knew quite well what he was talking about. "I see," he said, with his equably modulated intonation, "that you look surprised. I am glad to have been the means of bringing such a piece of good fortune in your way; and I know also that I was giving to your aunt a greater pleasure than to yourself; for you, I think, have always been rather careless of money."

"But, my dear Doctor," said Pole, "this sounds like a fairy-tale. By what process of alchemy can you have possibly worked this miracle?"

"That," replied the Doctor, "is precisely what I desired to explain. I have, as you know perhaps, served two Governments. My former chief, Sir Joseph Pilkington, to whom I owe my appointment, and who was pleased with what I did for him, was always of opinion that the stipends of myself and of one or two others were not commensurate with our work; and he was anxious to have them raised. But this he found impracticable. Subsequently he went to Australia, where he is at the present moment. You have heard of the Ridgehill and the Mount Mackinnon mines, the owners of which are now some of the richest persons at the Antipodes. Well, Sir Joseph Pilkington was the moving spirit in this enterprise; but the capital required at starting, for various reasons, had to be raised in England. Firmly convinced of the enormous fortune that would be realized, Sir Joseph offered to myself and one or two of my colleagues the privilege of raising among ourselves or our friends a certain part of this capital, placing us in a position similar to that of holders of founders' shares. I invested myself every available penny I possess, and for the past five years I have been receiving twenty-five per cent. Well, owing to circumstances which I can explain by-and-by more fully, the opportunity has been offered me of investing a yet further sum, not to exceed fifty thousand pounds, either on my own behalf or that of persons nominated by me—investing it on terms not indeed the same, but yet approximately similar to those which I have mentioned. Interest will be guaranteed to the amount of fourteen per cent.; and when I show you the names of some of the guarantors, you will see that this now is no speculative business, but something as safe as Consols. Now, I was on the point, six months ago, of offering my only brother the opportunity of investing thirty thousand pounds, but he, poor fellow, died, and his son has turned out ill. I was, therefore, glad to offer the same opportunity to Miss Pole; and for your sake she embraced it gladly and, I am sure, wisely. Of course, as I said, the sum is twenty thousand, not thirty. The remaining ten thousand—I tell you this in confidence—has been invested by Canon Bulman; but he would not wish it to be spoken about."

"But are you sure," said Pole, "that the whole thing is sound? A safe fourteen per cent. really seems hardly credible. Would it not be better, before the money is actually sent, to talk the matter over with old Mr. Whilks, my lawyer?"

"Of course," said the Doctor, "the opportunity is exceptional; but founders' shares constantly pay much more. As to your lawyer, I only wish we could have consulted him—for your own satisfaction, I mean. But there is one point which I must impress on you. It is absolutely necessary that this entire transaction should be kept private, as the favoured position which has been accorded to me might, were it known, excite—you can easily see how—any amount of angry feeling, not against myself, but against Sir Joseph

Pilkington. And this brings me to the point which I want to make quite clear to you. The money has been placed in my hands absolutely—it has already been sent, so we cannot recall it now—and thus, plain as the nature of the transaction will be, when you have heard its details, your reliance ultimately will have to be on my own integrity."

" Of course," said Pole, touched by the Doctor's manner, " I rely upon that implicitly. My only doubt has reference to the accuracy of your information."

"About that," said the Doctor, "you shall be satisfied very soon. But to return to yourself. I felt that, though I was sure you trusted me, I had no right in an important . matter like the present, to force this trust upon you. I have, therefore, arranged that, should you not approve of this investment, you will be able to withdraw your principal at the end of the current year, or any subsequent time, at two months' notice. If you are wise, I think you will leave it where it is. In my bedroom at the farm I have documents which will explain all to you."

The bedroom, when they came to examine it, they found to be clean, but almost Spartan in its simplicity. There was no carpet except a strip by the dimity-curtained bed; the chairs were hard and cushionless; and on the dressing-table, ornamented with tufted mats of crochet-work, was a looking-glass, in which the Doctor's face assumed the proportions of a spoon. The Doctor, however, welcomed the accommodation as delightful, and the room was littered already with various little properties belonging to him.

"See," he said with pride, " there is my new type-writer, and my patent reading-lamp, which I hook on to the blinds of the railway carriage. That is the oil-stove in which I can cook my breakfast—four and sixpence it cost; and here is my latest acquisition. See this lamp! I light it. It makes my coffee; then, when my coffee is made, whip!—up this catch goes, and out goes my lamp."

The Doctor was a great collector of small patent inventions, and had frequently testified his gratitude to his hostesses at Glenlynn by presents of ingenious button-hooks, tooth-brushes, and new kinds of soap. Having done the honours of his coffee-boiler, he resumed his airs of business, and briskly unlocking a black leather despatch-box, on which his address at Whitehall was printed in gold capitals,

he produced a number of letters and other papers, and one
after the other submitted them to Pole's inspection. The
Doctor's method of explaining financial matters surprised
him by its precision and its unostentatious lucidity. By the
time the various documents had been put back in their
places Pole's dominant feeling was a cordial sense of gratitude, which almost put out of his thoughts the actual
advantage which had been conferred on him; and, though
not an effusive man, he spoke his thanks with a sincerity
which Dr. Clitheroe, by his expression, showed that he
understood. They remained at the farm no longer than
their business kept them; and when they began to walk
back, the Doctor, as if considering himself thanked enough,
delicately turned the conversation to general and indifferent
topics.

Of the world, in the narrower sense of the word, the
Doctor had seen nothing; but his professional experience
had given him much knowledge of life, and his plans for his
own future seemed to be modestly extending themselves.
He talked of buying a yacht, to assist him on his official
journeys, and asked Pole's advice as to the choice of a house
in London.

"How soft the wind is!" he said, raising his tall, silk
hat; "and how marvellous is the beauty of these views!
See, here is a bench. Shall we sit down for a moment?"

They did so, and after a pause, emitting a few "hems,'
he began again, not without a certain shyness.

"There was one other little matter," he said, "which I
wanted to name to you; and I hope—indeed, I think I may
even say I am sure—that you will take what I say in the
spirit in which it is said. I know from experience that
persons who come into an inheritance frequently find themselves, for a not inconsiderable period, poorer than they were
previously, instead of richer. In the case of yourself, for
instance, and of your mother, the duties will be very heavy;
and I was thinking this morning that you would possibly—
it is no uncommon case—find your ordinary balance at your
banker's hardly equal to the calls on it. I have, therefore,
made bold to pay into your account a half-year's dividend in
advance, on the twenty thousand I have invested for you;
and this will enable you, in case the necessity arises, to help
your mother with any advances she may require. The

cheque I have sent is for fourteen hundred pounds—a sum
which I think will be sufficient to make things quite easy
for you."

"My dear Doctor," exclaimed Pole, "you positively take
my breath away! But, indeed, I cannot accept all this
overwhelming kindness."   .

"So far as I am concerned," said the Doctor, "you may
assure yourself that I feel no inconvenience. I only wish
I did, because I should feel in that case that I was making
some more adequate return for the kindness of your family
to myself. Listen now. To convince you how easy it is for
me to do this, and how little scruple you need feel in accepting so small a favour, let me tell you what my own income
has been for the last five years. You must remember that
this is in confidence."

"Certainly," Pole replied.

The Doctor proceeded in a soft, emphatic undertone,
letting the syllables follow each other slowly. "Eleven
thousand a-year," he said. "It is more, far more, than I
know how to spend. I am, therefore, quite sure that you
will not hurt me by refusing this trifling service which I
have so much pleasure in doing you."

"My dear Dr. Clitheroe," answered Pole, speaking with
more emphasis than was usual with him, "by refusing your
kindness I feel I should be making you an ill return for it.
You have made it easy for me to accept it, but difficult to
thank you adequately."

"Very well, then," said the Doctor, in a gratified manner,
"let us speak no more about it; though by-and-by there are
a few more business details which I shall have to mention
to you. It's late," he exclaimed, drawing out his watch.
"Bless me, how late! But wait here another moment. Let
us look at the view once more. How marvellously beautiful,
how marvellously peaceful it is!"

Pole, though he had hitherto showed no signs of exhilaration, began at last to feel the influence of the Doctor's
news, and the pleasure of unexpected wealth possessing him
like an armed man. The scene itself contributed to this
effect, as he sat for some minutes longer silent by the Doctor's
side. Before them was glittering an oval of breezy sea,
bordered in silver by the bark of a shining birch-tree. On
the steep banks that embowered them, and descended below

their feet, clumps of heather bulged between hazels and slender tree-trunks; above miniature horizons of tall grass ferns raised their antlers, and gorse in the intricate twilight lifted its yellow stars.

CHAPTER VII.

If Canon Bulman's anxiety to stay on at Glenlynn was due to the wish he had expressed for the society of his former pupil, his wish was one which apparently he took small pains to gratify: for though, like a Christian and a gentle-man, he was sufficiently civil to Pole, he never again sought him as a companion, or attempted a confidential conversation with him; but contented himself with aiming at him occa-sional darts of sarcasm, in the hope of shaming him back to his old allegiance. The Canon in fact was a person—and the type is by no means rare—who was not only offended by men who ignored his influence, but was also attracted to them by a sort of hostile fascination, till his self-esteem should be pacified by getting the better of them. He had, however, in prolonging his visit, other views of a less militant nature: and in these—as he learnt at luncheon on the day before the funeral—in these, at all events, he was not going to be disappointed.

"Lord Wargrave," said Mrs. Pole, speaking with an air of half-distressed amusement, "comes quite early this after-noon, and he tells me he is determined to stop over to-morrow. I can't think how we shall keep him quiet, and I know he'll be discontented with our cooking."

" He stayed 'ere twice," said Miss Drake, "in Miss Pole's time, and he liked our four-year-old mutton, which he said ate so juicy."

" I'm glad of that," said Mrs. Pole. " And then there's the old Madeira."

" He stayed with me once at Cambridge," said the Canon, " when I was a Fellow. I had a famous cellar in those days, which Lord Wargrave appreciated. He is a cousin of yours, I think," the Canon added abruptly, as if suddenly afraid he might have spoken with too great freedom of so important a man to a lady who had the importance of being his relation.

"He's my husband's cousin," said Mrs. Pole. "I am glad
to find you know him. You and he will amuse each other.
He's wonderful. He knows everybody. But this is not the
worst. The Duke—the old Duke of Dulverton "—the eyes
of the Canon glistened—"is also coming—not, however, till
later. At first he meant to have gone straight to the church
from Lyncombe. But I am sure that Lord Wargrave, who
is staying with him, has made him alter his plans. He is
such a cross old man—the Duke is, except when he's in a
good temper. I suppose you would know I was Irish, because
I said that." The Canon's radical soul swelled with reverence for a woman who could speak so naturally of a duke
as a "cross old man"; and his just appreciation of merit,
even in a great magnate, led him to observe how much he
had heard of the Duke's talents. Then he silently meditated
on what Mr. Godolphin had said—that the Duke also was
somehow connected with his hostess's family. The world in
general seemed to grow warm with sunshine : and however
Reginald Pole might rub him the wrong way, he felt, as he
surveyed the dining-room, that he was sitting in the right
place.

Pole, Dr. Clitheroe, and the Canon were still sipping
their coffee, and the Canon had taken a cigarette from a case
of ruby-coloured enamel—"a present," he observed incidentally, "from Prince George of Finland—such a good fellow—
a right good honest fellow "—when a boisterous peal came
clanging from the front-door bell, and Pole rose, exclaiming—

"There he is ; that's Lord Wargrave! "

Lord Wargrave was a man who had achieved European
celebrity, not so much for his own gifts, as his appreciation
of the gifts of others. He had never attempted to distinguish
himself either in literature, science, or politics, or in any of
the idler pursuits which give brilliance to fashionable life.
He had, indeed, once been devoted to the study of architecture, and had been anxious, at his own expense, to add a
chapel to Westminster Abbey; but his only solid achieve-
ment had been an Elizabethan house for himself, which was
so much too large for his means that he lived usually with
his friends. He had never made a speech in the House of
Lords; he had published nothing except some gossiping
notes of his travels ; but he knew the motives, the aims, and

the histories of half the public men and beautiful women in Europe far better than they knew them themselves, and he certainly divulged them with infinitely greater candour. He was master of a fair property and a very presentable pedigree, and wherever this last happened to be defective, he had thoroughly repaired it by the aid of his vigorous imagination. All this produced in him a satisfactory dignity of deportment, which was, when he entered the dining-room, much admired by Canon Bulman. His hair, his whiskers, and his eyebrows were so many sandy-coloured bushes. His face, in repose, possessed a certain massive gravity, but took a hundred expressions when he spoke, like lights in disturbed water. Liking, as he did, men of most sorts and conditions, the clergy were far from forming any exception to his rule, and often, when laying down the law in the study of some country parsonage, he had, except for the want of a white tie, every appearance of being an admirable clergyman himself.

He greeted Canon Bulman, taking him by both hands. "This is," he exclaimed, "a quite unexpected pleasure." And when the Doctor was introduced to him, he said, "I was reading your last report yesterday. It's by far the most masterly thing of its kind I know."

He then seated himself, awaiting the advent of his luncheon, and, looking round the room with a slow, judicial scrutiny, said—

"I tell everybody that this is the oldest house in England. It is the only house where the life is three generations old. If your aunt, Reginald, had not been a rich woman, I always maintain that she might have made a large income, merely by showing herself to American tourists as the one survivor of our old county aristocracy." He was here interrupted by some dishes being placed in front of him, and the voice of the old butler, which murmured in his ear, "What wine, my lord?"

"Madeira," said Lord Wargrave, with sharp and unhesitating brevity, as he transferred two chops with their rosy juices to his plate.

"I see," he began, pausing between his mouthfuls, and addressing Canon Bulman, "that you are still active as a captain of the national conscience."

His utterance was grave, and Canon Bulman was much

E

gratified by it; but under the corners of Lord Wargrave's
nervous mouth there lurked, in company with a few crumbs
of potato, a certain ambushed humour, which a keen observer
might have detected.

"You," said Canon Bulman, leaning forward with an
ingratiating smile, "I am sure, must be of our opinion, that
it is impossible for a man condemned publicly in the divorce
court to remain the leader of a great Parliamentary party,
especially considering the way the whole thing was done.
Why, he used to drive—I am told this for a fact—down to
Palace Yard with the partner of his guilt, in a brougham."

"Did you ever meet the lady?" asked Lord Wargrave,
peering up at him.

The Canon frowned and bridled. "Never," he answered;
"I am thankful to say, never."

Lord Wargrave looked at the ceiling, and murmured in a
reflective voice—

"A delightful woman, a most delightful woman! The
Archbishop of Monaghan used to call on her every day.
She wrote that Report on Ireland which he sent to the Pope
—the whole of it."

The Canon knew not how to receive this speech. Various
expressions were in a state of civil war on his face, and the
eyes of Lord Wargrave twinkled for just a moment.

When the latter had finished his luncheon, his expression gradually altered. He leant over to Pole, and said in a
resounding whisper—

"My dear Reginald, let me look at your poor aunt's body."

Lord Wargrave was an amateur of all kinds of emotion,
and before he had left the dining-room he had pulled out a
large silk handkerchief, so as to be ready for the tears which
he meant presently to shed; and when, five minutes later,
he emerged from the chamber of death, solemnly wiping the
remaining moisture from his eyes, he felt as much warmed
and exhilarated as if he had had another glass of Madeira.

The Canon, meanwhile, had recovered his equanimity,
and sacrificed the craving of his muscles for a long walk to
the unselfish pleasure of entertaining Lord Wargrave in the
library, and helping him to examine its rows of curious and
forgotten books.

"By the way," said the Canon at last, hastily closing a
volume of French engravings which had held him for a

minute or two in fascinated indignation, "do you happen to know and remember a certain pastel portrait here, which hangs in the next room?"

"I suppose you mean," said Lord Wargrave, "the portrait of the divine Thyrza. Beautiful, beautiful! That picture at Christie's would fetch at least a thousand guineas."

"I was not," said the Canon, dryly, "thinking of the merits of a picture whose presence in this house I consider to be in itself an indecency. What made me allude to it was a very curious fact." And he then described the appearance of the young lady in the garden, her singular resemblance to the portrait, and what he had gathered as to her family history. Lord Wargrave pricked up his ears. "And she was," the Canon continued, "not only like this woman, but she looked as if her career either had been, or would be similar. One of the family, Pole tells me, has gone desperately wrong already."

"Humph!" muttered Lord Wargrave into the space between his coat and waistcoat. "I've not the least doubt she's an extremely fascinating woman." Then, turning to the Canon, he said, "I should like to see her. I have in my own mind not the least doubt about the matter. Tristram Pole had a daughter by Lady Thyrza Brancepeth. Byron saw the girl, and mentions her in an unpublished letter. She was brought up in a convent, and married one of her mother's relations—a fire-eating count who fought under the first Napoleon. I've not the least doubt that this girl is her grand-daughter. With such a grandmother she has every right to be charming."

The Canon's face grew frigid. Out of the corner of his eye Lord Wargrave perceived this.

"Did you ever," he said, in a very serious voice, "hear these verses?

'Those myrtle-blooms of starriest birth
   Were dim beside her breast of snow;
And now it sleeps beneath the earth
   From which their sister blossoms blow.'

They come from the poem which Byron wrote on Lady Thyrza's death."

What would have happened to the Canon had the strain of the situation been prolonged, it is very difficult to say;

but at this juncture luckily the door opened, Lord Wargrave's eyes wandered, and he exclaimed, with extended hands—

"But, God bless my soul, who's this? Why, my dear old friend the Dean!" And the next moment he was very nearly embracing a stately gentleman in gaiters and snowy necktie, whose face was fresh as a foxhunter's, and who walked like an archbishop.

"I think, Canon," said Lord Wargrave, "you must know Dean Osborne Pole. This, my dear Dean, is the celebrated Canon Bulman."

The Dean, though a high Tory and a hater of clerical radicalism, greeted the Canon with much fraternal condescension, and the Canon returned the greeting with a courtly, yet independent deference, which showed him in his best light.

"I see, Wargrave," said the Dean, "you have been having an afternoon among the Muses. In this library there is, if I remember rightly, a remarkably fine collection of early editions of the classics." And the three gentlemen discussed books for an hour or so, till Mrs. Pole entered, and was shortly followed by tea.

"I hear," said Lord Wargrave by-and-by, as he finished the last tea-cake, "that half the county will be at the funeral; not only men, but ladies; and perfectly right, too. Such a death as this is like a Dissolution of Parliament. The Duchess is coming, and old Lady Taplow with her. That," he murmured, patting the Dean's apron, "is one of the reasons that brings the Duke here." Then followed some story told in a whisper, which the Dean received with an expression of not very severe reproof.

"Ah, well," said the Dean, "dukes have their ducalities. Augusta," he continued, consulting a large gold repeater, "I will, if you will allow me, ask to be shown my room."

"Let me," said the Canon, with alacrity, "act as groom of the chambers." And he sprang to his feet like a boy; but just at this moment the door opened again, and a new arrival was announced—an old man, short and fragile, who stooped somewhat, and shuffled rather than walked. His clothes hung on him loosely; his grey hair was thin; and a pair of smoked glasses which eclipsed a good half of his face, made it hard to conjecture the meaning of the smile which hovered about his mouth. The moment he spoke, however, he gave some clue to the mystery. His hollow voice, his pronunciation, which bore the traces of some far-off dandyism; his elocution, which was emphasized by sententious pauses, and punctuated by soft and semi-malicious chuckles, all combined to render the smoked glasses transparent, and to betray the light beneath them of an alert but benevolent cynicism. This was the Duke of Dulverton, who had inherited from his father one of the most celebrated names in Europe—a name which he was wont to say with a caustic modesty, had been for himself an extinguisher rather than a pedestal. When Mrs. Pole went up to him he shook her by both hands; he greeted the Dean with benignity, and nodded at Lord Wargrave curtly; but most of his graciousness seemed to have been kept for Canon Bulman. The Canon was delighted, though the ducal words had been few; and he was by no means so anxious now, as he had been a few minutes previously, to quit the library and escort the Dean to his bedroom. The Dean, however, held him to his promise, and the two dignitaries departed. The Duke eyed the Canon's coat-tails as they disappeared through the doorway, and turning to Mrs. Pole, he said to her, "Is that your sniveller?" This was his private generic name for a clergyman; but though it certainly betrayed small reverence for the pulpit, there were few men in England from whom a larger number of clergymen had received greater and more thoughtful assistance than from himself.

"Oh, ho!" he said, when Mrs. Pole had set him right. "Canon Bulman, is it? You introduced him to my deaf ear. A shocking fellow, I know him—a shocking fellow! I thought he was too well-groomed for one of your hedge-parsons. To tell you the truth, I like the hedge-parson better."

In spite, however, of this opinion, when the party reassembled for dinner, the Duke's attention to the Canon was even more marked than before, though a certain spirit of mischief underlay his urbanity.

"I have listened," he said to the Canon, who sat next to him, "with great attention to your sermons in the Chapel Royal." The Canon bowed. "I invariably agreed," continued the Duke, "with the beginning of every one of

your sentences." The Canon bowed again, with a puzzled
and yet a gratified expression. "Would you like me to tell
you why I didn't agree with the rest?"

"If you please," smiled the Canon, gravely.

"Because," said the Duke, laying his hand on the
Canon's arm, "because I could not hear it." And he
stopped abruptly, and glanced round the table. "Augusta,"
he continued presently, mouthing out the name in a tone
which suggested the beginning of a speech in the House of
Lords, "have you heard any more of that defaulting bailiff
of Miss Pole's?"

"Nothing," said Mrs. Pole. "It is you, Duke, who
should have heard, if anybody. It was your kindness which
helped him to go off to the Colonies."

"Miss Pole," said the Duke, "had him on my recom-
mendation, so I felt bound to look after him. I heard from
him this morning. Do you know what he is now? Not
one of you here will guess. He has just been elected a
member of the New Zealand House of Lords. Dishonest
men are dishonest only for one reason; that's because they
are poor."

At these words the Canon actually started with delight.

"That," he exclaimed, "is the very doctrine which I am
always preaching from the pulpit, and now and then from
the platform; and that's why some people see fit to call me
a radical. I'm glad to find that your grace is of one mind
with me. Men are dishonest only when society makes them
poor."

"Then in that case," said the Duke, facing round to the
Canon, and speaking in a voice that had the air of being
confidential, but which was nevertheless distinctly audible
to every one, "in that case, if I were you, I wouldn't be so
hard upon the rich."

Delighted as he was with this sudden thrust, he had no
wish to discompose the Canon seriously; so, to cover the
confusion he had caused, he addressed himself to Reginald
Pole. "Reginald," he called out, "if I were a poor man
you would probably find, when I am gone, that three or four
of these silver candlesticks were missing. If you or Canon
Bulman," he continued, "ever pay me a visit at Dulverton
—if you will, Canon, I shall be very happy to see you—"
at this the satisfaction in the Canon's face shone out again

after a momentary eclipse—"I shouldn't advise you or any one else," said the Duke fiercely, "to make away with any of the spoons or forks *there*."

"Why so, your grace?" asked the Canon a little stiffly; and all stared with wonder at the Duke's sudden ferocity.

"Because they're not silver," said the Duke, and closed his mouth with a snap. Having enjoyed for a moment the surprise which this explanation caused, "Most of my silver," he said, "is in the cellars of Childes' Bank. What I use at Dulverton is a copy in electro-plate. See, when you come, Canon, if you can tell the difference."

To the Canon's ear there was magic in the last words; and, on the whole, he enjoyed his dinner: but after Mrs. Pole had left the gentlemen to themselves, he began to be galled afresh in a place that was already aching. When Pole moved from his own end of the table and seated himself by the Duke, the Duke turned round, and edging as close to him as possible, became deaf to everybody else, and talked to him exclusively. He began questioning him about various European capitals, with most of which he himself had had formerly some acquaintance; and Pole's answers, which were more audible than the Duke's questions, betrayed an intimacy with the beauties of so many Courts, and with so many distinguished Continental families, that the Canon, who knew nothing of Europe but the peaks and table d'hôtes of Switzerland, felt—he could hardly tell why —as if he were intentionally shut out in the cold. This alone was a disagreeable thing to bear; but it was worse still when the Duke, dropping his voice, made one or two remarks which apparently related to ladies. It was an axiom with the Canon, who had the charity which believes all things, that every whispered remark about a woman was either cynical or indecent, or both; but his righteous anger was directed in the present case not against his ducal neighbour for making the remarks in question, but against his former pupil for being the recipient of them. Lord Wargrave, too, was annoyed, though for very different reasons. He was annoyed at being debarred, owing to the presence of the three clergymen, from a feast of philosophy and anecdote, in which he would have gladly joined; but his sense of propriety constrained him to make the best of the situation, and as he could not well take part in the gossip about

Berlin and Paris, he entertained the Dean, Canon Bulman, and Dr. Clitheroe, by trenchant accounts of the immorality of the country priesthood in Spain.   The implied tribute to the superior morals of Protestantism hallowed this subject in the eyes even of the Canon; but before long the discussion of it was interrupted by the voice of the Duke, whom the interest of some reminiscence had made unconscious of how loud he was speaking, and who was heard saying, in his most pointed and deliberate accents, " Her mother was my father's favourite mistress."

" Reginald," said the Dean, rising, " don't let me interrupt the Duke.   I am going to have a little talk with your mother."

The events of the dinner-table had a double effect upon the Canon.   They left him when he rose from his chair, and from contact with the Duke's elbow, elated with a delightful addition to his stock of social self-complacency; and they also left him more dissatisfied with Pole than ever.   But Pole's offences against him were not even yet complete.   The Canon's tenderest spot had thus far been only grazed by him. Before the evening was over he was destined to plunge a dagger into it.   Some business about the funeral, which necessitated an interview with the bailiff, kept him for a quarter of an hour from following his guests into the drawing-room.   When he did so, his mother and the Dean were talking together in low tones; Dr. Clitheroe was smiling silently; the Duke was apparently asleep; and the principal sounds in the room were proceeding from the Canon and Lord Wargrave.   The Canon, with the air of a complete man of the world, was discoursing to Lord Wargrave about society in the neighbourhood of Windsor; and as he saw Pole approaching, he unconsciously raised his voice.   " No," he was saying, with reference to a well-known clerical liberateur—the author, amongst other things, of a manual of private prayers, which a crowned head had rendered popular by offering them up to Heaven—" no," the Canon was saying, " I don't think I exactly like him.   Rather snobby, I fancy—rather fond of great people."

" I am never quite certain," said Pole, at whom the Canon had cast a lofty glance, " what it is that people mean by a snob."

" I mean," said the Canon, " and so I believe do most of

us, a man who estimates others by who they are, not by what
they are."

"I," replied Pole, "should venture to differ slightly from
you. So far as the accidents of position have any effect on
us at all, everybody's social judgments move roughly to the
same tune; but the men whom you call snobs play each note
a semitone wrong; they distort the tune with false expression and emphasis, and very often," he added as an after-
thought, "they pretend that they are not attempting to play
the tune at all."

In his mind as he spoke there was no thought of wounding
anybody. He was not even trying to put the Canon argu-
mentatively in the wrong. But the Canon, for some reason,
grew crimson to the roots of his hair. He bit his lip, and
was stammering for some retort when a hollow voice sounded
from the depths of an armchair. The speaker was the Duke,
who, if he had slept at all, had certainly managed to sleep
with one ear open.

"Canon," he said, "Mr. Pole is perfectly right. Mr. Pole
had you there, I think. When the nation honoured my
father by making him a duke, did they mean to give him
something which others should not respect? No one," continued the Duke, in his best aphoristic manner—"no one
deserves an honour who despises it; and no one despises it
who receives it. Wait, Canon, till you're a bishop—as you
are perfectly sure to be—and tell me what you think then."

So far as the Duke was concerned, Canon Bulman's
feelings, outraged by the beginning of this speech, were
charmed by the end of it into a state of renewed satisfaction;
but it was only by all the efforts of mundane and Christian
self-control combined, that he was able to be courteously
civil in saying "Good night" to Pole, and in accepting from
his hands a copy of the Lyncombe paper, which contained an
account of the arrangements for Miss Pole's funeral on the
morrow.

CHAPTER VIII.

A GOOD deal of arranging had indeed been necessary to facilitate the attendance of the large numbers that were expected. The church where the burial was to take place was some two hours' drive from Glenlynn, hidden in a deep valley : but a couple of miles on the Lyncombe side of it was a spot on the moor where several rough roads met, one having been a coach-road seventy years ago. Here stood a bald old inn, which had, since the days of coaches, been kept disconsolately alive by the patronage of a few stag-hunters ; and at this spot the mourners from all quarters were to assemble. Here the hearse was to await them at half-past eleven; and here, in a room where travellers once break-fasted, they were subsequently to solace themselves with the funeral baked meats.

By the hour appointed the place wore a strange aspect. The lines of hedgeless road were black with flies and carriages, the warm gorse-scented wind blowing all August through their windows. Some of the carriages were empty, but most had sable occupants : and a number of figures also were standing about the inn-door. Chief amongst these was Mr. Pole, the head of the family, six feet four in height, with a clean-shaved commanding face ; recalling a past age by his voluminous white choker, and black, swallow-tailed coat, buttoned across his chest tightly. A little in the background was the undertaker, taking charge of the waving hat-bands, with which he had contracted to decorate the principal male mourners, and, little as he thought it, to give to the day's solemnities another touch of an age that has almost vanished.

The last arrivals were the party from Glenlynn. Their advent caused a considerable though subdued sensation ; and the carriages then began to be marshalled in proper order. The family and their immediate friends meanwhile entered the inn ; where the hats of the favoured males were indued with the insignia of sorrow. The Duke alone was exempt, for the exceedingly simple reason that he wore an old soft wide-awake, on which no hat-band could support itself ; and the undertaker on realizing this would hardly have recovered from his bewilderment, if it had not been for Lord Wargrave,

who, with an impatient grunt, tendered his own hat to
receive the orthodox treatment.

At length it appeared that the preliminaries were settled:
and the undertaker, backing like a Lord Chamberlain, led
his lugubrious procession out to the line of carriages. In
front the plumes of the hearse slowly waved and nodded, and
wild bees and butterflies passed and repassed between them.
Presently a word was given; the dark plumes moved
onwards, and the carriages began to follow like a train of
crawling caterpillars. The nature of the road in itself was
enough to make the progress slow; but in half an hour it
suddenly grew yet slower, this being partly due to the steep-
ness of a descending hill, and partly to a fact which was
announced by the sight of some low-browed cottages, and
then by the throbbing note of a slowly-tolling bell. Presently came cottages clustering more thickly; men—mostly
old—were walking along in black: the note of the bell grew
clearer: the carriages at last stopped.

There was hardly a cottage within fifteen miles of Glenlynn which Miss Pole's charity had not either cheered or
pauperized: and a small, but sympathetic, crowd was
assembled at the churchyard gate. The scene was singular.
The church and the straggling village said to the stranger
from every roof and window that progress never as yet had
entered this secret hollow; indeed, the primitive aspect of
everything almost appalled the mind, whilst captivating it.
The church, for some reason lost in parochial history, was
large and out of all proportion to the present number of the
parishioners. It had been built in the fifteenth century;
but its fine pointed windows showed, both in their glazing
and their tracery, the repairing hand of the eighteenth; and
its old-world air was most probably owing to its suggestions
of that nearer past rather than of the more remote.

And now, from its opened door, what figure was this that
was given forth to the light, and advanced between the
mouldering tombstones—a figure whose old wig and dusty
tumbled surplice made it seem as if both they and their
wearer had been taken out of some forgotten cupboard? He
shuffled in walking; his proportions were somewhat portly;
and about his nostrils hung shadows suggesting snuff. His
face, indeed, produced the impression of a man who was
walking in his sleep; till suddenly his lips moved, and the

following well-known words rose from them, distinctly audible, though thin, in the open air : " I am the Resurrection and the Life, saith the Lord. He that believeth in Me, though he were dead, yet shall he live." And the palled coffin, with its bearers, had begun their movement towards the church.

The mourners followed—a long column of infantry—brushing the forlorn grasses that leaned over the grass-grown path, and defiling into the building through a porch, on whose whitewashed walls notices hung about ratepayers and licences for dogs and guns. Within the spectacle was one of which soon there will be no example left. The old square pews of the eighteenth century, some of them lined with moth-eaten green baize, filled the body of the church; and one of the aisles was dwarfed by a brown gallery. The clerk's desk, the clergyman's desk, and the pulpit, rose above one another, crowned with a huge sounding-board, on which stood a gilt angel blowing a dusty trumpet. The lion and the unicorn hung in a black frame, with the royal arms between them, over the middle of the chancel arch; and a meagre altar, adorned with two velvet cushions, was flanked by a dingy board inscribed with the Lord's Prayer, and the table that begins with, " A man may not marry his grandmother."

Whilst the coffin, in the central passage, rested on its high trestles, the alien company gradually found places, stirring up, as they did so, odours of old prayer-books, musty bassocks, and many past congregations. Pole, who, on entering, had observed the gallery staircase, made his way alone to a solitude amongst the upper seats; and filled with a swarm of thoughts, which he feared to betray to others, was able unnoticed to gaze on the scene below. Meanwhile, a sudden and unexpected sound had startled the ears of almost all those present. It was the sound of a fiddle, from which an old village musician, who supplied with his instrument the place of organ and organist, began to elicit the tune of a funereal hymn. To those, who, like Pole, knew the West of England well, and were aware that till up to the middle of the present century, a village band of flutes, fiddles, and clarionets, continued in remoter places to supply the sole church music, the wail of these notes was as music coming out of a grave. To Pole it rose pungent, like some bewitched incense, fraught with everything that was dear and past and impossible; and his own life, with its secrets, whatever they were, enlarged themselves, till his personal consciousness was little more than a heart, beating and palpitating with the hopes and losses of generations. Then his attention strayed to a mural tablet facing him, bracketed on coats of arms, and surmounted by a willowy female, whose straight Grecian profile drooped over a marble urn. Straining his sight somewhat he spelt out the inscription, the very phrasing of which was sufficient to fix its date. "In the adjacent vault, according to his own directions, are disposited the mortal remains of Tristram Pole, Esquire, eminent alike for the genius and the elegant accomplishments which endeared him to his Sovereign's son, and for his public services to his country. He was for many years Member of Parliament for this county, and owner of Pole Park and its large appendages. Reader, learn from hence the vanity of all earthly possessions; but be also taught, by the signal example of one whose charitable hand was ever open to the poor, to cultivate that special virtue which, more than any other, recommends man to his Creator and covers a multitude of sins."

But he had hardly come to the end when he realized that the fiddle had ceased and a single voice was snuffling through the musty silence. "Behold, Thou hast made my days as it were a span long; verily every man living is altogether vanity." Then the voice sank to a long monotonous murmur, interrupted only by the lilt of two doxologies, to the shame-faced singing of which the assembly was stimulated by the fiddle.

Pole had been listening in a fit of vague abstraction, moved by his surroundings he hardly knew how or why: and at length he leant forward, half kneeling, with his face buried in his hands. His mental condition, in common with that of so many, was such that the service could not possibly mean to him what it has meant to those who have listened to it for so many centuries. Its formal meaning for him was the form of a myth or fable; but there was something in it—a something not to be crystallized into words—which sank deep into his being and touched those roots of life from which all religion springs—all religion that is more than a lost chapter of chemistry. With a painful tenderness his thoughts began to fix themselves on two other lives connected with or dependent on his own, and he mentally began to offer up his own happiness for the sake of theirs, placing it, as it were, upon an altar, and offering it for his own sins also; until, as he knelt in spirit, it seemed to him as if a fire from heaven streamed through the cold and darkness, and consumed the sacrifice and accepted it.

But such visions are transient whatever their meaning or their effects may be; and Pole was roused from his by a rise in the clergyman's voice, which brought the following syllables poignant and piercing to his ear—"It is sown in corruption; it is raised in incorruption"—and reminded him, among other things, of how far the service had proceeded. At the same moment he distinguished what before had escaped his notice—a black wound gaping in the pavement of the aisle opposite; and he then recollected that the interment would be inside the church.

The open vault, however, was not all that he saw. On turning his head slightly, he perceived with some surprise, that he was not, as he had thought he was, alone in the gallery any longer. In the pew next to his own were two female figures. But he probably would not have bestowed a second glance on them if he had not been roused by a breath of some incongruous perfume. He looked; and a slim hand, delicately gloved in black, caught his attention resting on a mildewed prayer-book. Then he realized the crisp curves of a figure which a dark jacket emphasized with fastidious outlines; and, on raising his eyes, a pair of eyes met his which held his own in one long astonished scrutiny. They were the eyes of the pastel portrait; only far down in their depth, shining between their long lashes, there was, mixed with feeling, a faint sparkle of *espièglerie*. Of what he did he was altogether unconscious; but he knew he must have made some sort of movement towards her, for, shaking her head slowly with a gentle smile of deprecation, she just raised for a moment one reproving finger. But at this juncture a stir took place below. The coffin was being lifted, and numbers were making their way towards the vault. Pole, with a hasty gesture, prepared to do so likewise; but in the act of going he hesitated, and, leaning towards the fair stranger, he said in a grave undertone, "Would you care to come down too? I know you. I am Reginald Pole; and you are Countess Shimna O'Keefe." She was like a woman who is encountered in a dream, and who is surprised at nothing. She replied in a tone that was even lower than his own, "I would rather remain here. Go—you must go alone."

A moment later he was standing by the dark aperture. The sentences of the Burial Service were being read at intervals like minute guns, and the coffin was being lowered slowly. In the gloom underneath were lights, and by means of a dirty ladder the Squire, Lord Wargrave, and several others descended. Pole followed them. The cold walls of the vault lisped with unwonted echoes as men shuffled and pushed each other, settling the coffin in its place. At last somebody touched his sleeve respectfully, and put into his hand a trowel filled with something. He saw it was earth. He threw a little on the coffin lid, and the words, "Ashes to ashes," were heard in the air above. As he performed this office the words "Margaret Pole" gleamed up at him in silver as yet untarnished; and at the same moment the candle-light revealed another inscription, which now was quite close to this one, and which he stooped down to examine. What he saw was a text somewhat abbreviated from the original: "The mother may forget her sucking child, yet will I not forget thee." This struck him as sufficiently, though not signally appropriate, until through the thick dust he made out a few words more—"Tristram Pole," with the date of his birth and death; and then it dawned on him that the dead man might have chosen the text himself, with a meaning somewhat different from that which his orthodox relations must have attributed to it.

As he climbed the ladder again the elocution of the officiating clergyman struck him as having grown unaccountably more impressive and sonorous. It imparted the vibrations of a bell to the overwhelming sentence that was being uttered. "I heard a voice from heaven, saying unto me, Write, From henceforth blessed are the dead which die in the Lord: even so saith the Spirit; for they rest from their labours." Pole stared at the speaker, and instead of the old incumbent who had, as he heard subsequently, been seized with a fit of hoarseness, and had retired to suck lozenges in the vestry, his eye rested on the form of the Rev. Sunderland Godolphin, arrayed, it is true, in a surplice much too short for him, but, in spite of this trivial detail, more imposing than ever, and at last doing justice to Christianity, to his auditors, and to himself, by showing how the Church of England could bury her children when she chose. For him, at all events, the solemnities had not been performed in vain.

The concluding prayer at the grave had not come to an end before Pole had escaped from the crowd, and stolen back to the gallery; but he found it entirely empty. He had scanned the figures below, but failed to distinguish what he was seeking. He descended the stairs hastily, and at the bottom was an old bell-ringer, who asked him " if so be he was looking for two ladies; " and who, on being answered " Yes," replied, with a senile grin, " That the ladies had left in a carriage ten minutes ago."

A moment or two later everybody was once more in the sunlight. The sky glowed with blueness, the air smelt of grass and summer, and faces hitherto rigid brightened into discreet smiles. By the time the inn was reached again the smiles had rippled into laughter. Clergymen, lawyers, doctors, and tenants on the Pole estate exchanged greetings with the great county magnates; and Lord Wargrave, who alone stuck to his waving hat-band, looked about him fussily, as if surprised at not being recognized. Canon Bulman, by an unconscious instinct, hovered in the Duke's neighbour-hood, and found himself sitting next him when the party settled down to their refreshments. Old Lady Taplow, however, who was on the Duke's further side, took possession of the ducal ear, and the Canon could only listen.

" It was very touching and picturesque," she began in her gruff, masculine voice. " I am glad that you made me come. By the way, Duke, I ought to thank you for the cheque you gave me for my bazaar. It was kind of you, You're a good man, Duke."

" And you," said the Duke, " are a good woman—so far as I know, that is to say—so far as I know." The Canon swelled with anger at the tone of this flippant innuendo, and, cultivating the emotion, felt proudly that he was no syco-phant. He turned away, and found that his other neighbour was Pole.

" Somebody," he said sarcastically, as he glanced round the table, " will be proposing the bride's health soon. People

are far more cheerful here than at most wedding break-
fasts."

"Well," replied Pole, "is not that as it should be? A
death is the ending of sorrow, and a wedding is generally
the beginning of it."

CHAPTER IX.

CANON BULMAN, when the funeral feast was over, instead of
returning to Glenlynn, was claimed by Mr. Godolphin, and
his place was to be taken by the old family lawyer. The day
being Saturday, the rest of Mrs. Pole's visitors were to stay
till Monday; and Mr. Godolphin had been rendered happy
by her promise to bring them all to his Sunday morning's
service. As they were standing by the carriages and settling
how to seat themselves, Dr. Clitheroe, with a little nervousness of manner, touched Pole's arm, and said to him in a
confidential whisper, "Do you think you would care to walk
the last two miles of the way? We have had no exercise,
and I should be glad of a few words with you."

"Certainly," Pole replied. "Let us get in here then with
Miss Drake." And by-and-by, when the swelling downs
were reached which hid Glenlynn between their bare
shoulders and the sea, he and the Doctor descended, leaving
Miss Drake alone—a little abstracted bundle of silence, and
crape, and tears.

"I have had," said the Doctor, "during the last few days
no opportunity of explaining a small matter to you. Your
mother understands it. She, naturally, has my entire confidence; but the whole arrangement—I am sure you will not
forget this—must rest a secret between our three selves.
Your lawyer, Mr. Whilks—I presume he is coming here for
the purpose—will presently take possession of your aunt's
will, and explain its provisions to yourself and others. Now
I want to tell you beforehand that in the will itself you will
find no money left to you till after your mother's death.
The reason, of course, is that your twenty thousand pounds
had to be realized during Miss Pole's lifetime, and, as I have
explained already, placed in my hands to deal with. Well,"
the Doctor proceeded, "the difficulty in our way was this:
how to ensure your succession to the sum in question, and

F

yet to keep the transaction secret, as I was bound to keep it. Your aunt wished to confide entirely in my own honour, and to leave in my custody all the papers connected with it. That proposal, however, I could not entertain for a moment. She and I, therefore, hit upon this device. A document, signed by me and accompanied by a letter from herself, was placed in a sealed packet. It was directed to you, and deposited with other valuables in a safe, and this packet is expressly left to you in the will, described 'as containing certain papers and memoranda, explanatory of my conduct with regard to the said Reginald Pole, which packet I desire that he open and read in private.' If you will look here," said the Doctor, pulling out a large pocket-book, "I can show you a duplicate of a formal document, in which the receipt of the money is acknowledged by me, and the terms on which I received it are stated."

The Doctor produced a large sheet of foolscap paper, which bore the stamp of the Government Office to which he belonged, and on which the following form was engrossed in a clerk-like hand, the names and dates being faintly written in pencil: "Received for investment by me, the undersigned, from Margaret Pole, of Glenlynn, spinster, on behalf of her great-nephew, Reginald Osborne Pole, Esq., the sum of twenty thousand pounds. I undertake to pay interest quarterly on the above sum, at the rate of fourteen per cent. per annum, the same to be paid to the aforesaid Margaret Pole during her lifetime, and after her death to the aforesaid Reginald Pole, his heirs, or his assignees. This arrangement is to hold good for eleven years and five months from the present date, at the end of which period I reserve the right of repaying the principal. Further, after five months from the present date, I engage to repay the principal, should this be desired, at any time that may be named, two months' notice having been given me. In the event of my death, the above arrangements will be carried out for me by my colleague, Edward Stuart Michell, Esq., Inspector of Technical Schools for England, who will represent me in this transaction."

Pole looked the paper through, and gave it back to the Doctor, merely observing, "I am glad that my mother understands. She would else have wondered at my having been left nothing. As it is, I suppose old Whilks, who knew something of my aunt's affairs, will be puzzled at the personal property being less than he probably imagined it."

" I don't think," replied the Doctor, " we need have any fear of that. This last will, like the former one, was drawn up by Mr. Whilks himself, and your good aunt explained to him that she had spent a portion of her capital. The statement was strictly true, for, as you will see from the paper I have shown you, the twenty thousand pounds were virtually transferred to you during her lifetime. No," continued the Doctor, rubbing his hands gently, " since you and your mother understand the transaction, there is nothing in the will which will elicit comment from anybody." The Doctor's prediction in this respect proved substantially, though not literally, true; for when the contents of the will came to be known in detail, so many were the legacies left to old servants, and so far beyond her humble hopes was the provision made for Miss Drake, that the sense of Miss Pole's loss, which had thus far been a grey cloud, was already illuminated by the spreading light of resignation.

By the following morning the progress in Christian cheerfulness was remarkable, when Mrs. Pole, in a large open waggonette, conveyed her party to Mr. Godolphin's church. Mr. Godolphin, too, when he saw through the vestry window the heads of the Pole horses tossing themselves at his churchyard gate, felt his heart agreeing with the text of the sermon he was about to preach, and acknowledging that death had been partially swallowed up in victory. His own chancel, with its altar and surpliced choir, its brass lectern, its crosses, and brilliant scrolls, seemed by contrast with the one he had visited yesterday, more perfect than ever to him in its modest catholic beauty. It touched him afresh by the effect which he felt it would have upon the strangers; and when his organ, from its rows of spruce blue pipes, began to flute forth a very creditable voluntary, he silently thanked Heaven at being thus permitted to offer to it such music as would not ascend to it from any other village in the county. But the climax was reached when his choir, being duly robed, poured through the vestry door and took their appointed places. Then, slow and stately, came Mr. Godolphin after them, the sleeves of his surplice swelling with some wind of the spirit. The organ reverently hushed itself, and " Dearly beloved

brethren" prolonged, and, indeed, outrivalled, the music of
its silenced diapason. Mr. Godolphin proceeded with his
ministrations, as if conscious that the service was not prayer
only, but a lesson in prayer; and when he reached the
passage, which always had been his favourite, "High and
mighty, King of kings, Lord of lords," he produced the
impression, as Lord Wargrave observed subsequently, of
being "himself the great Sublime he drew." Nor was his
sermon unworthy of what preceded it. It was really in
excellent taste, and instinct with unfeigned emotion; and no
dispassionate student of human nature could have avoided
feeling, in spite of his guileless vanity, an affectionate respect
for him, as his periods hung and echoed amongst the rafters.

When all was over the party from Glenlynn waited to
speak to him in the churchyard, where they were first met
by his wife—a lady whose native kindness expressed itself
in a county accent. Mrs. Godolphin had a pronounced taste
for colour; and she usually celebrated Sunday with a display of glittering ribbons, which made her look like a yacht
on the morning of some grand regatta. But now she was
all in black, and her ribbons hung their heads, as she held
Mrs. Pole's hand, and, glancing shyly at the others, said
that "Dear Sunderland" would be there in another moment.
In another moment he came, glossy in long black cloth, and
standing bareheaded, as if, whilst he was on consecrated
ground, he was, in some special and spiritual sense, indoors,
he bowed majestically on being introduced to the two peers;
and turning to the Dean, told, though he hardly knew it,
one of the few untruths of his life. "Had I been earlier
aware," he said, "that there was any chance of your being
here, I should have asked you if you would have preached
this morning. Canon Bulman," he continued, "has taken
a service at Lyncombe. I trust, Mrs. Pole, that you—all
of you—are going to stay for luncheon. We counted on
your doing so—Mrs. Godolphin and myself." This invitation was entirely unexpected; and Mrs. Pole was on the
point of refusing it, when a vision rose before her of a table
laid for ten, covered with pies and chickens, crackers, and
coloured jellies, and of the sadness of two human beings, if
they alone sat down at it. After a little hesitation, therefore, the proffered hospitality was accepted, and the whole
party bent their steps towards the Vicarage.

Mr. Godolphin turned inclusively towards the Dean, Lord Wargrave, and the Duke. "I hope," he said, "you were pleased with our little service."

"Very much so," said the Duke. "I shall take your chancel for a model, whenever I have the courage——" He paused.

"The courage to do what, Duke?" said the Dean.

"The courage to deprive the Duchess of our old family pew."

"I don't know, Dean," said Mr. Godolphin, elated by this praise, and betraying in his voice a gentle amused triumph, "if you have seen the letters about me in the last week's 'Western Times'? There I am, gibbeted—as near Rome as possible." And as he spoke he shone with all the delights of martyrdom.

It was shortly after this that Lord Wargrave, nudging the Duke with his elbow—an attention which the Duke hated—muttered his observation about Mr. Godolphin and "the great Sublime." The Duke, however, entirely ignoring the witticism, replied sententiously—

"I thought the passage remarkably well read. I'll tell you what," he continued, with a little malicious laugh. "You, Wargrave, have seen a good deal of the world. Did you ever observe this, that bad men may have many follies, but only good men have foibles? Mr. Godolphin is a thoroughly good man. If I were the Deity, I should listen to him with a great deal of pleasure; and if he were a poor man I should give him my best living.'

Lord Wargrave felt the dig; he received digs very often; but nothing wounded him, and he was rarely even perturbed. He was not so now; and when he seated himself in the Vicarage dining-room, and perceived the amplitude of the hospitable repast before him, his friendship for Mr. Godolphin almost surpassed the Duke's. After luncheon, Mr. Godolphin happened to mention that he was sending his carriage to bring back Canon Bulman. Lord Wargrave, on hearing this, went up to Pole confidentially and said to him—

"Would you be disposed to come into Lyncombe with me? We can get a lift, and return to Glenlynn in a fly. It occurred to me I might as well take the opportunity of going and calling on my old friend Countess O'Keefe."

" You know her then, do you ? " exclaimed Pole, with surprise and interest.

" I've known half the family," said Lord Wargrave, " at one time and another; and I've not a doubt when she sees my card, she'll remember me. Besides, she's your own relation. It is only proper you should call."

Pole, however, required no pressing. Mr. Godolphin was delighted that the services of his carriage were appreciated, and the two gentlemen drove off in it triumphantly. When they reached Lyncombe, and descended the precipitous hill, which zigzags down to the port between villas and hanging gardens, the very first object that glittered at them and caught their attention was a smart-looking steam schooner lying near the primitive pier, and lighting up all the prospect with its awnings and flashing hand-rails.

" I thought," said Lord Wargrave to Pole, when the carriage had set them down—and he took his arm and spoke in a confidential mumble—" I thought it as well not to mention this visit of ours to your mother. She was not particularly warm in her wishes to meet these ladies; but when we have seen what they are like, I have no doubt we shall be able to tell her they're everything that is correct, well-bred, and delightful."

Pole was somewhat amazed at Lord Wargrave's speculative condition with regard to a person he had spoken of as an old friend; but he had not fully realized that this remarkable man, who had thrown the net of his acquaintanceship over most of the civilized world, assumed that he knew everybody, till events proved the contrary, and that he would then make a new friendship in discovering it was not an old one.

" We must get a boat," said Lord Wargrave, as with a somewhat imperious gesture he tried to attract the attention of an old, somnolent fisherman. But Pole interrupted him and pointed to a couple of figures, lounging at a little distance, with caps scarlet as poppies, and spruce blue jerseys, which were seen, on a nearer view, to carry in white letters the outlandish word "Moshiska." Lord Wargrave, always happy to exhibit his accomplishments as a linguist, addressed the men in Italian and then in German, as if taking it for granted that they were natives of Trieste or Fiume. They answered, however, in the tongue of the Isle of Wight. "The Countess," they said, "was on board;" and in a minute or two more he and Pole found themselves at the yacht's side. Lord Wargrave's hand was in his pocket, about to produce his card-case, when a fit of shyness, rare as an angel's visit, urged him to shift the burden of self-introduction to his companion. "Send up your card," he said, "and I will write my name on it." The card was sent, and with a very flattering promptitude the visitors were invited to ascend. They found themselves in a world of deck-houses, deck-chairs, and plump red cushions littered with Parisian novels. Amongst some of the cushions in the stern, there was, as they followed their conductor, a disturbance of blue serge and bright cherry-coloured bows; and a tall lady had risen and was coming forward to meet them. Her figure was full but had not lost its outlines; an infantine straw hat, with "Moshiska" written on its ribbon, surmounted rippling hair which recalled the yellow of a mimosa blossom; and her face, though it showed the lines and contours of sixty, was radiant—thanks to her powder puff—with the dust, not of age, but of youth. Both her hands were extended in gracious welcome, to Pole first, and to Lord Wargrave after him. Her voice was charming; she had a faint foreign accent, which produced the impression that she would have been very sorry to lose it; and her manner had just that one unnecessary degree of *empressement*, which betrays in a woman that civility has an added value for her, because, for some excellent reason, she no longer always receives it. "I was so distressed," she said, ringing her r's, "to hear, Mr. Pole, of your poor old aunt's death. My daughter and her maid went to witness the funeral. And your mother—she wrote me such a pretty, nice, kind note. I knew her as a girl. She is well now? Yes? That's right, then. Lord Wargrave, do be seated. We have met, you say. Was it at Baden?"

"That's the worst," said Lord Wargrave, who was in the depths of a chair by this time—"that's the worst of meeting a charming woman. The fact remains so vivid it makes one forget the circumstances."

"You were staying then with the Grand Duke, were you not?" said the Countess, helping him out. "We had not time, I think, for much conversation together. It was the year when that silly little Ladislaus—a perfect boy he was, a baby—you remember him with his great *boutonnière*—was said by everybody to be *au mieux* with the Grand Duchess."

Lord Wargrave remembered. At once he was on solid ground. "The united ages," he said, "of the Grand Duchess's lovers, would make a smaller total than those of any other women in Europe." He and the Countess now perfectly understood one another; and even if, as seemed possible, they had never so much as spoken previously, they were soon conversing as though they had been lifelong friends. Nor was Pole by any means left out in the cold. She said to him, "Will you order tea for me? You see I treat you like a relation. And be a good man, do; and fetch me my cigarette case. It is lying there by a book— oh, such a book, mon Dieu! It is called '*Les Lèvres de Violette.*' My cousin Bobrovski sent it me."

"Is that the prince—the traveller?" said Lord Wargrave. "Why, God bless my soul, I met him by the Dead Sea, when he was straining his eyes to distinguish the submerged public buildings of Gomorrah. I saved his life, I remember, by giving him a package of tinned pigs' trotters."

"He's coming here soon," said the Countess, with the faintest air of embarrassment. "The yacht is his. He is a dear fellow, and he lent it me. I was," she went on, as if hurrying over delicate ground, "told that the sea air would be good for my daughter's health; and this place was particularly recommended to us. She's been nervous lately, and there's been a little something wrong with the chest; and she would, for many reasons, like a place that was quiet. We've seen a little thatched cottage with which we are all charmed; and when some of our servants—our old servants —can arrive, we shall most likely leave her here for a couple of months."

"And where is Countess Shimna now?" asked Pole, who had been patient hitherto only because each moment he expected the young lady's appearance.

"She's gone with her maid to church," said the Countess, poising a cigarette between two fingers laden with pearls and diamonds. "She sets you a lesson. You should both be hearing a sermon, instead of sitting and talking nonsense here with me. You laugh! I should have heard mass myself at eight o'clock this morning, but the carriage did not come, and I am forbidden to walk uphill."

"Well," said Lord Wargrave, "here are two father con-
fessors, eager to hear your sins, and to tell you in absolution
that they are far more charming than the virtues of other
people."

"Ah," said the Countess, with a gay ripple of laughter,
"that is good now! I'm afraid they'd be a long catalogue."

Pole meanwhile was beginning to think wearily that,
since Countess Shimna was away, the visit was a waste of
time; so, consulting his watch, he said, "If we wish to be
back for dinner, I fear we must say good-bye, and ask to be
put ashore. My mother, Countess, is hoping so much to
see you; but if business prevents her this week from driving
over to Lyncombe, perhaps you and Countess Shimna will
come one day to us at Glenlynn."

"Your dear mother!" exclaimed the Countess, evidently
pleased at this overture, but once again betraying some
slight embarrassment. "As for me, I am not strong enough
for visiting. I must wait, too, and see what my cousin
Bobrovski has settled for me. But as for Shimna—she, I
am sure, will be delighted to see your mother. Write—do
write—and tell her a day for coming."

Pole was by this time standing, ready to say "good-
bye"; but Lord Wargrave, who seemed each moment to be
sinking deeper in a quicksand of cushions, was far from
showing the smallest inclination to move. "My dear
fellow," he said, "you are happily young and active. Will
you order the carriage for us? and when I see it on the
pier, I will join you."

Pole readily assented, feeling now that the visit had been
a success. Though his mind, since his meeting with
Countess Shimna, had been occupied with other things, the
memory of her at odd moments had been frequently shining
through them at him, and he was conscious of a curiosity
with regard to her which surprised him, and which he tried
to stifle. At this moment, however, it was possessing him
unreproved, and his thoughts were busy with her appearance
in the old church, when the boat that was taking him back
bumped against the harbour steps. As he landed he heard
that the men said something; but he did not realize what,
till, on reaching the topmost step, he saw that the subject
of his thoughts was herself standing before him. Again for
a moment, just as in the gallery of the church, their eyes

exchanged an unflinching and full regard. Then her lips
smiled, like an opening rose-bud. She put her hand out to
him. He took it, and held it lingeringly.

"I have been," he said, "to call upon your mother. Lord
Wargrave is with her still. We are just starting for
Glenlynn. I am going to get a carriage. My mother means
to write, and ask you to come and see us." The sentences
came with a sort of unconscious shyness. Something of
shyness showed itself in her also, for she several times drew
breath as if meaning to begin a sentence. She was silent,
however, until he came to an end, and then she said simply
and almost tremulously—

"I should like that. Good-bye; I must go now." She
again gave her hand to him, and, withdrawing it with the
soft slowness of a wave withdrawing itself from the sand,
she went down to the boat, and the water was soon between
them. He made no attempt to keep her. He did not turn
to watch her even. On the contrary, he walked sharply
away, anxious to make sure of the memory before it had
time to alter—the memory of that butterfly of a moment,
before a detaining touch had been able to brush from its
wings one of their fragile colours.

"The mother," said Lord Wargrave, as they drove home
together, "is a dear, delightful woman. Her cousin Bobrovski is evidently of the same opinion. Perhaps we can
hardly expect your own mother to agree with him. But as
for the daughter—well," he grunted, as if fumbling about
for a phrase adequate to his meaning, "she's the sort of
woman to make any man under fifty mad."

That evening on the terrace at Glenlynn he again returned
to the subject. He and Pole had, both of them, after dinner
been tempted out of doors by the moonlight and the breath
of the verbena beds; and Lord Wargrave, who was devoted
to poetry though he was shrewd enough never to write any,
talked by turns of the beauty of Countess Shimna with her
singular family likeness to Lady Thyrza O'Keefe; of various
moonlit scenes — of Venice, of Constantinople, and the
Alhambra, with which, he hinted, he had tender associations
of his own; and of various distinguished ladies who, being
dead, could never contradict him, and whose acquaintance
with himself had caused much romantic disaster, though
whether to them or to him he left chivalrously undetermined.

"If I were your age," he said, "I should, instead of being here, be in a boat in Lyncombe harbour watching the lights of the Mo-hiska. If you want to keep young," he continued, thinking of his own career, and diverging from particular reflections to general, "you should never attempt to marry before you're forty. You should be humbly content till then with women who are married already. You won't," he said, having debated for a moment whether he should give his wisdom a cynical turn or a sentimental—"you won't be disappointed then by expecting too much of marriage. But look. Your butler is at the window. Is he looking for us for family prayers? You have them, I know, on Sundays. On such occasions I never miss being present. I prayed with Brigham Young every night I was in Salt Lake City."

Pole replied that prayers would not be for another hour, and Lord Wargrave found there was time to relapse into sentiment and philosophy. Pole, however, was not responsive; and the very thought of Countess Shimna, for some reason, appeared to have grown wearisome to him.

"You don't," grunted Lord Wargrave, having congratulated him on possessing so fascinating a neighbour, "seem aware of your *bonne fortune.* Young men of the present day have no love, and no religion. They marry at twenty-five, and cease to say prayers at twenty."

"I," said Pole, with a laugh, "at all events, am not married. And as for praying, we shall all of us pray again when a Royal Commission reports upon what to pray to."

"A night like this," said Lord Wargrave, "is a creed and a religion in itself. What makes religion is feeling."

"Yes," replied Pole, "and it lasts while the feeling lasts. Religious belief in these days is a Penelope's web, which is woven by the soul in emotion, and which the mind unweaves in meditation."

"And in spite of the mind," said Lord Wargrave, "the soul weaves it again."

"Is Saul among the prophets?" murmured Pole; and moving away from his companion for a step or two, he looked out over the sea. "And I, too," he said to himself, "have still a religion left me. It is buried, but buried in my heart; and for me it will still live, till memory no longer sits by the holy sepulchre."

CHAPTER X.

TWENTY-FOUR hours later Mrs. Pole's guests had departed,
and a new chapter of life was opened at Glenlynn, after the
final closing of one which had lasted for sixty years. But,
so far as externals went, the immediate future promised to
be merely an unbroken prolongation of the past. The sole
innovation was that Miss Drake, who was to remain on, had,
after much pressing, consented to dine downstairs.

Pole, who for many months had been engaged on the
preparation of a Blue-book, in which the results of his long
labours were to be summarized, resolved to take every
advantage of a seclusion so favourable to work, and finish
the volume, by dint of determined application, before the
House reassembled for an imminent autumn session. He
had already been corresponding about it with his excellent
official chief—a retired manufacturer of stockings, whom
the wisdom of the Tory party had converted into a peer,
under the homely title of Lord Henderson; and Lord
Henderson, a man of extreme practical shrewdness, had
exhibited an interest in the task, and a keen sense of its
importance, which inspired Pole's resolution with new vigour
and spirit. There was, indeed, at present nothing to distract
him from it. Countess O'Keefe had written to Mrs. Pole to
postpone Countess Shimna's promised visit for a week, as
they were going with Prince Bobrovski for a cruise down
the coast of Cornwall; and Pole had received the news
without visible disappointment. If useful and congenial
work, prepared under agreeable circumstances, really contains, as it is said, the secret of human happiness, he had
apparently every opportunity of working out his own
salvation. His advantages were not merely those of common
quiet and comfort; they comprised almost everything calculated to nerve and gratify the ambition and the faculties of
an energetic man, and caress the feelings of a sensitive one.
Well connected, and bearing an ancient name, already
possessed of a reputation, intellectual as well as social, and
engaged in an absorbing occupation, which might lead him
to a brilliant future, he had not only just succeeded, in the
vigorous spring of life, to a beautiful home, which, being his

mother's, was his own, but he had also found himself possessed of a private income, so infinitely exceeding his expectations as to seem like a magician's gift. And this new life, despite the suddenness of its advent, joined itself to the old, not with any crude abruptness, but with a noiseless and gentle coalescence, reaching his earliest years with a thousand uniting fibres. Indeed, the rooms and passages, musky with ghosts of departed scents, the old books and the wall-papers, the silver and the flowered china, and the mysterious cupboards into which he had once peeped fearfully, not only brought him back again to his own boyhood, but seemed to exhale upon his spirit the calm of an earlier generation.

It was a calm, too, that was alive with freshness. He would wander out into the early hours before breakfast, when the air was quick with smells of shaven grass; when the scythes swished through the dew on undulating, green declivities; when the flower-beds were censers, with the soul of the earth rising from them, and the silver gravel on the walks rustled beneath his footprints. He would watch the gardeners, bent by one lifelong service; their moorland lads beginning the same career, and one or two wrinkled old women in sun-bonnets, kneeling to grub up weeds. Their very rakes, and spuds, and wheelbarrows—he had known them all since childhood. They were all like objects in prints of a hundred years ago; and he felt, as he walked alone among these surroundings, that an unlooked-for peace was for a time enfolding him in its wings. This peace even came to possess, or to simulate, a spiritual character. Dr. Clitheroe, whose work in that district was not yet finished, had taken on his room at the farm for some weeks longer; whenever he was not absent on business he had his meals at Glenlynn; and each morning and evening the gentle inflection of his voice now filled the dining-room with the murmur of household prayer. As Pole knelt and listened to the well-worn phrases of faith, the heaven, which had long grown visionary, again appeared above him, and sheltered him, like a kindly roof-tree, from the horror of the inhuman Infinite.

But this was not all. Before many days were over, new ideas, new schemes of activity, began to develop themselves in his mind, and revealed sources of happiness to him deeper, in some respects, than any he had known hitherto. Familiar though he had been, and also profoundly interested, in all contemporary problems affecting the prosperity of the masses, and frequent as had been the cases in which, prompted by his kindness, he had given assistance to individual sufferers, his view of the helpless and the suffering had been that of the scientific inquirer, whose business is to supply knowledge to others, rather than set an example by applying it practically himself. Indeed, his position, and the very nature of the duties he had undertaken, had prevented his feeling the existence of any personal relationship between him and the groups of men—themselves so widely separated—whose conditions he studied, and whose evidence he so often took. But now, for the first time in his life, he was no longer a wanderer; and he found himself, in addition to being possessed of a home, surrounded by human beings, who, instead of being specimens and examples, had with that home and himself a vital and a personal connection. Intellectually all this was, of course, a truism to him, of which from the very first he had been aware; but it was some days before accident revealed it to him as a moral truth, and he hardly knew its face when he looked at it thus transfigured.

He was an active man, accustomed to long walks; and often, to refresh himself after work, he would ramble for many miles, renewing his boyish acquaintance with the beautiful country round him. He thus passed through several of the moorland villages, contrasting them with the villages whose condition he had studied in other countries. Here the farmers, as he knew, lived in the patriarchal way, which is, in the West of England, not even yet extinct. They worked with their labourers, and ate often at the same table with them; and the aspect of the cottages, and of the simple people themselves, filled him with the feeling that round the tranquillity of his own home was a zone of social tranquillity equally undisturbed and deep. At first, in fact, they affected his mind no further than by supplying it with this sense of passive and almost indolent satisfaction: and he had looked on these scenes as a pensive observer only, being taken by the villagers for a tourist who had lost his way.

But one day when he was struggling to open an unhinged

gate, a woman came out from a cottage, and civilly offered
him her help. He thanked her with equal friendliness, and
was intending to pass on, when he noticed that on her door-
step a diminutive child was standing. It was a boy about
three years old, clean and pretty in spite of its poor clothes.
Pole asked the woman if it was hers. With a smile she
answered, "Yes;" and he, going up to it, patted it gently
on the cheek, and began to talk to it in very creditable
infant English. It looked up at him as if it had found a
friend, and presently enlivened its half-articulate syllables
with that most delightful and mysterious sound—a little
child's laughter. Pole had never, to his own knowledge,
possessed that most valuable gift of conversing easily with
persons out of his own rank of life, unless there happened to
be some definite reason for doing so; but now sitting down
on a bench and taking the boy on his knee, he began to talk
to the mother about it, and presently to question her about
herself.

At last she said, "You're so good, sir, to my little boy,
it may be, perhaps, you've a little boy of your own."

Pole's face saddened. "I am not married," he answered.

"It's not often, sir," said the woman, "that a stranger
comes our way. You'll be staying somewhere in these parts,
I suppose?" He told her who he was. "Indeed, sir!" she
exclaimed with a curtsy. "I'm sure I beg your pardon, in
case I have been too free."

"I have spent," said Pole, rising, "a very pleasant half-
hour with you. I hope I shall see you often. Come, little
boy, good-bye. One of these days I shall bring you a pretty
top."

He felt as he walked home that suddenly, and without
any effort, his knowledge of things had been enlarged by
this chance interview; and those roots of life, the simplest
human sympathies, were revealed to him pushing their fibres
through the whole human soil, and binding together all
classes, however otherwise divided.

It so happened that, in an equally accidental way, the
same grave fact was forced on him again next morning;
only now it was under a different aspect. Close to the
home-farm there lived a labourer's family, which was well
enough known at Glenlynn as improvident, and always
poor. Pole had himself known many of its members, in his

childhood; and they and their helpless ways had, during Miss Pole's lifetime, excited disapproving amusement, far more than compassion. Dr. Clitheroe, when he appeared at breakfast, brought news that the father was dying, "And I fear," he said, "that the wife and children will be in a very sad plight."

"The Westerns," said Mrs. Pole, with a sigh, "have been a trouble ever since I can remember. The more Miss Pole did for them, the less they did for themselves."

"Well," said Pole, as he sipped his coffee indolently, "I suppose we must sin against our principles and help them once again."

He had taken up one of his letters and was amusing himself by looking at the postmarks, when the Doctor observed casually: "I was told that they really have nothing to eat at all, and that the children are at the door crying. I have promised to give them a little help myself."

"And has no one," exclaimed Pole, "given them even a crust already? Mother, what can I take? Give me some bread and milk—meat, butter, anything. I will go with it myself this moment."

He rang the bell; the required orders were given; and half an hour later he found himself in the cottage kitchen, dispensing his provisions to the children and the mother also; the hunger of the father having just been appeased for ever. Hitherto he had been conscious of that shrinking from the sight of pain which often makes sensitive men more selfish in action than the callous; and he had even now experienced a momentary nausea on first coming face to face with the slatternliness of the misery he was relieving. But the pleasure of giving relief made him forget all else. The cheeks of the children, squalid with dirt and sores, became delightful to him as he offered each mouth its portion; and the youngest little creature he fed with his own hands, watching the smiles sprout on its lips like mushrooms. He promised to see what could be done further; and the widow's face was a blessing, which went with him when he turned away.

This incident started him on a career of new activity. The sentimental aspect of the scene he had just witnessed soon passed from his mind; but it left behind it a suddenly awakened sense that some of the very evils whose nature he had been so long studying, were here at his very doors, calling on his experience for a cure; and a resolution leapt to life in him, that he would apply practically to these, the remedies which his observation had shown him to be most successful elsewhere.

He explained his ideas to his mother, who was shrewd enough to see their value, and who promised him her help and sanction in any schemes that might be advisable. He sent for the bailiff, and consulted him as to the best means of ascertaining the exact condition of the poor in the surrounding villages; and with a view to obtaining not only information but counsel, he begged his mother to invite Mr. Godolphin to dinner—him and his wife, and all her array of ribbons.

The invitation was sent. Mr. and Mrs. Godolphin came. The dinner was at half-past six, this early hour having been chosen in order that afterwards they might enjoy the evening out-of-doors; and for the same reason, all were in morning dress—Mrs. Godolphin being, for her part, a perfect Golconda of jet beads. After dinner Pole in the twilight garden drew Mr. Godolphin away with him, and began to unfold his plans, which comprised an orphanage, with an industrial school attached, and perhaps a lodging for widows; and explained how such modest institutions had been tried with success in Belgium. He then asked Mr. Godolphin for advice and help, deferring to his practical wisdom, and superior local knowledge.

Mr. Godolphin was not only touched by this appeal, he was flattered by it. But his vanity was of that rare and delightful kind which stimulates its possessor's best qualities only; and he listened with the keenest attention to Pole's plans and prospects, criticizing them at the same time with great practical shrewdness. At last he stopped short in his walk, put his hand upon Pole's shoulder, and looked at him with generous eyes. "I am thankful," he said, "to see that your aunt's spirit lives in you." He paused, and then with a tremor in his voice, continued: "Canon Bulman was telling me that you had become a free-thinker. I confess I am not quite able to tell what that word means. The more freely I think myself, the more firmly do I believe in Christ. And, Reginald—may I call you that? for I knew you when you were quite a lad—I spoke just now of your good aunt's

spirit living in you. I ought to have said that what lives
in you is the spirit of Christ; and I will not forbid you, if
in doctrine you should not exactly follow me."

In width of knowledge, and in intellectual · power generally, Pole was, beyond comparison, superior to Mr. Godolphin; but what most helps and encourages even the greatest
of practical thinkers, what braces the sinews of their will,
and makes its strength a reality instead of a wasted possibility, is the support and appreciation of ordinary simple
men; and Pole experienced the reality of this great truth
now. Mr. Godolphin, moreover, possessed, in addition to
his simplicity, a temperament which, in some ways, was as
active as Pole's own. Many men who like him had spent
most of their lives in the care of the poor, and who had
done so, as no doubt *he* had, with a special, even if humble,
complacency, might have felt some jealous distrust of a
young layman like Pole, who was thus presuming to intrude
into their own department, and whose ideas, whatever their
value, were an implied criticism of theirs. But to such
feelings as these, Mr. Godolphin was a total stranger.
Much that Pole said to him was to him certainly new; but
he welcomed its novelty as a help, not an insult to himself.
In especial he welcomed Pole's practical suggestion that
they should provide themselves with the large-scale ordnance-
maps of the neighbourhood—maps which showed clearly
each individual cottage, and compile, with this to guide
them, a list as complete as possible, of the families inhabiting
each, with their wages and condition generally.

Intercourse between Glenlynn and Mr. Godolphin's
vicarage was of daily occurrence whilst these preliminaries
were being settled; and formed for Pole the pleasantest
element in his life. He did not, however, allow his official
work to suffer; and he found time also, with the aid of a
Lyncombe architect, to make some rough plans for his proposed simple buildings. His mother, though hitherto all
her ideas of charity had been nearly as old-fashioned as those
of Miss Pole herself, welcomed his projects with a sympathy
not unlike Mr. Godolphin's; and meanwhile, in private, he
had resolved on setting aside for these philanthropic purposes, and for another, more secret, but equally unselfish,
most of that additional income which had so unexpectedly
come to him. In this way he was carrying into action the

kind of resolve which his mind, at Miss Pole's funeral, had
laid as an offering before he knew not what Power; and the
charm of his home, and the interest of his official work,
were supplemented and increased by a contentment whose
source was deeper.

But in spite of all this, a certain portion of his being
was tenanted by a distress or melancholy, which work,
ambition, the approval of conscience, and the mere pleasure
of living, might often reduce to silence, but could not dis-
lodge. To have detected this fact would have required a
far acuter observer than any of those persons by whom he
now happened to be surrounded, and most of its signs,
indeed, were beyond the observation of anybody. But any
one who could have watched him in the solitude of his own
bedroom, or followed him on the lonely rambles which he
every day took, would have seen reason to be convinced that
all the liberal sunshine which the outward and inward world
had combined to pour on him was constantly made cold and
grey by some cloud of anxiety or of sorrow.

Like many men suffering in the same way, he would
frequently, when alone, talk aloud to himself in broken
sentences. Several times, in the morning, when his letters
had been brought to him in bed, he exclaimed, as he looked
them over, " Nothing—not a single line ! " and this would be
succeeded sometimes by some ejaculations such as these—
" I have given all I have, and I get not even a word; ' " I
did not think it was in human nature to be so cruel; " or
again, " I feel myself cut off from everything that is best in
life, as if I had been a murderer." There was, moreover, a
certain path clambering along the heathery cliff-side, to
which each day he would betake himself; and, seating himself on a lonely rock, he would look out over the sea, on
which now and again some white wave would flower, and
which whispered far below, with its foam, upon curves of
shingle. From here, high on the horizon the form of a coast
was visible, where Wales opened to the Atlantic a succession
of visionary forelands; and the eyes of the lonely watcher
would fix themselves from time to time on their distant and
elusive shadows, which were hardly distinguishable from
clouds. Here, too, he would not unfrequently talk to himself, in phrases which were similar to those just mentioned,
and which any one who overheard them could not have

failed to attribute either to unhappiness of the deepest kind, or else to the most ridiculous affectation of it. That it was not affectation, however, would have been proved sufficiently by the fact that the moment he was in the presence of others, his demeanour entirely altered, and he assumed the appearance of equable, and often of buoyant spirits. His aspect, indeed, would brighten occasionally even when he was alone, as though the natural hunger for happiness, inherent in a sensitive and vigorous nature, would insist on satisfying itself, despite all opposition from the mind; and he would view the scenes around him with the pleasure which is characteristic of a poet, and which is heightened, rather than disturbed, by a melancholy which has lost its sting.

Cloudless intervals like these were the result and the reward usually of some exceptionally hard, or exceptionally successful work, whether this were connected with his Blue-book or his philanthropic projects; and after ten days or so of life under his present circumstances, there came to him a morning of work that was exceptional in both ways. A letter from his chief, Lord Henderson, was brought to him, when he was still in bed, begging him to send, by return of post, if possible, certain comparative tables with regard to artisans' house-rent in Paris, Berlin, and other continental towns. As the first post left at one, and it was desirable to catch this, he ordered his breakfast to be brought him in his own room, and working there without intermission, just finished his task in time. This close application happened to be all the easier to him because a succession of light showers deprived him of any temptation to go out. But when he was placing the document in its envelope, he saw that the sky was clearing, and he rose, rejoicing in the prospect of a half-hour's stroll before luncheon.

He was, however, a little surprised when Miss Drake, whom he encountered in the hall, congratulated him on this change in the weather, with what seemed a disproportionate emphasis; and it also occurred to him, when he came to think it over, that her face was starched into an expression of unusual preciseness, and that the body of her black dress was unusually rich in crape. But these reflections quickly passed away from him as he went into the open air and smelt the soil of the garden in it, and saw about him the soft silvery mist assuming the dazzling whiteness that breaks

into blue and gold. He forgot his statistics; he forgot all
definite sorrow; and his mind for the moment became a
garden of hopes and feelings, vague and delightful as the
scenes of the garden round him. All those feelings which
the beauty of Nature, as distinct from her grandeur, touches
in us, are connected directly or indirectly with religion, or
else with love; and to Pole, who had known romance, it
seemed that the flower-scented air around him held vague,
diaphanous memories, without passion or regret in them,
of women who had charmed him, and of the scenes that had
been impregnated with their presence. His mind thus
pleasurably agitated, he was strolling, almost heedless of
where he went, down one of the little walks that descended
tortuously to the shore, when the bough of a rose-tree, bent
with its weight of moisture, arrested his course, stretching
across his pathway like a bar. It was bright with blossoms,
and he stood still to look at them. His gaze lost itself in the
depth of the crumpled shadows, where far down were
flickerings as of diamonds in crimson caves; and in every
drop that was globed on the upper petals, he detected a
miniature universe of colour and leaf and sky. From this
state of contemplation a sound of footsteps roused him.
They seemed to be near at hand, but he could not distinguish
where. He hastily raised the branch and proceeded as the
path led him, hoping to avoid a meeting with anybody—
even with his mother. A yard or two lower down the path
took a sharp bend, and brought him to a view of the sea,
framed in an arch of trellis-work. The waves shone in
streaks of purple and of green turquoise; high in the air
the arch was a curve of passion flowers, and beyond were
rocks and myrtle, and the spikes of one large grey aloe. It
was a view for which he entertained a special affection,
seeming to unite, as it did, the beauties both of Italy and of
England. But, in addition to these, it revealed to him
another beauty now, which brought him to a surprised
standstill. This was nothing else than Countess Shimna
O'Keefe, with a figure daintier than any that Watteau
dreamed of, and a dress redolent of the sea, as the sea is
understood at Deauville. During the whole morning the
thought of her had not so much as crossed his mind; but,
on seeing her, he remembered that she was expected to-day
for luncheon, and he realized all at once, with a certain

sensation of amusement, the true explanation of Miss Drake's aspect and demeanour. He was sure that she had been alarmed by the Canon's description of the stranger, and he augured that the reality would alarm her even more.

But this faint sensation of amusement was not his sole experience. For a moment his face grew grave, as he thought of how he had met this stranger last, and how her hand had lingered in his on the landing-steps of the Lyncombe pier: and shame at the interest she had excited in him passed through him like a shuddering spirit, whose place was again taken by the very interest which its passage had reproved.

CHAPTER XI.

COUNTESS SHIMNA at first was not aware of his presence. With an absorbed attention she was looking at the scene before her, and the simplicity of her attitude and expression was rendered doubly striking by contrast with her toilette, which, though in its own way equally simple, betrayed in every detail the subtleties of Parisian art. For a few seconds Pole had time to watch her. Then she started and saw him, and he came forward to meet her. Their greeting, so far as words went, consisted of inevitable commonplaces. He hoped she had not been rained upon, during her miniature voyage from Lyncombe, and they congratulated each other on the fact that the weather had so completel. cleared. But meanwhile he was receiving impressions of her which had little to do with what she uttered. Her skin and complexion, free from the least trace of cosmetics, had yet the unnatural daintiness of a face on an old French fan; and her English, though perfect, had yet the faintest of foreign accents, which made it like Sèvres china, as contrasted with common ware. Her touch, too, once more thrilled him with its almost unconscious lingering, and her dress, as he looked more closely at it, roused a new train of associations in him. Various points in it, for which, man-like, he had no name, ambushed coquetries of colour and fit and fold, filled him with thoughts of far-off continental dissipation, of the glitter of casinos, and of whisperings under lamp-lit foliage. But thoughts and impressions like these were at once chastened and intensified by others of a different order. If much in her air and aspect suggested an artificial world, in her face, as she looked at him, was an almost tragic sincerity. Her upper lip had a certain lift in in its curve, as if she were ready to gasp with acute feeling; and the look of her eyes was that of a heart's-ease wet with morning.

"I am glad I met you," she said, when the first civilities were over. "I should have been shy of making my way to a strange house all alone."

Any man who has been accustomed to deal with women, and has shared with them the beginnings and endings of a certain class of experiences, may have divided himself, as far as possible, from his past by change of id;as and conduct; but whenever he meets a woman whose history has been similar to his own, the past of each has the inevitable and unsought effect of producing between the two an unrecognized, and even unconscious, freemasonry. The man's knowledge of other women becomes knowledge of this one, and the woman is endowed similarly with an instinctive knowledge of the man. Pole, though he was no more aware of the fact than of the tone of his own voice, was himself an example of this truth now. He looked at Countess Shimna without a trace of freedom or familiarity, and yet he spoke to her as most men would not have spoken to such a stranger.

"I confess," he said, "I should never have thought you shy. You seem to me like a most perfect woman of the world."

She returned his look with a sparkle of quiet comprehension between her eyelashes.

"Of one world, yes," she said; "but not of a world like this. You may not know it, Mr. Pole, but to-day is a great day for me. For the first time in my life I shall be entering an English home. I am half English myself. English governesses have educated me. I have read English books —poetry, philosophy, novels—all of it; and I know, or think I know, what an English home must be. That is what makes me shy. Or suppose that I tell you plainly—I feel shy of your mother."

"Why ?" asked Pole, watching her as she dropped her

eyes and played with a sleeve-link formed out of two black pearls.

"There are many reasons," she answered, as if she were addressing the gravel—"reasons I can't explain. But here is one, and that one is quite simple. She represents a life in which I have no part."

"You have met me only twice," said Pole, "and you are not shy of *me*."

"No," she said; "but you are different. Would you like me," she continued, laughing, "to tell you what I mean by that? I have, as you say, met you only twice. How do I know you are different? How do I know what you are? I can tell you in an original way. In a Warsaw newspaper, which we got yesterday morning—you know the stupid things that are always coming in newspapers—was a letter stating that the eye retains, after death, the picture of whatever object it looked at last when living. That, of course, is nonsense; but there is something like it which is true. Eyes which have been familiar with certain sides of life, retain an expression produced by what they have seen; and other eyes, which have seen the same things, recognize it. I recognize something like this in you—in your whole expression—no matter what you look at, whether at a funeral service, or at this garden, or—you must not think me a coquette because I say this—or at myself."

"I am glad," said Pole, "that you feel me to have something in common with you; but I should like to think that the feeling rested on anything rather than the fact that your past had been like mine."

"My present is like yours, at any rate," she replied, looking slowly round her. "We are both of us seeing the same side of life now. Is your home as beautiful as your garden?"

"Come," he said—"come and see. I am glad, at any rate, that you like my favourite view. Look at those colours that float upon our western sea."

"Ah!" she answered, sighing, as if entering into his mood instantly; "that *nuance* of blue, far out! I have been looking at it all the way from Lyncombe."

They now moved away, and she followed him up one of the climbing paths, he apologizing for its unsociable narrowness and its difficulty.

"Ah," she exclaimed, as if nothing but trifles had passed between them, "here is your house! I can see the roofs and chimneys."

At this moment the sound of his own name reached Pole through one of the laurel hedges, and presently, at the end of the path, he caught sight of his mother, who called to him a little out of breath—

"Reginald, I've been looking for you everywhere. I wanted to ask you to meet Countess Shimna at the landing-place."

"Mother," he said, "she is here."

With a slight gesture of surprise Mrs. Pole looked beyond him, and scanned for an instant the delicate figure facing her.

"My dear," she exclaimed, "I've been wishing so much to see you."

"And I, too," said Countess Shimna, "have been wishing so much to come."

Pole watched her curiously. He saw how she had advanced with a kind of calm timidity, far more finished in its *aplomb* than any possible boldness, and he said to himself, "If this is shyness, it is shyness become a fine art." But then, on his mother's speaking to her, he saw all her expression change, and its dainty conventionality became transfigured into childlike gratitude. He saw the change go home to his mother's heart. He saw the gentle curve of the girl's lips appeal to her, and, bending with a maternal welcome, the elder woman kissed the younger.

"My dear," said Mrs. Pole, "you look like a living flower. With you on its walks, our garden will hardly know itself. Hark! that bell means luncheon—what you, I suppose, call *déjeuner*. Come and see how your English relations live."

Pole followed them, delighted at the success of the meeting, and very soon he saw, under his mother's influence, an entirely new side of Countess Shimna's nature show itself.

"You will find," Mrs. Pole said to her as they drew near the front door, " me and my son alone, except for one other person, a strange old *dame de campagnie;*" and she then proceeded to give a description of Miss Drake. "I've no doubt," she continued, "you've seen a great many things

and people, but I am sure you have never seen anything in
the least like her."

Countess Shimna stood still and broke into a ripple of
laughter, which showed her hearers that, whatever she had
seen or not seen, she grasped the idea of Miss Drake, and
saw her with her mind's eye now.   Her appreciation was so
unexpected, and the effect of her mirth was so contagious,
that her laughter was joined in directly by the two others,
until Mrs. Pole said, " Hush! It would never do if she
were to hear us."   And they passed indoors into the hall.

"Ah," said Countess Shimna softly, as at Mrs. Pole's
suggestion she laid down her sunshade, with a parrot's head
for a handle, on the cool surface of an old marble table, and
glanced at the busts, at the glimmering china bowls, and the
carpet mellowed with its hundred years of wear, "this is
what I knew a home would be."

"Look," whispered Pole.   "There Miss Drake is."

And there, sure enough, in an inner hall she was,
illuminated by the staircase window and standing at an
open door, as if waiting for the others to pass into the
drawing-room before her.   As they did so, Mrs. Pole introduced the Countess, and Miss Drake dropped a short curtsy,
which resembled the collapse of a concertina.   Limited as
the social powers of this estimable lady were, she contributed
more than any one to make luncheon pass off easily.   One
of her earliest emotions had been horror of the first Napoleon,
and she still clung to the idea that everybody not English
was French.   Countess Shimna had read of people like this
in books; and nothing could exceed her delight at coming
across a living specimen.   She divined at once that in Miss
Drake's eyes she was a Frenchwoman; and drawing her out
in the prettiest way imaginable, had at last the satisfaction
of hearing herself asked if frogs were not, when one ate
them, exactly like skinny chicken.   Miss Drake, in fact,
promoted conversation much in the same way that a cat, a
dog, or a child does, to whom everybody conspires to talk.
She had never been the recipient of so much attention
before, and indeed of the pleasure she caused she was herself
perhaps the chief participator.   Unwonted smiles made
novel wrinkles along her cheeks.   Her curls, which were
so prim this morning, now frisked with satisfaction; and
the outlandish young lady, who she fancied would smell of

brimstone, seemed to her by the end of luncheon little less
than an angel. But opinions suddenly changed are proverbially unstable. As the party were on the point of rising,
out of the corners of her provincial eyes Miss Drake saw
Countess Shimna take her gloves from her lap—long, delicate
gloves, with hands that were yet more delicate; and she felt
a sudden shock at the girl's physical beauty. It seemed
wicked to her, like some strange form of luxury. Then in
an instant came another shock worse than this one. She
recollected that this alien must be a Roman Catholic, and a
worshipper of saints and idols. Her mouth grew rigid with
religious and moral Protestantism; and as soon as they left
the dining-room she fled to her own chamber.

"My dear," said Mrs. Pole, as she took her guest into
the library, "I have a few letters to write, which I could
not finish this morning. I will get them off my hands now,
and return to you with a clear conscience. Meanwhile I
will leave you to the care of Reginald."

She went, closing the door. Pole and Countess Shimna
were alone.

"Well," he said to her, with a look full of the questions
that grow only from the soil of a mutual understanding.
To his considerable astonishment he saw gathering in her
eyes, not actual tears, but the dimness that comes before
them.

"I should," she said, "love your mother, if only I knew
her better."

"I know her," said Pole; "and she is devoted to you
already." His manner was different from what it had been
in the morning. There was for the moment nothing in it
but simple responsive friendship. "Tell me," he went on,
"do you like our home also?"

She began to look slowly round her, taking in every
object, like a person who is half stifled, inhaling a draught
of air. "Being here," she said, "is like being in church.
Your house surrounds me, as a church does, with a life
unlike my own, and there is some quiet of old times floating
in the air like incense. You won't know what I mean when
I say that. You will laugh at me; but I am made up of
nerves and senses; and with me one sense is always speaking for another. Do you understand that? One of my
governesses used to tell me I mixed my metaphors. For

me, scents speak, colours sound, and sounds flash like colour."

"Well," replied Pole, "come and see how the colours are sounding out-of-doors." And a moment or two later they went out together into the summer. The golden air was fresh with a wayward breeze, that came in sighing puffs from every quarter indifferently, and seemed to be laden with the spirit of moorland honey. "This," said the girl, "is all a new life to me. I have felt nothing exactly like it before—so lonely, so civilized, and yet so free." She seemed to Pole to understand the place as he did. He watched her with a curious interest, delighted to see her happy.

As they went they began talking of various matters. She mentioned that she had noticed in the library the works of some of her favourite writers—of Byron and Shelley amongst the number, and of one or two men of science— these last being volumes which Pole had himself brought down. "I saw ' *Werther*,' too, she said; " but that is silly and morbid—and Wordsworth. My first governess used to make me learn his verses."

The extent of her reading surprised him; and still more than her reading, the way in which she had made her own the intellectual meanings of most of it, so that they mixed themselves with her lightest thoughts, and moved familiarly with them. He hardly made an allusion to which she did not respond. She caught what he said as if it had been a ball tossed to her; and sometimes her mind, as through it his thoughts, came back to him, seemed like a prism which had dyed them with deeper colours.

" See," she exclaimed, as a turn in one of the walks gave her a new view of the singular and precipitous garden, "there is the wild heather shining above the lawns and laurels ! "

" I will take you to it," he answered ; "you shall lie on it. But you must not mind a climb."

He led her up walks that mounted through sloping thickets of laurustinus. They left the garden ; they passed through a wood of larches, and presently found themselves on the slanting wilderness of the cliffs. From the heights of the rocks above them down to the waves below, was heather, stretching before them in miles of headlong purple. Here and there on a crag some mountaineering sheep glittered; and above them a seagull passed, like the drifting petals of a magnolia. "The heather is dry," said Pole. "Try it: it is a bed of velvet."

She sank down amongst the tufts, with the supple gracefulness of a fawn; only as she did so, from her dress came a breath of perfume, which again in Pole's mind connected her with a far-off artificial civilization. He sat himself on a stone close by. The heather had half hidden her.

"From where you are," he said, "you can see nothing."

"On the contrary," she answered, laughing, "I can see an entire world. I can see—shall I tell you what? I can see little flowers—a nation of them—yellow, and white, and blue, showing me their faces through the grass. On each side of me is the heather like great hills. I can count the lights and shadows streaking the highest bells; and beyond these is the sky. And now I am looking in front of me. There my heather hills dip into an inverted triangle; and this is filled up by a lilac wall of sea. And I smell the earth. Ah!" she exclaimed, raising herself, "why should we consider it a reproach to be called of the earth, earthy? Why should we be ashamed of a parent through whom the violets are our sisters?"

When they re-entered the house, Mrs. Pole was still upstairs. They went into the silent library, where the blinds, which were now drawn down, filled the room with a cool luminous dimness. Her face and eyes, seen in this different light, startled Pole by their expression of meditative melancholy. He went up close to her, where she stood in an undecided attitude, and said, "Will you do me a favour? Will you turn round to the light? Thank you. Forgive me for staring at you. Come with me, and I will now show you the reason."

Not unnaturally puzzled, she followed him into the room adjoining. There he surprised her further. He seized her arm abruptly, and led her to the pastel portrait. "Look at that," he said. "Perhaps you will understand now."

For some moments she stared at the picture silently; then, hastily turning to him, "Do you mean," she exclaimed, "that is like me?" He took from a table a little ivory looking-glass and put it into her hand for answer. She looked alternately at the picture and her own reflection, and at last said, "Who is she?"

"She is," replied Pole, "some distant relation of both of us. But the thing so like yourself in her is the whole air and the expression."

"It is strange," she said, looking at the picture, and evidently not displeased at the thought of its being associated with herself—"it is strange how likenesses are handed down in families : and I suppose our characters, our feelings, even our little half-thought thoughts, have their family likenesses in just the same way—only likenesses to counterparts which nobody ever knew or painted. I often wonder which of my thoughts are my own, and which are echoes from my ancestors. Do you know these verses? I think you must. They express what I feel, in this way, with regard to my own nature sometimes.

> " ' Will no man tell me what she sings?
> Perhaps the numbers flow,
> From old unhappy far-off things,
> And battles long ago.' "

My governess I told you of, made me learn that. But the portrait—— You didn't tell me what the name of the lady was."

"The lady," said Pole, "was the celebrated Lady Thyrza Brancepeth. She ran away with the man who built this house—my great-uncle. She died only a year afterwards. She is mentioned in Byron's Letters."

Countess Shimna sank into a chair, with her eyes still fixed upon the picture. "Yes," she said presently, "she died in Italy. And so that was your great-uncle!" For a few moments she was silent. Then she spoke again. "I am amused," she said, at your asking me if I ever heard the story. Some day I can show you a picture which has a story also. I can show you a miniature of Lady Thyrza Brancepeth's daughter. You will not wonder then why I should be like that picture. If you care for science, you ought to be pleased to see me. Judging from that picture, I am a good instance of atavism. "See," she said, interrupting herself with a laugh, "I have dropped my pocket-handkerchief." He picked it up for her. A curve of her lips thanked him. "Consider," she said, smiling, as if to escape from seriousness, whilst her gloved fingers played with the film which she called her handkerchief, "consider the things of which I am the child, or rather the great-grandchild—of elopement, and of sorrow, and of passion, and of early death. My shield has all those *quartiers* to make up for the one that is wanting."

Pole looked at her, puzzled and fascinated. He could not tell what to make of her. How, he asked himself, did she come by thoughts like these—this flower of an idle world, who by turns seemed bud and blossom; and who sat there brilliant among the faded colourings of the room, with lips that were like a kiss, and eyes that were like an elegy. But the last words were hardly uttered, when he saw her expression alter, and the dancing light of childhood leapt back again into her face. Before he had himself perceived it, Mrs. Pole had entered, and coming to Countess Shimna, laid a gentle hand upon her shoulder. "You are not tired?" she said. "Ah, here comes Martin with the tea. But now tell me this. Your mother, of course, will allow you to stay to dinner? The nights are warm, and the launch will go back on moonlight."

It struck Pole as a strange, incongruous thing to hear their guest questioned about a mother's permission; and yet, when he saw how her face was suffused with childish pleasure, as she told Mrs. Pole that she was perfectly free to stay, she again seemed to him to be a mere child, after all. This impression was presently completed, when the figure of Miss Drake appeared, and grim with shyness, advanced slowly towards the group, moving along the carpet like a clockwork mouse on wheels. Countess Shimna's face lit up again with the light of a half-mischievous amusement; and Miss Drake's lips and cheeks had presently crackled into smiles which showed that this daughter of Heth had made her once more a captive.

After tea, Mrs. Pole proposed to Countess Shimna a drive in a pony carriage up the long approach; "Which will show you," she said, "how we are shut out from the world. The carriage holds only two. Reginald will perhaps ride." It was done as Mrs. Pole suggested. Pole, on an Exmoor pony, for most of the way followed them at a little distance, so as to let his mother and her guest cement their friendship by themselves; and he listened with puzzled pleasure to their soft intimate laughter. On their way back, when they had almost reached the house, they came upon Dr. Clitheroe, trudging from his lodgings, washed and arrayed for dinner, and carrying in his hand a little paper parcel. "Stop!" cried Pole, to his mother. "I want to introduce him to the Countess. Dr. Clitheroe, here is a lady who has never known an English clergyman, though she has had the privilege, I think, of seeing you once in the garden."

"I wish," said the Doctor, as he raised his dignified hat, "that the Countess saw before her a worthier member of his profession. Mrs. Pole," he continued shyly, still glancing at her companion, "I have brought you a present—one of those little patent strainers, for fixing to the spout of a tea-pot, and catching the leaves."

"How delightful," exclaimed Countess Shimna, amused by him as she had been at Miss Drake. "Dr. Clitheroe, how delightful!"

The Doctor, like Mrs. Pole, was already a victim to her charm; and at dinner his conversation displayed a demure sparkle, by which poor Miss Drake was eclipsed, and which came as a surprise to everybody. Whatever else might be in Countess Shimna's nature, there was one thing in it, at all events, that was completely genuine—the buoyancy of spontaneous girlhood, mischievous without being malicious, caressing even in its audacities, perfectly trained by the world, and yet supremely natural. She forced on Pole the impression of a child adorned with diamonds, which became her and increased her beauty because she was quite uncon-scious that she was wearing them.

But by-and-by when the time came for her to go, and, when wrapped in a fur-lined cloak that had been sent up to her from the launch, she went out alone with him, and they found themselves in the scented night, his impression of her changed suddenly. She was once again for him a woman, as she had been when he met her in the morning, with whom, in virtue of her past, he was conscious of some un-defined intimacy. Her eyes said it, as they looked at him, dim and liquid in the moonlight. Her lips themselves could hardly have been more eloquent, no matter how she had used them: and when they spoke her voice was in harmony with her whole bearing. "You must help me every part of the way," she said; and quietly took his arm.

The effect of this slight action was to fill him with a fantastic jealousy. How had she learned to take a man's arm so easily? What other man—what other men—had taught her? Such was the question he asked himself till the sense of her hand leaning on him, reminded him that he, at all events, possessed this treasure now, and showed him also that his support was not by any means superfluous. The sloping paths and the broken lights and shadows were enough to make his guidance necessary; and until they were close upon the shore he had hardly opened his lips to her, except to say briefly, "You will come to us soon again?" For a second, as he said this, she leaned on his arm more heavily. So at least he thought. If so, it was her only answer. But now when the waves were glimmering within a few yards of them, and they heard the spitting of steam from the launch by the rude landing-place, she paused in her walk, she turned to him, and she took his hand. "Would you like to see me again?" she said. "Perhaps you had better not; but by-and-by, if your mother asks me, I will come. For two strangers, I think, we know each other very well. And now—you must not hold me. Come, help me on board, and make quite sure that you have got rid of me."

She hardly needed his help, she stepped into the boat so lightly. The screw churned the darkness. Water began to gleam between them. She raised her hand, until—so he fancied—it nearly touched her lips; then she waved it in his direction—about this there could be no doubt; and he watched her drifting away from him over the wattled black and silver.

The house, when he returned to it, seemed to be unusually quiet; and himself disinclined to talk, he took up the day's papers, which, until that moment, he had not found time to glance at. His eyes wandered over the columns carelessly, till at last he leaned towards the light, and made the whole sheet rustle, as his attention was quite accidentally caught by the following paragraph.

"Amongst the passengers last Saturday by the *Umbria* for New York, was Sir Hugh Price Masters, who succeeded recently to the baronetcy, and to the ownership of St. Owen's Castle, one of the most curious though least visited of the historic mansions of Great Britain. Sir Hugh, who has been long known in sporting circles, and who fractured his thigh last year, when riding Gallipot at Frankfort, is understood to have some big venture afoot in the United States, which, since he is acting in conjunction with Mr. Julius K. Van Skink, we may, though the nature of the project hitherto has been kept dark, conclude to be not unconnected with the noble animal horse."

This elegant piece of literature was enough for Pole that evening. It did for him what could have been done by no other piece of literature in the house. It completely put out of his head the events of the last nine hours: and it certainly was not of Countess Shimna that he was thinking, when he muttered as he went to bed, "And has she gone too! Gone, and without a single word!"

CHAPTER XII.

He passed a restless night; but towards morning slept so heavily that when his servant brought him his letters, he had some difficulty in rousing himself, or in seeing distinctly what had been put into his hand. At last, however, he perceived on one of the envelopes, an address in untidy, but by no means weak, handwriting. As if something had stung him, he started up in his bed, and staring at the address again, broke the envelope open. The words written were few, being nothing more than these—

"Laburnum Lawn, Windsor.

"My Dear Mr. Pole,

"I deserve anything you can say of me. I am an abominable correspondent. But lately I could not have written, I have been so busy; though you won't believe me. I had to come to London with my husband, who has gone back to America; but I have been so knocked up and ill, with what I have had to do at the Castle, that I have come down here for quiet. I shall stay here for a fortnight, unless I am wanted at home before. I am in lodgings. If you should be in London, do run down and see me, on any day that is convenient to you. Post is going. No time for more. I am ever your sincere friend,

"Pansy."

He read this twice, then leapt from his bed, and his face

as he entered the breakfast parlour, where Dr. Clitheroe was finishing prayers, had a look of eager pleasure upon it, that was tempered by vague sadness. The Doctor, however, was shadowed by no such cloud. He rose from his knees, and closed Bishop Bloomfield's manual, which, with much ingenuity, he had been propping up against the sugar basin, bright and twinkling as if he had been getting out of his bath; and as soon as he had said "Good morning," he remarked, with much Christian briskness, on the manifold charms of the young lady who had last night· been dining with them. Mrs. Pole, too, seemed to be in quite as good spirits as the Doctor; and she, like him, was still full of Countess Shimna.

"I am so glad to hear," she said, "that she is going to be left at Lyncombe. I told her she had better come here; and so she will for a day or two. But the doctors advise her that bracing air is what she wants, and insist on her being established high up on the cliff."

"By all means," said Pole, with an indifference that surprised his mother. "Let her come when it best suits her. But till next Wednesday I myself shall probably be away. I have just had a letter which will oblige me to go to London to-morrow."

"Very well, then," said Mrs. Pole; "we will ask her to come next week. By the way," she continued, "I have heard from Ethel De Souza. She and Mrs. Steinberg have just come back to Thames Wickham. Perhaps you will go and see them. You will not find many friends in London."

"Indeed!" exclaimed Pole, with animation. "Of all women in the world, Mrs. Steinberg is the kindest, and Miss Ethel De Souza the most gifted. The one is a genius in friendship; the other a genius in every way. These, Dr. Clitheroe, are friends whom we first knew in Paris. Steinberg and De Souza were the great Brazilian bankers. Miss De Souza is Mrs. Steinberg's niece. She is an orphan, and keeps house with her aunt. Mrs. Steinberg, mother, has so often asked me to stay with them, that I think I will telegraph to her, and ask her if they can have me now."

A message was despatched accordingly; and in due time came an answer. "To-morrow, by all means; it will be, indeed, a pleasure."

Early next morning he started, and was speeding along

the high coach-road, whilst the dews and the gossamers
were still glittering on the gorse, and the purple dyes of
night were wet on the distant hills. The sight of a train
was strange to him, after the quiet seclusion of Glenlynn;
but his thoughts were already travelling faster than steam
could carry them. It seemed to him that the London
express, for which he had to wait at a junction, would never
come; and he looked down the line impatiently. At last
he saw in the distance a something like a slim black horse-
shoe, cut against the sky, with pennon of white fluttering
from it—a something that seemed to enlarge, but not to
advance nearer; until, with a sudden sound, it swelled to
a hissing engine; and the train came sweeping in with its
roaring wall of windows.

His journey, it so happened, was not without incident.
When he reached Reading, at which station he was to
change, his attention was caught by a considerable bustle
on the platform, taking place in front of a carriage near
that he had just left. There was a group—or a little crowd
—of men, well-dressed in black, clustering eagerly round
the door of a first-class compartment. Some of them were
evidently clergymen; whilst those, who as evidently were
not so, rivalled their reverend brethren in the edifying
gravity of their demeanour. In another moment there were
bowings and a great shaking of hands; and over one clerical
wide-awake, whose wearer had the stature of Zaccheus, Pole
perceived the well-known countenance of Canon Bulman,
florid with recognition of the distinguished welcome he was
receiving, but stamped at the same time with a look that
portended business. As the circle of his admirers opened
to allow of his being conducted out of the station, he
happened to perceive Pole; and quitting his companions,
came up to him. Flushed with the many successes which
he had achieved since he left Glenlynn, Canon Bulman was
determined to make one effort more at reducing Pole to his
former flattering allegiance, or, at all events, to show
himself to him in all the pomp of victory.

"My dear boy," he exclaimed, with a geniality almost
patronizing, "I'm delighted to see you—quite delighted!
Are you stopping in this neighbourhood? If you are, I
wish you would come to-night and hear my address on
'Democracy and Personal Purity.'"

Pole explained the reason why this pleasure would be impossible for him.

"Then come," said the Canon, "and lunch with me at my new house to-morrow or the day after. I'm only just out of Windsor, and you can reach me from Thames Wickham easily."

This invitation Pole cordially accepted, promising that that evening he would send the Canon a telegram; and presently, as he renewed his journey, in spite of other thoughts that had been occupying him, he began to give his mind to the friends whom he was so fast approaching. His early acquaintance with Mrs. Steinberg had been kept up by him ever since; and her niece for the last ten years he had known intimately also. Miss De Souza was indeed a remarkable woman. Born amongst surroundings the very essence of which was luxury—the sort of luxury that aims at turning all life into a bon-bon box tied with ribbons and lined with quilted satin, and herself by no means free from a certain sensuous appreciation of it, her existence had yet been that of a spirit in a world of matter. A singular quickness of insight, which outran curiosity, and had very little to do with it, had early revealed to her, almost against her will, the realities of human nature; and a gift of sympathy, equally quick and delicate, had taken her through the shadows, where others sinned or suffered, purifying what it touched of impure, not defiled by it. And yet, little as her friends suspected it, she had been herself a victim, not, indeed, to the sins which she looked on with such cleanly pity, but to one of those sorrows to which she seemed to be so superior. Wise for others, she had at one time been simple for herself; and her heart, having been left unguarded, because she had never imagined it to be in danger, had been yielded up by her almost without a struggle to the last man in the world who would have seemed calculated to attract her. Her own tastes and feelings were to the highest degree intellectual and sensitive. He was a soldier and sportsman—a son of the open air, with little to recommend him to the eye of ordinary observation, except gallantry and a semblance of reckless frankness. He had, however, as events showed, a certain fastidiousness of taste, with which few of his friends would have credited him. Captivated by Miss De Souza, who, besides being wealthy,

well-dressed, and distinguished by much mundane charm.
was also in many ways beautiful, he had also experienced a
genuine desire for her affection, which appealed to him as
something mysterious and indefinitely above himself, and
which roused him for a time into a state of stupid adoration.
But no sooner had she, who, if she gave her heart at all, was
a woman to give without reservation or distrust, surrendered
to him the treasure that had lately seemed so inaccessible,
than he little by little began to disregard and weary of it ;
and their engagement, which had not been made public, was
barely a month old, before his conduct had forced on her
the invidious responsibility of dissolving it. Availing himself of the excuse thus given him for posing as the aggrieved
party, he engaged himself a month later to a wealthier
woman, whom he married ; and thus this secret episode in
Miss De Souza's life ended, except for its effects upon
herself, which were not suspected by even her closest friends,
and which she never mentioned to any human being. The
sole outward sign was an increased sympathy for others.

The image of this charming friend was occupying Pole's
mind, and bringing to it a sense of rest, when the train
stopped ; and he was roused from his reverie by his servant,
who appeared at the carriage door, and informed him that
they had reached Thames Wickham. A few minutes later,
an open suburban fly, as dirty and as old as any that had
figured at Miss Pole's funeral, was wheeling out of the dusty
road, and conveying him between tall brick gate-posts, into
a space of turf and gravel which was shadowed by old cedars,
and revealed beyond the cedars the pillars of a large portico.
The vehicle drew up before a flight of wide stone steps ; and
the bell had been hardly rung before double doors were
opened ; and a footman, the excellen e of whose place was
visible in his mien and movements, was vying with Pole's
own man in assisting the visitor to descend. Pole glanced
about him with the natural curiosity of a new-comer. There
slumbered on every object the bloom of a placid opulence. The
house was old as suburban villas go, having been built by a
Lord Mayor during the reign of George II. But although
its exterior, which structurally had been hardly changed,
formed still a fine specimen of the stately taste of that period,
it was so well coated with paint and shone with such bright
plate-glass, that it suggested the last spring-cleaning far

more than the last century. A corresponding impression was produced also by the interior. The ceilings, the mahogany doors, and the curving stone staircase, were indeed left much as they had been; but the walls were modern with all the white and gold, that the most florid of contemporary decorators could muster courage to put on them. The old oak floors had been covered with new velvet carpet; and Pole, as he entered the vestibule, saw through two *portières* the fronds of palms distending themselves in the central hall of palms.

A large consequential butler, who was as well stuffed as a pincushion, and whose slightest gesture was a compound of a reverence and a benediction, having taken Pole's hat from him, as an acolyte takes a priest's vestment, conducted him past the palm trees, and a retinue of candelabra, into the drawing-room, and left him with the solemn information that the ladies would be there presently. Pole, though he had known his hostesses so well, and for such a long time, had never till now, visited them in their present home, which they had indeed acquired only within the last five years. The general decoration of the house he had taken in at a glance; and he had recognized with a smile the profuse spirit of Mrs. Steinberg. She, as he knew, had been cradled in the financial world, and her taste, as here exhibited, was an embodied chapter of her biography. He was aware, however, as he looked more carefully round him, that other tastes of a very different order also showed themselves by abundant signs everywhere. When his eyes had grown accustomed to the ormolu clocks and china, and to the many-coloured satin chairs that were quilted and stuffed like bon-bon boxes, he realized that, on every table where china or flowers left space for them, books and reviews of various kinds were lying; and standing by a piano, at one end of the room, was a harp—that instrument whose shape in itself is music. Moving from table to table, he began glancing at the volumes, all of which evidently lay there for daily use; and these, too, made in his mind an intellectual music of their own. Mrs. Steinberg herself was a woman of talent and cultivation; but the mental musician Pole knew was her niece.

He was absorbed in these impressions when one of the doors was pushed open, and Mrs. Steinberg appeared, shining with smiles and welcome, and cased in black satin, which

did justice to her exuberant outlines. She was a woman
whom few people had ever looked at without liking. The
upper part of her profile suggested that of a parrot, and also
a parentage not entirely English; but its keenness was
softened by a considerable number of chins, which would
constantly send their contours far up into her cheeks; and
she looked like what she was—an unruined spendthrift in
benevolence.

   "Ah!" she exclaimed, opening her eyes wide, and prolonging the syllable, till a dozen greetings were comprised in
it, "and here you are at last!   I have posted back at such a
pace—and on foot too—to receive you. I was really so
touched by your kindness in thinking of us, and proposing
yourself as you did. And how is your sweet mother? and
that dear old man, Lord Henderson? I knew him well
when he was quite a little humble lad. And I hope you had
luncheon in the train, or else you must be completely fam-
ished. But tea will come immediately. Hark—I can hear
the cups—such a clatter that second footman makes with
them."

   All this was said with so much rapidity that Pole was
hardly able to insert a word of acknowledgment, much less
to answer any of Mrs. Steinberg's questions, except, indeed,
the one which had reference to his own luncheon; for if he
had not assured her that he had eaten two large packets of
sandwiches, she would then and there have ordered for him
a collation of poached eggs. "Because, dear Mr. Pole," she
said, as she glanced at what was being brought in by the
servants, "there is absolutely nothing here for you."

   She pronounced the word "nothing" with so pathetic an
accent of complaint, that Pole looked about, to see what
the nothing was. The sight positively overwhelmed him.
Whilst he and Mrs. Steinberg had been talking, the corner
of the room where they were had undergone a transformation
not dissimilar to that which a bare rock undergoes when it
is covered by a flock of seagulls. Not only was the tea-table
itself laden with butter and toast, but on every table in the
neighbourhood had descended some form of food—cakes
covered with cream, with almond, with sugar, or with
chocolate; and a plate of Scotch short-bread was reposing
on an edition of Dante. "Come," said Mrs. Steinberg, "you
really must have something. No? You won't? I declare

it's too bad of you starving yourself. Well, here is your tea, at all events. Cream?" she asked. And before waiting for an answer she had given him an allowance so generous as to render his cup undrinkable.

Presently there rose from outside a sound of feminine laughter. "Ah!" exclaimed Mrs. Steinberg, "there is Ethel at last." And three shortish young ladies, accompanied by a fourth, who was tall, entered the room through one of the open windows. The shortish young ladies were pretty and pleasant-looking enough, but were all so much alike that it was difficult at first sight to distinguish them. Their clothes, with a humble rashness, aimed at the latest fashion; their refractory fringes flapped and frolicked upon their eyebrows; and their laughter rose and fell with a somewhat redundant gaiety. They fell back, however, to make way for the fourth, whose dress, whose bearing, and whose aspect were all singularly different. As soon as she saw Pole she came forward to meet him with a figure whose curves were graceful as those of some tall lily; and she gave him a welcome—for this was Ethel De Souza—genial as that of her aunt, but subdued, chastened, and etherealized. She was, indeed, a woman striking in her whole appearance, not having regular features, but instinct with a noble graciousness which showed itself in every movement, and focussed itself in her dark soft eyes; whilst her voice, equally gracious, had also a pathetic note in it, which made it vibrate with sympathy, and to some ears might have seemed to ask for it.

"I want so much," she said, "to hear about all that has happened to you—about your place in the country, which I am told is perfectly beautiful; and your work, which I see referred to every week in the papers. But I won't," she said, dropping her voice, "ask you about these things now. Bring up that chair, won't you? And here are the Miss Cremers—Molly, Dolly, and Folly. I think you met them once, when you were staying with us at St. Leonard's."

With an effort, Pole remembered; and, indeed, he felt remembrance necessary; for the three young ladies, with eyes full of recognition, were waiting to overwhelm him with mute reproach, if he did not. The Miss Cremers were daughters of a half-pay Indian Colonel, a man well-connected, but, owing to the narrowness of his means, reduced to seek for solace, as he approached the grave, in the sherry,

the bitters, and the billiards that offered themselves to him
in a third-rate yacht-club; and he was always delighted, for
urgent reasons of economy, when his daughters were absent
from him, and quartered on some opulent friend. As for
them, they were girls who naturally were sensible enough,
nor were traces of good birth and breeding ever absent from
their manner; but they had suffered from their circumstances.
They had not seen much of the world, except the society of
the watering-place in which they lived; and the little else
which they had seen had hardly been an unmixed advantage
to them; for their visits to a few country houses, and an
occasional week in London, stimulated them to flavour their
conversation with abortive attempts at worldliness, and to
excite by an elaborate meekness the criticism which they
meant it to disarm. Pole dimly felt all this in the somewhat
unnecessary effusion with which, one after another, they all
gave him their hands; and the eldest almost directly said
to him, with a confidential gentleness, " Mr. Pole, I was
staying last week with a mutual friend of ours, Lady Caterham—Jane Caterham. You will be glad to hear that she is
quite strong again now, and looking—oh, so beautiful!"
As Pole had met Lady Caterham only twice, as he had set
her down in his mind as a singularly vulgar person, and had
never thought of her since, except when he had refused her
invitations, he experienced some difficulty in responding to
Miss Cremer's communication. He managed, however, to
murmur, with a very creditable show of interest, " It is a
long time since I met her. I suppose you were staying with
her in the country?"

" Yes," exclaimed Miss Cremer; "and such a dear old
place it is—what I call a mellow place—just like Jane
herself." And she was proceeding to describe to him the
glories of its park, its museum, and its ball-room, when Mrs.
Steinberg happily caused a diversion by asking her niece if
"the man had come about the harp." Miss De Souza said,
" Yes." " Oh," cried the three Miss Cremers, "dear Mrs.
Steinberg, do ask her to play!" "Mr. Pole," continued one
of them, looking at him with ecstatic eyes, "don't you think
Ethel on the harp the most wonderful thing imaginable?"

" He never has heard me," interposed Miss De Souza,
laughing. "And if he had, he'd have thought it wonderful
only for its badness."

A sigh of "How can you?" broke from the three Miss Cremers; and Pole, who had for a moment looked away from them, saw that they now had seated themselves at Mrs. Steinberg's feet, holding her hands coaxingly and caressing her satin knees. "Oh," they repeated, "do ask her!"

"Mr. Pole," said Mrs. Steinberg, "these are the dearest girls in the world. I've no doubt, children, she'll play to us after dinner. Don't trouble her now. And listen, I'm sure that one of you will pick Mr. Pole a nice rose for his coat."

"We all will," they exclaimed, and as if by magic they were on their legs again. "Or perhaps, Mrs. Steinberg," said the eldest, "you would like me to find Birkett and get him to show Mr. Pole to his room."

"Molly, dear," smiled Mrs. Steinberg, "that will be very kind of you. Birkett is sure to be in the serving-room lecturing the gardener about the flowers. Indeed, we all must be thinking of going to dress soon. By the way, Mr. Pole," she continued, as he was departing under Miss Cremer's guidance, "to-night we have a treat in store for you. We've an evangelical minister dining here, a friend of Martha Blagdon's. You recollect Mrs. Blagdon, my old school-friend, don't you? She'll be down to dinner. This morning she was a little poorly."

"Over eating!" whispered Miss Cremer to Pole as they left the room.

He was punctual for dinner to a minute, but Mrs. Steinberg was down before him; and by her side was another lady equally stout, who, by imitating her dress, was invested with a superficial resemblance to her. Before Mrs. Steinberg had uttered a word of introduction, Mrs. Blagdon, half rising, and speaking with a solemn huskiness, said, "I have had the pleasure of seeing Mr. Pole before. Perhaps he does not remember an old woman like me. Mr. Pole, how are you? Are you well? I'm sure you're looking so." He had taken the fat and flaccid hand she offered him. It closed on his like a lobster's claw, and she fastened a moist glance on him which affronted him like an unasked-for kiss. Very rarely had he been more delighted at anything, then he was at a voice, which freed him from his present situation—the voice of a servant announcing Dr. Mogg. Dr. Mogg was a gentleman with white hair and a stoop, and a white beard which confused itself with the crumpled undulations of his shirt. His shaven upper lip was nearly as spacious as his forehead, and together, with his mouth, formed his principal feature. "I'm sure, ma'am," he said, in response to Mrs. Steinberg's greeting, "I am very happy to have the honour of dining with you. I've been blessed for many years with the friendship of Mrs. Blagdon." His natural solemnity was on the present occasion accentuated by a certain shyness; and his mind, which was really busy with the splendour of Mrs. Steinberg's chairs, had given his face an air of unusual thought, when Miss De Souza and her three young ladies entered, and reduced him to a nervous uncertainty as to what to do with his hands. Mrs. Blagdon, however, with the watchful tact of a friend, relieved him of this perplexity by herself taking charge of one of them, and by saying to the Miss Cremers, with a certain chastening tartness, "Well, girls, I hope that this afternoon you have been doing something a little less frivolous than usual." But Miss De Souza had now come to the rescue, and by the magic of her manner she so wrought upon Dr. Mogg that he presently was as much at his ease as he would have been in his own pulpit.

"My dear," whispered Mrs. Blagdon to Mrs. Steinberg, "I know that in fashionable society grace is often forgotten; but I beg you to ask Dr. Mogg to give a blessing."

Mrs. Steinberg nodded, and they presently passed into the dining-room, where the table was gorgeous with flowers and Venetian glass. There Dr. Mogg was given the place of honour, with a *menu* in front of him beginning with two soups, comprising three *entrées*, and ending with Strasburg *pâté*; and just as the Miss Cremers were on the point of seating themselves, Mrs. Steinberg duly asked her reverend companion for a grace. The Miss Cremers straightened their knees; every one remained standing; and for a moment there was a solemn pause, whilst Dr. Mogg considered how he might best improve the occasion. "Oh, Thou," he began at last, clasping his hands before him—" oh, Thou that sittest between the Cherubim, and whose glory is so exceeding that even the Cherubim cover their faces with their wings, consecrate to their appointed use these poor morsels that are before us, and make them humble instruments in the great scheme of our sanctification."

Mrs. Steinberg cast an involuntary glance at her *menu*; the three Miss Cremers appeared to be on the point of tittering; but Pole, who never laughed at any exhibition of religion in the presence of any one who could possibly take it seriously, was pleased at noticing how a look from Miss De Souza's eyes reduced the young ladies at once to a state of demure decorum. As dinner proceeded, indeed, they were quite unable to refrain from many whispered witticisms as to the number of poor morsels which found their way to the lips of Mrs. Blagdon. But Mrs. Blagdon, although she occasionally looked suspicious, was filled by food with a spirit of Christian gladness that made her impervious to most worldly annoyances.

"Martha," said Mrs. Steinberg to her, "you're eating positively nothing. Don't pass that jelly. You'll find it is excellent."

"Thank you, dear," said Mrs. Blagdon, with an air of meek resignation, and with two stalactites of cream hanging from her under lip as she spoke, "don't mind me. I assure you I am doing very well. John," she said, turning to the footman, "you may give me a piece of that, please. Yes, dear, this is really good—so well tasted and so wholesome." And as she finished it and returned her spoon to her plate, she looked round the table, smiling and almost frisky with content. "Seeing you all, dear," she said, turning to Mrs. Steinberg, "has made me ever so much better than I was. I think you are all of you a sight for sore eyes. I've had," she continued, with a species of hallowed jauntiness, "a series of blessings since the sun rose this morning—a good breakfast, good friends, a good dinner, and a good day. Do you know, deary, what I did with myself in my bedroom? I lay on my sofa and read Dr. Mogg's sermons?"

"I hope," said Dr. Mogg in slow, rumbling accents, "that those poor words of mine may prove efficacious with souls which need rousing far more than Mrs. Blagdon's. Madam," he whispered, leaning towards Mrs. Steinberg, "might I venture, as I am under an earthly physician's orders, to ask for a glass of brandy, just——" he coughed and paused as if hunting for a sufficiently delicate phrase, "just," he said, "to compose my stomach."

Again the Miss Cremers, who all were remarkably sharp of hearing, were just on the point of indulging in a trio of titters; nor did Mrs. Blagdon, who regarded them with equal disapproval on account of their worldly minds and

their want of worldly goods, tend to calm their risibility by
the black looks she cast at them. The situation, indeed,
was rapidly becoming strained, and Mrs. Steinberg, who
understood it, but was at the same time annoyed by it,
became so anxious to get the young ladies into the drawing-
room, that she quite forgot to ask for another grace, and
left Dr. Mogg, before he had realized what was happening,
to the company of Pole and the wine bottles, and the chance,
if he cared to use it, of composing a suitable thanksgiving
for the benefit of a single auditor.

Pole might, under ordinary circumstances, have found
it difficult to entertain so uncongenial a companion; but the
way in which that duty had been performed by Miss De
Souza—her tender consideration of the old man's feelings
and position—had put in his heart an example which he felt
constrained to emulate; and Dr. Mogg, though probably
regarding him as a brand for that bonfire of the lost, which
is for ever to celebrate the triumph and enhance the gaiety
of the saved, could not help feeling about him that, judged
by human evidence, he was a friendly and kindly gentleman,
full of all Christian courtesy. "After you, sir," he said, as
Pole opened the drawing-room door for him, the result being
that Pole, with a friendly violence, pushed Dr. Mogg forwards,
and entered holding him by the arm. As he did this he
saw that Miss De Souza was looking at him, and her face,
as she did so, brightened with surprised approval.

Come, Doctor," said Mrs. Steinberg, slapping her sofa,
"sit down here, and talk to me and Mrs. Blagdon. Those
young people are settling what to play to us. Go, Mr. Pole,
and help them."

As Pole approached the group which had clustered about
the harp, he found the Miss Cremers apparently fuller than
ever of wit and laughter, the zest of which was only intensified by suppression. "Ethel," said one of them, "play him
something from Don Giovanni." "No, no," said the second,
"Mephistopheles' serenade in Faust." "What will he do?"
said the third. "What effect will it have on him? I don't
suppose he ever heard an opera in his life;" each of which
observations was accompanied by smothered mirth.

"No, no," said Miss De Souza, speaking gently but firmly,
and yet accommodating herself to their mood so far as to
answer them in a whisper. "Why should we hurt his

feelings when he gave us such a delightful grace? Mr.
Pole, what shall I play? Look here—I have thought of
these."

"You couldn't," said Pole, "have possibly chosen better."

"Now, girls," said Miss De Souza, "go away and be
audience." And seating herself at her instrument, she
played with unusual power and feeling, "The Last Rose of
Summer," and "Oft in the Stilly Night"; and, finally,
when asked for more she concluded with "Home, Sweet
Home."

"Ethel," exclaimed the eldest Miss Cremer when the
Doctor had taken his departure, and she and her sisters had
again surrounded Miss De Souza, "you ought to be a lion-
tamer. Mr. Pole, oughtn't she? Do you know what Mrs.
Blagdon said when you finished the first piece? She said
to Dr. Mogg, in a fat wheezy whisper—no wonder it was
wheezy after that disgusting dinner of hers—'I often think
all these talents are a very great snare.' And what do you
think he answered? 'So,' he said, 'are our spiritual talents,
unless we employ them properly.'" "One for Martha, that
was!" said the second Miss Cremer, delighted. "And then,"
resumed the eldest, "when you had finished 'Home, Sweet
Home,' there were actually two tears in the good old gentleman's eyes."

"Mr. Pole," said Miss De Souza, lingering at the foot of
the stairs, as the rest of the party were going up with their
candles. "We haven't had a single word. But I want to
thank you for one thing—your kindness to that old man,
who must, I am sure, have bored your very life out of you.
We shall have a long talk to-morrow, I hope."

"To-morrow," he answered, "I fear I shall have to be
away at Windsor. I have told Mrs. Steinberg about it."

"Listen to the clock," she said. "It is only a quarter
past ten. The servants hardly ever put out the lights till
half-past. Come back with me into the drawing-room and
help me to find a book."

He felt her presence affect him as a man with an aching
wound is affected by the touch of some cool and healing
herb. Every look, every movement of hers was mesmeric
with assuaging sympathy. He followed her into the
drawing-room.

"You are not," she said, "looking well or in spirits. I

hope that all your affairs are going as you could wish them."

"So far as my affairs go," he answered, "everything has been beyond my hopes."

"And you are," she said, "famous already—famous for useful work."

"I could hardly," said Pole, "if I had had the choosing of them myself, have chosen external conditions more favourable than my own; and I also have done some work which I think is really useful. But I only show—though unhappily I show nobody but myself—how little external conditions are able to ensure happiness. You speak of my work too; and you think, perhaps, it must give me a good conscience. Let us suppose it does. Let us make that supposition, which so flatters me. \But our good consciences do not give happiness to us. Their utmost power as comforters is to help us to bear the want of it."\

CHAPTER XIII.

The following morning Pole received two letters in answer to telegrams he had sent the night before. Both letters were short. The one ran as follows. "My dear Reginald,—Come to lunch or dinner, whichever suits you best. If you do not come at one o'clock, I shall expect you at half-past six. Yours, Randal Bulman." The other was not much longer. "My dear Mr. Pole,—If you please, not luncheon. Come at three, or so soon after as you can. If you don't mind a bad dinner, dine." And there was a signature scrawled so hastily, that had this alone been his guide, it would literally have told him nothing. Reading this last note, he contemplated the careless writing, first with sadness, then with a passing scowl; and there came into his mind the image of Miss De Souza. He saw before him her face, so sensitive that she seemed to wince at even the passing thought of suffering borne by others. He had noticed her expression as she had asked him after his own welfare, and drawn his confessions from him by the mere magnetism of her sympathy. He recalled it now. He recalled her solicitous kindness towards the old clergyman, and her anxiety to shield him from any accidental mortification; and he said to himself half aloud, " What a strange thing is human nature! Here is one woman, on whom I have no claim whatever, except the claim she gives me by her own natural kindness: and yet she is unhappy at detecting the mere shadow of that suffering which another woman, not only sees with apathy, but inflicts on me without compunction." An hour later, however, when he appeared at breakfast, he was duly arrayed in that garment of calm cheerfulness with which men, in polite society, cover the indecency of sorrow.

"And so," said Mrs. Steinberg, "you are going to lunch with Canon Bulman. There's an account in the paper, I see, of a speech he was making yesterday. And oh!" she exclaimed, taking the paper up, "look at this! They have had their way at last! Well, I'm very sorry, I confess; and as Martha is not here I can say so."

"Who?" exclaimed the Miss Cremers in chorus. "Dear Mrs. Steinberg, who have had their way?"

"Who? Why, my dears, Canon Bulman and his meddling friends. You know how they have been clamouring that the unhappy man should resign." And she named the political leader who was the object of the Canon's antagonism. "He has not resigned, I see; but two-thirds of his supporters have repudiated him."

"The Canon," thought Pole to himself, as he set off for the station, "will be so full of his triumph, there will really be no holding him." And he managed to divert his mind from other subjects by speculating in the train as to how his host would receive him, and what would be the character of the canonical house and household. As for the house, it was very much what he had foreseen, except that it was a good deal larger. It was Gothic, as Glenlynn was; but yet with a wide difference. The Gothic of Glenlynn—the Gothic of a hundred years ago—was the toy of an aristocracy playing at mediæval feudalism. The Gothic of Canon Bulman's abode, with its piebald arches of red and yellow brick, was the toy of a reformed church playing at mediæval Catholicism. The building was divided from the road by a frill of turf only, and a cast-iron railing, ornamented with dwarf crosses, over which two excited cats were vulgar enough to be playing leap-frog. The pointed windows were white with muslin curtains, between which were glimpses of

I

ornaments under glass shades; and the brass knocker on
the varnished surface of the front door, was so brilliant that
it shone all across the road.   Pole's ring at the bell was
answered by a dark-eyed parlour-maid, as spruce as the
house itself, but considerably less ecclesiastical.   He, like
Mr. Godolphin, had heard from Dr. Clitheroe, that the
Canon was said to be blind enough to retain in his service
a domestic whose innocence or whose reformation was by
no means so complete as he believed it to be; and the
moment Pole looked at the young lady by whom the door
was opened, the Doctor's gossip came back to his mind.   He
gave to her appearance a very cursory attention; but a
glance was enough to suggest to him as an explanation of
her presence, that the Canon, like many of the emotional
apostles of chastity, had a special zeal for souls which resided
in attractive bodies.   This reflection, however, did not occupy
him for a moment, and was quite driven away by the interior
of the Canon's mansion.   The hall was imposing with woodwork of pitch-pine, scooped and scalloped with various
Gothic devices, which all had a tendency to be more or less
cruciform, and suggestive of sacerdotal asceticism.   The
Canon, however, who was very far from being a sacerdotalist,
had neutralized this effect, by hanging the walls with magnificent Alpine photographs, photographs of the Cambridge
Eight, and engravings of a few crowned heads; whilst a
new Turkey carpet covered the floor with comfort.   Pole
had hardly had time to look round him, when out came the
Canon from a library, and bid him welcome, with a muscular
grasp of the hand.

"Lunch, Sophie," he said, "as soon as you can let us
have it.   And now, Reginald, come in and see my den.   A
simple place, this, but not bad in its way.   Look—those
rows of classics—eh—do you remember them?   Sit you
down there.   You will find that chair comfortable.   Prince
Ferdinand was sitting in that chair last week, and he said
he liked it better than anything they could boast of in the
Castle."

The Canon, in fact, was in singularly good humour, and
that for four different reasons.   One was the downfall of
the detested and peccant politician; another, the success of
his own last evening's eloquence; a third—and perhaps the
chief—was the sense that the position of things at Glenlynn

was reversed, and that both as a host and a public man he was once again Pole's patron: and the fourth was the pleasure he took in his new house, and especially in displaying its merits to a fresh spectator. And indeed, when Pole reflected that one of the Canon's favourite missions was to lead the crusade of Labour against property, place, and luxury, he could not help feeling that the bitterness of the Canon's spirit was hardly caused by any want of the main advantages which he attacked.

"That," said the Canon, on their way across the hall to luncheon, "is the drawing-room;" and he opened one of the doors and disclosed a spacious apartment, divided in the middle by something like a chancel arch, and fitted with rosewood tables, and albums on bead mats. The Canon was blessed with an exceedingly healthy appetite, but he had neither the grossness of a greedy man, nor any of the refinements of a dainty one; and his table, in these respects, was a very fair reflection of himself. A turbot, a chicken, and an apple tart with cream, followed by a German cheese, the gift of a royal patron—such was the fare he offered; and it was served with appropriate nicety. The silver, though modern, and of very vulgar, inferior design, was plentiful, and well polished; the porcelain plates were adorned with the Canon's monogram; and though the Canon himself took only lemon and soda-water, he provided his guest with a bottle of first-rate claret.

"Well," he said, looking at Pole, with a smile in which the reproving tutor not ungracefully mixed with the triumphant public man, you see that I and my friends have had our reward at last, and to our credit as a Christian nation that scoundrel has had to efface himself. I thought, my dear fellow, when I was at Glenlynn, that you treated this and other matters too lightly, or were a little inclined to soften their true features by throwing over them a veil of sentiment—a very tawdry and betinselled veil at the best. I wish, my dear Reginald, you would always beware of sentiment. Next to the absolute temptation of the brute senses themselves, nothing is more dangerous to true and healthy manhood, both in the individual and to society. It does indeed prepare the way for corruption; and it does so by no means more efficacious and fatal than by leading us to judge gently of the sins and of the corruption of others."

"You are not then," said Pole, "of Bunyan's way of thinking, who was accustomed to say, 'If it were not for the mercy of God, I myself should be in that sinner's place!'"

"I am not," said the Canon, giving a slight thump on the tablecloth. "The mercy of God has implanted in us His own image. He has given us eyes to see filth and avoid it; and it is idle to say that we should all of us choose to walk in it unless, besides giving us eyes, He also kept us in leading-strings. If a man chooses to trifle with his own eyesight by putting on his nose the coloured spectacles of sentiment, which will prevent him distinguishing the clean places from the dirty, all I can say is, his dirt be on his own boots; only I don't want his boots to be trampling on my carpet. My dear Reginald, if your friend Bunyan's words mean anything, they mean this—and see how it sounds put this way—If I followed my own inclination I should be a thief, a forger, a murderer, an adulterer, a suicide. In fact it is only by a miracle that I am not one and all of them, as it is. I'm certain that if any one were to say that to either of us we should answer, 'That may be true of you, sir; but I can assure you it is not true of me.'"

It may be inferred that whilst the Canon was discussing these delicate subjects, his two parlour-maids—for the fair Sophie was aided by a sister handmaiden—were not in the room to listen; or, if they were, they were hidden behind a screen, which a hardly audible laugh made Pole think not improbable: and as at this moment their services happened to be requisite, the Canon was obliged to summon them, and give a new turn to the conversation.

It was easy to see, however, that his thoughts had not strayed with his words; for, as soon as his attendants had disappeared, he returned to his previous subject.

"I have," he said, "been doing all I can to encourage football and athletic sports in this neighbourhood. There's no better means of keeping our young men out of temptation. The unlucky thing is, that one gets only at the lower classes. One doesn't get at those which are really the worst offenders—the classes which make these riverside towns the sinks of iniquity they are."

"Indeed!" said Pole. "Are they worse than other places?"

"Oh," said the Canon, "it is deplorable! Artists and men boating—down they come, bringing all the vices of society with them. I tell you, in some of these towns there is hardly a pretty girl who gives you what you can call a really modest look. But that is not the worst of it. All these pretty little villas, looking on the river or hidden away in gardens—these are put to the very worst of purposes. Profligate men take them as summer homes for their mistresses. Wives take them as places where they may meet their lovers. The very Thames itself has become the most immoral river in the world."

The turn of the last phrase almost made Pole laugh; but he composed his muscles, and merely said, "How do you know all this?"

"Ha!" exclaimed the Canon, ironically. "I know, my dear Reginald, because I make it my business to inquire. Some of the landlords of those very villas I was speaking about—God-fearing, clean-minded men; there's one man named Snaggs, especially—a capital fellow, a right-hand man of mine—come to me with pretty stories. I heard from him only yesterday about a woman, who, whatever she is, is not here for any good. But come," he continued, as if ridding his mouth of some nauseous taste—"come, I'll give you one of Prince Michael's cigars. I am sorry to say I have an engagement at three."

Pole was pleased to hear this, as it simplified his own departure; and he could not help smiling, as he bade the Canon good-bye, to think in what a notorious way the giver of these choice cigars was unworthy, on the Canon's principles, to set his boots upon the Canon's carpet. Unwilling to be cross-questioned as to where he was now going, or—more embarrassing still—to be accompanied for any part of the way by his host, he had managed to take his departure when it was hardly half-past two; and, hurrying to the nearest cab-stand, desired to be driven to a house of whose position he knew little, except that it was outside Windsor. When he mentioned the name, the driver seemed well-acquainted with it. It lay on the outskirts of the town; and Pole, from his slight local knowledge, divined, when the cab turned down a narrow lane, that the river Thames could not be very far away. His conjecture proved correct, and soon between two garden walls he saw a boat flash by on

the volume of sliding water. At the same moment the
vehicle drew up at a wicket, which bore on its green woodwork the words "Laburnum Lawn."

CHAPTER XIV.

POLE dismissed the cab, and pushing the wicket open, entered
a pathway, narrow but trimly kept, which went for some
dozen yards in a curve between tall bushes. He walked
very slowly, as if shy of emerging from this seclusion, and
once or twice he hesitated and stood still. But soon—in a
few seconds—the sheltered path had done with him, and he
found himself facing a red little brick house, covered with
creepers, shining with white window-sills, and looking on
a lawn which was studded with brilliant roses, and which
opened out by a shy aperture on the stream. In the porch,
at the top of some steps, leaning against a pillar, was a
woman. When Pole appeared, she at first remained quite
motionless, but as he came nearer he saw that her eyes were
following him, and her lips were relaxing into a soft gradual
smile. Her dress was a blue silk shirt, and a skirt of rough
Scotch cloth. In her blue shirt was a rose, and her face
was a rose still fresher. Her eyes had the brooding light of
a clouded day in June, and in them and on her face, with
its soft infantine curves, there rested two expressions—that
of the child looking at its mother, and that of a mother
looking at her child. When Pole reached the steps, she
straightened herself with a little jerk that was half playful
in its abruptness, and ran down to meet him; and her eyes
had now in them a faint dancing sparkle which child and
mother, when they look at each other, never see. She held
out both her hands to him with a frankness that had something timid in it, and looking him earnestly in the face she
said, "Are you glad to see me?" Her voice was singularly
sweet, and trembled with a deprecating laugh.

"I think," said Pole, gently and yet sadly, "it is I who
should ask whether you are glad to see *me*."

"Yes," she said; "yes. Of course I am very, very glad."

"I didn't," he answered, "venture to think you would

be. But now I look at you, I really think you are, Pansy. Dear, I believe you are."

She looked silently at him and merely nodded her head.

"How pretty," he said, "your garden is, and the little house, and everything!"

Her face brightened, as if she were glad to speak of some indifferent subject. "Isn't it nice?" she exclaimed. "Let us walk round and see it all. There is an arbour there, where I thought we would have tea."

They went together with slow, intermittent paces, pausing now and then to look at a bush or flower, and only breaking silence to exchange some trifling observation as to the name or the beauty of a rose, the neatness with which the place was kept, or some other obvious topic suggested to them by the surrounding scene.

"I often," she said, as they came in view of the river, "sit here, myself quite hidden, and watch the boats go by. What pretty spots of colour those men make with their caps! They row well."

Pole assented, looking vaguely across the water. Meanwhile she had dropped her head and was poking at a dandelion with her parasol. At last he asked if she knew the name of a house, half hidden in trees, on the other side of the water. She seemed for the moment as if she had hardly heard him; and then looking quickly up she uttered the two words, "What, dear?" The unconscious tenderness of her manner, and the way in which the endearing phrase slipped from her, made him turn abruptly round. She raised her eyes to him and his look transfixed her. Half unwillingly she was obliged to return his gaze. "Pansy," he said, "do you know that I think of you night and day? Tell me—do you know it? Dear, have you forgotten everything?"

He spoke low, but his voice shook with suppressed feeling. He did not approach her; but she shrank a little away from him, as a gentle half-tamed animal shrinks from a hand approaching it.

"Don't," she said, "don't—I beg you."

"Don't what?" he asked.

"You know," she replied. "Oh, Reggie, please be kind to me! Be nice and friendly. I haven't too many friends." Then with a light, quick movement she turned away from the river, and said to him, "Come, you have not seen half the garden. And the house—I must show you that—and my books, for I have quite a library." She had now summoned to her lips the shadow of a pouting smile. "You will let me show you my books," she said.

Pole's face and bearing showed signs of an internal struggle. His brows contracted, and the lines of his mouth grew harsh. Then, with an obvious effort, he overcame every bitter feeling, and spoke with a voice and smile that answered to her mood. "Show me," he said, "everything; I am longing to see it all." A little childish laugh fluttered amongst her syllables as she answered him. She touched his arm lightly and they went together into the house. There, amongst her books, the conversation came with painless fluency; and if Canon Bulman, in his zeal for the morals of the neighbourhood, had been peering through the window and had known nothing of either, he might have thought them brother and sister, or cousins who had long been separated. It is true that Pole, when her face was turned from him, sometimes looked at her with a wondering and half-pitying sadness; but he continued to laugh pleasantly, and talk to her with tranquil sympathy, as if intercourse such as this left no emptiness in his heart.

Meanwhile time had gone by quickly, and a maid now appeared at the door of the room where they were sitting, and said that tea had been taken into the arbour. "Will you," said his hostess to him as they rose, "bring out a book with you and read to me? Any one you like—Shelley, or that volume of Dickens."

He did as she bade him with a slight reluctant sigh, and slowly followed her out of doors. When they sat down in the arbour he was silent and his face was changed.

"Have I bored you," she said, "with talking about myself? I have! I know I have, and now you are going to hate me! But, Reggie, I've no one but you to whom I can tell my thoughts; and when I see you they all come pouring out; and lately, until I came here, I have had no time for thinking."

"May I," he said, "ask what has been occupying you?"

"Oh," she replied, "every kind of thing—practical things. You've no idea what a house the castle is; and everything comes on me. I shall have to work like this for another twenty years at least. Perhaps," she said gently, " you will be able to see now why I so seldom have time to write to you. You wouldn't wish me—would you?—to neglect my duties. You ought rather to encourage me to do them."

Whilst she spoke he looked straight before him, as if he did not hear her. She might have seen by the movement of his throat that he was agitated by some emotion. At last he said in a low, deliberate voice—

"It is right. You must do the duties that are claiming you on every side. Your new life—the life you have so gladly chosen—must take you and make you part of itself, surround you and absorb you, and raise you, and change you past my knowing you; and, better still, it will change you so that you will have no need of me." His voice, as he went on, had acquired a growing bitterness, and there was something in it almost fierce as, turning on her abruptly, he said to her, "Is not that so?"

She looked at him with a face that was frightened rather than angry, and bewildered rather than frightened.

"Dear," she exclaimed, "don't be rough with me!"

Those few helpless words in an instant disarmed his anger.

"Forgive me," he said; "do I ever wish to wound you?"

"No!" she answered. "No; you don't. Be kind and good, then, and read to me."

He took the book up and began to turn its pages; but as he did so, his eyes kept straying towards the tea-tray.

"What is it?" she asked.

"I was looking at the cups," he said. "I see there are only two. I thought those little cakes might perhaps be for some one else. Is no one else here, Pansy?"

She slowly shook her head. "There was," she replied, "but they both of them went to London this morning. They went with nurse, to see the doctor."

Again his face darkened, but he spoke quite equably.

"Come," he said, "I will read now. Here is a chapter that always made you laugh. I could hardly trust myself to utter my own thoughts."

These last words were muttered rather to himself than her, and he began his reading without more ado. He read well, and with apparent interest and willingness; and she, as she listened, kept her eyes fixed on him, and laughed encouragingly at every amusing passage. But in time it seemed as if he were wearying of some painful effort. The spirit went from his voice; his elocution became monotonous; and at last she stopped him, saying—

"You're not attending; no, not the least bit. You've made three mistakes in those last two sentences. There, put your book down and talk to me. We have read enough."

He put the book down with alacrity, and abruptly asked her a question which, to judge from his manner, had been in his mind some time.

"Why," he said, "would you not let me come to luncheon?"

"I couldn't," she said; "I was expecting the dressmaker, so if you had come earlier you would hardly have seen anything of me. Why do you laugh like that?"

"I was smiling," he replied, "at a picture which what you have said suggested to me—a picture of you holding a pair of scales, with a man's soul in one, and some new petticoats in the other."

"No, no," she said, trying to laugh lightly. "Your soul was not at stake, only your body. And I do hope that you managed to get lunch somewhere."

He told her he had.

"Where was it?" she asked gently. "Where did you have your lunch, dear? Won't you tell me?"

He answered brusquely. "In Windsor, at Canon Bulman's. He was my tutor once."

"Oh," she said, "the man who makes all those speeches? Very well, and what did Canon Bulman talk about?"

"Oh," replied Pole, "he talked about his usual topic. If you very much want to know, he talked about the virtue of chastity. He thinks a man who has lost it is very nearly as bad as a woman." Pole would have been seen by any careful observer to have been speaking at random, and to have been hardly conscious of a listener; but there was in his tone a certain contemptuous bitterness that gave his words an edge, although they were uttered absently.

Her lips parted with a hardly audible gasp, and her face appeared to be frozen with some sudden and uncomprehended pain. "I don't think," she faltered at last, "that you ought to say things like that to me." She paused and bit her lip, and her cheeks became slowly crimson. "It is not delicate," she said, getting out the words with difficulty. Then all at once her eyes filled with tears, and hastily rising from her seat, she stamped on the gravel with her feet, and turning her back on him she hid her face in her handkerchief. "It's too bad of you," she exclaimed in broken tones. "What did you mean by that? Did you mean anything? How dare you come down here and talk to me like this!"

"Pansy," exclaimed Pole, distressed beyond measure at this outburst, and at first bewildered as to the cause of it. "What have I said? You know I never meant to pain you."

But without noticing his question she began to walk away from him. "I am going," she said, "into the house."

"Shall I come too?" she asked humbly.

"As you like," she said, without turning her head. But a moment later, throwing him a glance over her shoulder, "No," she added, "you had better not. Go away—you had better go."

Instead, however, of accepting his dismissal, he rose, and unchecked followed her with deliberate steps. They presently found themselves once more in the drawing-room. As they entered, he closed the door. The slight sound made her turn round and look at him. "You needn't shut it," she said. "I am not going to stay here. I'm only looking for a book; I am then going up to my bedroom." And she began to examine the books with an attempt at ease and indifference, though her eyes, had he only observed them, were not in a condition to see. She took up a book at hazard, and began moving towards the door. "I am going upstairs," she said coldly; "will you kindly let me pass?"

"No," he said, with a hard determination that startled her. "I will not let you go till you hear what I have to say." She tried to laugh, as if in that way she might conciliate him, but the little sound she emitted was hardly audible. At all events he did not heed it. "Pansy Masters," he continued, grasping her tightly by the arm, "I order you to go back. Go! Sit down in that chair. Whatever happens, by God, I will be heard; and you shall not leave me taking a false impression." By this time she had obeyed him; she had seated herself in the chair helplessly. At the sound of his oath, she winced as if he had struck her with a horsewhip. "I see," he said, struggling to speak calmly, "I see

now what you fancied, when I spoke about Canon Bulman.
But when I spoke I was not thinking of you. You had
driven me back on myself, and I was thinking—I was thinking—of many things. Do you imagine for a moment I was
such a coward, such a brute, such a fool, as to apply to
yourself anything that the Canon said to me? The Canon!
My thoughts were busy with him for a very different reason.
He talks about chastity. He has no idea what the word
means. St. Francis preached to birds. I don't know if he
ever tried pigs. The Canon's ideas of virtue are those of a
converted pig. When I spoke to you just now, I was contrasting in my own mind what he would teach me with what
I have been taught by some one else. Some one else has
taught me to feel in my heart of hearts the holy and living
thing that this virtue really is—to feel that, in its highest
form, it is no refusal or negation, but the self-devotion of
body and soul at once—of the reasonable soul and flesh that
is one man. Chastity is the complete living of one human
being for another, which is merely the humanized form of
the Saints living for God. And who has taught me this?
Who has opened my eyes? It is you—you. Pansy, do not
you know that? Have I loved you so long in vain—to such
little purpose? It was for you I exiled myself all those
years in Germany; for you that I—— Ah, but I can't
speak of it. The thought of you has been always with me."
He paused; his voice trembled, and sitting down by her, he
leant his face on his hand. "Pansy," he said, "I can't
describe it. You have been a presence always dwelling in
me, softening all my hard thoughts and quickening all my
good ones, and giving my soul wings, and enabling me to
forget self. And now, what do you do?" he exclaimed with
returning bitterness. "I had not much to give you; but all
that I had I gave; and you have taken it all—all—everything in me out of which happiness might have been made.
And you—you leave me with as little compunction as if I
had been an upper servant. For six months you never write
a single line to me—although, Pansy, there are such things
as mails between England and America; and at last when
you do write, it is only a careless word or two. I could bear
that, if your unkindness ended there. But does it? Think.
I travel two hundred miles for the sole purpose of seeing you.
Of the few hours we might spend together, you give up three

to your milliner; and of the hours we have actually spent, you take up the larger part in gossiping about the monthly reviews, and making me read Dickens to you. I have tried to speak to you—the real you; but in vain. You elude me, you repulse me. You treat me as some stranger, whom you had seen for the first time yesterday. And there is something else I had wished and hoped to see; and you—you deny me that! You have no heart; but do you think that I have none? or that it is made o" wood or leather? Perhaps I had none once; but you have given me one, and you are murdering it! Woman," he exclaimed, "how can you treat me like this? Do you realize what relation I am to you?— what link must always bind me to you?"

All this while she had sat in the chair motionless; but at these last words she rose with her face rigid, and stumbling forward a step or two, abruptly stood still and faced him. "When you speak like that," she said, in a low constrained voice, "I hardly know where to turn. How can you? I will not submit to it. Oh! I hate you!" She remained looking at him with an expression that seemed to repeat her language; but as she did so her eyes suddenly filled with tears again. A little gasp broke from her. She felt feebly and in vain for her handkerchief; and then approaching him with a curiously natural movement, she took his from the breast of his coat, and she convulsively pressed it to her eyes. A second later she hid her face on his shoulder, her hands clutched his sleeve, and he felt her sobs shaking him.

They dined together like friends; but their manner was so subdued and quiet, that a listener could hardly have conjectured the precise terms on which they stood. "And I may then," he said at parting, "see you again before I go?" She replied in a half whisper, "The day after to-morrow. And I will—indeed I will—try to be better to you, and to write oftener. I ought to—I owe you everything. Dear, good night." His lips touched her, and he was gone.

CHAPTER XV.

He returned to Thames Wickham oppressed by a profound melancholy, his heart reproaching him with the hard language he had used, yet bruised and wounded itself by the treatment he had just received. "All my hopes," he said to himself, "are over. She has no wish to pain me. She has lost almost all sense that it is in her power to do so. Yes," he continued, "I am nothing to her; and except her, no one is anything to me. Will she ever know—never! how should she?—what I am doing for hers, if not for her?" Then again his imagination confronted him with the image of Miss De Souza; and the thought of her sympathy, as contrasted with the cruel heedlessness of another, embittered his mind afresh, and yet at the same time soothed it.

It was late when he reached Mrs. Steinberg's, and his friends had retired to bed; but the following morning at breakfast, he received the welcome news that the three Miss Cremers were going for the day to London; and Miss De Souza, as soon as they had taken their departure, asked him if he would like to come for a little row on the river. "And we might," she said, "rest somewhere under a bank, and talk." He fetched his hat—she had hers on already—and they went out together into the garden. "How different," he thought, "is the treatment I am meeting now from that which I met with in that other garden yesterday." And a short involuntary sigh reached his companion's ear.

Before them was a lawn sloping down to the Thames. It was shaded with old cedars and traversed by broad walks. Beds of geraniums glittered in appropriate places. There were steps of white stone, and bright coloured majolica vases, and a tribe of luxurious chairs with plump red cushions under the trees. Closing to a landing-place was one of the gardeners waiting, with a boat in readiness—a boat light but roomy, cushioned as luxuriously as the chairs and built for indolent drifting.

"We shan't want you, Walter," said Miss De Souza, as they embarked. "How is your wife? Is she better? I hope she liked the jelly that I made for her yesterday. This afternoon, if she will let me, I will come and read to her.

That man's poor wife," she explained to Pole when he dipped his sculls into the water, and they glided out into the stream, "has a terrible internal complaint. It relieves her sometimes being read to."

A better means of leading to unreserved conversation and of gathering up the threads of an old and intimate friendship, could not have been devised than an expedition like this. For the little discussions that were necessary as to where they should best go, together with the physical occupation which fell to the lot of one of them, enabled them, by easy degrees and without any abrupt transition, to pass from the subjects which lie on the surface of life, to those which are hidden beneath and which conversation rarely reaches.

"Your aunt," said Pole, alluding to a conversation which had taken place at breakfast, in the course of which Mrs. Steinberg had indulged in some vigorous language, "was very severe on Canon Bulman, and all his splendid speeches. And yet he's a man who has many excellent qualities."

"I," said Miss De Souza, "confess I have no patience with him. I could hardly read the speech which he made at Reading. But then, perhaps, I am prejudiced, and I have a reason for being so."

"I was not aware you knew him," exclaimed Pole with some surprise.

"No more I do," she answered. "But I used to know his wife. Poor woman, I pity her."

"His wife!" Pole ejaculated. "Do you mean to tell me he is married? How? when? where? I have known him for fourteen years; though, no doubt, there have been long intervals during which I have lost sight of him. Do you mean he has a wife alive?"

"His wife," said Miss De Souza, "was the daughter of a Cambridge surgeon. He married her on being presented to a living, when he resigned his Fellowship. Ten years ago this was. They were only together for a year; and then they agreed to separate. There was nothing wrong, as people put it with so much unconscious irony—as if what they call wrong were not of all wrongs the least. 'He was always preaching,' she said to me, 'about people saving their souls. He never treated me as if I had a soul at all.'"

"Where did you know her?" asked Pole.

"Abr..ad," said Miss De Souza, "at a little place in the
Pyrenees. I often think of one thing she said to me. 'I
shouldn't so much have minded had there been other women
in the case. I could forgive him for having broken my
heart; but I cannot forgive him for having hardened it.'
And then," Miss De Souza continued, "I must tell you one
more thing. It will show you the sort of terms they were
on. 'You are always flattering yourself,' Mrs. Bulman once
said to him, 'that you are not as other men are. It is lucky
for the happiness of women that most men are not as you.'"

"It's odd," said Pole, "I should never have heard of
this; but of course it is a thing he would keep as quiet as
he could. What made him marry the woman, I wonder?"

"I should think, from what she told me," said Miss De
Souza, "that on one side of his character, he was just the
man to be taken by a pretty face. By the way, I ought,
however, to mention this in his favour—that he made her,
considering his means, a very handsome allowance. She
died last year. I saw her death in the papers."

"And now, I suppose," said Pole, "her allowance comes
back to the Canon. His fine new house must be more or
less a memorial to her."

By this time they were opposite the mouth of a quiet
stream which came floating into the river by many curves
and elbows, and formed, under an arch of foliage, an avenue
paved with water.

"Shall we go up there," said Miss De Souza, "and stay
quiet under the willows?"

He assented; and before long they were stationary in a
shady place.

"How hot it must have made you," she said, "rowing in
that burning sun. Lie down and be comfortable. There are
any number of cushions."

The stern of the boat, indeed, was like an oriental divan,
alluring the mind, through the body, to placid dreaming and
meditation; and for some time they neither of them opened
their lips, except for some broken remarks on the sound of
the water or the reflections in it, or the summer sky, which
showed itself in dancing tesselations between the leaves.

At last Pole said, "I hope that I have not been speaking
of the Canon too hardly. To speak bitterly of any one
leaves a bitter taste in the mouth."

"Yes," said Miss De Souza. "I know how you feel that. You did not when first I knew you; at all events, not so keenly."

"That," he said, "is because as one lives on, one learns how little one could stand hard judgment one's self. But as for the Canon, in spite of what you say about his wife, there is only one thing in him which I really dislike personally. I mean those opinions on which he happens most to value himself."

"Canon Bulman to me," said Miss De Souza, "represents an idea of virtue which has caused far more misery than most men's lapses into vice. His own wife's history is an instance of this. You see, I speak as a woman; and I have known—well, only a few weeks since, I was seeing a friend of mine—such a noble, patient woman, whose heart, from morning to night—I do not exaggerate—never ceases aching. And why? On account of a husband who, because he does not ill-treat her in one way, thinks himself at liberty to ill-treat her in every other. He neglects her, he wastes her money, he has never a tender word for her. Oh! men never can know how a woman can be made to suffer by a husband whom our Canon Bulman would compliment as a model of fidelity. If a man loves you, and is what is called unfaithful, you can forgive him and take him back to you. If he does not love you, if his warmth is coldness, if his light is darkness, you have nothing of value either to lose, or to win back, or to keep. It has always seemed to me that to call a man a good husband because he does not do one particular thing, is as wise as to call him a good husband because he happens not to be a smuggler. I hope, Mr. Pole, you're not shocked at me for talking like this."

He watched her. Her voice was trembling, and her eyes, which were turned away from him, and were looking up at the whispering movement of the leaves, had in them the strained, and almost painful intentness by which alone eyes sometimes are kept dry. "Does," she continued, "what I say sound unchristian? I am a Christian; I say my prayers. I am not married, and I never shall be. These questions personally do not affect me; but they affect me through the way in which I have known them affect other women, and instinctively I know that in their place I should have felt the same. Please do not think—indeed, I am sure you will not—that I make light of that which is commonly called virtue :

K

but in man, and even in woman, it seems to me mainly
beautiful—how shall I put it ?—as a sign of something else,
as the blush which the heart sends to the cheek of a deeper
constancy."

"You asked me," said Pole, "a minute ago, if I thought
what you said unchristian. Who are the women whose faces
shine at us from the pages of the gospel? Of course there
is the sacred Mother, and Mary, the sister of Lazarus. But
who are the others? They are Mary Magdalene, the woman
of Samaria, and the woman taken in adultery. If you are
wrong," he went on, "I should say you were wrong because
your view of things is too high, rather than too low. You
can understand only the nobility of the flesh. Canon Bulman
can understand only its vileness."

For a time they were silent. At last he resumed, in a
different tone—

"You say that you yourself feel strongly about these
matters, because the confidences of two women have shown
you their practical bearing. I am not married, and, like
you, I never shall marry; so, like you, as far as that goes,
they do not concern me personally. But, like you, I have
had strange things brought under my notice. One was
brought under my notice the other day, and it has been in
my mind all the time we have been talking."

"Is it anything," said Miss De Souza, "that you could
tell me?"

"All I can tell of it," said Pole, "doesn't sound much
when told. It is only a little story which I conjecture or
divine to be taking place at this moment. A man of whom
I knew something—this is the long and short of it—became
connected three or four years ago with a married woman,
who had been practically deserted by her husband. The
man was devoted to the woman, and gave up everything for
her; and she, too, was devoted in the most passionate way
to him. Well, the lady's husband, who was at first very
much out at elbows, has since come into a considerable
family property, and now has induced his wife to go back
and live with him. Of course, there are a thousand reasons
why she should do so. An avenue is open to her full of
interests and duties, and no doubt she sees her soul saved
respectably at the end of it. But, of course, to walk in this
avenue with comfort, it is necessary that she should get rid

of her lover. She won't want to have him jumping out of
the bushes and joining her; and the process of getting rid
of him is what she is now most intent upon. He's not a
man who would for a moment keep her against her will. He
would probably urge her to take the very course she is
taking. But the curious question is, what will he think of
her past relations with himself, when he sees how easily she
can sever them? What will he think of the value of her
love for a new life, when it costs her hardly a pang to say
good-bye to the old? Will he think that her soul is more
likely to be saved because she hastens to save it with such
very little compunction?"

"Oh!" exclaimed Miss De Souza, "but a woman *must*
feel under such circumstances. She couldn't do as you say,
if she ever really had cared for him. She would only deserve
happiness, she would only deserve peace, in proportion to
the misery she felt in seeking for them without her friend.
Why, a woman such as you describe is a woman who would,
if she were shipwrecked, cling to a swimmer till she was
picked up by a boat, and then leave him to drown, exhausted
by his toil in saving her."

"Women," said Pole, "are always hard on women. I
felt angry at the thought of her when first I heard the
story. But women are weak—so are men too—and life is
hard; and whenever I think of complicated cases like this
I am inclined to cut the knot—though I am not a Christian
like you—by saying, "'God have mercy on us, for we all of
us need mercy.'"

He said these last words simply, and yet they dragged a
little in their utterance, as if he were unaccustomed to this
species of confession. For a time they were both silent.
Then he said, "It does one good to talk to you. I am not
going to compliment you on all the wise things you say. I
am thinking of the way you affect me, not by what you say,
but by what you are. I find myself expressing to you easily,
without false shyness, things which very often I can hardly
acknowledge to myself. Your presence thaws thoughts in
me which generally are cold and frozen."

"If that is so," she said, "it is only because, being so
weak myself, I feel doubly the troubles of stronger minds.
It touches me that you should be troubled—you who are so
much above me in every way."

"Ah," he said lightly, "if I am to go on telling the truth to you, you must never yourself say things so far from the truth as that."

When they reached the house again the midday post had arrived, and Pole found a letter for him lying on the hall table. The well-known, untidy writing brought the blood to his face.

"My dearest Reggie," it ran, "I am suddenly obliged to leave. I must go to-morrow, and shall not come back again. I am very busy to-day, and have hardly a spare moment; but come here this afternoon—about four o'clock, if possible —and see Pansy just for a few minutes. Dear, I am yours.

"PANSY."

His brain, as he read, was confused by a rush of thoughts, reproachful recollections amongst them of things which he had said in the boat whilst this letter was actually on the way to him. The gong for luncheon was sounding. He hurried upstairs to his room, and ringing for his servant sent him off with a telegram, containing the words, "Punctually at four o'clock."

He excused himself for his absence to Mrs. Steinberg— not a very difficult matter, as she took it for granted that he was going to London for an hour or so; and he found himself, at the time appointed, again in the narrow lane which led between the garden walls and the gate of Laburnum Lawn. When he was still too far off for the actual wicket to be visible, he fancied he saw some movement at the opening in which the wicket was. "Can it," he thought, "be possible that I shall find other visitors with her?" This fear was still in his mind when a movement was again apparent, and in another moment a figure emerged into the lane. It was her own. With a shy slowness, which yet had something that was eager in it, she advanced towards him. "Pansy," he said to himself, "how have my doubts been wronging you!" They met. There was a smile on her face like the flickering light that is reflected from water. It was tremulous with the affection of which her eyes were full. As he took her hand a tenderness filled his heart, like that felt by a man for a little helpless bird which has fallen from its nest and is too young to fly; and there broke from him, in a low tone, many of those terms of endearment which, when recorded, are colourless, or even ridiculous, but which, in the air of passion, have a life as vivid and beautiful as the sea anemone has in its own world of waters.

They went into the garden together. She told him all her plans. She explained the reasons of her departure, which he saw was both necessary and unwilling, due as it was to some difficulty with the servants in her new home; and then they stood almost silent, bending over a yellow rose, as if its scent and colour were a parting thought which they were sharing.

Presently she said, "I told you that I had my step-child with me. She is very kind to me now, and I hope I do all I can for her. But there is something else here which I must show you. Wait for me, and I will be back directly."

With a naïve, girlish gesture she ran across the lawn and into the house, and Pole could hear her voice calling out to somebody. Indistinctly the sound of an answer reached him, with another sound following this, pitched in a higher key; and then his companion reappeared in the doorway, and slowly descended the steps, leading a little boy. If the child of a woman he had never seen before had been enough to attract him as it played before the moorland cottage, much more was he attracted by the apparition now before him. He went towards it; he lifted it in his arms for a moment; and he and its mother led it between them to a seat.

"Take him," she said, "on your knee;" and they listened to it, watched, and talked to it.

It was a pretty child, affectionate to almost a premature degree, and the spirit of childhood laughed in its dark eyes like a star through a night of melancholy. The mother's gaze wandered from it to Pole, and, without saying a word to him, her hand grasped his. The child's presence, however, insured them against silence. The seat, thanks to it, was a centre of conversation and laughter. But this did not avail to drown the notes of a chiming clock, which caused the boy's mother to look at her watch and start.

"A quarter to five!" she exclaimed. "Dear, you must go; I can't stay with you longer And here in the garden I can't even say good-bye to you—at least, I can only say it. But," she said, "I'll tell you what I will do. He and I will walk part of the way up the lane with you."

Slowly and reluctantly they both rose and went, the mother gently leading her little boy, and saying to Pole, " You take his other hand."

" And you will," said Pole, as they passed through the garden gate, " write to me, Pansy, sometimes, and not make me feel that you have forgotten me, though I never will ask of you to think of me in any way which you feel to conflict with the life which you wish to lead ? "

" Yes, dear, I will write," she said. " I will not be unkind again. But don't look so sad. You will frighten him ; he is watching you."

Pole stooped down to the small figure between them. " Dear, dear little man," he said, " I wouldn't frighten you for the world ; and when I think of you I shall be kind to every little boy I see." He had just pressed his lips on the diminutive upturned face, when the mother exclaimed, " Reggie, there is some one coming. We must go back, dear. Say good-bye to us, and we must go."

He again embraced the child ; he wrung the mother's hand ; and as she turned away she hastily kissed the tips of her fingers to him. He was on the point of casting a last glance behind him, when he realized that a pedestrian was already advancing down the lane. The new-comer was a man with a confident, swinging gait. He twirled his stick as he walked ; his head was well thrown back ; his muscular lips gripped each other. A gold watch-chain and a gold cross gleamed on him. Pole saw with a start that the stranger was Canon Bulman.

For a moment Pole and the Canon stared at each other in silence.

" Ah," said Pole at last, " so you see me again in Windsor. I have just come over for an hour to call on an old friend."

" Your friend," said the Canon, " it appears, has been able to work a miracle and combine in her own person the charms both of age and youth." These words, which were accompanied by a certain inquisitorial scrutiny, converted the embarrassment, from which Pole was suffering, into resentment, and supplied him with resolution to cut short the interview.

" I, at all events," he said coldly, " have no miraculous powers, so I must not wait a moment, or else I shall miss my train."

CHAPTER XVI.

POLE had not proposed to Mrs. Steinberg to stay with her for more than a day or two. She was, therefore, hardly surprised, though she was voluble with hospitable remonstrance, when he told her that the following morning he should have to return home. So far as the friend was concerned to whom he had said good-bye, he would gain nothing by remaining at Thames Wickham, and he began to long for the seclusions and the ample solitudes of Glenlynn, where he would henceforth each morning, through the channel of a faithful letter, receive new life from an affection sublimated, not lessened, by distance.

Such being his happy belief, he was relieved, rather than disappointed, to learn from Mrs. Pole, on his arrival, that the visit of Countess Shimna O'Keefe would not take place for another week at all events. Her image, during his absence, had hardly crossed his mind; and now, when circumstances were naturally bringing it back to him, he was irked by recollecting the interest he had suffered himself to feel in her personality.

He knew, by a study of posts and by reflection on probabilities, that it would be a good three days before one of those letters could reach him from which he expected to derive so much comfort, so he was freed meanwhile from the anxiety which often, by its wear and strain, more than outweighs the comfort which such letter-writing really brings. He accordingly returned, with a new spirit and energy, to his official work and his local schemes of philanthropy ; and his mother, who watched him with a keenness of which she was hardly herself conscious, was pleased to observe in him a buoyancy which she only realized he had lost when its sudden return reminded her how in youth he had once possessed it.

A part of his good spirits, however, was attributable to another cause; and this was the presence of two little Pole twins, cousins of his, about seven years of age, who had been offered by their mother for a week to Mrs. Pole's care, and who invaded Glenlynn with their nurse on the day after that of his return. They were children of charming

manners. They moved about the house like sunshine, and
Miss Drake, in their honour, begirt herself with an antique
reticule, out of which, at odd moments, she administered
French plums to them. The very shadows in the passages
seemed to grow young at their presence. But to no one
was their companionship more grateful than to Pole. He
told them fairy-stories, which they were never tired of
hearing, and to which their imagination imparted the terrors
and the delights of truth; and they in return questioned
him about the Deity and the fall of man, about goodness
and free will, with the prodigious rationalism of childhood,
on which the shrewdest philosopher has never been able to
improve.

Thus for a time the hours danced along, and Pole found
that his work and his serious thoughts were caressed and
cheered by every incident of the day—by the sound of the
prayer which Dr. Clitheroe offered up, as he knelt before
the breakfast-things; by the object lesson in happiness
which the little children gave; and by the fair hope of a
letter which hovered over every morning.

At last the letter came; but the moment he took it in
his hands his heart sank a little, the feel of it was so unsub-
stantial. It consisted, in fact, of but half a sheet of note-
paper, on which were scribbled a few disjointed sentences,
thanking him for a letter which he himself had written, and
expressing regret at the hastiness of the present answer.
There was, however, this postscript, "Always be a friend
to me," and the writer began with "My very dear Mr. Pole,"
and signed herself "Yours, and indeed yours only." When
he thought of his own letter, here acknowledged so curtly,
when he thought of how frankly he had put his most intimate
thoughts in it, his face wore a look of pain on finding that
they were all ignored; but his mind at the same time was
framing excuses for his correspondent, and night again
brought hopes of something better from her next morning.
But next morning there was nothing from her at all. Many
mornings followed, and there was still nothing. Each day,
nevertheless, he wrote to her much as heretofore, except
that insensibly his letters grew somewhat shorter, and little
by little the spirits which he had recovered were deserting
him;—a fact detected by the children, and the children only,
who afforded him thus, what they had not done previously,

a certain ground for dissatisfaction with the precocity of their intellectual powers.

Meanwhile, if his body could have taken wings with his mind, could it have crossed the blue sea-levels, across which he looked so often, and reached the mysterious country hidden beyond the hazy headlands, he would have found himself amongst scenes which strangers seldom visit, but which, in addition to much that is picturesque and curious, would to him have exhibited something far more interesting than themselves.

At the end of a branch line which penetrates as far as the border of the scenes in question, is an odd little Welsh town, most of whose houses have an air of extreme antiquity, owing to the fact that their stones have been quarried out of a huge abbey, a fragment of which still towers above their chimneys. Had Pole arrived at the station of this town, and named to the solitary cabman, who met the infrequent trains, the place to which he desired to be taken, he would have been driven away into a country of hills and of shady hedgerows, with mountains showing occasionally their purple walls in the distance. He would have been struck as he went by the undisturbed simplicity of everything—of the soft-voiced countrymen who would have touched their hats to him as he passed: by the old barns and farmsteads; by the antique roadside inns, occurring at long intervals; and the microscopic village shops, displaying a dim vision of peppermint-balls, stay-laces, and streaky sides of bacon. Gradually he would have found these signs of human life grow rarer, and a certain bleakness would have stolen over the landscape, till at length he would have seen between some shoulders of bare plough-lands momentary glimpses of the sea; whilst as for the country itself, there would have been hardly a tree visible to him, except for one long belt of dark-green woodland in front of him, which bounded his view, raising its ragged fringes into the sky. As he neared this woodland, he would have noticed many fine and ancient trees; but what would have struck him most would have been the prevalent neglect and overgrowth. Presently he would have reached a pair of dilapidated gates and a carriage-drive, green with weeds, and shadowed by lean laurels. At the end of this drive, half hidden in leafage, he would have seen before him a gate-house flanked by two loop-holed towers, and an archway beyond whose shadows was a medley of old grey buildings.

Such was the entrance to the curious castle of St. Owen's, which for seven hundred years had never changed hands except through direct or indirect inheritance, and during all that period had never been uninhabited. The male line of Masters having ended in the reign of Charles II., it had passed, by marriage with an heiress, to a family of the name of Price, and the bridegroom, thanks to his services against Oliver Cromwell, had been turned by his grateful sovereign into Sir David Price Masters. For more than a century onwards the house of Price Masters flourished. Its baronets wore as fine lace ruffles and velvets as ever were seen at the courts of the first three Georges; nobody drank harder, had servants with finer liveries, or gained the esteem of ministers by the possession of more boroughs. But as though to teach the neighbourhood that not even the noblest qualities, and the most precious possessions, can insure permanence to anything here below, the family at the end of the eighteenth century, began obviously to decline. The then baronet was childless; and to solace himself for the want of children, he had resolved to spend as much as was possible of the fortune, which, had they existed, he would willingly have saved for and transmitted to them. He succeeded beyond his hopes; and not being a religious man, his chief solace on his death-bed was the reflection that the distant cousin, his heir—an obscure person who had married the daughter of a country doctor—would inherit hardly a quarter of the income he might have reasonably expected. The heir, however, proved heir to more than his amiable predecessor had anticipated; for he apparently succeeded to all the extravagant tastes of the family, without the means or the knowledge which might have enabled him to indulge them like a gentleman. The result was one to which there are many parallels. The house of Price Masters, though not actually impoverished, and though still continuing to possess and to inhabit its ancient dwelling, declined socially in habits, connections, and prestige, till its former position became little more than a memory. The Lovelaces and the Lotharios who had represented it in the last century, were followed by rude squireens who spoke and dressed like farmers, who exacted their *droits de seigneur* from milkmaids and farmers' daughters, who drove home drunk in gigs from the nearest market-town, and whose wives and sisters were even more provincial than themselves, and occasionally, like their brothers and husbands, developed an interest in the cellar. After two generations of this obscure profligacy, the property with its ancestral honours,—the former crushed with mortgages—devolved on a man of sixty, who, though too infirm to impoverish himself in the pursuit of pleasure, contrived to injure his castle by the gratification of what he called his taste. Having never been acquainted with anybody except himself who even professed to understand what taste was, his ideas of Gothic restoration were not of the most satis-factory nature. He surmounted the principal archways with certain devices in stucco, which purported to be the arms of the aboriginal kings of Wales; he spiked his mouldering turrets with a forest of stucco pinnacles; his baronial hall he wainscoted with varnished deal; he made his floors hideous with heraldic Brussels carpets; and a Bristol up-holsterer procured for his principal living-rooms a staring wall-paper, adorned with spurs and battle-axes. Death alone arrested him in this course of improvement; and Sir Hugh Price Masters, the new head of the family, was as incapable of discriminating between bad taste and good, as he would have been of discriminating between classical Latin and mediæval. An old castle to him was nothing but an odd and inconvenient house, the possession of which, nevertheless, imparted a fresh swagger to his shoulders.

In spite of improvements, however, St. Owen's Castle was a place of singular interest. It was built irregularly round two courtyards. It was roofed with weather-beaten shingle; and its structure, at odd angles, was diversified by staircase turrets, and squat crenellated towers. On one side of it was a deep and wooded ravine, in the bottom of which was a church half hidden by yew-trees; whilst the principal front opened on an old-world garden, which slanted down in untidy terraces to the sea, hiding its shape and extent in honeysuckle and neglected shrubberies. Totally indifferent as its new possessor was to everything in this place except the social importance which he attributed to it, his young wife, when she entered it, felt herself transported into fairy-land. The plumes of enchanted princes rustled on the winding stairs. Cavaliers with silken love-locks strayed

along the garden walks. Cromwell, who had occupied the
castle for six weeks, and of whose cannon some were still
rusting upon the lawn, would re-enter the dining-room, and
drink from a huge " black Jack."   Her step-daughter, now
about twelve, who had hitherto seemed somewhat stolid, to
a certain extent was excited by the influence of the place
likewise; and her little boy, for some unfathomable reason,
would laugh and clap his hands at the old walls and towers.

As for her husband, during the weeks when they were
there together, most of his time was spent in the stable-yard;
and except about practical matters he rarely exchanged a
word with her.   But they were both of them now, for the
first time in their lives, sensible of some common external
interest; and this provided them with a ground on which
they could meet either amicably, or indulge in impersonal
differences which masked the existence of more intimate
ones.   His sole idea, for instance, with reference to his
future establishment, was the idea that he ought to have a
great many more servants than he had ever had in his life,
and that as many as possible should be in livery; and
numerous battles were fought by his wife with him over
this, before she succeeded in convincing him that with less
than three thousand a year, a butler and a half-grown footman formed the utmost retinue that would be required by
them.   But as to most of their domestic arrangements she
had her own way entirely; and he not only did not contradict,
he did not even assist her.

Still, in spite of the household duties thrust on her, she
found ample time for the enjoyment of her novel dreams;
and now that her husband was absent, and she, with her
child and step-child, had returned to her strange kingdom,
with nothing left to jar on her, the beauty and the wonder
of her lot began to tinge her imagination every day with
brighter and more mysterious colours.   Constitutionally
gifted with shrewdness about many practical matters, and
carrying in her memory one great experience, she yet looked
at life with the eyes of a wondering child; and the newness
of her present situation fell on her heart like dew.   Every
room in the house was a new country to be explored; every
poor old cabinet or battered wardrobe was a mystery; and
as for the library, dark with neglected leather, when she
ran her eyes along the titles on the dusty shelves, sugges-

tions filled the air for her, like the music of some enormous organ. These experiences lifted her off her feet; she floated, she no longer walked; and others supervened presently, which, though seemingly more prosaic, touched her quite as deeply.

It was no sooner known that Sir Hugh had departed for America, than all the county neighbours, within a radius of fifteen miles, drove—and the distance was seven miles for the nearest—to call on the young and beautiful mistress of St. Owen's; and at the same time, she found that her acquaintance was sought also by other and very different visitors, whose number increased daily. These last were the poor of the neighbouring village, who came to her with their plaintive eyes, like so many hungry birds. Both sets of visitors, each in its own way, touched her. The squire's wives and daughters, most of them homely people, met her with a mixture of good will and respectful admiration, which filled her with a longing for the wifely excellences they imputed to her; whilst the poor seemed, by applying to her, to endow her with new faculties. She felt almost inclined to kiss the infirm old women; and discovering that some of them spoke only Welsh, she resolved to learn the language, and worked for three days at it, with an eagerness born of the idea that on the fourth day she would be mistress of it. Every hour, in fact, was filled with action, or the agitations of fancy; and duties, with shining breasts, came settling on her like flocks of pigeons. In a word, circumstances were so arranging themselves for her as to allow her nature, for the first time in her life, to satisfy its sensitive eagerness without any clandestine hazard, and to exercise many of its faculties, whose existence, till the present time, had made itself felt only in the vague restlessness that resulted from them.

This being her condition, it is perhaps not unintelligible that a certain part of her past, tragic alike in the intensity of its joys and sadness, should now begin to appear to her in a new and alien light, and that she should shrink from the memory of it for two opposite reasons—the one being the fear that she might find herself too faithless to it, the other the fear that she might find herself too faithful. Her instinctive policy was, therefore, to put it gently aside, and rock it to sleep in some shadowy corner of her consciousness;

and though she could not be angry, she was tempted to feel
aggrieved and fretful when a voice from without appealed
to her, and tried to disturb its slumbers. Such was the
mood in which she received the letters of one who a year
ago had been more than all the world to her; and who,
little as she knew it, had, on more than a few occasions,
supplied her with the means of living, when her husband's
extravagances or forgetfulness would have literally left her
destitute. It said much for his tact that she never even
suspected her obligations to him; nor was he in this way
less successful now, as was shown by the gratified, and yet
perfectly blank, surprise with which, about this time, she
received the following communication, bearing the signature
of a local firm of solicitors :—

    " MADAM—
          " We have the honour to write to you, in accord-
ance with the instructions of a client, who, for family
reasons, desires to remain unknown, except as regards the
fact that his conduct in this matter is due to an interest
arising from consanguinity. Our client has instructed us to
place to your credit, quarterly, at the branch in this town
of the Glamorgan and South Wales Banking Company, a
certain sum, the payment of which will be duly notified to
you, to be used by you at your discretion, for the benefit of
your eldest son; or, in the event of his death, for any
purpose, or in any way, you may deem advisable.
    " We have the honour to be, madam, your ladyship's
obedient servants,
                            " LLEWELLYN, RHYSS, AND LEWIS."

    When she received this letter her little son happened to
be with her, and, with suddenly brimming eyes, she stooped
down and kissed him; and she ran off, laughing, to an
interview with the old coachman. Every day in her veins
the pulse of life beat quicker; and every day the letters
which reached her from Glenlynn, though she read them not
without feeling, became more difficult to answer. It is
easier for the saint to be intimate with the chief of sinners,
than it is for hope and excitement to talk to regret and
sadness. Nothing in the world can harden the heart like
hope.

CHAPTER XVII.

Pole, accordingly, waited from day to day, happy only in his ignorance of how little he had to wait for. His first burst of happiness had faded like the rose of morning, and every barren budget of letters stung him like a drift of hail. The walls of Glenlynn, with all their friendly shelter, gradually grew transparent, and showed the outer darkness of the infinite and forlorn void. Dr. Clitheroe's household prayers fretted him like a feeble mockery; and when he went with his mother and the children to Mr. Godolphin's church, that hospitable house of faith seemed to him like a roofless cottage, and the altar like a burnt-out hearth, which would never again warm anybody. Finally, however, a day came when the second post brought him one letter only, and when he looked at it he could hardly believe his eyes. He saw on the envelope the writing for which he had so long hungered.

He hastened with his treasure into the garden; but the very beginning chilled him. It was "Dear Mr. Pole" simply, without even the kindly touch that would have been given to it by the possessive pronoun. It continued in this way—

"A thousand thanks for your news. How pleasant your life seems! I like so much to hear about it. Please go on writing, even if I can't reply. I am such an uncertain person—I mean so far as leisure goes. I have so much to settle and think about. Each afternoon, for instance—my only time for letters—I have had to ask neighbours here, or else go to tea with them myself. I was, indeed, to have gone somewhere to-day—to a luncheon party, ten miles off; but it rained so, I couldn't. In consequence of this, at last I have a few quiet hours; and the first thing I do—as you see—is to write to you. Shall I tell you about this place? I will, if it won't bore you. It is so big, I am almost frightened at it; and I and the chicks play hide-and-seek in the passages; and we never should find each other if it wasn't that we burst out laughing. I am getting to feel so grand; but of course it is very silly of me; and you, who have seen so many splendid places, would not think much of this, half-furnished and tumble-down as it is.   But there is one thing I'm sure you would admire, and that is the library.   It is forty feet long, and there are old brown books all round it. No one has used it for more than fifty years.   I spend hours here, and it feels like an enchanted forest."

The letter was, no doubt, one which could have been addressed only to a person for whom the writer had a feeling of close friendship; but of anything more than friendship there was not a single trace.

Stung with suffering, he hastened in to answer her; and as he wrote he felt his resentment grow.   Then suddenly he pushed the paper from him.   " No, no," he said, " I've not the heart to be hard on you.   Perhaps I shall get a kinder letter from you to-morrow."   He knew, however, how doubtful this hope was; and the following day it was extinguished. That day moreover the two children departed; and as he stood at the door, and saw the carriage drive away with them, he felt as if the last ray of sunlight had taken its leave also.   Then, retiring to his room, he slowly and painfully composed the following letter:—

" Do not be frightened," he began, " when you see the number of pages, which will, I know, be covered by what I am going to say.   It will be only for once, Pansy, that you will find me so prolix a correspondent; and you will find nothing here to make you angry, and very likely nothing that will make you even sorry.

" I must go back a little; but I will touch on things very lightly.   I will not dwell on the past.   I will only ask you to think of it.   Do you remember that unfrequented little German spa, with its shabby *Kursaal* and great strag-gling gardens?   And do you remember a tall, white house with net window curtains, and red velvet furniture, and distorting mirrors, and the coloured print of Bismarck that used to hang just over your writing-table?   And do you re-member a certain chair under some trees, not very far from the kiosque where the band played?   One day, soon after I knew you, and you thought that I was not coming, you sprang up from that chair when you saw me.   I can see your face now.   I thought that no one had ever been glad to see me before.   If you can forget those days it is useless for me to remind you of them.   If you do not forget them, it is unnecessary. I can only s y that you seemed to me more single-hearted and more intense in your affection than I imagined any woman could be; and the whole idea of love, through you, was transfigured in my imagination.

"Well, I will not insult you by doubting your absolute sincerity at that time; and I will not—I cannot—bitterly as I now feel i's consequences—dishonour that time, by condemning it. Deliberately neglected as you were—deliberately pushed aside out of his life —by the sole person who had any right to duty from you—— But why need I go on? You know it all, as well as I do. And if you came to me now, under the same circumstances, you should find me as you then found me, or different only because I should be more thoughtful for you.

"And yet, ought I to say this to you? But it is idle discussing the question; for those circumstances never can be repeated; and you and I can never again meet each other as we met then. We are both different. I am related to you, and you to me; and all eternity cannot expunge that fact. We never again can be as if our past had not been. There are some memories which you never can make not mine. The only question is, how this past is to be judged by us; for on that will depend our future.

"And now, listen to me. I am going to speak for myself. Whatever we may, or may not, have to repent of, of my past relation to you, in itself, I tell you frankly I do not repent. I cannot. I have been true to you. I have been more than true to you. All my thoughts of self I have subordinated to thoughts of you; not, Pansy, that there was much self-denial in that, for where self used to be. there you were instead of it. Have I not proved this? Think over all these years and let your thoughts answer. And if I thus respected my own attachment to you, much more have I respected yours to me. I have identified it with everything that is sacred in the impulses of the human heart. Dear, you can never know how profoundly I have believed in you. And if I were to treat our past relations lightly, I should be treating lightly everything that makes human life valuable.

"Well; so much for the past. Now for the present. Events have taken place which could never have been foreseen by either of us; they have opened before you a new

L

path, and perhaps have almost forced you to choose it. In moments of bitterness, I confess, it has seemed strange to me, that this mere chance advent of certain external things, should so easily draw you back to a partnership not in itself congenial to you. But thoughts like these are unfair. Things being as they are, I cannot but understand that the path you have now chosen is obviously the path of duty. You are right in choosing your big house and your library forty feet long, and in paying for them by renouncing me. You are right: you are right. How many people you will be able to help now! How much you will be able to do even for your companion! And, Pansy, no doubt there will be a simplicity in your inner life now, the loss of which, through me, was always a secret pain to you. I know all this. I feel it as keenly as you do, and I would not tempt you back to any more doubtful fate. For me, then, good-bye to much. Good-bye! Have you any idea of how much? I will not try to tell you. I will try to make you realize something which is quite different—not how much I say good-bye to, but how much I keep, and must keep, and would not get rid of if I could. Do you wish me to get rid of that longing for you which makes me stretch my hands towards you across the waves now dividing us? Do you wish that longing to diminish? Do you wish it to become less tender? And do you wish another thing, or do you think another thing possible? I mean, do you think it possible that I can forget a something that is not yours— but yours and mine—ours for ever and ever? Do you think that I have no feeling? Would you wish me to feel nothing? If you would not wish that, then think—have I no claim on you? Are there no links that still bind us together—links that are living still—links not dead but changed?

"I ask you this, because you act as if there were none, or rather as if you could take up your end of them and drop it at your pleasure, just as if they were a bell-pull, and there was nothing human at the other end. You ask me to come to you. I come. You tell me you are glad to see me; you beg me to help you and support you by my example and my sympathy. I go away. I write to you. I try to be all I can to you. I try to appeal to every thought and feeling which I imagine you hold sacred. And what do you do? You simply turn your back on me. I put my soul into your hands—I whom you used to watch and wait for—I who am related to you by the closest of all ties; and your only answer is to give me the dimensions of your library.

"You think, perhaps—for you have often said something of the kind—that because I am clever, as you say, and occupied with great interests, your unkindnesses either do not pain me, or that I ought to bear them philosophically. How little you know of the truth of things. Philosophy can influence love in one way only, and that is by killing it. So long as intellect and philosophy allow his love to live, the wisest man and the strongest man is as easily wounded as the weakest. I could perhaps kill my love for you. I could insult, defile, and then murder your memory, and free myself in this way of you and of the pain you cause me. But that is the only way. And do you think I would have recourse to it? I would as soon strike you with my fist on your lips, in your eyes, or on your breast, as dishonour my own feelings for you—those feelings which thus place me at your mercy. So you ought not to despise me when you see how you can make me suffer.

"But I have not yet said all I want to say—or even the chief thing. Did the pain you give me end with myself, I could bear it silently, or I would complain of it as little as I could. But the bitterest part of it does not consist of my own sense of being neglected by one I value. It consists in the altered view you force me to take of yourself, by showing yourself capable of treating me in this undeserved way. I believe the bitterness of all ill-treatment at the hands of those we love, springs not from any misery which they may inflict on ourselves directly: but from the injury they inflict on our cherished thoughts of them, by doing it. Ah, Pansy —all you can do now is to write to me: and if you do not write often, at least make me think that you would do so, if it were possible: and when you do write, say some words of human kindness to me. Is it a great deal that I ask of you? Would ten minutes each day, or every other day—ten minutes stolen from a visit to a country neighbour, or a game of hide-and-seek, or from dipping at random into old books, be too great a sacrifice for you to make when it would save me from days of misery? Would you not naturally make a much greater sacrifice to assuage the pain

of any stranger you might encounter by the roadside? Why
should you treat me so much worse than him?"

Whilst Pole was waiting for a reply to this, a letter came
to his mother from Countess Shimna, in which she suggested
a near day for her visit. It was impossible for him to object,
though his immediate impulse would have been to do so.
Ordinary conversation was becoming daily more difficult to
him, owing to the abstraction caused by his growing pain
and uncertainty; and he felt at first that the presence of a
comparative stranger—especially a stranger whom he had
treated with so much unconventional attention—would
demand of him efforts which he would be quite unable to
make. But second thoughts completely reversed this view.
Countess Shimna, he told himself, would at all events be a
distraction; and whilst waiting for an answer to his letter,
any distraction would be welcome. That day was Wednesday.
She proposed to come on Saturday. On Saturday morning
Pole received a telegram. Its words were these:—"Letter
arrived all right. Answer follows in day or two. P. Masters."
This message was half a relief to him; half a cause of anxiety.
Her telegrams once had been always signed "Pansy;" and
the torturing suspiciousness of disregarded affection made
him fear that her present use of initial and surname was a
sign that his appeal had estranged rather than touched her.
But then again, he reflected, this might not be so. She
might have had, quite possibly, to send the message by a
servant; and been so formal in her language on that account
solely. What could be more likely? And to telegraph at
all was itself an act of consideration. At all events he
determined to hope and to believe the best till her letter for
good or evil should turn his doubts to certainty. In this
mood he began with positive eagerness, to look forward to
the hour of Countess Shimna's coming; and to think of her
as a person who would keep his hopes intact by preventing
his mind from re-examining them too closely.

CHAPTER XVIII.

WHEN men or women suffer from any deep wound in their affections, they often repel the idea of any distraction whatsoever which an interest, however slight, in a new acquaintance may offer to them; but when once such an idea is admitted, and the opportunity of realizing it approaches, a thrill will sometimes pass through their shattered and aching nerves, which, although such inconstancy as it may imply, is expiated by the pain it causes, has more of fugitive pleasure in it than they understand, or are willing to admit. And thus Pole, when the hour approached which was to bring Countess Shimna with it, was alternately exhilarated at the thought of her, and miserable at discovering that he was so. His misery, however, was powerless to repel her image. Her slight foreign accent began to whisper in his ears. He remembered her teeth, her nostrils, the way her hair grew on her neck, the turn of her head, and other like trifles. She was to come from Lyncombe in the launch, and he had intended to have met her at the landing-stage; but when the moment came, his resolution, in spite of his recent thoughts, failed him. Instead of meeting her he went for a long walk, and did not return to the house till it was time for him to prepare for dinner.

On quitting his room as soon as he had finished dressing, he fancied he heard in the distance a rustle of silk and petticoats, whose faint rhythm differed in some subtle way from any that accompanied the movements of Miss Drake or his mother; and as he went down the staircase in the dim summer twilight, some strange perfume was just perceptible in the air. Faint as it was, it stirred his imagination like a breeze stirring a tree. Once more his mind was filled with music and lamp-lit gardens, with a movement of gay crowds and whispers in shady places. Theatres glittered; the voices of singers rang; the wild oats of his youth sprouted again, and looked like roses. This all took place in the course of a few seconds, whilst his feet, treading the old Brussels stair-carpet, were bringing him from the middle landing to the mat before the drawing-room door. When he entered the room, glimmering with its chintzes and the

backs of books, what first accosted his eyes was a white and
purple something which had the fresh and illuminating effect
of a great bowl of flowers.   Lightly, but without haste, this
coloured something rose, and Pole in another moment was
welcoming Countess Shimna.   He hastily looked round him.
Nobody else was down.   He and she were alone together
amongst the soft and diffused shadows.

They exchanged one look and one clasp of the hands,
which seemed like a recognition of some common memory,
not to be alluded to in any other way.   Then he talked to
her trivially about Lyncombe, and his recent absence, and
watched the evening light on her arms and hands and dress.
It was a dress of ivory-coloured silk, with the purple of a
heart's-ease relieving it here and there, and he recognized in
every fold of it the perfection of that evanescent art which,
whatever philosophers may say of it, is beauty's daintiest
handmaid.   Her presence filled the room with a troubling
and unwonted atmosphere, and distracted him, for the
moment, into forgetfulness of his own pain.   He glanced at
her fringe of hair curling crisply upon her forehead.   He saw
that there glittered in it a minute spray of diamonds, and on
a narrow band of velvet another was glittering at her throat.
But for some reason or other he shrank from again meeting
her eyes ; she, too, when she spoke, looked pensively on the
ground, and their voices became so low that any one standing
at the door would have thought them entirely silent, or
exchanging some impassioned confidence.

But their *tête-à-tête* did not continue long.   Mrs. Pole
soon entered, with Miss Drake waddling after her, and then
came Dr. Clitheroe, eager to be fascinated again, and smell-
ing of his washhand-stand, and brown Windsor soap.   Pole
and Countess Shimna changed their demeanour as if by
magic, and talked and laughed with a semblance of that
singular interest in trifles which forms the presumed foundation of all our social intercourse.   Pole was again struck by
the versatility of the girl's nature as shown in her sudden
transition from pensiveness to a soft vivacity.   At dinner,
when the candles shone on her, she attracted the eyes of
every one, lighting up the table like some delicate hot-house
flower.   She had many questions to answer with regard to
the Lyncombe lodgings, and it appeared that her mother had
taken for her the prettiest small house in the place—a

thatched cottage looking over the sea, and completely secluded in a little thicket of larches.   It appeared further—and
this was the most exciting part of her gossip—that some old
foreign servants were very shortly to arrive for her, and that
very possibly a little baby cousin was to be sent there also
with its nurse, its parents, for some reason, being unable to
do their duty by it, and Countess Shimna's mother having
generously undertaken to supply their place.   Mrs. Pole's
opinion of the rouged and yachting Countess rose for a
moment when she first heard this intelligence, but it came
fluttering down again, not without a sense of amusement,
when she realized that her kindness was to be done
vicariously through her daughter; and she admired the
daughter the more for the pleasure with which she looked
forward to doing it.

Later on, when Pole and Dr. Clitheroe, having been
unusually quick over their wine, found their way to the
drawing-room, the first thing which they saw was a card-
table with cards and candles on it, and Mrs. Pole, informing
them that Countess Shimna was well accustomed to whist,
and also that Miss Drake was willing to take a hand, proposed a rubber as a means of passing the evening.   Miss
Drake once more contributed to the hilarity of the company
by revealing the fact that she was far from an indifferent
player, having had considerable practice in Miss Pole's
earlier days, and when at last, excited out of her natural
stiffness, she exclaimed to Dr. Clitheroe that he had neglected
her call for trumps, Countess Shimna, with laughing eyes,
laid her delicate finger-tips on one of Miss Drake's mittens,
and said—

"Miss Drake, you must teach me.   Miss Drake knows a
great deal more than she is willing that we should any of us
suspect.   I'm sure, if she liked, she could teach a great deal
to all of us."

Whist is a game which either silences conversation or
creates it.   In the present instance it had the latter effect,
continuing to offer occasions for that easy and obvious
banter which promotes good fellowship so much better than
wit does, and almost calls to life again the irresponsible
spirits of the nursery.   At the same time Countess Shimna's
fan, which lay beside her, with its sticks of carved mother-
of-pearl, and powdered shepherds and shepherdesses kissing

each other on the painted chicken-skin, flavoured the hour
curiously with suggestions of an alien world.

The following day was Sunday.   Pole came down to
breakfast with all his sorrow renewed by one more disappointment.   He had hoped against hope for a letter, but
none had come, and his pain had been no more cured by the
distractions of his guest's company, than a broken leg is
cured by the process of not thinking about it.   Fortunately
for him, however, some urgent and unexpected business
claimed his attention, and forced him completely out of
himself.   He had, since his return from London, despite all
his personal vicissitudes, used his practical talents with so
much purpose and energy, that plans for his proposed buildings had been completed some days ago; and the bailiff
coming to him with a rough estimate for their erection, the
two were shut up together till very nearly dinner-time.
But this separation from Countess Shimna's society increased
his sense of its charm when he came back to it in the evening.   After dinner she sang.   The pieces she chose were
sacred, one of them being a hymn to the Virgin, called
"Stella Maris," whilst the other was supposed to be a
lullaby of the Divine Mother over her Child.   The singer's
voice was low and sweet and vibrating, like human passion
which had just been transfigured into prayer, and which
was still shy and humble with the newness of the untried
change.   Its echoes were in Pole's ears when he found
himself alone in his bedroom, and they kept him wakeful
and restless with new thoughts about the singer, investing
her with the depth and the mystery of a night with stars
shining in it.   In spite of the feeling exhibited in her last
song, she did not impress him with a sense of what the
religious world calls goodness; but rather of something else,
he could not distinguish what.   There was nothing in her
eyes or bearing with which a saint could have found fault,
and yet even in her girlishness there was freshness rather
than innocence.   But one definite impression she left in his
mind, at all events, and this was that she was possessed of
a certain kind of refinement which would occupy the ground,
should there be such, left vacant by conscience, and that she
would be as jealous of her dainty dignity as any woman
could be of her honour.   Before she arrived he had hoped
that her visit would be a brief one.   He was now conscious

of a wish that it might be prolonged. But his thoughts of her had nothing in them that conflicted with his thoughts of another woman, or that even relaxed the tension of these last, although for intervals they made him forget its tortures.

The following day his condition was worse than ever, but once again an unexpected pressure of work, kept him till the evening almost constantly occupied. He had lately been sending some sections of his official report as he finished them to his chief, Lord Henderson, who happened to be with the Duke at Dulverton; and there was one section of special importance and interest, which Lord Henderson was anxious, if possible, to have before he left for Norway. This, by dint of concentrated and unusual effort, Pole finished before the ringing of the dressing-bell, and despatched it by a groom, who would catch a night-train at Lyncombe, and, sleeping at Dulverton, return the following day.

His hard work was the parent of sound sleep. He slept till his servant woke him, and put into his hands a letter, and drawing the blinds up revealed a stormy morning. The letter was the one which he had been looking for all these days. He waited till he was alone and then he tore it open. He had hardly glanced at a line or two before his hand dropped heavily on the bed, and it was many minutes before he resumed his reading.

"Dear Mr. Pole," the letter ran. "Forgive me for having been so long in answering you, but I really have not known exactly what to say. At first, when I got yours, I began to feel so sorry for you; but now, when I have come to consider everything more calmly, I must confess that I think you most unreasonable. I had fancied, when I told you about the library and my games with my children, and my silly little gossip about my tiresome neighbours and their tea-parties, that you would have taken this as a mark of my confidence in your friendship, and that you would not have despised my day of little things. I thought you would have cared to hear of the details of my humdrum life. But if you want from me so much more than I can give, and are angry with me for not giving it, you will make me so shy and so afraid of you, that I shall be unable to write at all. Oh! do be reasonable and not make things unnecessarily difficult. Let me be myself a little, and feel myself of some use in the world. I hardly dare to tell you that even to write this to you, I have had to keep the gardener waiting for half an hour, and I must now go and see him about some new flower-beds. Most of next week I shall be visiting poor people; but I hope by-and-by I shall have more leisure, and be able, if you care to hear from me, to write to you more agreeably. I am ever sincerely yours,

"P. M."

He read this and thrust it back in its envelope, with the haste of a man touching a handle of hot iron; but throughout the morning he clung to the forlorn hope that when he came to read it again, it might seem less absolutely heartless. He was also distracted somewhat from the pain that was thus caused him, by the fact of the groom, who had been sent last night to Dulverton, not having returned by either of the two early trains. He was expected back by ten. Had he missed the first train, their was another which would have enabled him to reach Glenlynu by twelve. But luncheon time came and nothing had yet been heard of him. Towards the end of the meal, however, a letter was brought to Pole. "Robert," said the butler, "was detained at Dulverton, in order that his lordship might be able to send you this." Pole glanced at the contents. A phrase or two caught his eye, and he slipped the letter into his pocket where another was already lying. The phrases which he had realized and which remained photographed in his memory were these : "I have kept your servant waiting."— "I cannot adequately express my thanks to you for your remarkable promptitude."—"By far the ablest document I have ever had submitted to me."—"In the course of a few days an important proposition to make to you." The words affected him like a current of hot water suddenly felt by a man in a bath which is almost freezing. They did not lessen his unhappiness, but they brought into his mind a companion to it, in the shape of an unexpected excitement. With more animation than he had shown throughout the meal he turned to Countess Shimna, and said: "Will you come out by-and-by and see what the place looks like on a day like this?"

The weather had not cleared. The windows were blurred

with rain, and a westerly gale was making their woodwork rattle. Mrs. Pole protested against this proposal; but Countess Shimna leaped at it. "I can stand a storm at sea," she said. "I am not afraid of being injured by one on land."

She and Pole accordingly arranged a meeting in the hall; and at the hour appointed they sallied forth together.

They had gone, however, but a few yards from the house, when a voice arrested them quaveringly calling to him from the doorway; and they saw the old footman, standing there with a telegram. Pole's first hope had been that its signature would be "Pansy Masters"; and for a moment his heart was in his mouth and all its injuries were forgiven. But it turned out to be something that had been sent to his mother. She had answered it already; and had merely desired that it should be shown to him. "That will keep," he said, as he put it into the pocket of his macintosh; and he and Countess Shimna resumed their walk vigorously. The wild air which blew the wet into their faces was congenial to the mood of both of them, and made them laugh as it flapped the folds of their waterproofs, and sometimes nearly brought them to a stand-still. The drifting mist made all the objects near them grey and dim as if seen through a white crêpe veil; but overhead its texture was more dense, and the woods behind the house, distinct to a certain elevation, were gradually absorbed and lost in heights of impenetrable cloud. All creation indeed appeared to Pole and his companion to be blotted out of existence, except the objects which immediately surrounded them, and even these had the aspects of phantoms fashioned out of some wizard vapour. None of the servants were abroad, not a stray groom or gardener; and the two pedestrians felt as if they were alone in a phantom world.

Their wanderings first took them along the wooded and winding pathway, on which Pole had received the financial confidences of Dr. Clitheroe. The air was wild with whispers of shivering brush-wood; birch trees swayed their boughs with a glimmer of restless silver; clusters of ash berries tossed and rocked their scarlet; and a wave below at intervals bloomed like a beaten drum. Parts of the path were so steep and slippery that Countess Shimna had frequently to lean on Pole's arm for support. At first whenever the need for his help was over, she at once withdrew her hand, and proceeded with an emphatic independence ; but at length it so happened that after an exceptionally difficult scramble, at the end of which they paus d to look down at the sea, she forgot to free herself as promptly as she had done hitherto. Then instinctively he drew her more closely to his side ; and for a time which they did not reckon she remained there with her weight leaning on him. They might both have forgotten this seemingly trivial accident, if it had not been that from that moment, though they spoke no more than before, a new intimacy had crept into their words, and even more into their silence.

"I wish," she said by-and-by, "we could get nearer to the waves."

He told her there was a stretch of shingle not far from the landing stage, with rocks and caverns where the sea would probably be at its fiercest.

"Let us go there," she said ; and they began to retrace their steps. A cry of delight broke from her when they diverged into a narrow fissure, through which by some rude steps the shingle of which he had spoken was to be reached. Not without difficulty, though helped by his firm hand, she descended slowly in the teeth of the sweeping wind ; and now at her very feet were the waters with their foam and their endless vociferation. Smells of sea-weed were blown hither and thither. Pebbles screamed and rattled, drawn down by the surf, till they reached the shadows that hollowed themselves under the arch of the mounting breakers. Presently a puff of spray wetted her from head to foot.

"This is much too rough," Pole said to her. "You had better come away."

But she answered him with a laugh. "It is delicious. It drowns thought." Her mood communicated itself to him.

"If you are content," he said; "I am. Over there, there is a cave, which the tide never reaches. It will give us a wider view."

With his assistance she climbed up a ridge of rocks, which formed a wet promontory in the sliding and frothing water ; and here was a shallow recess in the perpendicular cliff. It was just wide enough for Pole and Countess

Shimna to stand in, and sheltered them a little from the
deafening tumult of the wind. With the lull which he thus
experienced there came back into his mind the memory of
the woman's letter, by which all his feelings had been outraged; and at the same moment he turned his eyes from
the sea, and let them rest on the face so close beside him,
on the hair whose crisp curls the storm had hardly ruffled,
and the cheeks whose delicate surface the rain and brine
had affected only by rouging them with a new carnation.
Presently he said to her, "Let us see what is in that telegram. Till now I had quite forgotten it." He put his hand
into his pocket; and she, responding to his invitation, turned
towards him and moved a trifle nearer. But just at this
moment through a crevice in the rocks in front of them
there rushed into the air a volume of leaping water, which
caught by the wind fell splashing heavily at their feet.
They both shrank back; and with a movement entirely
unpremeditated, he seized her arm, and drew her close to
himself. As he did so he felt her cling to him; and the
curve of the narrow cave compelled her to incline her head
till it was almost resting on his shoulder. The action of
the one was as involuntary as that of the other; and some
moments passed before they realized how they were standing
linked together. But time for reflection came; and neither
of them spoke or stirred, except that he held her with a
firmer pressure to his side, and little by little her weight
more frankly leaned on him. The solitude and the storm
spoke for them and freed their silence from embarrassment,
as if it were an anthem or oratorio which rendered speech
impossible; and their eyes found rest in watching the tumult
of the incalculable waters, whose wanness the dark cave
framed like an oval picture.

At last she said, "Are you going to show me the telegram?" There was in the words a tone which gave them the
quality of a caress; whilst at the same time their commonplace
meaning relieved the situation of its tension, without breaking its spell.

"Here it is," he answered; "help me to hold it, and we
will read." The message ran thus: "Expect me to tea.
Board and lodge me for night. Am bringing news of utmost
moment to your son." These words merely bewildered Pole,
till with some trouble he deciphered the name and address

of the sender, which a drop of water had rendered hardly
legible. The name was "Wargrave," and the address
seemed to be "Dulverton." Lord Henderson's letter again
shone out in his memory. It and this telegram must plainly
have some connection. What was in store for him? He
drew a deep breath as he asked himself, and a flock of wild
ambitions rose suddenly out of his heart, and mixing themselves with his consciousness of the storm, went floating over
the foam like sea-gulls. The girl's look of inquiry, and the
curve of her parted lips, added to the ferment of his mind.
"I never showed you," he said, "the letter I received at
luncheon. I have been doing work for the Government, and
they now want something more of me. I can't think what.
I suppose I shall know soon." With that quickness of
sympathy which was one of her great charms, she caught
his excitement, and it began to sparkle in her eyes.

"What is the time?" she exclaimed. "See, it is nearly
five; we must not stay a moment longer. It is very late as
it is. And yet, after this I feel that the house will stifle
me."

"Give me your hand," he said, as they moved forth from
their shelter, and their waterproofs once again were caught
by the sweeping wind. "My dear," he exclaimed, "be careful," as her footing almost failed her. "Rest there till I
find a firm place to stand on. Now, if you're not afraid,
put your hands on my shoulders." And she, committing
herself to his arms, was lifted down by him to the shingle.
The beach before them was white with a multitude of climbing fleeces. The tide had risen, and all but licked their
feet. But for some time they remained where they were,
stationary, she still clinging to him, though all need for his
support was over, as if both were reluctant to go back to
the world and quit the magic solitude which had drawn
them thus together. There had been a spell for both of
them in the noise of the winds and waters. It had drowned
so many voices in them which would soon again be audible;
and they still lingered, as if they were mesmerized by their
sensations, watching the waves which arched themselves
like the necks of Clydesdale horses and fell clothed with
thunder.

When they re-entered the house the first object their
eyes fell upon was a man's great coat, a dirty-looking knitted

comforter, an open paper packet with a half-eaten sandwich in it, and a hat with a discoloured lining, which Pole recognized as Lord Wargrave's.

CHAPTER XIX.

"HERE he comes; here is the saviour of society." Such was the greeting that fell upon Pole's ear as soon as, having changed his clothes, he made his appearance in the library. The words would perhaps have been even more impressive than they were, had Lord Wargrave's mouth when he spoke thus been a little less full of muffin. With an effort he rose from the cushions amongst which his form had entrenched itself, resting his hand, during the process, on Mrs. Pole's shoulder, partly as a token of his affectionate esteem for her, and partly as a means of assisting his own movements. "How are you, my dear Reginald?" he continued, extending both his hands, and gradually dragging Pole with him to the cups and muffins. "Sit down there," he said, subsiding into his former seat, and pointing out a chair to his host which was Spartan in its simplicity and hardness. "I hear you've been out bathing, and in very agreeable company."

"I'm glad," said Mrs. Pole, "that Shimna seems none the worse for her wetting. I'll take her up a cup of tea, and leave you two to talk together."

"Here," grunted Lord Wargrave, giving a push to the muffin dish, "take these also, Augusta, if you don't mean to ruin my dinner. My dear Reginald," he resumed, as soon as Mrs. Pole was gone, "if you're at all the man I take you for, I have every reason to congratulate you. I have been at Dulverton the whole of this past week. I have read your reports, and entirely agree with Lord Henderson about them. You're the first person who has accurately mastered these subjects, and has kept meanwhile a cool head on your shoulders. Most of our modern politicians who busy themselves with the question of poverty are as useless as a surgeon who sobs when performing an operation, and cuts an artery because his tears prevent his seeing it."

"I fear," said Pole, "that their blindness is a good deal more genuine than their tears"

"I was not referring," said Lord Wargrave, "to our
ultra-radical revolutionaries, who will probably, this autumn
session, so seriously embarrass the Government. I am," he
muttered, "a democrat in many ways myself; but these
men show us the weak spot in democracy. The distress of
the poor, in times of industrial depression, is not only the
most important of all political problems, but incalculably
the most complicated; but it is unfortunately a problem for
dealing with which in a popular way, ignorance, incom-
petence, and vanity are literally the first qualifications.
Well, the fact of the matter is this, though these men in
the House of Commons have no knowledge themselves,
it requires a good deal of accurate knowledge to answer
them. At present they are answered by nobody; they are
only outvoted; and nobody but a fool—and there are many
fools—will confuse the two operations. Now what the
Government wants is some one who has facts at his fingers'
ends, and who knows how to use them as arms of precision
against an opponent. When neither party knows facts, the
party wins which invents them; and the present Government, for a wonder, would prefer to win by knowing. Well,"
continued Lord Wargrave, "the long and short of it is,"
and he brought down his hand on Pole's knee as he spoke,
" the long and short of it is that there is a strong impression
at headquarters—the Prime Minister feels quite as strongly
about it as Lord Henderson—that the man who can best
supply what the Government is in want of is yourself.
There is, in short, a serious anxiety to have you in the
House of Commons."

Pole listened with grave attention, but without much
animation.

"I was once asked," he said, when Lord Wargrave paused,
"to contest one of the divisons of Devonport. I was not,
at that time, in a position to do this; but, had I done it,
I should have been beaten by a thousand votes."

"It is not proposed," said Lord Wargrave, "to ask you
to stand against anybody. Sir John Markham, the Under-
Secretary for ——, as you probably know, is going to resign
his seat. He sits for the Windsor Boroughs—a constituency
in which there has been no contest for twenty years, nor
will there be one when he resigns. The idea is that you
should take Sir John's place, and succeed him—I assure

you this is meant in all seriousness—not in his seat only, but in his office. I tell you," said Lord Wargrave, who sat on the cross benches, "I tell you, my dear Reginald, that it is more than eighty years since the Tories have shown such a quick appreciation of talent; and if you are only as remarkable for having deserved such rapid promotion, as you are for having received it, you will find yourself in a month or two the most distinguished politician of your generation."

Pole's face had, by this time, entirely lost its apathy.

"Do you mean," he said, "that such a proposal will really be offered to my acceptance? Or is this merely some idea that had occurred to yourself and Lord Henderson in conversation?"

"Ten days ago," said Lord Wargrave, "it was no more than that; but the idea has now been suggested to the Prime Minister. I have written to him," said Lord Wargrave, with consequential solemnity. "In fact, my dear Reginald, I may say it is I who have been your godfather in the matter. The Prime Minister is an excellent man. He rarely gives good advice, but he very often takes it; and he shares entirely Lord Henderson's views about you, and my own. I told him besides," Lord Wargrave added, "that personally you were charming, and that if he had a young wife, he ought never to ask you into his house. I need hardly inquire if you are willing to embrace fortune, though this is the very thing I have come here in this rain to do."

"Upon my word," said Pole, laughing, "I have hardly taught myself yet to believe that this is really true."

"You're too modest," said Lord Wargrave. "More men are so than most people suppose. My dear fellow, I should like you to remember this—that there is one point, and one point only, as to which the least influential man can lead the opinion of everybody—and that is his own capacity when he himself undervalues it. I'll show you, after dinner, the Prime Minister's letters. But where is our young lady? Where is the beautiful Countess? I suppose she is still drying herself, and we shall not see her till dinner. In that case," he said, rubbing his bushy eyebrows, "I think I will take a nap; and the new Under-Secretary shall show me up to my bedroom."

Lord Wargrave's nap was of so charmingly sound a

M

quality, that it trenched considerably on his usual time for dressing; but he sacrificed with a sublime indifference many minor niceties of the toilet, and when he entered the drawing-room his composure was quite unruffled by the fact that his shirt was deficient in two of its pearl buttons, and that the bow of his necktie was under his left ear. He was so over flowing with a mixture of importance and universal benevo-lence, that he almost embraced Dr. Clitheroe, and actually kissed Miss Drake; and he looked round the room with a curious twitching of his features, as if expecting in some corner to discover the presence of Countess Shimna.

"Don't be alarmed," said Mrs. Pole. "We have got her safe and sound for you. I made her go to bed after her wetting, which accounts for her being a little late; and I begged her, whatever she did, to come down in high dress. Here she is."

And as Mrs. Pole spoke, Countess Shimna entered, trail-ing a silken tea-gown of pink and pale green, and showing as she walked the tips of her pink pointed shoes. Her eyes were shining, her cheeks had a shell-like clearness.

"Here is a Venus," exclaimed Lord Wargrave, "who has literally risen from the foam." And he hurried forward to meet her with a species of paternal gallantry.

Pole realized the impression which the girl had made; indeed there seemed to himself to be a new brilliance in her aspect. As he looked at her, he thought of the hours they had so lately passed together, and a secret sense of possession passed through him with an electric thrill.

"Is she still the same?" he asked himself with a moment's jealous doubt: but as they went in to dinner and her hand pressed itself on his arm, his pulses received an answer. What filled his heart was pain almost as much as pleasure; but in defiance of a voice within him, he deliberately gave the pleasure harbour. His thought was, "I have suffered enough. I will free myself now at any price."

Every circumstance combined to assist in his emanci-pation, at all events for the time being—his intoxicating sense of the prospects which had just been opened before him, and which even yet he hardly realized; the look which now and again Countess Shimna cast at him through her eyelashes, and the animation of Lord Wargrave, who was half a dozen conversationalists in one. He talked of St.

Petersburg, of Warsaw, of Florence, surprising Countess
Shimna with his knowledge of them; and he described an
attempt at a revolution in the streets of a northern capital,
which he said he had seen extinguished by the bloodless
artillery of two fire-engines. "I never," he said, "knew
hydrophobia exhibited in so salutary a form." Then he told
an anecdote of the dignified Dean Osborn Pole, which one
of his auditors recognized as a myth that was told of many
people. The Dean, said Lord Wargrave, had, in the Close
at Exeter, seen a boy of exceedingly small stature, vainly
endeavouring to reach the Archdeacon's bell-pull. The
Dean with magnificent benevolence had lifted the boy up,
who lost no time in producing a peal like thunder. "Now,"
said the urchin, when the Dean had put him gently down,
"you run like Hell." Countess Shimna's amusement at
this, fanned the fire of Lord Wargrave's memory. He asked
Dr. Clitheroe if he had ever known certain bishops; and
proceeded to sacrifice them, hardly waiting for the Doctor's
answer; and he then alluded to the trial of a certain fraudulent banker, which had very lately been attracting public
attention.

"And everybody," said Mrs. Pole, "thought him such
a good man."

"I have a Prayer-book still," said Lord Wargrave quietly,
"which he gave to my poor dear mother. When he sent
her a 'Manual for Communicants,' and 'Meditations for
every Day in the Week,' I made her withdraw her balance."

"I'm glad," said Mrs. Pole, "we're none of us your
bankers. It seems you would have no faith in us unless we
pretended to be very wicked. Have you known many
swindlers that you're so quick in detecting them?"

"Intimately," answered Lord Wargrave. "I've known
every variety of them. Delightful men, most of them, ex-
cepting perhaps the Socialists."

"Socialism," said Pole, "and I speak from a good deal
of experience of it, is the same thing in these days that
patriotism was in Dr. Johnson's. It is the last refuge of
a scoundrel."

"Serious Socialism," said Lord Wargrave, "is something
much worse than that—it is the last or the first refuge of
inferior or ineffective talent. We have to thank our friend
Dr. Clitheroe here for most of it."

"May I," exclaimed the Doctor, surprised at this sudden attack, "venture to ask why?"

"Because," answered Lord Wargrave, "you're one of the ablest men in the Education Office. It is quite possible to educate anybody so as to make most of the necessary work of the world intolerable to him. A socialistic leader, as a rule, is active in the cause of Socialism, in proportion to the contempt he feels for the only useful work he is fit for."

Miss Drake's mouth was rigid with amazement at Lord Wargrave's eloquence. Mrs. Pole seemed amused at him rather than concerned in what he was saying; but Countess Shimna, on the contrary, somewhat to Pole's surprise, had all the appearance of listening with real attention. At last she said to Lord Wargrave, looking at him with her heart's-ease-coloured eyes—

"Are English Socialists—you see I know so little of this country—in any way like Russian Nihilists?"

"No," said Lord Wargrave, "except that they are both dreamers. One wants to destroy what is an accident of society in Russia; the other, what is the essence of all society everywhere."

After dinner Mrs. Pole asked Countess Shimna to sing. Lord Wargrave seconded the request, but in a somewhat perfunctory manner; as music at that moment presented itself to his mind mainly as an obstacle to the flow of his own conversation. At the first notes, however, of Countess Shimna's voice he rose from his chair, with his eyes brightening under his eyebrows, and strode across the room to the piano, on which he leaned, absorbed and motionless. The song to which he listened was in Russian. The air, with a curious accompaniment, came to the ear plaintively as a kind of barbaric wailing, and the soft, unfamiliar syllables rose and fell on the notes, wild and remote, like the lapping of the Don or Volga. Lord Wargrave's emotions were so deeply stirred that he made, when the song was ended, an audible sound in swallowing them.

"The Russians," he said, "talk every language so well they never would give me the chance of learning a word of theirs. What is that song? It's the most moving piece of music I ever listened to."

Countess Shimna looked up at him, her fingers still on

the keys. "It is supposed," she said, "to be the song of Nihilists on their way to Siberia. I have two Polish friends there."

"What a pathetic song, my dear," said Mrs. Pole's voice from a distance.

Lord Wargrave and Pole were the sole auditors at the piano, and for some moments neither of them made any answer. At last Pole said, "See what a lovely night!" Countess Shimna and Lord Wargrave both of them turned their eyes to the window. The curtains were but half-drawn, and they saw, through the glass and between the fringes, the tossing of troubled silver on a sea under silver clouds, and the full moon shining in an estuary of clear sky. Pole opened one of the casements. The air was moist and warm, and the sound of the waves, still unquiet on the beach, came rustling up to them through the foliage. The three went out, and stood on a broad stone step, which, despite the recent rain, was now perfectly dry. Lord Wargrave, under the combined influence of the song, the singer, and the stars, was a totally different man from what he had been at dinner.

"I once knew," he said, turning to Countess Shimna, "a young Polish Nihilist myself. He was noble, rich, accomplished; and had eyes as dark and wild as a forest on a stormy night. I have always thought of him as the last of the cavaliers. That's a type of man that can never be produced by Socialism. The aspirations of the Nihilist are impracticable; those of the Socialist are unreal."

"But surely," said Countess Shimna, with a ring of feeling in her voice, "some of your Socialists have had their sincere enthusiasms."

"I call Socialism unreal, as a creed," said Lord Wargrave, "for this reason. It demands what is not only impossible, but what every human heart knows and feels to be impossible – that men should seek the welfare of others exactly as they seek their own. If our sympathies were really so keen as to enable us to do that, instead of all being happy, no human being would be ever happy again One mother's bereavement would break the hearts of all of us. One case of cancer would madden us all with pain."

"And yet," said Countess Shimna, looking out towards

the sea, and seeming to speak to herself rather than Lord
Wargrave, "people do perform this impossibility for the
sake of their children daily."

"True," muttered Lord Wargrave. "But the Socialism
of the family is the only Socialism practicable; and this is
the very thing that all other Socialism would destroy. My
dear young lady," he exclaimed, speaking to her in a tone
which compelled her to look at him, "a man who tells you
he loves a stranger as much as his own son, really loves his
son as little as he loves a stranger. You speak of children.
Wait till you are yourself a mother. No woman has any
love for the children of others, if she has not a love, wh'ch
is immeasurably greater, for her own child. In fact," said
Lord Wargrave, clearing his throat impatiently, so as to rise
from the tone of emotion to that of calm philosophy, "we,
none of us, care for anything pertaining to our neighbours
unless we first care more for a similar thing pertaining to
ourselves. The only exception," he added, digging Pole
with his elbow, and sinking his voice to a sort of grunting
whisper—"the only exception is supplied by the case of
wives." The grimace which accompanied this speech presently died away, and his face resumed its gravity. "The
most moving thing "—he went on again, changing his tone,
and drawing Pole a little aside—"the most moving thing in
the whole world is the clinging of a mother to her illegitimate child. She not only does everything for it, but she
braves everything." Countess Shimna meanwhile had been
altogether unconscious of this by-play. She had apparently
even forgotten the very presence of her two companions.
Her face was turned away from them, her eyes were wide
and shining; and Pole saw, or thought he saw, the outlines
of her moonlit throat troubled, as if by an effort to master
some strong emotion.

At this moment the slight puff of a breeze caused Lord
Wargrave to look down at his shirt front. He saw that the
sole button which the energies of his laundress had left to
it, had slipt from its frayed buttonhole, and was permitting
the breath of night to visit his person with an undesirable
intimacy. "Come," he said to Countess Shimna, taking
her without the least ceremony by the arm, "it's getting
cold. You ought to stay out no longer." And partly
pushed by his touch, partly moving to escape from it, she

was with surprising rapidity shepherded back by him into the drawing-room.

What could be the meaning, Pole asked himself, of the sudden emotion which appeared a moment ago to have overwhelmed her? Was she thinking of the Siberian exiles? Had one of these been her lover? On what strange voyage had her thoughts and her feelings gone? As he said good night to her, her eyes were liquid and shining—so it seemed to him—with sadness rather than passion. And yet the slender hand which had clung to him that afternoon still left its pressure lingering and tingling on his arm.

He was not, however, permitted to dwell upon these sensations; for no sooner had the three ladies retired, than Lord Wargrave made preparations, with which all his friends were familiar, for sitting up and talking till two o'clock in the morning. "Send my servant," he grunted to the old butler.

"He's here, my lord," replied Martin; and in response to a whispered summons, a valet entered bearing a dirty quilted dressing-gown.

"I have here," said Lord Wargrave as soon as he was invested with this garment, "all those letters of which I spoke to you. I put them in these pockets before dinner, in order that I might show them to you now." He advanced as he spoke towards a tray, which gleamed with bottles and tumblers, and mixed himself a glass of strong brandy and soda-water. Provided with this, he at once went to business, and explained to Pole, with the aid of various documents, the exact position of affairs. "Sir John Markham's retirement," he said, "will not take place, till just in time to admit of your being elected before the Autumn Session. There will therefore be no necessity for you to move in the matter for the present. You will before long be approached from the proper quarter; and meanwhile leave the whole thing to me. By the way, your mother tells me you are making some experiments here. That is all in your favour; and I shall not forget to mention them, especially as we shall have you in your office before they have time to fail. You must tell me to-morrow what it is you contemplate. And now," he said, "let us talk about this lovely Austrian Countess. She's quite the most fascinating woman I ever met—I mean," he added with gravity, "outside the demi-

monde. She has every charm about her. She's *jeune fille*—
she's married woman—she's Magdalen—she's Madonna—
she's conspirator—all by turns—all together—all made up
of music and Dresden China. And her dress too—delightful! I have seen nothing like it since the last days of the
Tuileries. She made even Socialism interesting by the way
in which she listened to what I said about it. You know
who she is, don't you ? "

"How do you mean ? " asked Pole.

Lord Wargrave rubbed his chin, and shot out his under-
lip. "I've not," he said, "the least doubt in my mind about
it. I've been thinking the matter over since we paid our
visit on board the yacht. Her grandmother was the daughter
of Lady Thyrza Brancepeth by that most remarkable man
—that genius *manqué*—your great-uncle. She died in child-
birth and had a daughter who lived. I know the convent
in which the child was educated. The Mother Abbess was
a daughter of an Archbishop of Paris."

"You are right," said Pole, "about Countess Shimna.
She told me the same thing herself."

"God bless my soul ! " exclaimed Lord Wargrave. "You
don't say so ! Did you ever hear this ? " he added, and he
muttered forth the following verse :—

> "'Those myrtle-blooms of starriest birth
>   Were dim beside her breast of snow;
> And now it sleeps beneath the earth
>   From which their sister blossoms blow.'

They're Byron's lines," he continued, "written on Lady
Thyrza's death. I was quoting them the other day to that
male vestal of yours, Canon Bulman. And so, the young
lady knows the story herself, does she? I should like to
talk to her about her distinguished ancestor and ancestress."

"I dare say," said Pole, "she would not have any objection."

"Objection ! " said Lord Wargrave. "Objection to the
subject ! She knows far too much of the world not to be
fascinated by it. By the way, I have upstairs a copy which
D'Orsay gave me of a poem by your great-uncle. I thought
you might like to see it. I will read it to-morrow to you
both."

CHAPTER XX.

LORD WARGRAVE had told Mrs. Pole that his visit would be for one night only; but the charms of Countess Shimna, the romance of her parentage, and her evident appreciation of himself, so wrought on his mind that he announced his intention next morning of remaining another day, "in order," he said to Mrs. Pole, "to see the site of Reginald's buildings. And then," he added, "when I return to Dulverton, I'll take you over with me to lunch. We've shown Countess Shimna an English statesman already. We mustn't let her go without showing her an English duke."

When the visit to the site had been accomplished, and when Pole had retired to his work, Lord Wargrave had Countess Shimna all to himself till luncheon, and approached with complete success the delicate subject of her ancestry.

"I promised her," he said to Pole, as after luncheon they were smoking in the garden, "that if she would come to us here I would read that poem I was speaking about. I told her she was descended from the most remarkable romance of the century. An illegitimate birth celebrated by Byron is better than a legitimate one consecrated by the Archbishop of Canterbury."

He sat himself down on a bench and looked slowly round him. Before him was a verbena bed, and rose-bushes were on each side of him.

"Beautiful," he muttered, "this place is! Beautiful! You know, Reginald, that celebrated saying of Kant's—the only saying the world at large knows him by—that he was filled with awe by two things—the stars, and man's sense of duty. Had his eyes been sharpened by life as well as by philosophy, he would have mentioned three things, not two, and three totally different ones."

"And what," asked Pole, "would they have been ?"

"A flower," said Lord Wargrave, sententiously, emitting a puff of smoke, "a woman in love, and a woman praying. They are all expressive of precisely the same mystery—the universe breaking into life. A flower is earth's kiss to her human children, who have drawn a conscious life from her;

a woman's kiss is the longing of that life to renew and to
complete itself; a woman's prayer is the longing that the
completion may endure for ever. Kant talked about stars.
Words—words—words. Why did he take the trouble to go
so far ? The earth is a star to the people who live in Jupiter,
and it is the only star which for us is more than a huge tee-
totum. For us it is the one mouth of the universe. It talks
to us, and we are ourselves its language. Nobody, my dear
Reginald," he continued, shifting his position a little, " has
more affection for the moon than I have. But why do you
and I consider the moon beautiful ? Merely for the sake of
the lovers who have whispered amongst her lights and
shadows."

Lord Wargrave, when he had risen for a moment into
the region of sentiment, generally felt it incumbent on himself to descend somewhat heavily to earth, as if to show the
weight of the wisdom that could be thus lifted at will.

" The ancients," he now began, adjusting his voice afresh,
" were perfectly right in making the god of elemental passion
the god of gardens. The idea had nothing gross in it. It
was no insult to the gardens. It was merely a beautiful
expression—beautiful as the garlands which were offered
him—of the true character of the god. Protestant theology
——" But Lord Wargrave sharply checked himself.
" Hush ! " he exclaimed, " don't move for a moment. She
has not seen us yet. Did Greuze or Watteau ever paint anything daintier ? You ought to give her a lamb, which she
might lead with a blue silk ribbon, and a shepherdess's
crook set with diamonds. She has everything that the artificial world could give her except artificiality."

Countess Shimna, who had been advancing slowly along
the walk, now caught sight of them, and they both rose to
meet her. Pole looked at her with eyes sharpened by Lord
Wargrave's criticism ; and her appearance, he thought, certainly justified it. No English girl would in the country
have dressed as she did; and an English girl, so dressed,
would, in the country, have appeared constrained and vulgar.
But every movement of Countess Shimna's was grace and
nature itself; and her face, in the rose-coloured twilight
formed by a pink parasol, seemed to him like a mirror which,
though set in a jewelled frame, was filled with the reflections of the naked realities of life.

"I was," said Lord Wargrave to her, as they strolled towards one of the summer-houses, "on the point of observing to our friend here, how much better your Church understands hum in l'fe than ours does. Protestant theology, as I was just going to tell him, quite in opposition to the Catholic, regards soul and body as if they were oil and vinegar; the oil being specially manufactured for burning in the Protestant hell, the vinegar for giving its character to the genuine Protestant heaven. The true connection of the two is altogether different. Life is the flame of a lamp; and the body, with all its senses, is the wick by means of which the mysterious spirit burns. Do you understand that?" he muttered, peering at Countess Shimna.

"Who would not?" she answered, with a sort of pensive emphasis, which for some reason or other came as a shock to Pole. She spoke at times as if life were all behind her; and yet she looked as if it was all to come.

"Now," said Lord Wargrave, seating himself, "now for the verses of your ancestor. There's a curious thing about him, which few people ever knew. He was supposed to be a man of the most reckless and lawless tastes. No idea could be falser. He really had the same poetic passion for constructing a home that Byron had for breaking loose from one. Indeed, his imagination surrounded the legitimate satisfaction of the affections with all the charms which poets usually attribute to the illegitimate. Inexperience," muttered Lord Wargrave, parenthetically, "is probably the explanation in both cases. Well, listen to this now. It is quite evident from its date, as well as everything else, that it was written to Lady Thyrza before they eloped, and whilst she must have been still hesitating.

"What gift shall I give you? Suppose, if you please,
  I had houses, and acres, and fashion, and fame,
And a name. Need I tell you, my friend, that of these
  I could give you not one, dear, not even my name.

"But a something I must give—a something with qualities
  To prove you and move you. So since, as I said,
I can't give you things that the world calls realities,
  Let me bring you my hopes. Will you take them instead?

"They are excellent hopes. I can speak, for I know them.
  I have fed them and nursed them, through good and through ill;
And they in return—you can't think what I owe them,
  For when all things had left me they clung to me still.

" When the days and the nights became drearier and colder,
  When I slept with a sigh, or awoke with a moan,
They were by me to breathe with their cheeks on my shoulder,
  'Take courage, you shall not be always alone.'

" How simply they spoke! But they cheered my dejection;
  For they hinted of one who should come through the gloom.
To the hearth of my life with the fire of affection,
  And should turn to a chamber what else were a tomb.

" How simply they spoke! And yet all that was tragic,
  Took flight at their touch, and receded from life;
For they sang a redemption, a passion and a magic
  Into words like a hearth, and a home and a wife:

" Till what seemed to the boy like the vain iteration
  Of copy-book platitudes bought by the quire,
Was flamed on the man like a new revelation
  Of the glory of God in a scripture of fire.

' Yes—that's what my hopes did. Despair and complaining
  They turned into patience ; and day after day,
When my dark mood returned like the clouds after raining,
  They were by me, to cheer me and chase them away.

" Will you take them—my hopes, then—my gift that I'm bringing?
  But before you accept them, there's this to be said,
'Tis merely that now they have done with their singing,
  They are silent ; I've killed them. I bring you my dead.

" Nay, turn not away in disgust from their faces ;
  Look at least at them once, and I think you will see
That for you, dear, my mute ones still speak from their places,
  And you'll hear them, and murmur, ' He killed these for me.' "

If Lord Wargrave had wished to create an impression
by his reading, he succeeded, but not on the person in whose
special honour he had exerted himself ; and the effect being
unexpected, he altogether failed to observe it. Countess
Shimna indeed thanked him with expressions of appreciation and interest ; but the one listener who had really been
moved was Pole. "If I could write verses," he was saying
to himself, " this, and this, and this, is what I myself should
have written." And his thoughts for the time being were
with a woman who was far away. It happened, however,
that just as the reading was concluded, he caught Countess
Shimna's eyes. She seemed, as she looked at him, to be
penetrating into his very soul; and her lips, half parted,

and half pouting, seemed to send her sympathy to him, charged with remembered passion. His cheeks grew hot— he knew not for what reason: and like a relapsing wave his thoughts came refluent back to her.

"That girl," said Lord Wargrave to Pole, when by-and-by they were alone together, "is a remarkable instance of what we now call heredity. Her own character is exactly like her great-grandfather's verses. I can see it in her. These verses have that delightful and convenient quality of dressing up as a virtue what the vulgar would call vicious. In this case, as it happens, Tristram Pole was right. He and his Thyrza have my profoundest sympathy. But what he did in this case, our young lady would do in every case. She is quite incapable of doing what she thinks wrong; because she never would think wrong anything she might want to do. Before she had tried to judge it, she would have tied it up into a nosegay. If she wished to commit a murder, she would arrange the act to look like self-immolation."

This hasty criticism did not exactly please Pole.

"Do you, then," he said rather dryly, "believe in the theory of heredity."

"I have," said Lord Wargrave, "believed with so much enthusiasm in every false theory that has shocked the world since I was twenty, that I often wonder why I have not been taken in by this one. There's something in it—not much. Think for a moment. You have sixteen great-great-grand-parents. In producing you they are just like sixteen paint-brushes, each of which has been dipped in a different colour; and all have been washed together in one tumbler of water. Will the pink brush or the blue make the water blue or carmine?"

"It might," said Pole, "if the carmine or the blue were strong, and the other colours weak."

"My own theory precisely," said Lord Wargrave. "I believe that the race is saved by the intensity of its illegiti-mate unions. A couple like Thyrza and Tristram might transmit their colours for generations. I'm devoted to my own theories; but nothing surprises me so much as some fact, like Countess Shimna's character, which suggests that they may be really true."

At dinner Lord Wargrave handed Mrs. Pole a telegram.

It consisted of six words : " The Duchess will be delighted. Dulverton."

"I wrote to him," said Lord Wargrave, "last night, to say we would come to luncheon. I find we must leave this at half-past ten in the morning."

Mrs. Pole looked at him with a smile in which startled amusement just got the better of annoyance.

"I never," she said, "thought that you were really serious. But you have, it seems, settled it all yourself." And the expedition was arranged accordingly.

When the morning came, however, Mrs. Pole announced at breakfast that she was suffering from a severe headache and could not possibly go. Lord Wargrave seized her hand, in an outburst of sympathy and disappointment.

"Not go !" he exclaimed. "My dear Augusta, you must. The two best things for a headache are fresh air and sleep. You'll get one in driving to Lyncombe ; and you'll secure the other by talking to the Duchess after luncheon."

But Mrs. Pole was firm.

"Very well, then," said Lord Wargrave, "I must be Countess Shimna's chaperon. I've taken out three nieces and one daughter in London ; so I think you may trust this young lady to me for an hour or two."

Pole seconded this plea ; but his mother remained doubt. ful, till she saw that Countess Shimna's eyes were bright with a wish to go.

" Well, Shimna," she said, "you must promise to take care of Lord Wargrave, and you must begin with setting him an example of getting yourself ready this instant."

"You and Reginald," said Lord Wargrave to Mrs. Pole, when Countess Shimna had left the room, "must take a house in London this winter, and you should bring this young lady out."

"Me !" exclaimed Mrs. Pole. "I don't know twelve people there."

"I," said Lord Wargrave, "would see that she was asked everywhere. I'd take her myself to every ball that was worth going to."

"Yes," said Mrs. Pole, laughing, "and if she were not a foreigner, I've not the least doubt you'd present her."

To this repartee Lord Wargrave made no answer. He was meditating on the new social value he would himself acquire, if he could appear in London as the godfather of a new beauty. "I'll tell you what," he said, "when the autumn session begins and Reginald comes to London, you and he shall have my house in Brook Street, and your only rent shall be to bring Countess Shimna with you."

CHAPTER XXI.

Pole's impressions of his beautiful and enigmatic guest had been sharpened and multiplied by the various incidents of the day; but taken as a whole they were even less intelligible than before, and yet their mystery was becoming more and more fascinating to him. Under the sparkling surface of her girlhood, he had seen as if he had been peering into water, vague and fluctuating images of matured and almost sombre womanhood. She had shown herself possessed of an insight into life and sorrow almost as vivid as her discrimination in the literary matters of which from time to time she had engaged in discussion with Lord Wargrave. He fancied too that he detected in her opinion of George Sand and of Byron the same knowledge which had betrayed itself in that penetrating look which she had fixed on him, after the reading of Tristram Pole's verses; and Lord Wargrave's enthusiastic appreciation of her did much to intensify his own.

When they drove off next morning on their way to their lunch at Dulverton, he felt himself transported into the atmosphere of some hardly credible fairy-story, though an aching nerve in his conscience was still tethering him to his past. As he sat opposite to her in the landau, which was a Glenlynn heirloom, and saw her fresh as a flower against the old moth-eaten cushions, his imagination surrounded her with all kinds of shifting scenery. She was leaning her breast on a balcony of Italian iron-work; love-songs and the sounds of guitar-strings were rising to her from mysterious gardens; or wrapped in furs under frosty northern starlight, she was leaving a last kiss on the lips of some Polish exile. Then, through all these fancies her actual aspect would force itself on him, with the lips and the eyes that had begun to provoke and tantalize him; and

then he would remember the fact—now hardly credible—
that this form, which he persuaded himself had been longed
for by so many others, had almost, in the foam-drenched cave,
committed itself to his own arms. On the platform of the
Lyncombe terminus every eye followed her. There were
various ladies there of the kind common in watering-places.
Countess Shimna was as conspicuous amongst them as an
orchid in a bowl of buttercups; and many a feminine face
turned towards the carriage which she entered, attracted by
the silver braid which glimmered on her dark-blue collar.

An hour in the train brought them to the Duke's station
—a cottage and a gravelled platform, close to the lodge gates.
A footman, whose hat had a band of deep gold lace, but
whose long maroon-coloured coat was apparently far from
being of the newest, was there awaiting their arrival; and
they were presently speeding through the park in a large
but uncomfortable waggonette, whose springs, as Lord Wargrave explained apologetically to Countess Shimna, had been
injured when the vehicle was used at one of Sir Robert
Peel's elections. Lord Wargrave was now in a state of
complete happiness. He felt as if he were himself the
possessor of Dulverton and of the Duke also; and when
soon in the Duke's presence he should resign this vicarious
lordship, he looked forward to a comforting sense of a
property in the young lady he was bringing with him.

Dulverton Park was a long, low structure, whose
hundred yards of stucco and square windows stretched their
bilious line on a green and wooded slope, where it looked,
from end to end, like a placid but emphatic protest against
everything which modern taste considers as architecturally
tolerable.

"What an immense *château!*" exclaimed Countess
Shimna, as it came in view. Lord Wargrave was delighted
at her wonder. "I always say," he muttered, "that this
house is the most striking monument existing to the
Englishman's estimate of Consols. The nation bought the
property for the great Duke, and gave him a hundred and
fifty thousand pounds with which to build a palace upon it.
He kept the house as it was and put the money into the
funds. Everything inside is exactly as he left it. That
makes it interesting. Nothing could make it comfortable."

The carriage, as he spoke, drew up at the front door, and

Countess Shimna was presently testing the accuracy of his description for herself. The interior of Dulverton, though more modern by thirty years than that of Glenlynn, was in some respects like it. It produced the same sense as one entered it, of faded carpets and curtains, and constant dusting and polish applied to old mahogany. But huge equestrian portraits, which hung in the square hall, and a row of busts which stood under them on pedestals of red granite, each representing some celebrated statesman or soldier with whom the great Duke's name had been associated during the first quarter of the century, impregnated the air with all the savour of history.

"Where's his Grace?" said Lord Wargrave to a portly groom of the chambers. "I will take Countess Shimna O'Keefe and Mr. Pole to him myself." And he was preparing to push his way past several other domestics, when a short fragile-looking figure, which appeared to consist entirely of a soft wide-awake hat, an old cloak, and a pair of large smoked spectacles, became suddenly visible in a doorway, and shuffled forward towards the visitors. Lord Wargrave advanced rapidly, and meeting him half-way, caught him by the arm and injected a whisper into his ear, which all the walls and ceiling were unable to help echoing. "Here she is—our fascinating Austrian Countess." Pole observed how the Duke, with a little irritable gesture, freed himself from Lord Wargrave's grasp, and, bestowing on him no other notice, came straight to Countess Shimna, shook her hand benignly, and said, "How do you do, my dear? I'm very glad to see you. The Duchess will be glad to see you. She's outside on the terrace. Let us go to her. Come, Reginald." He began to lead the way, but, stopping short after a pace or two, and turning round to Countess Shimna, "That picture," he said, "is my father. The bust directly under him is the great Duke of Marlborough. Are you interested in these things? You shall see all of them after luncheon." They passed out to the terrace, through a billiard-room hung with chintz, and discovered the Duchess seated, with a little dog on her knee. She had heard the party approaching, and, with such speed as was possible to her, she was duly preparing to rise from her chair to meet them; but the Duke ignoring this perfectly obvious fact, called to her from the step of the window, with his utmost pomp of utterance, " My dear," he shouted, " when you have finished your siesta, you will find me waiting here to introduce Countess Shimna O'Keefe to you."

The Duchess was a woman mellow with the beauty of a faded tree, which still stands in November sunlit with all its leaves. She advanced wearing a smile, whose natural placid sweetness had been ruffled by the Duke's address into one of humorous resignation, and had then softened into one of conventional though gracious welcome. But when she saw Countess Shimna the conventional graciousness disappeared, and gave place to an expression in which surprise was mixed with admiration ; and Pole saw that she was fascinated very much as his own mother had been, only the Duchess's manner expressed something more than his mother's had done—worldly approval in addition to instinctive friendship. He presently saw her achieve a yet more difficult conquest. Old Lady Taplow, who was so exalted a great lady that she remained an intrepid Liberal, because she never could believe in democracy, emerged from one of the windows, tremulous with years, but unbent by them. " I heard the Duke's voice," she began, " and also Lord Wargrave's. One can hear Lord Wargrave from anywhere." And she looked at him with a malicious nod. Then she became aware that there were strangers present, and froze into silence till Countess Shimna and Pole were introduced to her. Pole she had met before, though she did not at first recognize him. " I knew," she said, " when I was young so many of your family. I can just remember that handsome but very naughty man, your great-uncle. And of course—to be sure—I saw you at your aunt's funeral." Then turning to Countess Shimna with a sort of tentative patronage, " I don't think," she said, " that I ever saw you before. If I had, I should have remembered your pretty face."

" I am sorry," said Countess Shimna, " that never having been in England before, I have had no chance of being honoured by a place in your memory." The answer was made so gently and yet with such perfect *aplomb* that Lady Taplow was unable to show herself offended at it ; but it effectually checked her preliminary note of patronage ; and as, in speaking to an unknown person, she had no other at her command, she was turning away and was going to address the Duchess, when Lord Wargrave entered the lists on behalf of his beautiful *protégée*, and said, "This young lady, though she speaks English so well, is Austrian."

Lady Taplow, who had heard nothing of Countess Shimna's expected coming, and who, being a trifle deaf, had not caught her name, again began feeling her way, by saying, with agreeable condescension, "I have a grandson at Vienna—Lord Taplow—perhaps you know him."

"My family," replied Countess Shimna, "never go to Vienna."

Lady Taplow on hearing this was again turning away from her, when a distant bang of the luncheon-gong caused a general movement.

"Lady Taplow," said Lord Wargrave, drawing Countess Shimna to him by her arm, "is a very interesting study. In your country she would be impossible. Her mother was the adopted daughter of the old Duchess of Southwold, but who she really was the old lady would never say. Were Lady Taplow an Austrian she could never even go to court. Her son, you know, married the heiress of a great Jewish banker."

A faint dimple showed itself on Countess Shimna's cheek, which became almost a smile when Lady Taplow, at luncheon, returned to the subject of Vienna, and spoke of the charms of its society. "I've never been there myself," she said, "but my grandson enjoys himself immensely."

"It's different," said Countess Shimna, quietly, "for a man and for a foreigner, especially if he's horsey, like your grandson."

Lady Taplow could hardly believe her own dignified ears. "My grandson," she said, "would, I think, be welcome anywhere." And she was swelling with preparations for a still further reply when Countess Shimna proceeded, "With us—with me—for instance," she said, "it would be quite different. I should always suffer from the fact that one of my great-grandparents was illegitimate." She alluded to this delicate subject with a quiet and modest self-possession, as if she were merely stating that one of her great-grandparents wore a wig. But the effect on Lady Taplow was remarkable. Completely giving up any further attempt at patronage, she leaned forward to the Duke and said to him, "What is the name of this very good-looking young lady?" The Duke told her, adding, "She's a cousin of Count O'Keefe, the minister."

"My dear," said Lady Taplow, "you ought to come to London. You'd be admired from morning to night. We could show you society better even than that of Vienna."

"Lady Taplow," interposed the Duke, blinking at Countess Shimna, "can afford to ask you to London; and I'll tell you why. Both her daughters are married—married for twenty years—so you couldn't cut them out. Nobody," he added, turning round to the subject of his compliment, "nobody could cut out Lady Taplow herself."

"I'm sure," said Lady Taplow, "if she'd cut out some of our young married women, it's the very thing for which we should all feel grateful to her."

"Now," exclaimed the Duke to Countess Shimna, at the end of luncheon, "I'm going to show you the house. The Duchess will give us some coffee in the drawing-room when we come back. Wargrave knows the whole. He doesn't want to see it again." And with a rapidity surprising in one of his infirm appearance, he left the room, taking Countess Shimna with him.

"My dear," said Lady Taplow to the Duchess the moment Countess Shimna had disappeared, "she has a charming manner, this girl has: but nothing would induce me to take her out in London. She'd have too many men—married and unmarried—at her feet."

"Humph!" grunted Lord Wargrave, addressing his glass of sherry, but at the same time by an adroit jerk of his elbow inviting Pole to share his muttered wisdom, "she'd have them, if it depended on them, not at her feet only, but at her lips."

At this moment a door was partially opened, and a deep voice through the aperture ejaculated the word "Reginald." The voice was the Duke's. "Come," it continued. "Come with me. I want to have a little talk with you."

Pole rose and went. He had seen the house before, and had heard from the Duke the history of every relic and picture; but he now heard it all again with a totally new interest. The Duke was renowned for his sensitiveness to youthful beauty; so there was nothing surprising to Pole in his gallantry to Countess Shimna as a specimen of it. But what did surprise him was the extent of Countess Shimna's information as to most of the battles, the generals, and the political events, to which the Duke had occasion to allude in explaining the memorials of his father. She understood him in a moment, questioning him with a charming animation; and Pole watched curiously how the manner of the old man changed from what at first was a mere superannuated tribute to a toy of the other sex, and brightened into the manner of a keen man of the world, conversing with a woman who was almost his equal in intelligence.

"Now," said the Duke to her, when at last he had brought her to the drawing-room, "there's the Duchess. She will give you some coffee before you go. I've got a little business to talk about with Mr. Pole."

The business, as Pole had anticipated, was connected with his political prospects. The Duke, who, though he was often amused by Lord Wargrave's company, could rarely speak of him without some furtive sarcasm, declared that in Pole's case his judgment had been singularly sound, "and for the first time in his life," said the Duke, "his whole conduct has been judicious. I've nothing to say in addition to what he has probably told you—except," he added, "and this is an important point—except that you will be justified in believing it. My dear Reginald, I congratulate you. I congratulate you on your political prospects, but still more upon something else."

"And what is that?" Pole asked.

"Your prospect," said the Duke, "of driving home alone with this very charming young lady."

CHAPTER XXII.

WHEN Pole followed Countess Shimna into the Duke's brougham, and, the door being closed on them, they drove off together to the station, he enjoyed a sense of possessing her which he had not before experienced. The way in which she had captivated her host and hostess alike, and still more the grace with which she had shown herself a match for Lady Taplow, had just been making him feel that she belonged to the world rather than to himself; and that he was but one amongst many on whom she exercised an involuntary fascination: but now when he felt her by his

side, imprisoned with him between the same windows, the
sense came over him that he had carried her away from
everybody—that he had taken her from the world—that he
had made her absolutely his own; and an inclination seized
him, as she sat there, to enfold her, a captive, in his arms.
But this inclination roused in him its own antagonist. It
roused again the image of a far-off woman, by whose side
he had sat in a garden with a little boy between them—a
woman whose eyes had then been as soft and tender, as her
letters since then had been selfish and hard and heartless.
All the rest of the journey the memory of her pleaded with
him, and fawned on him; and his first action as soon as they
reached Glenlynn was to make for the table where the
letters were, which had come by the second post. His mind
as he did so was breathless with a hungry hope. He saw
that there were three for him, and one other for Countess
Shimna. He handed hers to her, and retired to a window
with his own. They were all bills. Beyond the bills there
was nothing for him. Two separate pangs passed through
him in quick succession—the one of miserable sadness, the
other of impatient anger. An hour later, when he took
Countess Shimna in to dinner, he touched for a moment the
hand that was resting on his arm. The hand in response
clung to him a thought more closely; and he murmured to
her, almost in a whisper, "I hope that you are not tired."

The night was warm—almost sultry; and after dinner,
Countess Shimna, who with great good-nature had been
showing Miss Drake some beautiful Venetian lace, at last
moved, fanning herself towards a window that was wide
open. She cast as she did so, one momentary glance at Pole.
Presently he rose and followed her; and they stood by the
window confronting each other.

Her face, which had been bright just now, like the
sparkle of the sea at morning, changed as she found herself
practically alone with him, and became like the shadowy
moonlight that was actually flashing on the waves. He
looked into her eyes with a long passionate interrogation.
As he did so a burst of unheard music filled his mind, from
instruments vague as the harps of sirens. He dropped his
voice to a whisper, and said, "Shall we come outside?"
She slowly nodded her head. They stepped out on to the
terrace. He felt the music in the air floating and wheeling

round him, hardly to be dissociated from the perfumes of the night-smelling flowers. They went to the balustrade before them, and looked out together over the sea. Below them, waves belonging to this human world, kissed and whispered amongst the rocks; but the moonlight on the far horizon was washing shadowy continents where mermaids sing, and the foam shines like diamond dust. Countess Shimna presently turned her head away, and as if with the intention of bringing herself back from dreamland, drew a deep breath of the scented garden air. In a low voice she repeated a line of Baudclaire's—

"Chaque fleur s'évapore ainsi qu'un encensoir."

Then she turned to her companion and lifted her eyes to his. On one of her wrists was a bracelet he had not seen before.

"Tell me," he said, "what stones are those?" And as if to draw them nearer to him he took her unresisting hand.

"I have," she said abruptly, "something that I want to tell you."

He glanced round as she spoke towards the dining-room window, which was sending straight towards them a narrow oblong of lamplight; and he said to her, "Let us walk a little; or else we shall probably have Dr. Clitheroe joining us. Can't you see him there, pretending to be interested in those book-shelves?"

"Come," she responded quickly. She had glided out of the light already; and they left the balustraded terrace for a walk which was hidden from the windows, and wound in silvery curves between rose-bushes and clumps of evergreens.

"Well," he said presently, using her Christian name for the first time, "and what is it you are going to tell me, Shimna?"

"I had," she said, "a letter this evening—a letter I have been expecting every day."

Pole sought her face with a look of perplexed inquiry; and his heart startled him with a throb of formless jealousy.

"The letter," she said, "is not much in itself. It merely tells me about the arrival of two of our foreign servants; but it is connected with something more. It is connected—how shall I put it?—with a certain happiness that is coming to me."

The jealousy that was just now formless, took shape and stung him. He shrank a little away from her, and said in a constrained voice, "May I venture to ask what kind of happiness it is?"

He saw her in fancy claimed by some coming lover; he saw her face lifting itself to receive this lover's kisses; he watched her lips as if they were being thus deflowered before his eyes.

She seemed to divine something of his mood and of his suspicions; for she looked at him with a smile, and said, "I can at least tell you this. It is no kind of happiness of which you can possibly be now thinking. I shall tell you about it some day. Perhaps when you know it, you may not like me the worse for it. But I wish—I don't know why—to breathe in your ear this—I am not what you think I am."

These last words were spoken slowly, and in a very low tone; and yet there was in lingering utterance a sort of caressing hardihood.

They had paused in their walk. She had disengaged her arm from his; and she now stood before him, pressing to her lips the sticks of her folded fan, the carved mother-of-pearl glimmering in the moonlight as she did so; whilst her eyes challenged his answer. In spite of what she had told him, and in spite of the fact that he believed it, the air seemed electric round him with the presence of some unseen lover. He advanced a step nearer to her hand. Her eyes, her lips, her breast, were drawing close to his own. A determination filled him to take that conjectured rival's place, and drive him, if a reality, out of her remembrance, or, if a mere phantom, out of his own. The situation produced an effect on him which he had not himself anticipated. Without his being aware of it, his natural reserve gave way.

"Shimna," he exclaimed, "I am lonely—I am deserted and miserable. Come to my breast, and make it forget its aching. Touch me with your lips, and make me forget memory."

The words had been hardly spoken, before, so far as her own power went, both prayers had been granted by her, but with one last reservation. She suffered herself to lean on him, as a flower might lean on trellis-work, with an unabashed gentleness. She lifted her face to his, as it bent down

towards her; but between his cheek and hers she quietly
interposed her fan, keeping his actual touch from her with
the pressure of its cool surface. "I know you are unhappy,"
she whispered. "Do you think I should make you happier?"
He had in his nature a mixture of pride and chivalry, which
made him respectful of a woman's least reluctance; and he
made no attempt to break down the fragile barrier she had
placed between them; but her breath as she spoke touched
him, though her lips remained virginal. All the world went
mad in his brain, his nerves, his fancy; and he felt as if he
were holding in his arms, music, moonlight, and perfume.

He turned that night to the picture of a very different
woman, which memory had painted on his mind more than
four years ago, and whose tender and living colours it had
renewed day by day; and he realized that over this, like a
cataract spreading over the eye, a film had spread itself
bearing another picture. For the first time, next morning,
he was conscious, when his letters were brought to him, of a
feeling of relief that there was none in a certain well-known
hand.

That morning, contrary to her usual custom, Countess
Shimna appeared at breakfast.

"How well you are looking," said Mrs. Pole. "Your
expedition of yesterday must have agreed with you."

The compliment was not unmerited. In certain women,
a certain stir of the emotions gives to their complexion a
clear and delicate vitality, which never results to it from
mere bodily health; and Countess Shimna was an example
of this fact now. The tint of her cheeks made her eyes
seem darker and more bright than usual, and her lips redder;
and she had more than ever the air of being complete
mistress of herself.

Pole was, perhaps, a little surprised at this. Men often
are surprised at the *aplomb* evinced by women under circumstances such as these. They forget that some women are
then in their natural element. But an announcement, which
Countess Shimna made presently, surprised him a great deal
more.

"Dear Mrs. Pole," she said, "I have just received a
letter which makes me fear I must go back to-day to
Lyncombe. There are two foreign servants whom my
mother wishes to leave with me; and I hear they are to

arrive to-day.   Poor things, they are women, and speak
hardly a word of English.   I should like to be in the house
when they arrive."

"I wish," said Mrs. Pole, "I could come into Lyncombe
with you; but I am still a little unwell, and the jolting of a
carriage is fatal to me."

Countess Shimna looked at Pole.   "Never mind," he
said quietly.   "I will go with her.   I want to see the builder
about a slight alteration in the plans."

He reflected that at any rate he would, during the drive,
be alone with her; and he wondered all the morning, which
she spent in his mother's company, how this new drama
would develop itself in the afternoon.   He found, however,
that he had been reckoning without his host—or, in plainer
language, without Countess Shimna's maid, who occupied,
in company of a dressing-bag, the back seat of the carriage;
and who, understanding life as well as she understood hair-
dressing, prevented the interchange in her presence of any
but the commonest observations.   But Pole's consciousness
of the literal facts of the situation, was coloured by his
imagination, which from time to time bewitched them,
turning the English sea into the Mediterranean, the gorse
and heather into groves of lemons and oranges, and himself
and his companion into a pair of married lovers, borne on
their bridal journey along the Cornice Road: nor had these
fancies quitted him when the carriage stopped at the
builder's.

"I," said Countess Shimna to him, "shall be busy till
half-past five; but if, after that, you have time for a cup of
tea, no doubt I could then give you one."

"If I don't come," he answered, "you will know that I
have been kept too long here, and have been obliged to drive
home straight."

His fear on this last score proved to be quite groundless.
His business was soon settled, and he was once again in the
street, with half an hour intervening between him and his
promised tea—a sober refreshment which at that moment
meant for him the mystery of the lips which had been withheld, but only just withheld, from him.   What allurement,
he thought, could be comparable to that last refusal?   Would
this blank half-hour, he wondered, ever draw to an end?

On the side of the wooded hill below Countess Shimna's

cottage were some paths open to the public; and to while away the time he betook himself to one of them, where, lighting a cigar, he sat down on a bench. He now recollected that just as he was starting in the carriage the second post had arrived, and that his pockets were full of business-letters. He pulled them out, and began to examine their directions. But before he reached the last, his hands holding them became motionless. Staring up at him from a square chocolate-coloured envelope was the penmanship for which he had so long been waiting. The blood rushed to his face, and for a moment or two his ears tingled. At last he broke the seal and drew out the letter that was within, opening the sheets gradually, as though he feared they might have contained a scorpion. Finally he summoned resolution to look at the opening words. He had hardly done so before he thrust the letter back in his pocket. But another action had intervened. He had first pressed it against his lips. The words which he had read were only four in number; but they had been these—"My own dearest Reggie." These for the present were enough for him. Without some mental preparation he felt he could endure no more. Hardly master of himself, he hastened to the hotel where the carriage was, not to the house above him, and gave orders that the horses should be got ready at once. Then he wrote a line—"I cannot come to tea—I am detained," and despatched it, before he started, to Countess Shimna by a messenger.

All the world was changed for him as he went home alone. He had left Lyncombe, and was ascending the wild hill outside it, before he allowed himself to look once more at the letter. Then he read it through—"My own dearest Reggie, I am so hurt and surprised at having heard nothing from you for so long. Except when I have been travelling, and you could not write, you have always written to me till now. What does it mean? Have you quite forgotten your poor Pansy? Or are you cross with her about something? Reggie, don't be cross with me. I am trying to do my best here, but things sometimes seem so hard, and I have no one at all to help me; and as to worldly things, in some ways I feel myself as ignorant as a child. But perhaps I am partly distracted because you have stopped writing to me. If you leave me I shall be indeed alone. But don't let me be a burden on you. I would sooner never have from you a single line again than one which you wrote unwillingly, thinking it a duty, a mere irksome duty. Forget me quite before that; but, oh, do not forget me."

Once, on a former occasion, Pole had spoken to the writer of the above letter as follows : " Since I have known you the thought of you has wrapped me round like a cloud, and all other women have been outside it, like so many bloodless shadows. They are nothing to me. I can hardly even see them clearly." The feeling which he had thus expressed, and which had of late left him, now, as he read her letter, returned to him once more. As if by magic, all the work of the past few days had been undone. Countess Shimna, indeed, remained still in his thoughts as an attractive and interesting woman; but every passionate feeling with regard to her which had developed itself under the spell of her presence, disappeared at once, like gauze when it catches fire, and left nothing behind it but the ashes of self-reproach and of regret. He feared that he might have wounded her by his conduct, and he wondered to what extent. He was also conscious that in relation to her his own position was embarrassing. But as to any wrong he might have done to that other woman, the very idea that he had been unfaithful to her for a single moment, was completely lost in the sense that after long sorrow she was restored to him. His arms were round her; he was caressing her with a gratitude that could not be told. Her eyes looked at him from the tender evening sea; her breath came to him in the air that was sighing over the heather, stirring his faithful thoughts of her as if they themselves were heather-bells. The better to realize the incredible happiness that was possessing him, he got out of the carriage and walked the last half of the way, with the moon floating above him, a semi-transparent film, coloured like a bruised primrose-petal in the purity of the quiet sky.

He left the road for a sheep-path ; and its short elastic grass brought him to a swelling eminence, which showed him for miles and miles the cliffs and promontories of the coast. Here he paused, and, seating himself on a solitary boulder, he bethought himself of his other letters. He took them out and began again to look at them. Amongst them, he saw, was one from his chief, Lord Henderson. Having reason to believe that Lord Henderson was by this time in

Norway, he was surprised at finding his envelope bearing the London post-mark. The contents of the letter revealed the reason of this. " Unexpected business," said the writer, " has forced me to give up every idea of leaving England. Lord Wargrave has explained to you the substance of the conversation we had together, and I learn with satisfaction that our suggestions, which are those of the Prime Minister also, are acceptable to yourself. I have forborne to write to you, until I knew with certainty what Sir John Markham's intentions really were. But his resignation is now an absolutely settled thing: and we may congratulate ourselves that so far as you are concerned all will be plain sailing. No one, however, knows better than you do, or knows to better purpose, how essential to success is a complete mastery of detail; and there are a number of points with which it is highly desirable that you begin to acquaint yourself at as early a date as possible. I write, therefore, to ask if you could come to London on Friday next, and arrange to stay several days, in order that we may have ample time together. I shall myself be tied to my office desk for at least a fortnight more: so your case will at all events not be so hard as mine."

This letter, in addition to the excitement which its contents caused him, was welcome to Pole for a yet more immediate reason. To-day was Wednesday. His summons to London was for Friday. The day intervening would be necessarily filled with business; and he was accordingly relieved from the possibility of again seeing Countess Shimna, before they should have both had time to realize and reconsider relationship. To her accordingly he wrote the following simple note:—

" I had hoped, when we parted to-day, that I should see you again almost immediately; but I am called away to London by the political work of which I told you, and in which it will always be a pleasure to me to know that I have your sympathy. I shall finish my business and return by the earliest day possible. Whatever happens to us, think of me as your friend, Reginald Pole."

But there was another letter which cost him considerably more trouble—his answer to that which had caused him his new happiness, and to which no adequate answer could be well committed to note-paper.

" I can hardly," he wrote, " thank you enough for yours which I received to-day. Repeat this to yourself over and over again. You cannot repeat it half as often as I do. You ask me why I have not written. It was only because I feared my letters had ceased to interest you. But to-day it happens I can tell you a piece of news. A letter reached me, by the post that brought me yours, from an old friend of mine, who I thought had quite forgotten me. She used to write to me constantly ; and then, for some reason I never could understand, she seemed to grow tired of me, just as I thought you had done of my correspondence. I have mentioned her before to you, and I dare say you have understood the truth—I mean, that she is more to me than any other woman in the world. Well—at last, after I had thought her dead to me, a letter from her came to-day. I wonder if you will be able to feel with me, and rejoice with me, in the happiness—the more than happiness—I have received from those few lines. Since you care to hear from me, you shall hear again very soon, if only you will be good enough not to think me in my dotage because I can to-day write only about a little thing like this. On Friday I go to London. You know the club at which letters will always find me. Send me a line when this reaches you, if only to ·tell me that you understand why I can write no more now."

On Friday, when the long lights of morning were damp and yellow on the downs, he was speeding on his way to London ; and the evening found him at dinner in his almost deserted club, his ears singing with that curious and pro-found silence which permeates Western London during the closing days of August.

CHAPTER XXIII.

POLE soon discovered that he had not come to London for nothing. There was a mass of information which, as Lord Henderson showed him, it was highly desirable that he should acquire and digest at once ; and he presently sur-prised his chief by the way in which he pointed out to him that, voluminous as this information was, it was deficient in many particulars, and that with regard to these, he would himself undertake to supplement it.

In this way almost all his moments were occupied; and a week slipped by like a single day and night. But though he had not time for much sentimental reflection, his mind was still permeated, as it was when he left Glenlynn, by the thought of the woman who had sent such a welcome letter to him; and his renewed faith in the depth and the fidelity of her nature was like a spiritual food to his whole inner being, making him see the world as a place that was worth working in, and nerving his will and mind to endure and to exert themselves to the utmost. His past experiences had, by means of many disappointments, taught him one useful lesson; and this was that the woman in question was a constitutionally bad correspondent. He had accordingly resolved not even to expect an answer from her till at least a week after his own letter should have reached her. It is true that, being a man, in addition to being a philosopher, he did, every morning, in spite of his resolution, inquire for his letters at his club in the hope that one from her would be amongst them; and finding none, it is quite true that he was disappointed. His disappointment, however, hitherto had been less keen than his hopes, and had not appreciably damped his spirits during the day. But now a week had passed; a second week begun; his correspondent still was silent; and anxiety began to supervene. Anxiety in a few days more developed into a wretchedness equal to anything —indeed greater than anything—which he had ever suffered in the past, and it never for a moment left him. It did not interfere with his work; it rather made his industry the fiercer: only, sometimes when at his desk, with his official papers before him, he would drop his pen in the middle of some elaborate calculation, and murmur to himself "How little it is I ask of you! I will never disturb your life, or trespass across your path of duty. Only do not become quite dead to me. Write me some word of kindness."

The strength of his feelings, however, was equalled by one thing; and that was a haughty and almost sullen self-control in concealing them. No one who had met him at dinner during those dark and desolate days, would have judged from his conversation that his mind was otherwise than at ease. But what manner or conversation may hide,

health, that *enfant terrible* of those who suffer deeply, will in
time partially betray, although this breach of confidence will
be necessarily discreetly vague : and some alteration in Pole's
general appearance at last attracted the notice of his shrewd
and observant chief.   Lord Henderson was a man full of a
homely friendliness ; and this natural characteristic had been
fostered by his gratitude to a scheme of things which had
resulted in the provision of so respectable a position for
himself.

"I don't know," he said one evening to Pole, peering at
him through his spectacles, and noticing a paleness in his
cheeks, and a faint line in his forehead, "I don't know what
may be your powers as a parliamentary orator : but from
the very first day since we began doing work together, I
have felt that you will have to speak worse than the worst
speaker I ever heard, if the quickness of your reasoning
powers, and your extraordinary command of facts—and I
may add your industry—do not very soon bring you into
the forefront of public life.   But there is one thing, my dear
Mr. Pole," he continued, " of which I should like to warn
you.   Do you know what that is ?   I wish this warning was
very much oftener needed.   It is a warning against a
tendency to do too much work, and—if you won't be shocked
at me—too thorough work.   You are growing to look
unwell—run down.   That's why I say this to you.   Go
home to bed, and be as idle as you can manage to be to-
morrow : and very soon we shall both of us have earned our
holidays."

Pole, when this advice was given him, had been dining
tête-à-tête with Lord Henderson ; and he left the house, and
started to walk home, with the compliment just paid him
still ringing in his ears, and the waters of his own bitterness
surging up in his heart.

As his steps carried him rapidly through the clear night
air, two subtle influences began mounting up to his brain—
a sense of his own wretchedness, and a sense of his own powers,
which last his own proud modesty had hitherto underrated ;
and the two together produced an effect upon him that was
not unlike a certain kind of intoxication.   The brilliant
future promised him as the result of his own exertions, and
still more the knowledge that these exertions would be really
useful to his country, seemed suddenly to lift his self-respect

above the levels of his private conscience, and set it high up
on some broader and firmer pedestal; and then on the glow
produced by this mental experience, there followed with
extraordinary rapidity a feeling of vague recklessness, as
though whatever he did with his own poor private life, his
self-respect would no longer be jeopardized. His thoughts
began to dart from one source of pleasure to another,
embroidering golden patterns on the dark sackcloth of
sorrow; and yet for moments this fever would come to rest,
and sorrow unrelieved shadow his whole heart. Indeed,
by-and-by he heard himself, as if he were another person,
betraying his own condition, by muttering these well-known
words—

> "Blow, blow, thou winter wind,
> Thou art not so unkind
> As man's ingratitude."

By this time he was in Piccadilly, along which lay his
way home. Its vista of pavement, wan in the September
moonlight, was hushed and was almost vacant. Only at
intervals some wandering figures blotted it. A cab rattling
in the stillness from one of the side streets detained him for
a moment at one of the many crossings, and he heard on
resuming his walk a light step behind him. He looked
round, and close to him he saw a girl—a graceful figure,
dressed with studious quiet. She raised her eyes to his with
a curious kind of modesty, valuable in the calling she
followed, and often not destroyed by it; and as if half afraid
of speaking, she faltered a faint "Good night." Pole's first
impulse was to pass on without noticing her; but her accent
was refined and gentle, and involuntarily he returned her
greeting, She quickened her steps, and was at once walking
by his side. "And what," he thought, "has been this poor
child's history? And what fate is in store for her?" His
mind as he scanned her was occupied by a mournful and
moody pity, and he wondered at the possibility of the drama
which, for one of its principal characters, is almost certain ·
to have a forlorn end like this. But his whole nature at the
moment was in unstable equilibrium. Before he and she
had walked many yards further, her modest eyes had
achieved their intended victory. "What does it matter?"
was what he was saying to himself now. "She will at least
help me to forget, as drink helps the unhappy poor." A

minute went by, during which he was quite silent; and then abruptly stopping, he said to her, "I beg your pardon, I have suddenly remembered something. I must say good-bye to you and go home. Let me give you this for walking with me when I felt lonely." And pressing into her hand the few pounds he had with him, he left her.

"Oh, thank you!" the girl exclaimed, with real gratitude in her voice. "I'm sorry he's gone," she murmured, as she resumed her hurried walk. "I liked that man. There was something in the way he had with him that was a little bit like Charley's."

Pole meanwhile was nearing his own door. "Pansy, Pansy," he said to himself, "it matters little what becomes of me; but I respect all women for your sake, and even if you really have left me I will not make myself unfit for you to call me back again." A similar thought possessed him when he woke the next morning, and he was thankful that last night's episode was a mere phantasmal memory. He was doubly thankful for this, when at last, on going to his club, he found amongst the letters handed to him the one he so long had waited for. His heart leapt at the sight of it; and he said to himself as he took it in his hand, "My dear, forgive me for having doubted you. Forgive me for all my bitterness."

The contents of the letter for which he had thus thanked the writer in anticipation, were as follows—

"DEAR MR. POLE,

"I have not been able to answer your note before. Some friends—neighbours, to whom it is right that I should be civil, have been staying here for a county ball; and I have hardly a moment in which I can call my soul my own. You, no doubt, are very busy also, though you don't say how. Write and tell me some day when you can find time. Your note was very kind, and I am glad that what your friend said pleased you. She must, I think, have been in very low spirits when she wrote. But don't tell me anything of that kind again, I entreat of you. My letters when they come lie about on the hall-table, with all the bills and circulars, and with the visitors' letters, and with my husband's letters; and by accident, or by design, they might be opened by any human being. Yours,

"P. MASTERS."

The first effect on Pole of this letter was bewilderment; and then came a feeling that he had sustained some deliberate, some unprovoked blow, the cruelty of which, when he began to reflect upon it, reduced him once more to bewilderment; and bewilderment began now to smoulder into forlorn anger. It seemed to him that he had reached at last the dregs of the cup of misery. But though more miserable than formerly, he had become, since last night, wiser, if wisdom consists in realizing the byways by which we escape from pain. His mood gradually came to resemble that in which he had last night left Lord Henderson. His respect for himself as a man of action, hard-working, successful, and—as his conscience told him—disinterested, appeared once more as a licence to comport himself in other matters as he would; only the licence now was of a more liberal character. Why, he asked himself, should he not return to Countess Shimna, freed from the half-hearted scruples which had hitherto chilled his wooing of her, and seek in the chalice which her untouched lips had offered him, relief at all costs from his present disastrous wretchedness—a wretchedness from which, it appeared to him, no relief was possible, so long as he clung to the faiths and fidelities which were its foundation? The dove-like eyes, and the soft face made of rose-petals, with gentle expressions playing across its curves like cloud-shadows—the eyes and the face of the woman he had loved for years, looked at him steadfastly for a moment; and with a shudder he turned away from them. It was now the face of a Medusa, turning his heart to stone; and then, more mysterious, more brilliant, more dainty than ever, there shone before him the image of Countess Shimna.

Whilst this sad, but yet not singular, drama was taking place within him, he had left his club, and, having strayed into the deserted park, had been wandering there aimlessly he knew not for how long. Then at last, with the same aimlessness he left it, and was just issuing from the gates at Hyde Park Corner, when he heard behind him a burst of feminine laughter, and mixed with the laughter, the exclamation, " I said it was Mr. Pole!"

He was obliged to stop and turn round, and there, with all their eyes on him, were three excited young ladies, hustled close together, and so exactly alike in their dresses, their ribbons, and their parasols, that they seemed like a single creature with three agitated heads. By the time, however, that one of them had detached herself from her two companions, he had realized that he was in the presence of the three Miss Cremers, and that, though he could count on the fingers of one hand the days which he had spent in their company, they were greeting him with as much effusion, coupled with as much surprise, as if he had been a favourite brother, and they had stumbled on him in the middle of Africa.

"Mister Pole!" they exclaimed one after the other, with an arch and vigorous emphasis laid on the word "Mister." "Who," continued the eldest, in admiring and serious accents, "would have thought to see you in London at this time of the year? Even we," she continued—"poor little humble we—are only shopping for the day. We came up this morning from Thames Wickham, to do some commissions from Ethel; and Mrs. Steinberg—did you ever hear of such vigour?—insisted on coming too. We are now on our way to meet her at the New Piccadilly Restaurant, where we're going to lunch early—the place for luncheon. Of course you know it well. Do come there with us and see her—that is to say, Mr. Pole, if you're not too grand to walk with us."

"And on the way," said another of the sisters archly, "we'll reward you for being so good, by telling you about dear Martha."

"That," he said, laughing, "is quite an unnecessary inducement; though it alone would have been sufficient, supposing there had been no other." The company of even the Miss Cremers was at that moment a relief to him. "Well," he said, when they had started, "and what about Martha? Tell me."

"We have never," said Miss Folly, "found her so pleasant before. She has been shut up with a bilious attack for a whole week in her bedroom. The only doctor she will tolerate is Dr. Mogg, and he comes every day with a new spiritual prescription."

"No," interposed Miss Dolly; "you mean with a new spiritual meal. I'm sure her soul overeats itself, just like her vile body; and next week, if her vile body is well enough, she is going to indulge in a regular spiritual banquet. Dr. Mogg has given her a platform ticket for a meeting at Thames Wickham of your friend Canon Bulman's League."

"And what league is that?" asked Pole.

The youngest Miss Cremer could give him no very precise information; but the eldest, peering up at him with the consciousness of superior knowledge, first expressed her wonder at his really being ignorant of anything, and then told him that the league in question had only just been formed; and that its object was to inquire into the moral antecedents of every Parliamentary candidate in every constituency in the kingdom, and, should any shadow be found to rest upon the character of any one of them, to make him either disprove the charges brought against him, or retire. "Did you not see," she continued, "what one of the papers said—that the secret aim of the League must be to abolish Parliament altogether?"

By this time they were nearing the Piccadilly Restaurant; and Pole stopping said, "I must really go no further with you; but will you give my card to the head-waiter, who knows me? I am writing an order on it for my luncheon in a quarter of an hour, and then when I come, I shall be certain to see you all. I cannot go in with you now, and inflict myself uninvited on Mrs. Steinberg."

The matter was arranged accordingly; and when the quarter of an hour had expired, Pole was entering a room, which seemed, with its lace-curtained windows, and red velvet seats, to have been transported whole from Paris, like the miraculous House of Loretto. In spite of the emptiness of the streets, the Piccadilly Restaurant was crowded. In all directions were hungry and talkative parties, whose members were eating and laughing and helping each other to champagne, and ostentatiously enjoying themselves at a minimum of ten shillings a head. They belonged for the most part to that mysterious travelling class, which seems born to disprove the assertion that, even in these mercenary days, mere wealth can secure for its possessors any resemblance to ladies or to gentlemen; and they bore the various hall-marks of the provinces, of the Continent, and of America. Pole looked about him, bewildered by this motley throng, and was advancing amongst the tribe of tables, in search of his friend the head-waiter, when he heard a commanding voice, which, although neither

loud nor harsh, pushed its way to his ear through a chorus
of other noises, as an experienced dowager pushes herself
through a crowd at an evening party.

"Waiter," the voice said, "bring that gentleman here—
here, I tell you—that gentleman in the tall hat. I think,"
it added to itself, "he's the only gentleman in the place."

This flattering comment was loud enough to reach Pole's
ears; and his eyes had only a little way to travel before
they encountered Mrs. Steinberg, in gorgeous raiment, who
beckoned him to a table variegated with half the delicacies
on the *carte*.

"Here's your luncheon," she exclaimed. "Dear Mr.
Pole, how are you? Child," she said to Miss Cremer, "move
a little that way, and make room for him. I call it most
unkind and wicked, Mr. Pole, to think of sulking by yourself.
Here are three young ladies who say you are too proud to
eat with them. If there had been only an old woman here
I could have understood you, though I shouldn't have forgiven you. I have punished you as it is, by countermanding
your solitary meal; and I told the waiter that, if he served
you, I wouldn't give him a penny for himself. Come, now—
begin with some of this *omelette au caviare*. It is quite hot
still, and has been only five minutes on the table."

Pole felt himself caught and absorbed in the vortex of
his hostess's welcome: and seated himself and eat exactly as
she directed or suggested.

"Well," she said presently, "and now tell us your news.
What brings you to London?"

He explained as briefly as he could, that he was engaged
on some official work, and also mentioned the possibility of
his eventually entering Parliament.

"Dear Mr. Pole," exclaimed Mrs. Steinberg, "that is
really very nice for you—the very thing you are made for. I
congratulate you a thousand times. Shake hands with me,
if you can do so without knocking down that siphon. And
poor good Lord Henderson—I hope he is wearing well.
But, dear me, you must be dreadfully alone in London; for
an hour each day of Lord Henderson is hardly gay society.
Come down and stay with us. We'll give you a room to
work in; and whenever you're wanted here, you can easily
run up by train. And then, by the way, I'm expecting a
great friend of yours—Lord Wargrave. He's coming to us

for a day or two, because he knew he'd be so bored in town.
Now," she continued, turning to the three Miss Cremers,
"don't you young ladies think that we should secure our
gentleman while we've got him? Ah! Mr. Pole, you see
what their eyes say; so have your portmanteau packed,
come down to us to-night, and stay till you find our society
more tiresome than solitude."

In Mrs. Steinberg's kindness there was a sort of conquer-
ing sincerity, which would have compelled Pole to accept
her invitation, even if it had been less agreeable to him than
it was. The Blue Book at which he had been working was
now nearly ready for publication, a copy in advance having
been sent already to *The Times;* and the work which at this
moment claimed him was the final revision of the proofs—
a work which he could accomplish at Thames Wickham just
as well as in London. He accordingly left the four ladies,
when he parted from them at the door of the restaurant,
promising to be with them again that evening by dinner-
time.

CHAPTER XXIV.

WHEN he reached the house, and found himself in Miss De
Souza's presence, he once more experienced a sense of profound gladness that he had not to blame himself for his
conduct on the previous night; and his recent thoughts with
regard to Countess Shimna, though blamable only in a very
vague way, were pushed away by him with a sense of
contemptuous shame, in order that he might meet frankly
the regard of Miss De Souza's eyes, which for him were,
if not the most beautiful, yet the noblest, he had ever
known.

Mrs. Steinberg and the three Miss Cremers had arrived
an hour before him. Mrs. Steinberg, as was hardly wonderful,
had gone upstairs to rest herself; but the three Miss Cremers,
unwearied in effusive usefulness, were all of them clustered,
when Pole was ushered into the drawing-room, round a
deeply-cushioned sofa, on which Miss De Souza was lying,
one of them holding her hand, another holding her scent-
bottle, and a third beseeching her to have another cup of

tea. They all on Pole's entrance rose like a flock of birds, first emitting a burst of welcoming laughter, and then joining in a sort of elegiac trio, and sighing, "Oh, isn't it too bad! She's knocked herself up again! She has over-walked herself taking jellies to poor old Sally; and now her back aches so she can hardly sit upright. Ethel, I call it quite wicked of you, sacrificing yourself like this."

"Mr. Pole knows," said Miss De Souza, "that I am not generally so fragile, and he won't waste his sympathies on a hardy young woman's backache. I want to forewarn him of a far greater catastrophe, and one from which he will suffer a great deal more than we shall. Now, girls, don't tell him. Let him give three guesses."

"Mrs. Blagdon is better," said Pole, "and is coming down this evening."

"Oh no," said the Miss Cremers, "not quite so bad as that; and from that *we* should suffer a great deal more than you."

Pole meditated; and drawing a bow at a venture, he said, "Dr. Mogg is coming again to dine here."

The three Miss Cremers shrieked till the glass chandelier tinkled, and blurted out "Yes, that's it," amongst gurgles of stifling laughter. At this moment the eyes of the eldest strayed to a clock on the chimneypiece, who face was almost lost amongst bouquets of Dresden china, and exclaimed with a gasp to her sisters: "We must go and arrange the table. The gardener's ill, Mr. Pole, and we do the flowers now." Pole secretly felt himself delighted to hear they did; for a minute or two later he was sitting alone with Miss De Souza.

The room was growing dusky; but in Miss De Souza's eyes as they turned to him, there floated a light like a gleam on a slowly-flowing evening river. "And now," she began, "we can talk for half an hour in quiet." There was in her voice, as there was in her whole air and in all her move-ments, a subtle something which always seemed to say, "The joys and sorrows of others are so much more to me than my own." And they seemed to say this to P. le with peculiar emphasis now. "I saw," she continued, "in *The Times* yesterday, a short paragraph about this Blue Book you have been preparing; and there was an allusion at the end of it to some experiments of your own at Glenlynn. Tell me all There is no subject in the world half so inte-resting as those that are now engaging you."

Pole, in many respects, was a man of unusual reticence. To the woman he had loved he hardly mentioned these subjects at all; and he had mentioned them to Countess Shimna only because, when she happened to be with him, they were engaging him in obvious and unmistakable ways. But with Miss De Souza he felt it would be as hard to keep silence about them as with other women it would be to be confidential. He drew his chair closer to her, and with an eagerness like that of a boy, he began to describe the matters with which his Blue Book dealt, the appreciation which cert in parts of it had already met with, and the sudden and surprising political prospects that were before him. She could not have listened with more delight and animation had all the beatitudes of life been announced to her as in readiness for herself. They hardly knew, indeed, how time was passing, till the gong for dressing began to thunder like Sinai; and silently following the thunder a couple of housemaids entered, bent on obliterating from the room every sign of its having been occupied during the day.

Miss De Souza and Pole retreated with the precipitation that is invariable under such circumstances; and when the latter returned dressed, and found the candles lighted, and every cushion as smooth as if it were in an upholsterer's shop, the room was empty except for the figure of Dr. Mogg, who was rubbing his black-coated shoulder-blades against the rim of Mrs. Steinberg's chimneypiece, and was apparently endeavouring to catch sight of his shirt-front through his beard. He straightened himself as Pole entered, and relaxing into a ponderous smile, he said, " I am pleased, sir, to have the honour of again meeting you." Pole answered him with corresponding cordiality, which was, however. touched with a more mundane cheerfulness; and Mrs. Steinberg, when she appeared, trailing several yards of satin, was delighted to find her two gentlemen on what seemed to be the most satisfactory terms.

Dr. Mogg, despite his severity towards most forms of enjoyment, was by no means bigoted against the grave pleasures of the table. He sucked up his first spoonful of soup with a noise like an incarnate sigh; and before long, encouraged by his two hostesses, he was expressing his opinions, which were by no means wanting in sense, about all sorts of matters connected with public and private life. It happened, however, that the name of Canon Bulman's *béte noire*—the politician who so lately had fallen by his private sins, was mentioned in connection with political questions; and this unfortunately led Mrs. Steinberg into a whispered conversation with him, which had reference to the moral side of the incident. The three Miss Cremers, who had excellent ears for a whisper, realized presently that he was referring to the heroine of the whole mischief, and remarking with wonder on the incredible turpitude of women who not only yielded to temptation, but actually were them-selves tempters. "When we hear of such," he proceeded, "it makes us the more thankful to think of such elect vessels as the admirable lady upstairs, who, as we may humbly venture to say, have never in their whole lives known what it was either to tempt or to be tempted."

This was too much for the Miss Cremers. The youngest of them without warning burst into hysterical laughter; the two others spluttered; even Mrs. Steinberg struggled, with her muscles. Pole was the only person who was abso-lutely grave and calm. Mrs. Steinberg, however, saved the situation by calling to the youngest Miss Cremer in a voice of extreme sharpness—

"Put your napkin up to your nose directly, Folly. Her nose is bleeding. Can't you see that—any of you? Take her out, and lay her flat on a sofa. These silly girls," she continued, turning to Dr. Mogg, "are always giggling over some foolish joke of their own. Come, Ethel, if Dr. Mogg will excuse us, we had better go and see what they have done with her, and he and Mr. Pole can join us when they have finished their wine."

Dr. Mogg could hardly conceive that such a subject as feminine virtue, which had in his mind severely limited meaning, could raise a smile except in the most abandoned company; but, all the same, a suspicion crept over him that the only person present who appreciated him seriously, was Pole. Pole accordingly rose high in his favour; and raised himself higher still by the topic which he introduced now. This topic was Canon Bulman's League, with which he gathered that Dr. Mogg had some connection. And such indeed proved to be the case. Dr. Mogg was delighted at the interest which Pole exhibited in the subject; and

proceeded to answer his qustions with eagerness, yet with a
certain reticence.

"Canon Bulman," he began solemnly, "is a Churchman;
I am a Nonconformist; but we both represent one particular
opinion in which multitudes of churchmen and nonconformists agree. We are of opinion that a man who breaks
a certain commandment has broken all; and it is not for
nothing that in a special and emphatic sense we give to this
commandment the name of the moral law. I don't say that
other men may not pay some respect to it; but what we
insist on is its enormous and overwhelming importance. It
is for this reason we are so jealous of all forms of pleasure
and frivolity. Well, sir, the object of our League is to
organize the latent righteousness of the nation, so as to
make it impossible for any man to enter Parliament, whose
life and conduct have shown him to be careless of the
law I speak of; and I am sure you will sympathize with
us in our object, even should you not deem it to be
practicable."

"Do you think," said Pole, "that if it were so, and you
were in reality to attain it, you would materially improve
the Government, and consequently the condition, of the
country?"

Dr. Mogg scratched his head, and wiped his mouth with
his napkin.

"Probably," he said—"probably. I certainly incline to
think so. But, Mr. Pole, I won't disguise it—the point you
have raised is, for us, merely a side issue. What we want—
if you will forgive the phrase—to be down upon, is not bad
government, but the luxury of immoral living. We want to
reach criminals whom the law cannot reach. We want to
strip them of their false decency, and, in a word, to show
them up—show them up," he repeated, bringing down his
hand upon the table-cloth. "We want, Mr. Pole, to bring
them to open shame."

"I don't know," replied Pole, "whether you have considered this question:—You say that the law cannot reach
those criminals: but may not the law of libel reach those
who endeavour to expose them? Unless a man has appeared
publicly in the Divorce Court, or has otherwise made any
irregularity in his conduct notorious, it passes my wit to
see how any League whatsoever can damage his character,

without running the risk of getting into legal hot water
itself—and very dirty legal hot water too."

Dr. Mogg frowned meditatively at some peach-stones
that were lying on his dessert plate, and paused for a
moment or two before making any answer. At last he said,
with a sort of resigned sigh—

"Every cause has its dangers. As to this, Mr. Pole, I
would answer you, if I could, more fully; but our exact plan
of action is not yet ripe for disclosure. If, however, you
would attend our meeting here next week, we shall, I assure
you, be fraternally glad of your presence; and you would
hear Canon Bulman explain as much as can be explained at
present. Meanwhile, I may point out this to you. The
objection you have suggested has less application to the case
of a Parliamentary candidate than to any other. A constituency, or any section of constituents, has a *primâ facie*
right to inquire into the private character of a man who
publicly asks them to entrust their vital interests to him,
which it might not have, judged by mere worldly standards,
to inquire into the character of an ordinary private citizen:
and I believe it is this fact, quite as much as his strong
political feelings, which has influenced Canon Bulman—a
man of the world in its best sense—to withdraw his services
from a Vigilance Society, called the Lily League, whose
members were accustomed to follow any immoral man in
the streets, and devote himself to founding the League of
which we are now speaking."

"Well," said Pole, civilly, "should I be able to attend
your meeting, I will, with your permission, write to you for
one, or even more tickets."

"And indeed, sir," said Dr. Mogg, "I shall be much
gratified in sending them. You, Mr. Pole, I am told, belong
to one of our most ancient families. I should like to tell
you that the English Nonconformists, as such, have no
objection to an aristocracy. What they do object to is a
frivolous and licentious aristocracy. I can assure you
honestly that the winning of a horse-race by a peer, which
is always associated with all manner of private profligacy,
does far more to rouse the antagonism of conscientious
Radicals than any action of the Lords as a political body.
Indeed," Dr. Mogg continued, as if imparting a State secret,
"there is in our Radicalism a strong Conservative element.

We resent the profligacy and the frivolity of the aristocratic classes partly because they tend to bring all wealth into contempt in the eyes of those whom God has not elected to be the possessors of it."

Pole could not help admiring the astuteness of this last remark. "I see," he said, as they rose to go into the drawing-room, "that you have the wisdom of the serpent amongst you, as well as the purity of—well, I can't say more—of women like Mrs. Blagdon."

<h2 style="text-align:center">CHAPTER XXV.</h2>

POLE's life for the next few days was wintry and flowerless enough; but it was made tolerable by constant application to his work, and sometimes more than tolerable by the sympathy and companionship of Miss De Souza, whose influence was peculiar in being at once stimulating and soothing, and came to him like a breath of spring between bitter and frost-bound branches.

At last the evening arrived that was destined to bring Lord Wargrave. He and Mrs. Steinberg had been intimate friends for years; and when he entered the drawing-room they very nearly embraced.

"It is centuries," exclaimed Mrs. Steinberg, "I declare it's positively centuries, since you've dined with me in my own house. Come now, you faithless man, confess when you did so last, if you are not ashamed of admitting how long ago it was."

"I remember," said Lord Wargrave, "your dinners so well, that the last one always seems to have taken place yesterday."

"Listen, young ladies," cried Mrs. Steinberg to the three Miss Cremers. "When will you, I wonder, have such a compliment paid to you as that!"

Lord Wargrave meanwhile having wrung Pole by the hand, and compressed his verbal salutations into a mere muttered "God bless you," walked hastily to a table on which the papers of the day were lying, and began, with some impatience, to push them about, examining them,

" You haven't *The Times* here," he granted, turning to Mrs. Steinberg.

" Dear Lord Wargrave," said Mrs. Steinberg, " I'll ring the bell and send for it. It is most likely upstairs in bed with poor Martha Blagdon."

" No matter," said Lord Wargrave, with an air of being not altogether discontented. " I've a copy of my own somewhere. I'll send for it after dinner."

Whatever his interest in this paper was, dinner was enough for the time to put it out of his head; and as soon as he and Pole were left together over their wine, he began to discuss what he called a "little bit of family business."

" I should," he said, " have written, if I had not heard I was to meet you here. What I want to say to you is this. Before many weeks are over Parliament will have re-assembled; and from all I can hear there will be a very unusual thing—not only an Autumn Session, but something like an Autumn Season. Our friend the Duchess of Dulverton is actually going to give a ball, with a view to keeping in town till the critical division is over, all the respectable Whigs, as well as the Conservatives. The idea, I need hardly say, is not hers, but the Duke's. All the same, if it succeeds, it will prove, what I have always maintained, that the part of the great lady in politics is by no means played out yet. Well, my dear Reginald, the practical point is this. You really ought to persuade that excellent sweet mother of yours to come for a month or so to my house in Brook Street, and bring up with her your delightful Austrian Venus, who rose, under such respectable auspices, out of the West of England foam. The only rent I shall ask will be that you shall bring some servants, as I've nobody there myself but my own man and a housemaid. Your mother need have no scruples in accepting what I propose. I should profit by it quite as much as you and she would."

To Pole for many reasons this proposal was pleasing; but whilst he was assuring Lord Wargrave that he would do his best to recommend it to his mother, a folded copy of *The Times* was put into Lord Wargrave's hand. " Come," said Lord Wargrave, waving the paper like a *bâton*. " I'm going to tell those charming ladies something about you, which, so far as I can gather, you don't even know yourself."

Completely mystified, Pole rose and followed Lord War-grave, who, on entering the drawing-room, took up his position on the hearthrug, and confronted the company, with *The Times* still in his hand. "At dinner," he began, "Mrs. Steinberg was talking to me about our friend here, and saying that he was a rising man. I'll read you something to show you how far she was right."

"Dear Lord Wargrave," said Mrs. Steinberg, who had not quite followed him, "oh, do read to us. That will be too delightful of you. I remember those charming ballads of Alfred de Musset, which you used to read to us long ago in Paris."

"Listen," said Lord Wargrave, when he had found his place in the paper. "This is from a leading article. I need read you only part of it.

"'Government Blue Books and the Reports of Royal Commissions frequently fail to be useful even to the professional politician. They rarely affect public opinion directly, for the general public very rarely read them; and still more rarely do they reflect any personal lustre on their authors. The Report on Trades Unionism on the Continent, which is just completed, and will be laid next month before Parliament, promises to be a signal exception to these general rules. The subject is far wider than the title indicates. It embraces nearly all the questions relating to the condition of the working classes, which a certain extreme party in the country are at the present moment endeavouring to make their own; and the crude theories which, borrowed from France and Germany, the more reckless of our own politicians are now beginning to advocate, are not only stated here with the utmost fulness and lucidity, but accurate and brilliant accounts are given of those social experiments by which, in different countries, and at different times, the value of these theories has been tested.

"'The writer of this volume, Mr. Reginald Pole, is to be congratulated as an author, as a political philosopher, and as a statesman; for the qualities which make a man great in each of these three capacities, are present throughout his pages to a high and most unusual degree. They are sufficiently rare when separate. They are rarer still in combination. Mr. Pole's name has hitherto been little before the public; but in the inner circles of the political world his

abilities have been recognized as remarkable for some years
past, though their full extent has not been suspected till
now; and we are much deceived, and the country will be
much disappointed, if their full development has even yet
been reached.   Whether Mr. Pole, in the party sense of the
word, may call himself a Liberal or a Tory, we neither know
nor care; but his support, in whatever way it be given,
would be a support, we do not hesitate to say, of which any
moderate Government, when dealing with social questions,
might feel proud.'

  "There!" said Lord Wargrave, bringing down his hand
on his knees.   "What do you think of that?"

  "Dear Mr. Pole," exclaimed Mrs. Steinberg, "this is
really delightful.   This is fame running out to meet you.
It is such a joy to me to think of all your talent being appreciated.   My dear husband used to say, when speaking of the
career of talent, 'Appreciation is opportunity.'"

  "Humph," muttered Lord Wargrave, "that's exceeding
well said.   Yes—yes.   To be appreciated at the right moment,
is the rarest luck for ambition, and it's positively the elixir
of vanity.   However, our friend here is not, I think, vain;
so half the value of it, I'm afraid, will be completely thrown
away on him.   By the way," he continued, "I see in the
papers that our good friend Canon Bulman and Dr. Mogg,
of Manchester, have started a League, as they call it,
which is to unite all ugly Christians in blackmailing
Conservative candidates who are better looking than themselves."

  "To be sure," exclaimed Mrs. Steinberg—"to be sure—
what am I thinking of?   There's going to be a meeting of
this wonderful League to-morrow—here, Lord Wargrave,
here in Thames Wickham; and Mrs. Blagdon intends to
exchange the comfort of her bed for the honour of a chair on
the platform by Dr. Mogg's side.   Dr. Mogg has promised
Mr. Pole as many tickets as he wants, in case you or he
should either of you care to go."

  "Ethel," exclaimed a Miss Cremer, "let us all go!"

  "Not from this house," said Mrs. Steinberg, with much
decision, "that is to say," she added, "if you want to sit on
the platform: though of course Mr. Pole and Lord Wargrave never would think of that.   As for Canon Bulman, no
doubt he may be charming socially; but his public opinions

are really very reprehensible—hardly fit, indeed, for young ladies to listen to."

"There is," said Miss De Souza, "an organ-loft in the Town Hall. Perhaps my aunt will allow us to hide our blushes there."

"Well, dears," said Mrs. Steinberg, mollified, "the organ-loft, I know, is dark; and if you got places there, you would none of you be observed by anybody. We could send to Dr. Mogg, and no doubt he would have the seats reserved for us."

Lord Wargrave, whose curiosity was omnivorous, had already determined to be present: so a letter was sent to Dr. Mogg, and an order for the seats obtained. When the evening came, Mrs. Blagdon, wheezing under a cloud of shawls, was despatched in a hired landau, having dined in her own room. Then the rest of the party, after an interval of ten minutes, followed unknown to her, in a couple of four-wheel cabs, and entered the building unnoticed, by a door in a side street.

When they reached their seats, the proceedings were just about to begin. The body of the hall was gloomy with the backs of a middle-class crowd, on whose black coats and bonnets the gaslight made no impression. But the platform, though its occupants were attired with no less severity, was lighted more strongly, and was speckled with pink faces. The chairman, a local minister, dressed like a High-Church curate, was pulling his long black beard, and was looking at the clock nervously, whilst his mouth, with its bitter smile, was twitching with preparations for speech. Dr. Mogg was on his left, grim but yet benevolent. Next to Dr. Mogg, and so far overlapping her chair that she seemed to be leaning on the shoulder of her ghostly counsellor, was Mrs. Blagdon, crimson with devout importance; and on the chairman's right, his head well in the air, his lips firmly clenched, and his eyebrows knit defiantly, was the principal speaker, and the hero of the occasion, Canon Bulman.

When the minute-hand of the clock pointed to half-past eight, the chairman jumped up, and addressing his "friends, brethren, and sisters," announced that before going further, they would sing three verses of a hymn, a copy of which would be found on every seat. He had hardly spoken when just over Lord Wargrave's head, the organ began to rumble;

P

and the hymn in question was started by some trained voices
on the platform.

> " Let every home a Salem be !
> Let doubt and discord prove
> Its chastening guests if Jah so wills,
> But not unlicensed love."

Such was the opening verse; and what followed was
suitable. The closing Amen was still echoing in the roof,
when the chairman, who possessed at least the merit of
promptitude, had rapped the table in front of him, and had
begun to inform his hearers that he would confine himself to
the business of introducing the principal speaker of the
evening. He said that most of those present were, he
believed, Nonconformists, whilst the principal speaker would
be a clergyman of the Established Church; and this fact
was typical of the purpose of the meeting, which was to
unite Christians, no matter how divided otherwise, in defend-
ing one principal equally dear to all of them. That principle
was the principle of moral spotlessness. They knew what
he meant by that. It was one thing, and one thing only.
Let there be no vagueness about the matter. Party politics,
he said, were to be strictly excluded from the meeting; but
he felt he should be justified in alluding to one bright sign
of the times—a sign like a star, which to-night was shining
close to them. This star was Canon Bulman himself. Canon
Bulman, highly placed as he was in the hierarchy of the
Established Church, courted by earthly princes, whose favour
he valued at what it was worth—Canon Bulman was in
favour of Disestablishment. An Olympian smile of assent
passed over the Canon's lips, and a cheer, as solemn as an
Amen, rose from the attentive audience. It was therefore,
the chairman observed, peculiarly cheering to them, to know
that when the Established Church should be called on to
divide her temporal riches, as well as renounce her temporal
supremacy, they had one before them, who, though personally
he had much to lose, was prepared to cast his all into the
great National treasury. He would now call on Canon
Bulman to address the meeting.

The Canon, whose face during the last few moments had
undergone a slight change of expression, now rose, and
coming forward with a not ungraceful movement, began to

speak in a voice which by its refinement and cultivated modulations, formed a striking contrast to the utterances of the preceding speaker. Nor was the difference in his tone less striking. The Chairman's speech had had in it a vein of acrid piety. The Canon began as though he were nothing if not business-like.

"I rise to speak," he said, "having two objects in view, an immediate object, and an ulterior object. I shall explain the latter best by dealing first with the former. My immediate object is to claim your support for a resolution which will be submitted to you at the close of to-night's proceedings; and the terms of the Resolution are as follows:—' In the opinion of this meeting no man, whatever his abilities, is fit to sit in parliament and legislate for a Christian country, who is in his own person a violater of the moral law, and such being the case it is desirable that a League should be forthwith formed for the purpose of inquiring, wherever any doubt exists, into the private morality of persons offering themselves for parliamentary election. Furthermore this meeting is of opinion that when any candidate, no matter what his party, is shown on inquiry to be a person of immoral life, it is the duty of all Christians, no matter what their party, to secure his withdrawal, or to record their vote against him.'

"There," the Canon continued, "is the Resolution you will be asked to pass. I will now briefly explain to you the practical points implied in it. A League of this kind, if it is to do practical work, must have a careful organization, a variety of competent officers, and fitting local habitations. It must furthermore have a definite policy, and must be content to begin with limited, but definite and concentrated effort. And here," said the Canon, taking up a piece of paper from the table, "I pause to answer a question, which has been submitted to me at the beginning of the meeting, in order, I suppose, to make sure of my being explicit as to the subject it refers to. The question asked is, ' What means do you propose to take, firstly to discover the offences of an immoral candidate, and secondly, to bring them publicly home to him.' Well," said the Canon, not with the best grace in the world, "it may perhaps have occurred to the gentleman who put that question—I am sure with the best intentions—that it is a question which must have many

answers. When the offence is notorious—as in a case lately
before the country—our course is simple. When it is an
offence not legally proved, but notorious nevertheless, our
course will be simple still. Our only difficulty will arise
where the offence has been more artfully concealed, or is at
any rate less widely known, or where its commission may be
reasonably doubted. Well, gentlemen, in such cases,. the
nature of the courses to be pursued will depend altogether
on the exact circumstances, and will have to be left to the
judgment of such judicious and Christian men as may be
elected to the task by the League, in each constituency. All
I can say is, that in such cases, our first endeavour will be
to deal with the offender privately, and either assure ourselves of his humble repentance, or attempt to force him
back into the obscurity of private life, before taking any
steps to make his offence public. As for evidence, in such
cases, it is rarely far to seek. The immoral man sins less
secretly than he imagines. My own experience of him is,
that he is like the ostrich with its head in the sand." These
last words were received with a long mutter of applause,
being taken as an allusion to the gallantries of one of the
sitting members for Thames Wickham. "And now," continued the Canon, "I will return to my former point. We
propose, I was saying, to begin with a limited but concentrated effort. We propose to begin with the formation of
three, or perhaps four branches, in the constituencies near
London, one of them being the constituency in which this
meeting is held; and it is hoped that, if we are supported,
as we hope to be, we may very shortly be in working order.
Of the reasons which have induced us to think that our
efforts would be exceptionally useful here, it is not necessary
that I should speak. I will rather," he continued, encouraged
by a sympathetic groan, "proceed to the more general aspect
of the question; and show you how the application of this
great moral test will, besides subserving the cause of purity,
tend indirectly to liberalize"—the Canon stopped and hesitated for a moment, feeling that he had inadvertently slipped
into party politics; but putting a bold face on the matter,
he repeated the word emphatically—" to liberalize, I say,
in the best sense of the word, the whole course of legislation."
He proceeded to do this with a skill that was suitable to
the occasion. He drew a series of pictures, familiar to the

youngest person in the audience, which he said would be
recognized as types of the various kinds of men who had
figured in politics hitherto—men who affected care for the
welfare of the poor and suffering, but whose own lives were
a round of pleasures, of frivolity, and of intoxication; who
openly divided their time between dancing, sport, and the
card-table, or worse still, the blackguardism of the execrable
race-course. The Canon, in fact, indulged in a time-
honoured caricature of the ways and amusements of those
whose society was most sought by himself.

"And in order to secure, or in order to protect such
pleasures," he exclaimed, "these men are ready to depopulate
whole districts in Scotland, to tear the roof-tree from the
hovel of the wretched Connemara peasant, to prop up the
fraudulent cause of Capital in its war against Labour." At
these words there occurred a slight disturbance, and cries of
"No, no," were heard from several parts of the building.
The Canon saw that oratorically he had made a false step.
"The cause of Capital," he repeated, correcting himself,
"even when that cause is fraudulent; and to employ a body
of selfish and irresponsible legislators, to undo the work of
those who really represent the people." The expressions of
delight with which this last sentence was greeted, more than
atoned for the hostility which had manifested itself a moment
ago. "These then," continued the Canon, "are the men
whom our moral tests will exclude; and now having put
before you—I solemnly and sincerely trust without reference
to party — the political bearings of the movement, and
awakened in you—as I trust I have—a desire to support and
to assist it, let me do what will stimulate that desire still
further. Let me reinforce the agreements of the political
organizer with those of the Christian minister, and dwell on
the enormity of that special sin, in comparison with which
all other sin is venial, and against which our League is a
moral, far more than a political, protest."

The Canon was a born orator. Having roused the feelings of his hearers to what they had felt to be a climax, he
was now working them up to a yet higher pitch, the force
of his words being heightened by their obvious influence in
himself. All along he had spoken with a certain trenchant
energy; but hitherto it had been the energy of a partisan;
it was now that of the religious or moral revivalist. His

face flushed, his gestures became more marked, and the white
of his eyes occasionally was seen glittering above the pupils.
His audience, the women especially, began to lean forward,
eager to have their hatred of sin intensified by as clear a
description of it as the indiscretion of enthusiasm could
supply them with. Nor did the Canon disappoint them.
The solemn men with puffy and pasty faces, and their solid
wives, with boas and corkscrew curls, and square cameo
brooches glimmering under their treble chins, opened their
ears wide to the waters of the Canon's eloquence. Drops of
perspiration began to bead themselves on his forehead, as he
emphasized the vileness of man's physical nature, until it
was transfigured by the respectable magic of matrimony, and
as he adjured every husband to perform the feat of imagining
his partner's honour assaulted by some perfumed scoundrel.
This indeed was a singularly successful point; for though
the husbands may have found their imaginations hardly
equal to the demand thus made on them, the ladies found
little difficulty in imagining such a calamity happening to
themselves: and still less in imagining their lords exposed
to a corresponding peril. The Canon did his best to assist
the imagination of the most sluggish. Mrs. Blagdon, de-
voutly delighted, beat time with her silk boots, and the light
of ecstatic virtue oozed from her upturned eyes.

At last he began to work up to his peroration.

"False sentiment," he said, "masquerading as Christian
charity—charity, the extreme virtue which, being such, is
the most near to sin—false sentiment, I repeat, developed
and cultivated amongst the rich in the interests of the rich,
will endeavour again, as it ever has done in the past, to
make us think lightly, mercifully, even kindly, of this hideous
thing, immorality. It will even try to garnish it with the
fair colours of poetry. Horrible prostitution of that noble
and lovely art!" The Canon for the moment seemed to
have forgotten the kind of assembly he was addressing, and
impressed them all the more, by following his own thoughts
over their heads. "Launcelot and Guinivere," he exclaimed,
"and those blots on the Divine Comedy, the figures of Paolo
and Francesca, for which poets beseech our sympathy—
what is there under it all? I will tell you. There is nothing
under it but the feelings of pigs for pigs! There is nothing
at which the Christian stomach will not vomit! I do not

mince matters, and I dare not. Oh, my friends, this false
sentiment would even go so far as to plead with us that we
are all human, all liable to temptation, that we might ourselves at any moment be even as these are whom we are
invited to condemn. I tell you that this is not so—that
these insidious pleadings are sophistry. Would any one of
us here—God-fearing men and women—not resent it as an
insult were it to be said to him or her, 'To-morrow you may
be picking your neighbour's pocket; to-morrow, for all I
know, you may be shooting your neighbour in a fit of anger;
or in a fit of petulance taking your own life!' In the same
way we should resent the voice of that false humility which
may say to you, 'To-morrow you yourself may be guilty of
an immoral act.' If anything is voluntary it is this—it is
immoral conduct; it is this deliberate stepping out of the
clean and straight high-road into a seething and filthy ditch:
and when we presently ask you to pass the Resolution which
will be put to you, that immorality in our legislators shall
be no longer tolerated, and that you will join with us heart
and soul in refusing to cast your votes in favour of any man
who has not a clean moral record—I say, when we ask you
to pass this Resolution unanimously, let no false charity
unnerve you or make you hesitate. All that we shall be
really asking is that each one of you say in his heart, Whenever an immoral man shall solicit my parliamentary suffrage
I will do to him only what I would do for a like offence to
my own wife, to my own daughter, to my own son. So far
as in me lies, I will cast him off; I will cast him out!"

The Canon sat down amidst a noise of umbrellas that
beat the floor: and before this had subsided, Miss De Souza,
who had for some time been biting her lip with disgust, contempt, and indignation, felt her arm seized violently by Lord
Wargrave. His hat was already on his head, and looking
at her under his bushy eyebrows, he simply said, "Come,"
and bustled towards the door. The others followed him.
Their cabs were awaiting them in the street; and in ten
minutes more they were back again in Mrs. Steinberg's
dining-room, where their hostess, who welcomed their return
as if they had been gone for years, had provided a supper of
soup, cold chicken, and oysters.

"Well, dears," she said, when she had learnt, in answer
to her inquiries, that Mrs. Blagdon was still enjoying the

delights of purity on the platform, "and what was the Canon like? I do hope he said nothing very shocking."

"I feel," said Miss De Souza, "that if I heard many more speeches such as his, I should be ready to elope with the first man who asked me."

Mrs. Steinberg was an odd mixture of primness and worldly common sense. "How did it strike you?" she said, in an anxious voice to Lord Wargrave.

Lord Wargrave answered her with a placid and leisurely sententiousness. "So far as the people are concerned for whom the speech was meant, it was," he said, "the greatest success that can be imagined. It was admirable. The Puritan middle-classes never read French novels. They get all their literary immorality in these protests against it."

CHAPTER XXVI.

THE following day Lord Wargrave departed; but before doing so he extracted a renewed promise from Pole, to write to his mother on the subject of the house in Brook Street. As for Pole himself, he remained for a week longer at Thames Wickham, distracted by his pressing employments, and elated by the recognition he had met with, but still aching with the frost which had bitten below the surface of his consciousness. Every morning he had, to his own surprise, found that the hope of a letter with the signature of Pansy Masters, had sprung up in his heart, like a solitary and shivering snowdrop; and every morning on the arrival of the post, it had been killed. But hard work, together with Miss De Souza's companionship, had enabled him to get through the hours with a certain semblance of cheerfulness, inward as well as outward. At the end of the week, however, the work that had till now been absorbing him was accomplished; and left him face to face with his own blank unhappiness. His sense of having been abandoned and finally cut adrift by the woman to whom for so long he had given and been so much, did not indeed become sharper; but it sunk yet deeper into his mind, and pervaded it more completely; and it was against this darkening and extending background of loss that Countess Shimna's image gradually grew more glittering. Miss De Souza's charms would very often dissolve it, or make it dim; but whenever he was alone it would come shining back to him, growing brighter and brighter, as if by hidden witchcraft: and meanwhile he was growing conscious of a fact which at once surprised and pained him. He was growing shy of Miss De Souza's sympathy, and anxious to escape its influence. It touched too nearly, despite its healing qualities, that part of his heart which had been so torn and wounded. Countess Shimna's image on the contrary lured him far away from it.

All his thoughts accordingly were now turning towards Glenlynn; but unwilling to leave Mrs. Steinberg abruptly, the moment her hospitality ceased to be an obvious convenience to him, he did not for a day or two, say anything to her about his departure. At last one evening a small packet arrived for him, which he forebore to open till he was in his bedroom dressing for dinner. It contained, as was evident, a photograph; and in extracting this his hands trembled. At first sight of it, he drew a long and bitter sigh; then holding it to the candle he began studying it minutely. It was a photograph of Countess Shimna. He became breathless as he looked at it. The curves of her throat and figure, and the delicate moulding of her hands, the lines of her evening dress half hidden by a fur-trimmed opera-cloak, stirred his imagination by the perfection of their insolent daintiness; whilst her eyes, dim and velvety with some exquisite languor, gave to this flower of the world the bewildering scent of passion. The sound of her voice, as he looked, was again echoing in his ears; a moonlit memory of her lips fluttered and trembled upon his own; he heard the music of her barbaric Russian melodies. Presently the question occurred to him of who had sent the picture. Was it she herself or his mother? He examined the direction of the packet; most of it had been torn away, but as he handled the paper a note fell out of its folds. He opened it, and found these lines:—

"Dear Mr. Pole,

"*Tout passe, tout lasse, tout casse.* By now, no doubt, you have very nearly forgotten me. This, perhaps, will prevent the forgetfulness being quite complete. The photograph was done in Paris, and some copies have just reached me. I have often seen your mother, and I learnt your address from her.

"SHIMNA."

A breath came from the paper of the peculiar perfume which he associated with her. He had already written to his mother to say he would return presently. He now said, as he dressed himself, "I will go down to-morrow."

It was easy to excuse himself to Mrs. Steinberg for leaving her at so short a notice; but he decided, in order to seem as little abrupt as possible, to remain till the following evening, and to travel by the night mail. He would thus arrive at Lyncombe in the early morning; and it occurred to him that he could dress and breakfast there at an hotel, and, before driving out to Glenlynn, call at Countess Shimna's cottage.

The sun was brilliant in the east, though the dew had not yet begun to dry, when the train came sliding along the craggy and tortuous valley through which Lyncombe was reached—it seemed almost miraculously—by its railway. High on the slopes the shadows were clinging to the headlong woods; shining sheep were dotting precipitous pastures; whilst here and there, from the greenness, some limestone rock protruded itself. Then came houses rising among banks of foliage, and showing the quiet whiteness of windows not yet awakened; and then the train arrested itself at a long gravelled platform, beyond whose prim palings were one or two cabs and omnibuses.

To Pole fresh from the suburban atmosphere of Thames Wickham, there was something singularly invigorating in the impact of the free West-Country morning, amber with summer sunshine, and yet smarting with a breath from Autumn. He drove up the hill to the hotel where he meant to breakfast, surprised at the vigour with which his spirits rose. His bath in the hotel bedroom was delightful to him; and the hotel coffee-room with its mutton-chops and its clumsy toast, had something exciting in it, as though it were in some strange country.

Reflecting that he ought not to call on Countess Shimna too early, he lingered long over his meal and the local newspapers; and then sauntered slowly through the air, which was now warm, to her lodgings, timing himself so as to reach her door a little after eleven o'clock. "It can hardly be too early now," he thought as he rang the bell; and yet as he waited before the porch admiring the picturesque dwelling, he was conscious of a feeling that nearly resembled shyness. This feeling, however, gave place to another, when a pink-cheeked English maid-servant appeared presently in the doorway, and informed him with a stolid smile that the Countess had gone out already, and would not be back for luncheon.

"Was she driving?" asked Pole, sharply. "She has gone possibly to Glenlynn."

"I could not say," was the answer, "where the Countess has gone. She was on foot, and had her maid with her."

Pole reflected for a moment, and walked away rapidly. He ordered a fly, and despatched his luggage by it to Glenlynn, sending a message, by his servant, that he himself would walk. Countess Shimna, he thought, might perhaps be going out in the launch, which had, as he knew, been left at Lyncombe for her use. He descended the hill briskly. Lyncombe was still full; and here and there some moving figure with a parasol beguiled him for a moment into fancying it the woman he sought. But each, as he approached it, resolved itself into some ordinary holiday-making visitor; and at last he saw the launch lying idle and empty in the harbour. This second disappointment being completed, he set out for Glenlynn. Instead of going by the coach road, he chose another way, which, though somewhat longer, was in parts of it more beautiful, and gave him—so he persuaded himself—one more chance of overtaking her. It lay through a wooded valley, in the bottom of which was a rock-strewn river. About a mile and a half from Lyncombe this valley divided itself into three; and through each of these from the moor came a leaping and pouring stream. The spot where the three united was known as "The Meeting of the Waters;" and its nut-brown sleeping pools full of reflected woodland, and its lines of falling foam, which flickered under the sylvan twilight, formed the subject of countless photographs on sale in the Lyncombe shops. Pole, until his feet had brought him thus far on his journey, had been buoyed up by the thought that he might discover Countess Shimna here. But when he reached the Meeting of the

Waters, where the narrow path expanded itself, and offered a space for some rustic seats and summer-houses, everything was deserted. There was not a human being anywhere.

He stood still for a short time, meditating. He then resumed his walk, taking a path yet narrower, which ran up one of the glens, burrowing amongst trees and underwood. Not having succeeded in obtaining Countess Shimna's society, a sense, as he went, came pleasantly stealing over him of rest and ease in the ever-deepening solitude; and by-and-by he began to talk aloud to himself. "No doubt," he said, "my heart is shipwrecked; but it shall save its life as Ulysses did; and she shall make a home for it—the Calypso of a magic island." The scene around him at that moment, might have been in some such island itself, so far away did he feel himself from all human ears. The only sound was the fall of the rustling stream, or the faint lisp of the leafage as it played with the midday sunlight, and dappled with shadows the silken silver of the beech-stems, or the mouse-coloured ground that was under them, bare amongst slopes of vegetation. He had hardly uttered the words, swinging his stick as he did so, and picking his way amongst the rolling stones that were on the path, when, on turning a corner, he was startled by a flash of colour, red as poppy, and extending itself at the foot of a beech-tree. It was a scarlet cloak or shawl, and a female figure was reclining on it. By her side was lying a parasol with a gold handle; and a soft, dove-coloured hat was tipped over her dusky hair —hair which shone where crimping had given it an intermittent curve, and which caressed the nape of her neck with a little curling wave; whilst her insteps, arching like a ripple on the brook close by, were showing their outline through the bronze of the leather that was laced over them. She had been looking down at her lap, but the sound of Pole's tread roused her. She raised her eyes to his. From his lips came a single unpremeditated exclamation—"Shimna!"

Of how she answered him he had no very clear idea. It might have been by a word: it might have been by a mere cry: but these sounds interchanged between them had said more than either realized. Before she had time to rise, he was close to her, and their hands were joined. Her eyes were pools of purple, with a tremulous light laughing in them. In a few breathless sentences he explained to her that he had just arrived; he thanked her for her photograph; he told her he had been to call on her; and she in return imparted to him the striking and original information that walking was her favourite exercise. Then there was a lull in speaking. He stood before her in the shade, and looked down at her. She seemed to him like Rosalind, as Watteau would have conceived and painted her, had the Paris fashions of our day been the court fashions of his. This fanciful thought had hardly had time to shape itself, when something happened in her eyes. It was as though the buoyant lights there had been suddenly put out, and depths of melting darkness had as suddenly opened themselves before him. They were depths which, as he looked at them, seemed to expand and deepen.

Had he been told an hour ago that he would find himself in this situation, he would have been puzzled considerably to know in what way he would comport himself—above all, what words he would use, and the tone of voice which he would adopt. But once more the impulse of the unexpected moment solved his doubts before he had begun to be conscious of them. He presently uttered to her, hardly knowing that he spoke, one of the most ordinary, but at the same time one of the most intimate terms of endearment, which exists in the vocabulary of lovers. The sound was less like a word than a thought which had involuntarily become visible. As for her, her lips relaxed like a bud that is about to open. She extended her hand to him and murmured, "Come, and sit down here by me."

He slowly obeyed her, extending himself on the sloping ground at her side. But even as he did so, his thoughts took a rapid and sorrowful flight to another woman; and over his mind, lightly as a bird's shadow, there passed the memory of Virgil's undying line, which describes the lost Eurydice, but which Pole appropriated to himself: "*Invalidasque tibi tendens, heu non tua, palmas.*" The syllables, however, had hardly quitted his consciousness before he realized where he was; and a touch of Countess Shimna's hand recalled him to the actual moment. She had raised herself into a sitting attitude, and she now was looking down on him. He held her hand, and drew her gradually towards himself. As her jacket came nearer, he breathed again from her dress that subtle penetrating perfume, which seemed to have been distilled from the petals of a hundred passionate memories.

"Shimna," he exclaimed in a low, hurried whisper, "I have come back to you. Do you care to see me? But first I should tell you this. You may perhaps have guessed it. I do not come alone. I can never come alone to anybody. I have certain sorrows which I live with, and they have limped after me to your very feet"

His eyes were aware that she made some gentle but abrupt movement; but they were aware of nothing more. The next thing that spoke to him was the touch of her lips on his. The touch was as gentle as the touch of a leaf, swayed by a light wind; but there was no shyness in it.

"I will," she said, "ask you nothing about your sorrows. I like you the better for having them:—only now—now— forget them—forget them—forget them!"

She spoke like a mother bending over a suffering child; and with each repetition of the words, her lips once more brushed his. A few seconds later she was looking at him with an expression which was full of tenderness, but the quick light of *espieglerie* was again dancing in her eyes: and she said to him with a soft laugh, "Come now—let us talk about other things." She pressed his hand as she spoke, and gently withdrew hers from it. He could for a moment hardly believe his senses. What bewildered him most was not the consciousness of her kisses, but this almost magical change from a passionate to a laughing tenderness; and it delighted him even more than it bewildered him. She seemed, by some fairy art, possessed by no other woman, to have turned what poets describe as "the wine of passion," into a light elixir, which, instead of intoxicating the pulses, thrilled them with a new vitality; and to have removed the weight from love, without attenuating its strength. He had seen much of the world; but here was a new experience. The next moment, however, he had recovered his self-possession; and his mood was answering hers like an instrument in tune with another.

"What is the time?" she said presently. "It is nearly one o'clock. I have come out here to picnic. My maid has gone on in front of me. She has a basket full of sandwiches. There is plenty for all of us, and you and I will lunch

together. Take my shawl, and let us climb the hill. I
have," she continued, as they began to walk, "been here
once or twice before, and I have always had my feast farther
on in the sunshine. Clarisse knows the place. We shall
find her there waiting for us."

In five minutes' time, the path, through an arch of woodland, began to show them a vision of open country, with
shadeless sunlight brilliant on slanting heather; and there,
as Countess Shimna expected, close to where the trees ended,
was her maid seated on a heather tuft, with a stream
babbling close to her.

"Clarisse," said Countess Shimna, in clear little crisp
accents, that were at once caressing and imperious, "open
your basket and give Mr. Pole some *déjeuner*. He is walking
home, and will faint if we do not feed him."

With trained agility the maid obeyed her orders. The
contents of the basket were set out on a napkin; and then
she herself, receiving her own portion, retired to a distance
with a tact which suggested considerable experience. Pole
and Countess Shimna seated themselves on cushions of
purple bells, laughing like children as they undid the pack-
ages, and shared a single tumbler and a small bottle of claret,
tempering the last with water dipped up by him from the
stream.

At last Pole began. "I have so many things to say to
you." But she shook her head and interrupted him. "No,"
she said, "not now. Let us for the present be content with
the present moment."

He divined in her words a shrinking from anything like
serious speech. "What I want to say," he answered, with
a half-bantering laugh which reassured her, "is something
that must be said; it is so commonplace and practical. You
must come to us at Glenlynn. My mother wishes to have
you. You must come soon—do you hear?—soon, soon.
You will do that, won't you?"

"Perhaps," she said, "perhaps—if your mother really
wishes for me."

"Well," he replied, "I am not going to press you now.
But to-morrow or next day a letter from her will come for
you; and you must let me go with the belief that your
answer to that letter will be Yes."

"Good-bye," she said, as he rose to resume his walk;

and not committing herself to any distinct promise, she waved her hand to him as he went, and looked after him with laughing eyes.

CHAPTER XXVII.

He turned away from her with an unnatural summer in his heart. His progress home was marked by one outward incident only, and this took place not far from Glenlynn, at the spot where the path which he had been following joined the coach road. Here his ears were greeted by the sound of advancing wheels; and he presently saw a farmer's spring-cart rapidly coming towards him and carrying two persons. One of them, as they drew nearer, proved to be a country lad; but it was not till the cart was just about to pass him that he recognized the other as Dr. Clitheroe.

"Mr. Pole," exclaimed the Doctor, as the vehicle drew up abruptly, "I hadn't an idea that you had come back from London. I am glad—glad indeed, to have thus chanced to meet you. I have been suddenly called away—called by telegraph; and I have not had even time to say good-bye to your mother. I shall write of course; but pray thank her for me for all her kindness; and I, *vivâ voce*, thank you also for yours. Work, work, work," he said, pointing to two despatch-boxes. "With me, you see, it is always the old story." Pole saw that the cart was laden with other luggage as well. "Yes," continued the Doctor, answering Pole's glance, "I shall, I much fear, not be coming back again to Glenlynn. I must not delay a moment, or else I shall miss my train. Once more, good-bye. Now, Jemmy, drive on."

On reaching home Pole found a second luncheon awaiting him, for which his exhilarated spirits provided him with a good appetite. As his mother watched him eating, he told her of Dr. Clitheroe's departure—an event which surprised her considerably; and then of his meeting with Countess Shimna, though his account of this last was naturally not quite complete. These bits of news being disposed of, the two began at once discussing, first the question of

Lord Wargrave's house in London, and secondly, the question of their asking Countess Shimna to share it with them. The result was that a letter to Countess Shimna was sent in to Lyncombe the following morning by messenger, begging her forthwith to pay them another visit; and ending with the postscript, " There is a certain little plan which my son and I are very anxious to propose to you." A letter moreover was duly posted to Lord Wargrave, which contained, on Mrs. Pole's part, a definite acceptance of his proposal, and also said to him, " We will, if we can possibly manage it, bring our young lady with us, whom you are very right to admire. I have just written to ask her to come and stay with us to-morrow; and I shall lose no time in putting the plan before her."

Countess Shimna's answer came duly back by the messenger. She accepted the invitation with expressions of pleasure and gratitude, mentioning, however, that she could not arrive before dinner-time; and Pole accordingly, as on a former occesion, did not encounter her till he had dressed and had gone downstairs.

He had been wondering, not unnaturally, in what way she would receive him. Would she show any memory of what had passed between them under the glimmering beech-trees? And what should be his own demeanour supposing that hers were doubtful? But all these questions, so he found, were rendered unnecessary by the fact that, when he entered the drawing-room, her arm was round Mrs. Pole's waist, and the two were talking and laughing together like an aunt and a caressing niece. On seeing him she disengaged her arm, and advanced towards him with the frankest cordiality; and for all that her manner would have shown an observer to the contrary, she might have been merely a young lady in a ballroom welcoming a favourite partner.

His position he felt was strange. To what would his intimacy with her lead? The past and the future alike became incalculable. But his inability to speak to her in private left him more time to observe her; and the result of his observation was not a surprise only, but a shock to him. It began in the form of a mere vague consciousness that she disappointed him. At first he attributed this to the cordiality of her welcome, which might, by its frankness, have suggested

that it had nothing warmer to conceal; or else to her affection
for his mother, which might have suggested that to him she
was a sister.   But he soon saw that it was due to a very different cause.   She fascinated him still, not as a relation, but
as a woman.   She fascinated him as she had done under the
beech-trees; and even more now than then.   But she did
nothing beyond fascinating him.   Another woman, he reflected, bound to him by a tie which all churches condemn,
had touched the sources in him from which all their religion
springs.   And yet the more Countess Shimna suffered by
this comparison, the more were his eyes, by a perverse
attraction, drawn towards her; whilst his doubting thoughts
as he looked, became more and more distinct.   Her dress,
which clipped her waist, but fell from her back loosely, had
the delicate pink and the waxy gleam of a begonia; and as
she stood by the fire, slightly lifting her skirt, the pink was
fringed by a delicate foam of lace.   It was a dress which
she herself would have probably called a tea-gown; and as
such, no doubt it was theoretically suited to the occasion;
but whether owing to any quality of its own, or to the way
in which its wearer wore it, it struck Pole as somehow being
too perfect.   The little spray of diamonds which he saw
trembling in her hair, and the paste buckle which called
the eye to her instep, emphasized this effect.

"Don't," said Pole to his mother, when Countess Shimna
was occupying herself with Miss Drake, "don't let us trouble
her to-night with any mention of our London plans.   Let
us wait till to-morrow, when we can talk it over with her
quietly."

Mrs. Pole nodded.   "The subject," she said, "might as
well be broached by you.   I am longing that she should
come.   I tell you I'm quite in love with her."

And indeed at dinner, Pole, though his own impression
of her remained unchanged, could not wonder at the effect
which she produced upon his mother.   Her liking for the
elder woman—a woman so different from herself—was
evidently altogether genuine, and produced in her a wish
to please, almost as though she were bent on the conquest
of some man.   She told Mrs. Pole stories—one after the
other—of her past life in all kinds of places and societies—
of journeys in sleighs over the wintry snows of Poland—
of autumns on the Italian lakes—of summers at French

bathing-places; and each description she gave was shining with life and colour, and also had in it somehow the bloom of a brilliant innocence.

After dinner Mrs. Pole and Miss Drake, each by a little work-table, settled themselves down to knit before the warmth of the peat fire, whilst the lamplight glimmered on rows of old gilded books, made folds of shine and shadow amongst the faded roses on the curtains, and slept on the larger blossoms of the old Axminster carpet. At Mrs. Pole's request Countess Shimna played a little on the piano; then she tried a verse of one of those French songs in which passion, sadness, and levity play at hide-and-seek amongst the cadences; but she stopped, saying that this evening she was not in good voice: and finally she and Pole settled themselves to a game of chess. "I would," she said to him in a low tone as they arranged their pieces, "if we were by ourselves, sing to you something else—a song I have just learnt."

Thay played almost in silence, and were so leisurely over their operations, that their game was far from finished when the clock struck half-past ten, and the butler entered with his tray of tumblers and bedroom candles. This was Mrs. Pole's invariable signal for retiring. She and Miss Drake raised each the lid of her work-table and committed her knitting to its tomb in a pendant bag below. Then, seeing that the chess-players were still busy, and were, as far as appearance went, much absorbed in their occupation, Mrs. Pole stooped down, and kissing Countess Shimna's hair, said,

"Don't get up or disturb yourselves. You, Reginald, will ring to have the lamps put out when you have finished."

The two antagonists, as soon as they were left alone, began to regard the chess-board with more intentness than ever. They had, however, forgotten whose was the next move. A word or two settled the matter, and then they were completely silent. In a few minutes, despite the obvious fact that their eyes had never strayed from the kings and pawns and castles, they showed signs of a further forgetfulness, which was of a less usual character. They both seemed to have forgotten the elementary rules of the game. At last Countess Shimna moved a castle diagonally.

"You can't do that," exclaimed Pole, laughing.

She laughed also. They abandoned the pretence of playing. With a brusque movement she sprang up from her
chair; and, looking over her shoulder at him, said,

"I am going to sing to you. You must listen your best,
for I shall sing it very low. This is a silly little song. I
saw it yesterday in a music shop; and in the evening I
practised it. Its words, the shopman told me, were written
by a local genius, and came out first in a corner of the
Lyncombe paper. I bought it because it reminded me—
well—of the scenery between this and Lyncombe."

She dropped her eyes, and just touching the keys of the
piano, she sang softly into the following verses a significance
not their own :—

> "Spring is on land and sea, dear!
> If you would woo me still.
> Say how you'll live with me, dear,
> You may promise me all you will.
>
> "Spring is on heather and hill, dear!
> Joy is on gorse and steep!
> You may use my life as you will, dear,
> For you never will make me weep.
> Spring is on heather and hill.
>
> "Summer is warm above me.
> Think of our spring-time tryst.
> Oh, how will you prove you love me?
> You may do with me all you list.
> Summer is warm above.
>
> "Autumn comes with a sigh to me.
> What! Are you near me yet?
> Say, if you wish, 'Good-bye' to me.
> Only forget, forget!
> It is Autumn that sighs—not I.
>
> "Winter is come: and deep, my friend,
> Is its ice on my tears and blood.
> You never will make me weep, my friend;
> Ah, God, if you only could!"

When the song was ended, the singer, looked up at her
auditor with a laugh again in her eyes, and said, "Do you
recognize the *couleur locale ?*"

There was a low stool by the piano. He sank on it half
kneeling. She started as if she would have risen, but the
movement at once spent itself; and before either of them

had spoken or taken count of time, her lips had settled on his, and her eye-lashes slept content upon her cheek. At last, rousing herself, she murmured caressingly in his ear,

"The day will come when you will have to 'forget—forget,' even if I do not tell you to do so. But meanwhile—meanwhile—

'Use my life as you will, dear,
You never will make me weep.'

And now it is bed-time. Say, if you wish, good-bye to me! Indeed, you must say it, whether you wish or no."

She filled his dreams that night. She would not be driven out of them, no matter what qualities he might feel her to lack, or to possess; and the seal of sleep, when it touched him, touched him like Countess Shimna's lips.

The following morning he took her out for a walk. October was drawing near; but September to the last moment was keeping up a golden imitation of summer. They went by the wooded pathway that led to the home farm.

"Do you remember," he said, "what a storm there was on the day when we went here first?"

"That," she answered, "was the day when you got the telegram that told you—what? That you were going to be Prime Minister—wasn't it? Believe me it is much better to stay and be happy here. Look," she exclaimed, laughing; "how am I to cross this?"

A microscopic stream, obstructed by a dam of leaves, had made the ground swampy for a couple of yards in front of them; and in mimic embarrassment Countess Shimna halted. As a mere piece of colouring there was something in her that bewitched the senses, standing there amongst the glitterings of sylvan gold and green. Her dress was of blue serge; but her soft cap was scarlet, and was fixed to her hair by a long pearl-headed pin; her gloves were grey; and her boots were brown like an autumnal oak-leaf. These spots of colour to Pole were like so many notes of music, celebrating the exotic daintiness of this presence that was now alone with him, and joining with the whisper of the woodland to tell him she was all his own.

"See," he said, "by the bank is a ledge that is quite

dry; give me your hand, and I'll keep you from slipping. That's right—-so. Now get a little higher. Now give me both your hands, and you can jump down quite easily."

"No," she said, "that's just what I can't do, unless you stand farther off."

He did not move, however; but still holding her hands, he looked up at her, and said, "As soon as you do jump down, I want to ask you a very practical question."

His voice was only half serious; but it was changed from what it just now had been. At any rate, she seemed to detect in it some meaning from which she shrank; for shaking her head she said, "No, no—ask me nothing. Let us live for a little, and forget to question life."

"Don't," he retorted, laughing, "say 'No, no, no,' like that, before you are certain of the sort of question with which I am threatening you. I want to ask if you will come with my mother and me to London. My mother wishes it. I am asking you at her suggestion. There—the murder is out—the formidable question is asked; and now, if you are not the worse for it, jump down; and you and I will talk about it as we go along."

She seemed willing enough to listen, and he explained the whole plan to her. At last she said with a sigh, "You have conjured up before me such a pretty vision, and— Mr. Pole—if that is the name I am to call you by—such an unattainable one. Yes—unattainable. I wonder if I can tell you why. See, here is a bench. Let us sit down for a minute or two. I want to think how I can best explain my meaning."

She folded her hands on her lap, and for some time sat silent looking at them.

"What do you suppose," she said at last, "I have been thinking about all this while? About the things I won't tell you—not about the things I will. I could tell you that my coming to London is impossible on account of my health, or because I want sea air, or because I have presently to rejoin my mother in the South. I may have to say this to Mrs. Pole, but I won't say it to you. To you I will say frankly that I cannot come to London because, for special reasons, I am in no mood for the world. I want to avoid, not seek it. Look me in the eyes, and tell me—can you believe that?"

She raised her fringe of eye-lashes, so as to enable him to do her bidding.

"Of course," he answered, with a gaze full of interest and interrogation, "here in this quiet life amongst ourselves, I can form no judgment of you. But certainly the day when we went over to Dulverton, you seemed to take to society as if you had been born and bred for it."

"Oh," she said, "that was amusing; but it was over and done with in an hour or two. Besides one's old habits survive one's old feelings. Yes. I was born in society. It has been round me all my life. I came out at seventeen at a ball in the Winter Palace at St. Petersburg. I shrink from the world now because I have known the world so well."

"Most of us," said Pole, "have at times had the same shrinking. But if you met the world again—and the world under some new form—the feeling would pass at once. It is sure, indeed, to pass in time."

"Perhaps," she said. "So are most things. We shall all, if we live long enough, survive every feeling except regret. Ah, Mr. Pole—Mr. Reginald Pole—Reginald—I wonder very much if you have guessed one thing. Young as I am there is a certain story attaching to me. I am not like other girls. It is a story that I intend to tell you—but not to-day: you must let me wait till my visit is just ending. Meanwhile I will give your mother no definite answer. That will save discussion, and make our days pass more pleasantly. And meanwhile, too, let us both forget what I have been saying to you. Let both your secrets and mine be as though they had never been; and let these few days be a little happy island, in which all that we do or feel is cut off from the continent of consequences. Let me see how you take my proposition. You smile—your lips smile. Ah —and now ' Yes ' is in your eyes. You need not make any other answer. Come—we will walk on."

She rose from the seat, and, laughing, took his hand, and made him rise also. Her influence mixed itself with the freshness of the golden day, and impregnated with the spell of womanhood the leaf-scented air around him. For both of them the rest of the morning turned into a child's holiday; and they went back to luncheon taking with them children's appetites. Countess Shimna thanked Mrs. Pole for the invitation to London, telling her that in a day or two she

would know if she were able to accept it. "A good deal
depended," she said, "on whether or no her mother was
going, after all, to send her relation's little child to Lyncombe." But she certainly betrayed in neither her voice nor
manner, any trace of the quarrel with the world at which
she had so lately hinted.

"Well," said Mrs. Pole, " we have you in our possession
now ; and I hope that here, at all events, you will stay with
us as long as possible. Have you ever, Reginald, asked her
if she cares for riding ? "

"Indeed I do," she exclaimed, " for riding in an open
country ! Ah, Poland is the place for riding. I have ridden
there sometimes all day."

Mrs. Pole's suggestion opened for them a new excitement. "This afternoon," said Pole, " we will try our own
open moor."

A message was sent without delay to the stables ; and in
a short half-hour the equestrians, mounted on Exmoor ponies,
were slowly ascending from Glenlynn to the wild world
above. At last they reached the summit, and the moorland
rolled before them, a purple wilderness, out to the long
horizon, with streaks of elastic turf stretching away from
them amongst the heather.

"Now," said Pole, "for a gallop ! " And off they both
started.

" Ah," she exclaimed, as they paused at the brink of a
hidden valley, "that was pure delight. A moment more
and I shall have wings and fly."

" Down the hill ! " cried Pole. And they dipped into a
wild valley, which looked as if no one had entered it since
the creation of the world. It was littered with rocks, and
along it a stream came floating in lazy pools which were
linked by purring or prattling rapids. The voice of the
water alone disturbed the silence ; and the two adventurers
felt themselves pressed together by the intense solitude.
"At the head of this valley," said Pole, " there once was a
robber's strong-hold. We shall not be able to get there this
afternoon. In a mile or two we shall come to a sheep-track.
We shall have to ride back by that." They found the track.
It led them to the high ground again. The turf was good
for trotting, and now and then for a gallop ; and round them
the scented wilderness sank and swelled and sank. Suddenly

Countess Shimna checked herself, and broke into an exclamation. Below was a straggling village, with fields and some trees round it; and almost under her was a large dilapidated church. "It was there," said Pole, "that you and I first met; and Tristram Pole and his passions are lying there, under the pews and hassocks."

"Do you think so?" she said. "I fancy they may be still alive. There are more things than we suspect, which people when they die do not carry away with them."

They then descended to the village, and so trotted briskly home, following the road that had been taken by Miss Pole's funeral.

Glenlynn, when they reached it, seemed to be warm with welcome.

"I never realized till to-day," said Countess Shimna to Mrs. Pole, "what a lovely place this is. How delightful it is to be safe, and shut away from everything! Dear Mrs. Pole, this is far better than London."

"I," said Mrs. Pole, smiling, "certainly myself think so."

Countess Shimna and Pole that evening, true to the spirit of the compact made by them during their morning walk, avoided chess, as a game which might repeat their last night's experience, and jeopardize their present happiness, by leading them to face the cause of it. They therefore insisted on Mrs. Pole and Miss Drake joining them in a rubber of whist; and the time passed by with a sparkle of quiet entertainment, till the butler appeared as usual with his tray, his bottles, and his tumblers.

The drama of the day, however, was not yet entirely ended. The three ladies, having each sipped a little water, had said good night to Pole, leaving him alone behind them, when the door opened, and the Countess Shimna re-appeared.

"I have come," she said, "for my fan and my handkerchief. They must both of them be here somewhere."

"I am glad you forgot them," said Pole. "I will help you to find them presently. But I want first to say something which, I am sure, you will not object to. Come here by the fire. It will take a minute or two to say. Listen now—I have had a most delightful day with you: and I hope you observe how judiciously I choose my phrases. I hope for many like it: but in one way they must be a little different. I have work to do—work which I must attend to: so don't quite forget me if, for some hours each day, I shut myself up in my room, or am out with builders or with bailiffs. I pay you the compliment of thinking that you don't want to make a fool of me; and you would be making me a fool if you made me forget my duties."

"I quite understand," she said. "I like a man with a strong character."

"I think," he said, "you understand most things, and now listen to this. On looking over my letters I find that I shall, most probably, have to go away ten days hence, to see about my parliamentary election."

"And I," she replied, "may have to go even sooner."

"Well," he said, "let us not number our days. But whatever their number be, I want to tell you this—that you have made me happy already, and I am not going to ask why. Make the others equally happy, and I will still not ask—not till the days end. Shall I show you a proof of how sincere I am in saying this? I should like at this moment, Countess Shimna, to take you in my arms and kiss you. But I won't. I don't. I stand here decently by the chimney-piece."

"Hush—hush!" she said. "You must not speak like that. And yet I forgive you; for you make me say something that I want to say. You must not touch my lips again, till I go away—till this holiday is over—till I tell you everything. But I will not forbid you to remember that twice I have been less distant with you. Till I go, however, we are to live together like good comrades, who have a memory, if you like, which they never speak about, of something more than *camaraderie.*" She opened her fan, pressed it against her face, and looking at him with laughing eyes over its coloured and glittering arc, she held her hand out to him, and said, "Now, *mon ami,* good night."

CHAPTER XIII.

POLE was as good as his word with regard to his own work. Whatever might be the effect on him of one woman's neglect, and the unanalyzed compensation he was receiving from the companionship and caresses of another, he did not suffer himself to be distracted from the duties which he had set himself to perform. His coming career as a politician entailed on him both study and correspondence; but his buildings, the walls of which had now risen above the ground, and the mass of local information which he had from the first determined to collect, at the present moment absorbed him even more than politics. Nor did this preoccupation with matters so entirely unconnected with herself do him any harm in the eyes of Countess Shimna, or in any way interfere with the pleasure and the development of their friendship. On the contrary, it increased both. She did, indeed, as she had told him, respect strength of character, much as many women respect the strength that is merely physical: whilst as for him, an experience which he had frequently undergone in London, now repeated itself, only in a more delicate form. The natural self-approval produced in him by assiduous work, by the letters of applause and encouragement which he received from his official correspondents, by Mr. Godolphin's admiration of what he was doing on the Glenlynn estate, and the gratitude of several families whom he had already helped successfully—the self-approval produced in him by these causes operated once more, as a kind of absolution in advance, for any possible development in his relationship with his beautiful companion, which otherwise he might have been tempted to condemn.

"I have known," he said to himself, "what the love is which is religion. Let me play a little now with another love, which is its half-sister, and which comes to me here disguised as friendship, and looks at me laughing through a black velvet mask."

But as the days went on, the aspect of things changed. More and more he came to realize how in Countess Shimna were all sorts of attractions, which were not only fascinating but endearing; and her powers of thought, her taste, and the extent of her reading, which had, on his first acquaintance with her, so much struck and surprised him, began to form between them a genuine intellectual link. Whenever she was not with him she passed her hours in the library, except when Mrs. Pole accepted of her assistance in the character of secretary. She renewed her acquaintance with Byron; she learnt many of Shelley's songs by heart; with remarkable quickness of comprehension she glanced through

some books on science, and dipped into the pages of endless
old French Memoirs. Between her and Pole, therefore, there
was no lack of subjects for conversation; and they were
never tempted, by any awkward or *banal* silence, to have
recourse to the crudities of direct love-making. But a spirit
of *coquetterie*, or perhaps something even more serious, lurked
amongst her words and manner, flashing through them like
quicksilver.

They continued their rides; and he saw her, in a certain
limited fashion, begin to show some interest in his study of
the neighbouring poor. Lonely though the country was,
their way would often take them through one or other of the
primitive and scattered villages. These, by this time, were
all well known to Pole, who had studied the plans of each on
his six-inch ordnance map, and had made elaborate notes as
to the condition of the inhabitants of the cottages. Such
being the case, he would now frequently stop at one door or
another, either to make some fresh inquiry, or proffer some
kind assistance; and Countess Shimna, who would wait for
him with a good temper that was inexhaustible, naturally
elicited accounts of what he was either doing or hoping to
do. Every time that he issued from some rude cottage
kitchen, with its atmosphere of faint peat smoke, through
which dressers and mugs glimmered, the sight of his companion sent a fresh thrill through his imagination, as he
found her outside, displaying to the ragged village street a
habit and figure which invariably made him feel as if some
magician had deposited her there, fresh from the Bois in
Paris. And the brilliant eyes of this vision would smile at
him, a faint, foreign perfume would steal through the air to
him from her handkerchief; and he and she would gallop
home together between the vast horizons, which seemed as if
they held within their circle no other human beings.

Of his own interests, however, those connected with his
social and philanthropic schemes were the ones in which she
seemed least able to share. She could understand the idea
of helping some individual sufferer; but the need or the
possibility of any organized beneficence towards the poor, she
understood very dimly. For her the world was divided into
serfs and nobles; a Nihilist was a noble disregarded, not a
peasant oppressed. The lot of the people, for her, was like
the surface of the Steppes of Russia—equally natural and

unchanging. This was no symptom of any hardness of heart in her. On the contrary, the gardeners at Glenlynn, and the old women who weeded the walks, had never in their lives seen any one as captivating as Countess Shimna. By the old women especially she would stand and talk, questioning them about their work, their age, their ailments, their clothes, their food, and their husbands; sometimes taking their spades from them and doing a little work herself; and giving them, when she went away, a pat on their bent backs, as though they had been domestic animals who attracted her, and with whom she loved to play. One morning, indeed, she surprised Pole and his mother by producing a number of boxes, come by the parcels post, with yards of ribbon in them as presents for the old women, and an assortment of brilliant neckties for the delectation of the male gardeners.

The same goodness of disposition which showed itself in this little act, showed itself also in her appreciation—instinctive and almost unconscious—of goodness and of sincerity in others; and this, as Pole realized, was all the more remarkable, because her sense of the ridiculous was acute to an extreme degree. To some men nothing in a woman, to whom they are attracted otherwise, does more to enhance her charm than a sense of the ridiculous such as this, especially when free, as in Countess Shimna's case, of any personal maliciousness; and never had Pole felt her personality more delightful than he did when one evening, towards the end of her visit, the dinner-table at Glenlynn was enlivened by the presence of three guests—Mr. and Mrs. Godolphin, and their son, who had just done with Harrow.

Countess Shimna had seen them before for a few moments; but never before had she had so clear an opportunity of watching them. At every little oddity in their manner her eyes brimmed with amusement; but an amusement that to them had the happy aspect of appreciation. For Mr. Godolphin indeed she evinced an instinctive sympathy which delighted him to such a degree, that his manner, generally so majestic, assumed at moments the graces of a chaste flirtation; while as for the boy, with his cheeks embrowned by the cricket-field, he fell so deeply in love with her, that he begged, in a broken whisper, for the head of a rose which fell on the carpet from her dress, and

committed it with an adoring glance to some recess between
his heart and waistcoat.

"I hope, Countess," said Mr. Godolphin at parting, "that
you will honour us one day by coming over to luncheon, and
seeing the interior of a quiet English parsonage."

"Mrs. Pole," cried his wife, who, voluble though she
naturally was, was too shy to address the brilliant stranger
directly, "do, I beg of you, bring the Countess over, if she
won't think our house too humble a place to come to."

Countess Shimna blushed scarlet. "Dear Mrs. Pole,"
she exclaimed, as if to bury this last speech, "do let us go.
I have always been told, Mrs. Godolphin, that many of the
English clergy, with their gardens and fields and houses, are
far greater people than many continental bishops."

Mrs. Godolphin's face rippled into a web of smiles; and
her husband, stroking his beard, and laughing with a deprecating complacency, said: "I'm afraid, Countess, you'll find,
when you come to see us, that I'm a very humble minister
of the Catholic Church in England. Mrs. Pole," he continued, "no time like the present. Suppose you bring the
Countess the day after to-morrow."

This was arranged; and far into the silent night Mrs.
Godolphin arrested her lord's incipient slumbers with broken
conversation about the forthcoming banquet, which she
wished, as she expressed it, to make "nice and French for
the Countess." It is probable indeed that she would not
have slept till morning, if Mr. Godolphin had not suddenly
remembered an album containing mementoes of a tour taken
by them on the Continent; and in this volume, he reminded
her, were the menus of some hotel *déjeuners*.

"Dear Sunderland," cried his wife across the bed-clothes,
"capital. We shall not want soup. We will have French
names on the cards."

The meal, when the time came, was a delight and pride
to the hostess. It actually suggested to more persons than
one the fare of a Rhine steamer, or a large *table-d'hôte* in
Switzerland; and the finishing touch was put to it by Mr.
Godolphin, who, when coffee came, leaned towards his
foreign guest and asked her, with a playful obsequiousness, if
she would "have a *chasse*." When she said that she would, in
the quietest way imaginable, he was a little taken aback, as
the brandy was locked up in the cupboard. But he felt

that, though he had failed in a witticism, he had succeeded as a man of the world; and having produced the bottle, he administered a homœopathic dose to her.

As they were passing out of the room, his wife, who had watched this transaction, said to him in admiring whisper, " Dear Sunderland, I believe you know everything."

" Eh, mother," laughed Mr. Godolphin softly. " You do, do you ?" And he chucked her gently under the chin.

This little conjugal idyll was observed and appreciated by Countess Shimna. It increased the good will with which she regarded her host and hostess; and when the son, in the drawing-room brought her a rose to replace her own, she flushed the boy with happiness by asking him to pin it into her jacket. Then presently began the great process of sight-seeing, which included the best bedrooms, the stables, and some fine Alderney cows, and ended with Mr. Godolphin's pushing his church door open, and admitting Countess Shimna to a sight of his blue and crimson organ, his lace-trimmed altar, and his row of altar candlesticks.

" Do you know," she exclaimed, " it is almost like one of our own churches ! "

No human words could have pleased Mr. Godolphin better. He swelled as though a cubit had been added to his patriarchal stature; and, smiling down on this daughter of the Roman fold, he said to her, "The Protestants of England have given up burning their Catholic brethren; but there are many of them in this country who, if they only had their way, would be too delighted to tie me to a stake in Lyncombe." He had at first regretted that Countess Shimna was not, like himself, an Anglican; but the wish died a natural death: for, if she had been, he never could have received from her so weighty and so gratifying a compliment. To all concerned the day was a great success, and the memories which the Glenlynn party took away with them were as pleasant, though hardly the same, as those which they left behind.

When they reached home, however, a certain incident occurred which somewhat disturbed for Pole the tenor of these enchanted days. Having handed Countess Shimna a letter for her which was lying on the hall table, he found two for himself. One of these was from the Conservative agent at Windsor; the upshot of it being that he would

have to leave Glenlynn somewhat earlier than he had anticipated. This piece of news annoyed him; still he bore it
with resignation. But what moved him far more was the
other letter, though it contained no news at all, except such
as was connected with what seemed a very commonplace
question. "I have heard nothing from you for so long," the
letter ran, "that I feel quite shy of writing to you; but
perhaps you will be kind, and tell me, or find out for me,
what is the line of steamers to which *The Arctic* belongs. It
belongs to a new service, between America and Milford
Haven, which begins running some time in November. If
it is not too much trouble to you, will you write and tell
Pansy Masters."

On seeing the writing he had taken the letter into his
bedroom; and as he was opening the envelope his heart had
palpitated painfully. But when he had done reading it, he
threw himself into a chair, and with his hand pressed against
his eyes, he remained there almost motionless in a long
reverie of disappointment, which had hardly in it any distinct
thought. It was nothing indeed but a desolate and almost
drowsy pain: and when his servant entered to arrange his
things for dinner, he felt he had been roused from some
dream, the memory of which was clinging to him like a
chill.

Countess Shimna on the contrary at dinner seemed more
animated than usual; and by-and-by succeeded in restoring
him to his previous spirits. Any one, however, who had set
himself to watch her carefully, would have noticed occasional
signs in her of some abstraction of mind, due to some hidden
happiness, the source of which was elsewhere. Mrs. Pole
and Miss Drake in the evening were both too tired for cards;
and it thus came about that Pole and Countess Shimna were
once more left to a tête-à-tête at the chess-board.

Pole till now had not observed the change in her; but he
presently saw her to be playing in such a reckless way that
he began to suspect her of being either bored or preoccupied.
"Perhaps," he said presently, "you would sooner not go on.
Do you see the position in which you have put your queen?"

His words appeared to rouse her. She glanced furtively
at the clock; and answered him: "No, no, I want to go on
particularly. How stupid I was! Do let me have that back
again." She now made her moves with what seemed to be

extreme deliberation, and although her play showed few signs of improvement, she postponed her defeat till nearly half-past ten. "Now," she exclaimed with a vivacity which surprised her opponent, "one game more. Let me see if I can't beat you."

Pole assented, and a second game began. It had not proceeded far before the butler and the tray entered; and Mrs. Pole and Miss Drake rose with their accustomed regularity. "Ah," said Mrs. Pole to the players, "I see you have not done."

Countess Shimna laughed. "No," she replied; "this is a second game. Dear Mrs. Pole, don't let me keep you up. I am having my revenge. You must allow me to finish it."

"It is your move," said Pole, when the two elders had departed.

She laid her hand for a moment on one of the ivory pieces; but then, instead of playing, she sat back in her chair. "I wanted," she said, "to speak to you. I can do so now. I am a little cold. Let us go over to the fire."

They did as she suggested, and stood on the hearthrug facing each other. The letter received by him before dinner, had left a chill in his heart, which persisted like a physical chill through whatever warmth had followed it. It was a chill he dared not think of: and yet he shivered from it at this very moment. Would nothing, he asked himself, drive it out of his system; and send through all his thoughts the pulses of sanguine life? And there before him stood the answer, with every charm of fancy and flesh and spirit. She stood there close to him—already half his own. He looked down at the hearth, upon which the peat lay smouldering.

"Let me make a blaze," he said. "I am feeling cold also. Do you see that soft, grey ash which lies over the whole fire? If you touch it, you would find it as soft and as warm as bird's down; but its heat comes only from the fire under it, which it hides. Now look!" and with a few thrusts of the poker he loosed the leaping flames; and all the room grew rosy. "For the last ten days," he said, looking at her, "our life together has been like that downy ash. Stir it; and I can tell you, for my own part, that you will set free the fire again. Perhaps we have, both of us, let the ash accumulate over it, because we thought the fire a dangerous thing to play with."

She looked at him with expanding eyes, in which changing gleams floated; and as she looked, her lips slowly parted, the lamplight shining upon their coral. "And is it dangerous?" she said. "I am not afraid of it. Do you think I am?"

They moved towards each other softly, like two shadows. She put her hands upon his shoulders, and for a moment hung her head. She then lifted her face to him; but as she had done once before, she held his away from her, by pressing her fan against his cheek. Pole was one of the men who, in abandoning themselves to situations like the present, are compelled by their nature to consecrate the passionate impulse, by committing to its current the treasures of their mind and heart; and he suddenly found himself offering to this form that clung to him, a tenderness and a mental admiration, which surprised him by their depth and seriousness. Her kindness, her good temper, her wit, her moments of thoughtful melancholy, the poetry she had loved and quoted, all came thronging together into his mind and memory; and when at last he felt the pressure of her fan relax, and the chalice of her lips offered itself to him undefended, he felt that he had kissed some dream, or some verse of Shelley's.

At last she forced herself away from him, so far as to allow herself to speak. "Do you remember," she said, "one thing which I told you—that you were not to kiss me again till the time had come for me to be going? Well, I must go to-morrow. It was this that I wished to say."

"Go!" he exclaimed. "But why? I must go soon myself. Cannot you wait till then? And meanwhile, how much I should have to say to you!"

She shifted her position a little, and leaned her head against his shoulder, beginning to play meanwhile with one of his coat-buttons. Her self-abandonment had all the grace of self-possession. In every movement there was a certain dainty dignity—even in her hand, as it busied itself with its present babyish occupation.

"I cannot wait," she said, "and I can listen to nothing more from you. You ask me why I must go. I shall tell you before long. The immediate reason is that the little child-relation which I mentioned, comes to Lyncombe to-morrow; and I have promised my mother to do my best for it. That is enough to account for my abrupt departure to your mother. But to you by-and-by I shall have something very different to say. Come and see me at Lyncombe, the day after to-morrow; and I will say it then. Do you remember some time ago I spoke to you of a coming happiness, announced to me in a letter which I received? Well —that happiness is very near me now—a kind of happiness that you never would have imagined was in my reach. Why do you start away from me, as if I had shocked you, or as if you doubted me? Did not I tell you before that this is no happiness you need be jealous of? When you know what it is, you will understand many things. It may," she said, looking up at him, "take me far away soon; but it has not taken me even away from this hearthrug yet." He felt, as she spoke, her hold on his arms tighten. "Forget to-morrow," she said. "Hold me a little whilst you can!"

For a few seconds they remained like figures fashioned out of wax. Then Pole was aware that her arm was round his neck once more; and the flower of her face was his, in all its unfolded petals.

When next she spoke she was standing a pace away from him. She was perfectly self-possessed—mistress, as usual, of her own grace and beauty. "You will, perhaps," she said, "like me the worse for this; but not for the happiness that will come between this and us. For that you will like me better."

CHAPTER XXIX.

SHE went, as she had said. He offered to drive into Lyncombe with her; but for some reason or other she begged him not to do so. She left him restless with a fever so strange to him that he hardly knew himself; and he found himself, for a wonder, incapable of any kind of work. One letter he wrote, indeed, the address of which was "Lady Pryce-Masters;" but it was no longer than hers had been. He promised to get her the information, which she required, about the steamer; and he added, "As you say, it was indeed long since I had heard from you." But that was all. "I suppose," he said to himself, "she is interested in this steamer because her husband intends returning in it." Then, with a certain impatience, he thrust the subject out of his head; and he shrank from walking in the garden, or on any of the cliff-side paths, lest, in looking at the sea, he should feel the thought assaulting him, that somewhere behind the sea-line was this woman to whom he now was nothing. He chose instead some of the wooded slopes, where he and Countess Shimna had many a time scrambled, where her dainty syllables seemed to have left crystal echoes, and where the perfume of her presence mixed itself with that of the whispering pines.

At length the moment came, after luncheon the following day, when he might, without undue precipitation, set out for Lyncombe to rejoin her. The hour she had mentioned was five o'clock; and he thought with some impatience of how short would be the utmost time which, since he must return for dinner, would be thus allowed for their interview. He accordingly reached her door, punctually as the hour was striking; and rang the bell with a vigour which ought to have informed the household that he was resolved not to lose a moment in unnecessary waiting there on the gravel.

A foreign-looking elderly woman soon made her appearance, who seemed to understand neither English, French, nor German; though she evidently recognized Pole as an expected visitor; for she took him across a little lobby, decorated with shells and coral, and, without announcing his name, admitted him to a small drawing-room. He looked about him eagerly; but he saw that the room was empty; and so, to beguile the time, he began indolently to examine it. The cottage was comparatively old—one of the earliest of the houses that made Lyncombe more than a fishing-village. The drawing-room opened on a verandah, thatched, and hung with creepers; and the furniture, though worn with use, was better than what is usual in lodging-houses; and indeed it had about it a suggestion of bygone honeymoons. But what principally interested Pole, were the various exotic objects, with which it had now been filled, obviously by its present occupant. On some of the chairs were pieces of embroidered oriental silk; on a chipped rosewood table was a smart russia leather writing-case, and a little glittering litter of smelling-bottles, and silver ornaments. There were a number of books, some of them bound

beautifully in morocco of pale shades, and ornamented with
gilt monograms; others were in vellum, which lit up the
whole room; whilst here and there, glittering with satin
and tinsel, were boxes of Parisian bon-bons; and pots of
flowers were standing in some baskets of gilded wicker-
work, which at some Parisian Easter must have originally
been *bonbonnières* also. Countess Shimna's family, it was
evident, took such care of her that even in a lodging they
surrounded her with the breath of luxury. The room,
thought Pole, suggested the occupancy of one who had rarely
lived between walls not gilded or hung with silk. A hand-
mirror, in silver, was on one of the small tables; and lying
beside it was a copy of Dante's " Purgatorio."

For some time his examination of these details interested
him; but her continued absence gradually made him impatient; and finally, when a carriage clock musically chimed
the quarter, he began to doubt whether the servant could
have informed her mistress of his arrival. He went to the
window, which was open; he stepped out into the verandah;
he looked about him, pretending to himself to be interested
in the view; then he returned to the room, anxious, perplexed, and restless. At last he heard voices. He had been
sitting, and he sprang up at the sound, straining his ears to
distinguish where they came from. Whilst thus engrossed,
he was startled by Countess Shimna's voice quite close to
him. She had entered the room through a pair of dim chintz
curtains, which he now saw gave admission to some other
room beyond. She was dressed in blue, with a dainty little
sailor's hat. Her eyes were shining, her cheeks were like
flushed porcelain.

"Ah," she said, " have I kept you? Will you forgive
me? I could not help it. You will see in a minute or two
what I mean by that. And now listen," she went on, coming
closer to him, and holding him by his coat as she spoke, " I
believe that in some men's eyes, mystery gives charm to a
woman's character, just as powder very possibly in their
eyes gives charm to a woman's complexion. What I am
going to do now is to brush my powder off. Wait here one
minute more, and come to me through these curtains, when
I call to you."

She disappeared as she had come; and Pole again heard
voices, both of them hushed and gentle; and then he heard

a closing door. "Will you come?" said Countess Shimna's voice to him; and he penetrated to the room within. At first he saw nothing as the result of all this mystery, except the fact that she had the child, of which she had spoken, in her arms: and his only wonder was that she knew so well how to hold it. But a moment later he was enlightened. Bending down over the little sleeping face, she laid her lips on it with the low inarticulate murmur, which is produced by the passion of one sole relationship. A nerve in Pole's memory thrilled and vibrated at the sound. He looked at her without uttering a word. It seemed to him that they were silent both of them, for an indefinite time. In reality not many seconds elapsed before she found her voice.

"I see," she said, "that my secret surprises you; but I see in your face that you have divined it. I felt when I first met you—though the feeling then was vague—that you knew the deep things of life. Yes—here is my happiness—here is my secret in my arms. I sometimes feel that I shall never enjoy anything else. This little thing—this wonderful little thing—is my own. She is called Thyrza."

Pole was silent, not knowing what to say. "Well," she resumed, "the next question is, What do you think of me? Shut that door. Thank you. Now, sit down there." And she, as she spoke, reseated herself. "I will give you, in very few words, the means of forming a judgment."

Her face had become quite calm, and there was in it, as she now looked at him, a return of that soft brilliance which had so often provoked his admiration.

"My story is this," she said, speaking in a quiet, level voice. "Less than two years ago I was married. Four months before the birth of this little creature, it was dis-covered that my husband had another wife alive. Some time or other I can tell you more particulars; but these bare facts will show you my situation. I ought to add that it has this redeeming feature—It has dissolved a marriage which I shudder even now to remember, and which would have made my life even a greater ruin than it is. Don't speak yet. I have a few things more to say. My little child is not sup-posed to be mine. My mother, who is a clever woman, managed everything wonderfully. It is supposed to be the child of a cousin of ours who died; and my mother gives out that she herself has undertaken the charge of it from

kindness. It was her arrangement that it should be brought
here, so that I might have it for a time without exciting
observation. That is the reason of our coming to Lyncombe,
and of my being left here. I should add, that the man I was
married to, believed his wife to be dead. She was in hiding
for political reasons; but her story is neither here nor there.
And," she went on, hesitating, "there is another particular
I must mention. My husband was summoned to St. Petersburg the day after we were married. My mother's story is
that he had to leave me at the church door. She is accustomed to thank Heaven for this fortunate circumstance, and
most of the people who think anything about the subject
believe her. The marriage has been annulled. I don't feel
somehow that that makes much difference. Well—what do
you think of me?"

Pole could not speak. He did all that he could do. He
came to her side, kneeled down by her, and raising her hand,
kissed it. The grave respect of the action said more than
any protestations; and the young mother thanked him by
the expression of her face as she turned to him; but far
more by the quietness with which, he remaining close to
her, she continued to watch her child.

In her downcast eyes light hung like dewdrops. "Look
at it!" she said, "just look! Isn't it beautiful? Isn't it
wonderful? Bone of my bone—flesh of my own flesh!"
and she gently caressed the wax of its sleeping cheeks.

For a moment or two longer Pole watched by her in
silence; and then leaning nearer to her, he said, whispering
in her ear, "I like you better now than ever I did before—
far, far better."

The slight movement he had made woke the child, who
uttered a small cry.

"See," said its mother to Pole half sadly, half playfully,
"you have summoned her back to sorrow. Open the door,
and call upstairs for Anna, will you? Anna is one of the
nurses. She must take my baby now."

An old woman presently entered the room, who received
the child, smiling over it with withered lips.

"Take it, it's a good little thing," said Countess Shimna
to her, with a kindly carelessness. "It has hardly cried at
all. I have fallen in love with it already. Do you see?"
she went on, when she and Pole were alone together, "I

must not seem too fond even of my own baby. Perhaps,"
she continued, "you understand now why I have no heart
for London, and why I—— " she stopped, as though it were
vain to finish the sentence.

With an abrupt gentleness Pole took her by the arm.
"Come," he said, "sit down again. You have talked to
me thus far. Now let me talk to you. Bear with me a
moment. I want to collect my words."

During the last ten minutes a change had come over him
with regard to her. Through her extraordinarily attractive
qualities he had, during her visit at Glenlyn, been seeing
day by day lovable qualities show themselves : but till now
there had been a something wanting — some depth and
sanctity of nature, which he had known in another woman,
but till now he had missed in her. At last, so he said to
himself, he had found it in her—she possessed this also. He
was persuaded indeed that one woman had deceived the
faith he had put in her: but this experience, far from rendering
him cynical, had only made him the more anxious to believe :
and his heart now opened itself to Countess Shimna with a
trust that was at least generous.

"You could not," he began presently, "have found in
the whole world a better person than myself, to whom you
might tell your secret. I don't say this as a compliment to
my own trustworthiness, or as a means of making love to
you. If I want to make love to you, my friend, I can do so
in other ways. What I mean to tell you is, that I have a
secret too. When I saw that little bundle of white clothes
lying between your breast and arms, I knew that to you it
was the wonder of all wonders—the unimaginable mystery
of existence, still shining into your eyes with newness—
because I have seen such a burden in the arms of another
woman, and both our lives were mixed in it. It is far away
from me now. Its mother—his mother—is tired of me.
That little life I speak of—he lives in an old castle, and
plays in an untidy garden. I think about him so often,
and wonder what he is doing. I wonder all sorts of little
things about him—things too silly to tell you :—and nobody
tells me anything. Listen now !— You can never be a
mother to my first-born. Will you let me be a father to
yours ? "

"Hush ! " she exclaimed, " oh, hush ! hush ! hush ! Please

do not talk like that! I can never, never listen to it. I had a husband once—a husband for eighteen hours. He was seven feet high—a General. People said that he had the bearing of a hero. I have seen his face like a lantern, with the monstrous appetites of an animal in it. Oh," she said, shuddering, "cannot we sing and play among the flowers and in the sunshine as we have done? Must all that be over?"

She rose, and stood before Pole, with a glimmer of returning gaiety; and lightly stroked his cheek, as a little marquise in powder might have stroked on a painted screen the cheek of a kneeling shepherd. Men are composite creatures. Without his relinquishing one of his serious thoughts about her, Pole's temperament and manner responded to her change of mood.

"You forbid me a certain subject," he said. "Very well then—I will not talk of it. But I give you warning, I am not going to forget it. I shall lock it up in a jewel-case, with a lining of soft velvet; and one day or other, with your leave, I shall take it out again. Countess Shimna, do you hear that?"

"Come," she said, with a pout of her half-smiling lips, "come into the garden, and help me to pick some flowers. Will you have a chocolate? I don't often eat them myself, but my mother and Prince Bobrovski are never tired of sucking them. Here—take one; and now let us come out."

"There is," said Pole presently, "one serious matter—not the one that is forbidden, but another—which we have still to talk about; and that is the question of your coming to London with us. You have given my mother, I believe, no definite answer."

"I thought," she said, "that before definitely refusing, I would explain things all to you, so that you would understand my refusal."

"Now that I know all," said Pole, "I should understand it less than ever. I will find a lodging for your child. My mother won't go for three weeks or so. Everything will be quite easy."

Her expression was half relenting. "How could I?" she answered. "I may meet the world again some day. I don't think I could now."

"Well," he said, "I won't urge you more to-day. You

know that I go to London myself almost at once. Think the matter over, Shimna. Tell me you will do that; and before I leave Glenlynn, say 'Yes' to my mother."

"I will say 'Yes' to you," she replied, "meaning that I will think it over. And now, good-bye for the moment, else you will be late for dinner. Adieu!" she said on the doorstep.

"Adieu!" he answered. "*Je t'aime.*"

CHAPTER XXX.

A few weeks later Mrs. Pole was saying to her son, "Here is a letter, which has, at all events, the merit of being characteristic." And she handed him a mauve envelope, adorned with a huge gold coronet.

They were seated together at breakfast, in a panelled and somewhat dingy room, containing three portraits said to be by Sir Joshua Reynolds. The walls were lined by a serried row of chairs, whose leather betrayed the friction of many generations of diners. At one end were two windows, darkened with old rep curtains; and at the opposite end a pair of Corinthian columns formed an alcove where a great mahogany side-board reposed its respectable bulk in a dim sanctuary of shadows. Such was the dining-room of Lord Wargrave's house in Brook Street — a house which had hardly been changed since it was built in the last century, except by having been refurnished shortly before the battle of Waterloo, and having acquired unintended lines through the sinking of its floors and ceilings. It had, moreover, another speciality which it certainly did not start with. It was now beyond comparison the dirtiest house in the neighbourhood. Lord Wargrave's father had inherited it from an uncle, its original builder; and in Lord Wargrave's eyes its condition was a distinction as well as an economy. "In a London house nowadays," he was very fond of observing, "four generations of family dirt is the only decoration that money cannot buy."

Pole and his mother had arrived there two days ago; and the bags, books, and boxes which stood on some of the chairs, showed that the new tenants were but half settled in their quarters.

"I suppose," Mrs. Pole continued, as her son read the letter, "we shall have to ask her to dinner, or offer her some civility. I'm glad, at any rate, that she's pleased at our taking charge of Shimna; and there must be something good in her, in spite of her odd ways, since she takes so much interest in this poor little pretty baby, and spends—for the spending must be hers—so much money upon it."

Pole meanwhile had been reading the following letter :—

"My dear Augusta—for I suppose a cousin may call you by your *nom de baptême*—how shall I ever thank you for all you have done, not only for Shimna, but for a very little relation of ours, who is too young at present to be very interesting personally? I could not take the little darling about with me ; and it would have been too distressing to have left it alone with nurses. You may readily believe then, how delighted I was when my daughter—herself too delicate too travel—begged to be allowed to have it with her. But, on the other hand, except in a very quiet place, my daughter could hardly have been left alone either ; and quiet places are apt—are they not ?—to be *triste*. Lyncombe would have been *triste*. Any place would have been in which Shimna could have been left. But in London, under your care she can be happy—she can keep her spirits, and perform at the same time those charming and tender duties with which, out of the goodness of her heart, she has charged herself. And all this is owing to you. How many thousands of thanks must I pay you before you are paid in full, dear Augusta—kind kinswoman ? Ah! I can neither count nor pay them. But allow me, while I am here—and that is for a few days only—to call and renew my acquaintance with you, and at least thank you in person, though I never can thank you fully. To do so will be indeed pleasure to your very grateful cousin,

"YOLANDE O'KEEFE.

"Shimna tells me," continued the writer in a postscript, "that she joins you to-morrow or next day."

"If Lord Wargrave sticks to what he told you in his note," said Pole, "he will be here by two o'clock, from

Shropshire. Let us ask the Countess to luncheon, and he
shall get some friends to meet her. And now, what can this
be?" he exclaimed—"what exceedingly early visitor?"
For as he spoke a noisy rattle of wheels came to an abrupt
cessation immediately outside the windows; and, rising
from his seat, he saw above the wire blind the ruddy disc of
a hackney cabman's face, motionless with the gleams of
morning on it, and backed by a pile of luggage. Presently
the bell was rung with an imperious vigour, which made a
bell-wire rustle and whisper along the cornice: and Pole,
approaching the window, saw Lord Wargrave's servant busy
in extracting his master from the depths of a four-wheel cab.
Lord Wargrave emerged, like a portrait stepping out of its
frame, his figure swelled as it seemed, by several layers of
overcoats, and his eyes and his mouth just showing themselves between a muffler and a woollen cap.

"Where in the world can he have come from?" said
Mrs. Pole, laughing, for she, too, by this time, was contemplating her landlord's advent. "He looks as if he'd been
travelling for forty-eight hours, at least."

She had not long to wait for her question to receive its
answer. A moment later Lord Wargrave was in the dining-
room doorway, his scanty hair ruffled by the removal of his
head-gear, but his person not yet divested of any of its other
accoutrements.

"My dear Augusta, God bless you!" he said; and before
Mrs. Pole had had time to collect her faculties, his hand
was on her shoulder, and he had aimed a kiss at her
cheek, which, without his seeming to notice it, only hit the
air.

"Reginald, my dear, how are you? No, no, no! What
is it you're fumbling at? The other one first; not that
one."

This was addressed to his servant, whom he had, by a
shrug of his shoulders and a backward bend of his body,
silently ordered to free him of his superfluous garments.

"Now," he resumed, when he was reduced to his natural
dimensions, "now, Augusta," and he fixed an appraising eye
on the table, "I think I am ready for something in the way
of breakfast."

"Everything's cold," said Mrs. Pole in dismayed accents.
"We had no idea you'd be here before luncheon. Wouldn't

you like to dress first, and let us have something fresh got for you?"

This suggestion Lord Wargrave did not even condescend to notice.

"A chair," he grunted to his servant. "What have we here? Sausages! Reginald, I think I'll have one of those little fish as well, and—ah! what's this? The grilled bone of a chicken. I only," he said presently, "left Paris at nine o'clock last night. The train was late by three hours, at least. I never enjoyed the inconvenience of unpunctuality better. My dear old friend, the Chairman of the Dover Railway, was sharing it, on the seat next mine."

"Paris!" exclaimed Mrs. Pole. "You were in Shropshire when you last wrote to me. How many nights running do you ever sleep in the same bed?"

Lord Wargrave answered this question by a momentary glance at Pole, which gleamed with nebulous innuendo. And then, turning to Mrs. Pole, said, with an easy gravity, as if he were mentioning the most common of daily incidents,

"I had an engagement to dine with the President of the French Republic. He's the most ferocious Radical in Europe, with incomparably the best cook. I was specially asked that I might meet the newest Academician."

"Do you mean," said Mrs. Pole, "the man who writes those disgusting novels?"

"He's quite the most delightful man," said Lord Wargrave in unruffled tones, "the most tender, the wittiest, the most delicate man in conversation I've ever met since the death of the late Bishop of Aylesbury."

"Your letters, my Lord," said his servant; and in the space of tablecloth close to him, which happened to be freest from bread crumbs and broken crusts, a pile of envelopes was deposited as big as five packs of cards.

"That reminds me," said Mrs. Pole, "here is another communication for you. It's really written to me, but we mean it to be for you. We want you to entertain Countess O'Keefe at luncheon."

"Certainly," said Lord Wargrave, as he read the Countess's letter. "And the beautiful young lady comes to-morrow, or the day after? Capital—capital! I'll see about the lunch this morning."

He then turned to his letters, and having extracted them from their envelopes with as much dexterity as a kitchen-maid shells peas, he laid on one side a little heap of cards and invitations, and stuffed the rest carelessly into one of his baggy pockets.

"I told you, my dear Reginald," he said, "we should have not only a session but a season. As soon as I've done dressing come into my room and let me talk to you."

Half an hour later, in response to this invitation, Pole knocked at Lord Wargrave's door; and entering found the carpet littered with clothes and towels, and Lord Wargrave standing amongst them illuminated by a clean shirt.

"Sit down there," said Lord Wargrave, as, with chin well in the air, he was struggling to tug a noose of black necktie into something that might pass muster as a bow. "For the last few days I've not seen the English papers. Tell me about your own affairs. Your election, I suppose, is over."

"Yes," said Pole, "there was no second nomination, and my constituency has given birth to its member without a single pang of parturition. I have had, however, to be in London, hard at work for the past three weeks: and I think that by this time I am beginning to know my business."

"Well," said Lord Wargrave, "you'll take your seat to-morrow. I shall be there to witness the great event. I wish our fascinating young lady could have seen you enter the lists."

Pole replied that it was doubtful if she would reach London before Friday.

"Never mind, then," said Lord Wargrave, "she shall hear you make your maiden speech. We'll ask the mother for Sunday. I'll get a few members of the *Corps Diplomatique* to meet her, and some pleasant women; though that will be more difficult. When a woman like our Countess has such hair and such a cousin Bobrovski, of the women to whom *she* would be civil, there are only two sorts—in this country at least—who would be civil to her in return—those who stick at nothing, and those who know nothing. The gay ladies, I think, would hardly be agreeable to your mother; so I'll get, if I can, an old Catholic Marchioness, a Catholic Marchioness with a plain Catholic daughter. And as for Countess Shimna, I've a box for the L—— Theatre. The ticket is

just come, and you and I and your mother will take her on
Saturday night."

It was not till Saturday, so it proved, that Countess
Shimna would arrive; and Lord Wargrave meanwhile began
to busy himself with further schemes for her entertainment.
All that afternoon he was running over in his mind various
houses to which he would take her, and in which he would
acquire himself a fresh importance because he did so. The
thought of her gave to life a new social zest. The following
day brought to him an excitement almost equally gratifying.
He saw his protégé take his seat in the House of Commons;
and he enjoyed the cheering with which the new member
was greeted quite as much as if he had been himself its
object. One thing only in any way chilled his satisfaction;
and this, as it happened, was his protégé's own demeanour.

"My dear Reginald," he said to Pole next day, "to look
at your face you might have been in office for twenty years,
and been learning how little an Under-Secretary can do,
instead of dreaming of how much."

"If," replied Pole, "I have any qualifications for my
present office at all, it is that I know life too well to dream
about it."

"You ought to dream a little," said Lord Wargrave.
"Every statesman with any genius should. All actual
improvements have been the children of impossible hopes.
However," he added, "the same may be said of the worst
failures also; so the nation, perhaps, would be right in
congratulating you on your philosophy."

That evening Lord Wargrave, on coming back from his
club, was met in the hall by Mrs. Pole, who was dressed for
dinner, and who told him that Countess Shimna had arrived,
and was already preparing herself for the threatre. "And
you," she said, "ought to be dressing too : for you specially
impressed on me that we were to dine at seven punctually."

Lord Wargrave's toilet never consumed much time; and
on the present occasion he was even more rapid than usual.
Indeed, such was his eagerness to be again in Countess
Shimna's presence that he paid her the homage, which was
hardly obtrusive in its character, of not prolonging his
preparations by adorning himself with a fresh shirt. When
he entered the drawing-room his expectations were even more
than satisfied. If Countess Shimna had shone amongst the

faded furniture of Glenlynn, her brilliance was even greater
with the Brook Street drawing-room for a background,
especially as now she seemed to Lord Wargrave's eyes like a
butterfly whose wings were palpitating for flight into its
natural element. The quiet of her dress was, in every pleat
and fold, full of worldly knowledge of the exact fitness of
things; whilst her hair had that finished neatness which,
classic as well as modern, makes Greek beauty immortal in
the statuettes of Tanagra. A vision of the future flashed
upon Lord Wargrave in a moment. He saw this brilliant
fairy the heroine of a hundred drawing-rooms; he saw new
social light irradiating himself as her guardian; he saw
cards for a hundred dinners, to which he would be begged
to bring her; and the generous impulses of youth were
actually so far rekindled in him that he experienced a distinct
resentment against the obvious necessities of the situation
when the arm that rested on his, as he went down to the
dining-room, was not Countess Shimna's, but Mrs. Pole's.
At the theatre, indeed, he took fate into his own hands; and
no sooner where the party inside the glass doors of the
building than, frankly leaving Mrs. Pole to the dutiful
escort of her son, he tucked Countess Shimna's black-gloved
arm under his elbow, and hurried her off with him in her
rose-coloured opera cloak, proud of the glances that witnessed
its intimate proximity to himself. His feelings, however,
were by no means of such a nature as to interfere with the
pleasure he from time to time received on observing how
Countess Shimna would instinctively turn to Pole, and her
eyes say some silent word to him with their wet, velvety
heart's-ease. It was possibly with a generous wish of
facilitating this interesting by-play that Lord Wargrave
managed to engross so much of the front part of the box,
that Pole was obliged to content himself with the land of
shadows behind into which any number of glances might be
sent with complete security. But whatever might have
prompted this arrangement, Lord Wargrave was happy in
the results of it. The gas lamps which clustered close to
the box exhibited himself and his neighbour centred in a
common halo. As he scanned the house between the acts,
he swelled with the proud consciousness that a growing
number of opera-glasses were converging in his direction;
and whenever he felt himself to be specially under the public

gaze he would murmur some confidential observation into Countess Shimna's ear, that the mystified world might see how the unknown beauty smiled at him.

Such was Countess Shimna's first evening in London; and Pole, who had not seen her for more than three weeks, was pleased to observe, when they came home from their dissipation, both in the brilliant sparkle in her eyes, and the tint of enjoyment upon her cheeks, signs that she was being reconciled to the world, either by time or by the world itself—and if to the world, he thought, to the idea of marriage also.

The incidents of next day's luncheon party, which Lord Wargrave had duly organized, confirmed him in this opinion. The first guests to arrive were Lord Wargrave's Catholic Marchioness, old Lady Fermanagh, with her daughter Lady Editha O'Malley, the one lined with wrinkles and tottering in limp silks; the other erectly dowdy, and wearing a gentle smile, which seemed to say to the fashionable world in general that she only remained friends with it because it happened to be her near relation. These ladies whom Lord Wargrave had invited partly for the reason that they were distant cousins of Mrs. Pole's, well rewarded his kindness by the effusion with which they met her, in addition to pleasing him by their evident admiration of Countess Shimna. "Your mother," he said to Pole, nudging him with a confidential elbow, "will very soon find herself amongst a set of friends she likes. That's why I asked those two. I always tell Lady Fermanagh that she's the chaperon of the Roman Church in England. It's a pity your mother's not a Catholic. In that case she'd have a society ready made for her," At this juncture there was announced an *attaché* from the French Embassy, with brown suède gloves and hair cut like a tooth-brush; and then, a moment later, Countess O'Keefe entered. She was very different now from what she had been on board the yacht. She was all in rustling black, and though her hair was yellow as ever, the soul of Church and Sunday was fashionably embodied in her bonnet. Her very bracelets were heavy with a sort of mundane sanctity, and her hands were befittingly encumbered with a prayer-book, and a jewelled smelling-bottle. When Lord Wargrave welcomed her and conducted her to Mrs. Pole she involuntarily cast at him a glance of furtive freemasonry, but this

was the only sign of the old Adam which she exhibited, and to
Mrs. Pole, her manner was florid with Christian virtue.
She embraced her daughter, and gave her a scented kiss,
with a nice restraint that was a model of drawing-room
maternity. She greeted Pole as a cousin and good comrade;
and dropped Lady Fermanagh such a dignified continental
courtesy, that the elderly limbs of the latter involuntarily
did their best to imitate it. The Countess was now the
centre of a small circle, and began to rattle and ripple with
so easy a volubility, that she captivated her new acquaintances by saving them from the difficulty of talking to her.

"I fear I am so late," she said, in her best foreign
staccato, which she always employed as a shield against
English criticism, "but really the sermon of Father Burke
was so long—good, yes—but long, and I afterwards had to
see a very young little friend of mine—a bairn," she said,
laughing benignantly; "is not that what you call them?
Mrs. Pole knows. It's a baby relation of ours," she continued in explanation, "whose mother is dead; and it has to
be left in England. My daughter Shimna has been too kind
to it—an angel." And then the Countess, as if a chance
subject were done with, asked Lady Fermanagh if she too
had been listening to Father Burke; and paused with
deferential sweetness to let the other ladies speak.

"The Duke of Dulverton," said the voice of Lord
Wargrave's servant. "Luncheon," growled Lord Wargrave
promptly into his servant's ear; and by the time he had
done so, the Duke of Dulverton with his spectacles had
shuffled into the room, which he confronted with an inter-
rogatory smile. He found that he knew all present, except
the young *Attaché* and the Countess; and as the Countess
happened to be standing against the light, he had exchanged
words with the others before he even saw her plainly.
When he did see her and was presented to her, Pole noted
with amusement that a curious expression passed over his
face, as if he had been expecting something out of the way,
and had found precisely what he expected. "I'm sorry to
hear," he said, "you're paying London so short a visit; but
we are all of us very thankful to you for leaving us your
charming daughter. She is the next best thing, since we
can't keep her mother—the next best thing." A moment
later, when the Countess had turned away from him, he

pulled Lord Wargrave by the sleeve and quietly drew him
into a window. "Oh, ho," he said, "I know her. My dear
fellow, I recollect her well. She was staying at Spa twenty
years ago with D——. I never spoke to her; I was not
alone myself then: but I'll tell you what, Wargrave—I used
to think D—— a devilish lucky fellow. I should like to
occupy D——'s old place at luncheon." Lord Wargrave,
who avowedly set a high value on dukes, was only too
delighted to comply with his friend's wishes, and the Duke,
as he subsequently confessed, "had a monstrous pleasant
party." He drew the Countess and Lady Fermanagh both
into conversation with himself, and when the latter was
warming into friendly sympathy with the former, he would
allude to some *bal masqué*, some race-meeting, or some
question of gambling, and say, "Let us ask the Countess;
when the Countess played at Spa, or when the Countess
backed a horse, every one said she was always sure to win."
Countess Shimna, meanwhile, was admired and approved of
by everybody, and the Duke was constantly watching her
in spite of his preoccupation with her mother. To one of
the party, however, she gave a certain amount of uneasiness.
Her neighbour was the young *Attaché;* and suddenly between
him and her the discovery of some mutual acquaintance set
fire to a conversation which leapt up and burnt and sparkled,
and hardly ceased till they all of them went back again to
the drawing-room. The person rendered uneasy by this
occurrence was Pole. He was not jealous, but it was a new
and unpleasant experience to him to see Countess Shimna
show any particular interest in any one saving himself, who
was on the sunny side of fifty. The young *Attaché*, however,
was unable to linger long; and whatever uneasiness he had
caused went with him out of the street door. "Shimna,
darling," cooed the Countess, "I must say good-bye to you
now. Come and see your mother before she goes off on
Tuesday, and don't forget your pretty little baby cousin.
Dear Mrs. Pole," she added, "I must positively be hurrying
away. At half-past three I've an appointment with Father
Burke." And then turning to the Catholic ladies, whose
hearts she knew would be conquered by this communication,
"The best friend," she said, "that I ever had was a Jesuit."
The Duke, meanwhile, had just appropriated Countess
Shimna, to whom he had hitherto hardly spoken a word.

"I suppose," he said to her, "you have not many engagements yet. Very well—don't engage yourself for Wednesday fortnight. The Duchess will ask you to a little party at my house. You have seen my house in the country. I will show you my house in London. What—there's your mother going. I can give her a lift in my brougham—either to Father Burke, or to the Cardinal Archbishop if she wants him."

"My dear," said Lord Wargrave to Countess Shimna, when the last guest had departed, "if nothing else happens in the social world this autumn, you will at all events see two of the most brilliant parties possible. At the dinner to which you have just been asked, and the Duchess's ball to which you will be, you are sure to see the very best that the society of London can offer you."

Lord Wargrave thought that Countess Shimna was less impressed than she should have been: but he solaced himself with the thought that she would know better presently.

CHAPTER XXXI.

The Duke's invitation, so far as Countess Shimna was concerned, was very far from being the sole social result of the luncheon party. The two Catholic ladies, whose gentle and estimable natures recognized in Mrs. Pole an excellence that was akin to their own, were delighted to gather her under the dove-like wings of cousinship; indeed, the faith, the hope, and the charity with which they were so largely gifted, led them to see in her something better than a cousin, or even many cousins, namely, a possible convert; whilst as for her young friend, though they looked on her somewhat doubtfully, both on account of her dangerous beauty and of the justice her toilet did to it, she was at all events a member of the true flock already, and thus had a natural claim on them to shield her with a wholesome *entourage*. The consequence was that Mrs. Pole and Countess Shimna were themselves, the very next day, entertained at luncheon by Lady Fermanagh, and introduced to a circle of her intimates, of whom some in early days had been actually known to Mrs. Pole, whilst they all of them knew all about her.

Of the many sections that make up English Society, none is more charming than that composed of those Catholic families whose reverence for themselves and their religion has remained sufficiently high to keep them indifferent to the rivalry of contemporary gentile fashion. Countess Shimna's new friends, although they, like Lady Fermanagh, thought her manner and her appearance too finished for an unmarried girl, approached her with an air of deferential and yet motherly friendship, which called to her responsive face its expression of fascinating gratitude. It is true that the Catholic young ladies, to whom she was gradually introduced as companions, and who showed a strong inclination to whisper with her in confidential corners, did not succeed in penetrating very far into her sympathies by their restless ripple of talk about dresses and balls and knitting, or even about the horses on which they rode, or some lectures on literature which they attended. This prattle, light as feathers, and the eagerness of the girls' eyes, inclined Countess Shimna alternately to laugh and sigh. But so great was her perception of any good-will shown her, and she instinctively responded to it with such a caress of thankfulness, that her new playmates were charmed as well as a little awed by her; and she, for her part, had the not unpleasant sensation that she had, by some miracle, slipped back to her convent-school again.

As for her child and its nurses, a suitable lodging had been found in a place not far off, which Pole's ingenuity had suggested. This was a house adjoining the well-known Catholic Church, in which Countess Shimna's mother had so profited by her Jesuit's sermons—a house often occupied by various reverend Fathers, and possessing a door at the back which gave access to the ecclesiastical precincts. Here the child and attendants of a distinguished Catholic family were sure of advantages and attention which they could not have counted on elsewhere. It had also occurred to Pole that the young and unacknowledged mother, who would presumably select this church for the performance of her religious duties, would be able, by means of the private door that has been mentioned, to avoid inconvenient notice when she visited her little girl daily. He found that his forethought was in every way justified; and the frequency with which she was seen in the neighbourhood of Father Burke's

church atoned, in the eyes of her new Catholic friends, for
her excess of worldly charms, by investing her with a
reputation for devoutness.

Thus a week went by. Of society, in the sense of any
formal parties, neither she nor Mrs. Pole saw anything.
Indeed, in spite of Lord Wargrave's prophecies, there was
not much to see; and he himself had gone off to a fashionable shooting-party in the country. He himself never shot,
but he approved of sport in others, as a means of purging
houses of dangerous and inferior rivals. Quiet intimacies,
however, such as those that have been just described,
produced pleasant incidents for Countess Shimna every day ;
and the social atmosphere in which she now was moving—
an atmosphere placid with a sense of lineage and mutual
relationship—recalled much to her with which she was
instinctively familiar as an Austrian.

As for Pole, a number of days elapsed before any occasion
arose for his speaking in the House of Commons ; and he
was far too reserved, and in some ways far too indifferent,
to attempt to air his eloquence till the exigencies of business
called on him. But his life as a politician was full, and
was daily becoming fuller. He found that in private his
opinion was being sought and deferred to by many of the
most influential and most experienced members of his party ;
the Prime Minister had treated him with exceptional consideration and attention; and all this, together with the
manner of Countess Shimna, who still seemed to like him the
better because he showed he had a life apart from her, made
the present thrill in touching him, like a sort of ether spray,
which, not by its coldness but by its warmth, was an
anodyne for the sufferings of the past.

Countess Shimna, indeed, both in her own mental condition and in her demeanour towards himself, was beyond
what had been his most sanguine hopes. She was recovering, so it seemed to him, a healthy friendliness with the
world, without being seduced by its frivolities. He was
pleased to note the eagerness with which she read the papers,
in the hopes, as he divined rightly, of discovering his own
praises in them; and he had the stimulating sense that,
however strong might be her feelings for him, every fresh
distinction he won for himself would have a tendency to
make them stronger. The tint of her cheeks, her dress and

the grace that moved in it, the homage of the looks that
would follow her when she appeared in public, and the
tender memories swimming in her eyes when she looked at
him, mixed themselves with a faith that her life might in
every way complete his. She became a part of his ambition,
both for himself and for the public good; and when images
of success fantastically came to him in his sleep, the perfume
that always went with her came floating and lingering
through his dreams.

At length the day arrived when he was to make what
would be his maiden speech. Lord Wargrave, who meanwhile had returned to London for a night or two, and had
left it again in response to an invitation of the nature of a
command, was back, bustling with punctuality, in order to
be present at the event; and was brimming with anecdotes
of the various pithy phrases in which he had commended to
Royal interest the talents of the rising statesman. His only
disappointment was that Countess Shimna, being slightly
indisposed, was unable to go down to the House with him
—a disappointment in which she evidently shared. Pole,
however, who took a singularly impartial view of the amount
of general interest that would attach to what he had to say,
was far from sorry to think that her impressions of him as
a public man were not to be first formed from such an
exceedingly tame exhibition of himself. Nor, perhaps, was
this view unjustified by probabilities. The occasion of his
speech was a Bill that was to be introduced by a notorious
Ultra-Radical, relating to the regulation of certain East-End
industries. It was a Bill which, as was known, was limited
in its immediate scope, but it embodied principles capable of
far wider application, and fatal, in the opinion of its opponents,
to the elementary rights of property. Such a mass of sensational facts, however, such statistics of injustice and
suffering, had been got together by its supporters in order
to prove its necessity, and so telling an exposition of these
was expected in the Ultra-Radical's speech, that fears were
entertained by the Government lest some even of their own
followers should be led astray by it. The speech was made.
The expectations of the speaker's friends were exceeded by
what they heard. The facts and figures were there, sharp
in their detail, ominous in their significance, and enunciated
with a sarcastic calm, which seemed to make them bite and

burn. In spite of the rancour by which the whole was
disfigured, the effect it produced was powerful, and parts of
it seemed conclusive even to many who held the speaker in
detestation.

Pole's reply, therefore, was awaited with unusual interest.
If the House had expected anything that is commonly called
oratory, it was signally disappointed; for the manner of the
new speaker was deliberate and unimpassioned in the
extreme. It was soon perceived, however, that he possessed
three most valuable qualities—an unusual clearness of utterance, an absolute familiarity with his facts, and a command
of argumentative weapons, coupled with a contemptuous
good-nature in the use of them.

"The honourable member," he said, "has produced the
undeniably strong impression which he *has* produced, by two
distinct means—firstly, by his description of the distress
which he proposes to remedy, and secondly, by his description
of his remedies. If it is not invidious to compare them, I
will take upon me to say that the first of these have been
the most powerful. I will deal therefore with that first.
The statistics which he has put forward, with so much
energy and lucidity, do not come on me as a surprise; nor
has he quoted them without ample authority. So far as
they are concerned, indeed, though I am not in the honourable member's confidence, I venture to assert that I could
have written his speech for him beforehand: and I venture
to assert this because I knew beforehand the precise authorities which the honourable member would consult. They
are the authorities on which invariably he and his friends
rely. And as I have said already, they are ample. Their
only fault is that they are worthless. I will read a list of
the works, the articles, the pamphlets, and the political
leaflets, which I recognize, from the evidence of his speech,
as the sources of the honourable member's inspiration.
There is a set of pamphlets especially," he continued, when
he had read his list, "which the honourable member will
recognize as particularly intimate friends; because they have
supplied him not only with many of his figures, but with
more than one of his most remarkable and pungent sentences.
The author of those pamphlets conceals his personality
under a pseudonym. He calls himself '*Labour*.' The
honourable member is doubtless ignorant as to who his

authority is. I will inform him. He was formerly a sales-
man in Bethnal Green market. He was subsequently a
tout for a firm of East End money-lenders; then a secretary
of an East End Socialist organization; and at the present
moment his domicile is Dartmoor Prison. Had he signed
himself ' *Hard Labour* ' instead of ' Labour,' his *nom de plume*
would have been more felicitous. Well, amongst the honourable member's most stirring and startling assertions are the
following." Pole recapitulated them. "These," he said,
"occur in the original edition of ' *Labour's* ' pamphlets. I
presume, therefore, that the honourable member has studied
these pamphlets for a long time. He seems unaware, however, that every one of these special statements was withdrawn, as a libel, under threat of legal proceedings; the first
edition was suppressed; and in subsequent editions the
statements do not occur. It would be well, perhaps," the
speaker continued, "that the honourable member should
remember that first editions have a greater value for the
book-collector than for the politician."

Pole then proceeded to examine, with results very similar,
the rest of the facts and figures brought forward by the
radical orator. "The honourable member," he said, in concluding this portion of his speech, "asserts that he could
give us the names of fifty firms in the East End who have
been guilty towards their employees of the abominable
practices to which he alludes. I could forgive the honourable member of his ignorance of any authorities an appeal
to which would involve much research, or even much arith-
metic, but I cannot forgive him for having overlooked the
London Post Office Directory and those Trade Directories
which would have given him even ampler information. Had
he referred to all, or to any one of them, he would have
found that the London firms to which he makes allusion
are at the present moment only twenty-five in number, and
have never, during the past ten years, exceeded the number
of twenty-seven. That there is great suffering in connection
with the trades in question, I admit. A man may suffer
agonies if he happens to sprain his ankle : but the description of the situation as given by the honourable member
represents the truth of the matter not more nearly than a
description of a man with a sprained ankle would, which
represented him as having broken every bone in his body.

The honourable member, in short, is but one more example of the curious delusion so dear, through all ages, to the school of which he is himself an ornament—that because it may be impossible to exaggerate the pain of an injury, it is impossible to exaggerate its extent. This is the delusion of the Socialist; it is the delusion of the child who has had a tumble; it is also the delusion of the nursery-maid; but I trust it may never be said to be the delusion of this House."

Pole's victory thus far was an easy one, though he was probably the only person present who could have at that moment accomplished it: and a second victory followed, which, if as easy, was no less signal. Coming to the Bill itself, he acquainted the House with a fact of which no one present appeared to have the slightest knowledge—that in three Continental States experiments had been actually made of a kind precisely similar to those which this Bill aimed at introducing; and he then proceeded, with a mass of minute and overwhelming evidence, to show how in every respect these experiments had completely failed. Only once did his voice or manner betray the presence of the smallest feeling, or the smallest inclination to express it. His words began for a moment to vibrate with an impatient scorn; but he at once checked himself, as if guilty of some slip of the tongue, and he sat down as though the follies and errors he had been combating had been the faults of some damaged machine, and as if he had as little animosity against them. He went home with Lord Wargrave, who, gripping him affectionately by the arm, said—

"In many ways that speech was magnificent. It will be the foundation of a success for you, but it won't be the foundation of popularity."

The practical results of his eloquence need not be mentioned particularly. It is enough to say that, so far as he was able to judge of them, they were far beyond his expectations; and when he lay down to sleep that night, they filled him with a modest wonder, which was keener than his sense of elation, and also did much to deaden it.

The following morning *The Times*, in a leading article, reproduced with emphasis the principal points made by him, and observed sedately that he had already justified his appointment. Countess Shimna read this at breakfast with a pretty heightening of colour, which made her cheeks for a moment seem hardly perfect without a patch ; but what really excited and absorbed her were the far more personal comments which she found before dinner in a well-known evening paper. The paragraph containing them being as follows :—"The great sensation of the evening, however, was contributed by Mr. Pole, whose voice for the first time was heard by his brother members. Anything less sensational than his language, his matter, and his demeanour it is hardly possible to imagine. And it was partly to these very causes that the sensation, undeniably produced by him, was due. The evident apathy, almost amounting to boredom, which has, hitherto, been suggested alike by his face and his attitude, had been a source of considerable satisfaction to many enthusiastic Radicals, who had hoped to discover in his appointment one more folly of the Government. One of the principal points of interest in his speech of last night was the suddenness and the completeness with which it dissipated this impression. The House at once perceived that it was listening to a man whose perfect and minute knowledge and keen reasoning powers were made only the more remarkable by the sluggish self-possession of his manner ; whilst his refined and fastidious accents gave a similar prominence to the hard and business-like way in which he approached and gripped his subjects. In addition to all this, Mr. Pole's first appearance owed something of its success to various adventitious circumstances—to the unusual suddenness with which he had been pitchforked into public life, to the picturesqueness of his family connections ; and perhaps, also, to a fact which was commented on by certain critics in the ladies' gallery—that he had, when speaking, a certain air of abstraction, as though his deepest thoughts were engaged with distant and more serious matters—a criticism, which, we presume, if translated into bald masculine language, would mean that he was interesting because he seemed to be so little interested."

"Ah," said Countess Shimna to him that night, "you will be a great man ! You will make me proud of you."

"I," he replied, "should value another feeling more."

She was going up to bed, as she spoke to him ; and leaning over the banisters, extended her hand to him, which he pressed to his lips and kissed.

London had not even yet socially fulfilled the expectancy

of Lord Wargrave; but the following evening was to be the
evening of a great event—the dinner-party at Dulverton
House, to which Countess Shimna had been invited.   Mrs.
Pole, who had also been pressed to come, knew the world
and herself a great deal too well to be inclined for the sort
of society she would encounter on this occasion; so Brook
Street contributed but three guests to the feast—Countess
Shimna, Pole, and Lord Wargrave, who delighted in the
post of chaperon.   At five minutes to eight, a carriage with
jobbed horses, and with Lord Wargrave's coronet on the
panels, was standing patiently at the door; and Lord Wargrave and Pole were stationed at the foot of the stairs when
Countess Shimna descended, shimmering in her pink cloak,
and radiant with anticipations of the evening.   When the
ca riage drew up, not many minutes later, under the shade
of the portico with which Dulverton House was dignified,
when the opening door emitted a flood of lamplight, which
fell upon red baize and beaconed her on to brilliance, and
when Pole was following her as closely as the length of her
train permitted, that same newspaper paragraph which she
had read the previous evening, and which still remained in
her mind as a source of pride and pleasure, was coming, in
a house far off in the country, for the first time, under the
eyes of another woman.
  The woman was seated near the hearth of a large ill-
lit drawing-room, where a glimmer of burning logs was
playing over a thread-bare carpet—a woman with soft blond
hair, and cheeks tender as rose-petals.   Her head was bent,
and a shadowy smile was on her lips, of which the cause
was evident.   Her lap supported the burden of a little boy—

> "And like a star upon her bosom lay
> His beautiful and shining forehead."

  Whilst she was thus preoccupied a newspaper, just come
by post, was brought to her.   Close to her chair was a
shaded lamp, the one lamp in the room; and leaning
towards it she began languidly to read.   Suddenly she
started, her indifferent gaze became a stare; and for some
moments, motionless as if she had been petrified, she was
poring over the lines in which Pole was described and
criticized.   Then the paper fell suddenly from her hand;
she looked at her child's face, turned it tenderly in different

ways, scrutinized the curves of his mouth, and lifted his curling hair. All at once her eye became brimmed with moisture. With childish precipitancy she rubbed it help-lessly away, and stooping, hid her face on that of her little boy. A footstep roused her, and she looked up. "What, nurse!" she said. "And is it his bedtime already? Come, he must give his mammy one kiss more and go." When she was left alone she turned to a writing-table that was close to her, and her eyes again brimming over, she pulled to herself a sheet of note-paper. "I must write to him," she said. "I will write;" and she seized a pen. But all she did was to look helplessly at the paper, the quill for some reason remaining idle in her hand. At last, with a petulant melancholy, she dashed its points down upon the blotting-book and broke them. At the same instant a servant announced dinner; and rising abruptly, and snatch-ing up some book at random, she moved away through the shadows alone to a lonely meal.

CHAPTER XXXII.

DULVERTON HOUSE, though it would have been petty in Florence or Pisa, was yet a palace, as London houses go. The entrance-hall had a row of very respectable pillars, and caught the eye with a number of busts and bronzes; while to-night a long line of servants, majestic with powder and shoulder-knots, gave it an air of festival to which it had been long a stranger.

The guests were received upstairs, in a brilliantly lighted gallery, which was hung with magnificent pictures, was floored with shining parquet, and was furnished with nothing but a number of gold chairs. The organisms here assem-bled—if the terminology of silence may be borrowed—appeared to bear, for the time being, the impress of their stiff environment. Lord Wargrave, who could gauge at a glance the social value of an assembly, perceived in the bearing of everybody, the moment he entered the room, a certain formality and restraint peculiar to the class of entertainments in assisting at which he felt far less amused

than honoured; but honour of this kind was one of his
choicest pleasures. Most of the elder men wore stars on
their black coats. The Duke himself was blue with the
imposing ribbon of the Garter. The unmarried girls of
whom there was an unusual number, seemed to be adorned
with complexions made specially dazzling for the occasion;
and their mothers, sparkling with diamonds, had a grave
restlessness in their eyes, which confirmed the evidence
tendered by the red baize carpet, and betrayed a consciousness of the proximity of some royal personage.

Had Lord Wargrave devised in a dream his introduction
of Countess Shimna to the world, he could have devised
nothing better. He puffed with pride as all the company
stared at her. The gentle and pretty effusion with which
she was greeted by the Duchess flattered him like a tribute
to himself; and still more delightful to him was a slight
movement amongst the men, which was followed by her
introduction to the most august guest of the evening—a
Prince whose charm for every one was equalled by one thing
only, and that was the charm of every pretty woman for
him. Pole, who had met him in Germany, was received by
him with a friendly recognition and a flattering allusion to
the debate of two nights ago, which were not lost on Countess
Shimna, though they escaped the observation of the others;
and he presently found himself, when the Prince had turned
away from him, the subject of certain stares, which had
more of criticism than admiration in them. The stares proceeded from three jewelled dowagers, belonging to that
curious class of women who, despite good birth and connections, seem to be always on their promotion, and suspicious
of everybody who shares it. These particular specimens
had been invited on account of the beauty of their daughters;
and their hearts, swelling under their stays with the delights
of an exaggerated exclusiveness, were asking, with respect
to Pole, who this unknown man was. He had indeed for
some years been very little in London; but it so happened
that such friends as he had there belonged mostly to the
precise section of society in which his present critics struggled
in vain to naturalize themselves, though, to do them justice,
they often managed to appear in it. The consequence was
that when he came to look round the room he met with
welcome from the hands and the friendly faces of three or

four of the greatest ladies in the kingdom, whilst his critics
looked on and watched with rapidly changing feelings.
Their mouths relaxed, their eyes smiled behind their eye-
glasses, and one of them thawed into a distinct movement
of graciousness when the Duke introduced him to her, and
asked him to take her in to dinner.

"You will have," said the Duke, still standing by Pole,
"to divide mother and daughter. Your own young lady
has been ordered to sit by his Royal Highness. Do you see
Wargrave," he continued, pulling Pole by the sleeve, "em-
bedded in princely sunshine—eh?—like a fly in amber!
You wonder how the devil he got there! But he has got
there!—eh?—What a fellow that is! Listen now!"

The last exclamation was due to an outburst of royal
laughter, which Lord Wargrave had had the honour of
eliciting by some story or witticism. This incident, with
the exception of Countess Shimna's charms, constituted,
indeed, the first success of the evening, and imparted an
animation to the company which it had hitherto, perhaps,
lacked.

"I wish to God, my dear fellow," said a weary-looking
Knight of the Thistle, smiling at Pole decorously out of his
hollow eyes—"I wish to God we could all go in to dinner.
We're tired of standing here on our hind legs like this."

His devout aspiration was fulfilled with surprising
promptness. Two great doors at the end of the gallery
opened, and the company presently passed to another gallery
beyond, where a long table was glittering, starry with wax
candles, Pole's dowager scrutinizing during the transit
several of the ladies who were offensive enough to be sent
in before her. The Duke had inherited some of the most
remarkable plate in Europe; and the table to-night was
covered with groups, in silver-gilt, of soldiers, savages, and
artillery of all descriptions, emblematic of the armies which
his father had had the pleasure of annihilating. The
brilliancy of this historic, if not beautiful, decoration, lit up
each of the ladies like an additional set of jewelry; and
Pole's dowager, in particular, was exhibited to so much advantage, that every time she smiled at him he could have
drawn an accurate diagram of the network of little worldly
wrinkles in which the corners of her mouth ensconced themselves.

"Of course, Mr. Pole," she said, "we're all talking about your speech. I think you have spent a good deal of your time abroad. By the way, do you know my daughter? Adeline, this is Mr. Pole. You've been seeing lately a great deal about him in the newspapers. Tell him, dear, about your ball at the British Embassy in Paris."

The young lady turned on Pole a pair of very brilliant eyes, which seemed to hold in their depths the memories of a hundred balls, and of little else, Pole thought; but in this he found that he was wrong. The young lady was very observant of other young ladies, her competitors, and presently asked him—

"Who is the foreign-looking girl who is sitting between the Prince and that funny little Jacques de Pontorson? Everybody has been staring at her: nobody seems to know her."

"Do you think her pretty?" asked Pole.

"She is," said the young lady, "one of the smartest-looking girls I ever saw in my life. That dress came from Paris, I know. Pretty? Well—yes; I've no doubt some people would think her so."

"The Czarewitch," said Pole, "when he danced with her at the Winter Palace, declared she was one of the loveliest women who had ever been seen in Petersburg."

The young lady turned to him with animation. "Oh," she said, "do you know her, then?"

"She.is," replied Pole, "Countess Shimna O'Keefe, my cousin. Her chaperon to-night is Lord Wargrave, who is my cousin also."

The young lady's mother, who had been listening to all this with interest, felt that Pole was every minute rising higher and higher in her estimation; and she at last became perfectly satisfied, which she hardly had been hitherto, at having been taken in to dinner by a man who had no distinct precedence. She asked him if he were one of the Poles of the West of England, who she now recollected were a family of much provincial m gnitude. She expressed a wish to make his foreign Countess's acquaintance, and ended with proposing that he should join them at a party to the play next Wednesday. Men who are capable of appreciating genuine social flattery get it far purer and less adulterated by friendship from women who are near the social summit

than from those who actually stand on it. For the latter
can afford to feel friendship; the former only to show it;
and thus, when they do show it, it has the extended value
of representing the opinion of the world, not a private whim
of their own.

Pole was fully aware of this, and had his mind been at
ease, he had, being human, quite sufficient vanity to derive
considerable pleasure from the homage that was thus offered
him. But his mind was preoccupied, though not his eyes
or his manner. No one who watched him could have told
that he was thinking of Countess Shimna. As from time
to time he glanced at the faces opposite him, his impartial
attention never lingered on hers; but all the while he was
conscious of the kind of relations that were developing
themselves between her and her two neighbours. Towards
her Royal admirer she comported herself with a mixture of
self-possession and deference, animated with a sparkling
pleasure that was never out of her own control. To her
conduct in this respect Pole could take no exception; yet,
nevertheless, it disquieted him. It filled him with a jealousy,
not of any special man, but of the world. That other
jealousy, however, was not forgotten by him. It stirred in
him vaguely, when she turned to her other neighbour, the
identical young *Attaché* who had enjoyed her favour in
Brook Street. That for this young man personally she
entertained the smallest regard, was not by any means the
impression which she could possibly have conveyed to anybody. But she had evidently discovered that she had certain
intimate subjects in common with him; and as she discussed
these with subdued and confidential animation, Pole fancied
that memories with which he had no connection were calling
expressions into her face which he considered should have
been sacred to himself.

When a man is in love with a woman of a certain type,
it is not enough for him that her eyes should never be used
so as to convey to any other man any impression that he has
moved her. What the lover demands is that, except when
they are fixed upon himself, any sign of how they look when
she is really moved, should be absent from them. He
demands that treasures belonging to himself alone should
not only not be given, but not even shown, to others; indeed,
that in his absence, they should almost cease to be. And

T

such were the demands, imperfectly as he was aware of the fact, which Pole's passion, by this time, was making on Countess Shimna. The dinner, accordingly, brilliant though it was as a spectacle, and flattering as the tributes were that were paid to his own importance, yet offered him, as it dragged its course from one quarter of an hour to another, little pleasure but the prospect of its own conclusion.

The principal event of the evening, however, was not yet foreseen by him. When, after the enjoyments of claret, cigarettes and coffee, the men, in a straggling body, went sauntering into the state drawing-room, it became apparent at once that something unusual was in the air; and the news was presently communicated to the male intelligence that the young ladies of the party were preparing to justify their presence there by a minuet. The scene that ensued was one of singular beauty. The goddess of some new Pygmalion seemed to have endowed with life a bevy of statues made out of Dresden china. Girls, whose conversation at dinner required youth to excuse it, now had youth to avenge them with its gift of exquisite motion. Amongst these Countess Shimna was not only the most graceful; she was the most self-possessed, and was incomparably the most finished in appearance. But her greatest triumph was to come.

At the end of the minuet she was surrounded by some of her new companions, and was evidently being pressed by them to do something. "I think, sir," said the Duchess, in answer to a question from the Prince, "they want her to dance by herself some Polish dance she was describing to them."

"I am sure," he exclaimed, in a voice that brought all the young ladies to attention, "Countess Shimna will not disappoint us. She will never refuse to give us so great a pleasure."

With the prettiest manner imaginable she put all hesitancy aside. Her companions drew away from her. She was alone on the dazzling parquet which gleamed with blurred reflections of the silken colours of her dress. A musician, already instructed, lashed from a piano a couple of barbaric chords : a wild melody then began to swing and sway itself, and the figure of Countess Shimna was swaying and undulating to the music. To Pole, as he watched her, and saw the dance develop itself, she became a new creature. Something of the spirit of the wild Russian song, which she had sung to him and Lord Wargrave by the moonlit window at Glenlynn, had passed into her limbs and movements, and the flexure of her supple outlines. But other things were in them also. There was a delicate hardihood of abandonment to a tribe of untamed emotions, some of them fierce, as if kindred to savage warfare, some suggesting a languor that relapsed upon a bed of roses. And yet with all this her whole action was so restrained, the least look of her eyes, the least movement of head or wrist, showed such complete control of the passion with which she played, that emotions and forces which in themselves were almost tragic, became part of that drawing-room comedy in which passion is assuaged to smiles.

The Prince was delighted. The room echoed with applause. All the spectators present looked at each other in acknowledgment of a new sensation. Lord Wargrave was in the seventh heaven. "You," said the Prince, who was near him, " have seen most things. Have you ever before seen anything like that ? "

" Once, sir," said Lord Wargrave, sententiously, "but in a very different kind of house. A dance like that," he muttered, " is a provocation to one of two things—to run away with a woman, or to cut your enemy's throat." As it was difficult to imagine Lord Wargrave performing either of these interesting feats, the Prince rewarded him with a second ebullition of laughter, the memory of which, as Lord Wargrave drove away, lay on his expanding heart, sparkling like a new decoration.

CHAPTER XXXIII.

ONE of Lord Wargrave's chief difficulties in life was persuading himself to go to bed. To-night, as the carriage was turning, on its way home, into Piccadilly, he abruptly started out of what seemed a philosopher's slumber, pushed his head out of the window, and shouted to the footman, "Stop!" He then informed his companions that he was going to "look in," as he expressed it, at a certain club, which met every Wednesday night during the session, and discussed everything, from religion to "rare and curious" literature, in a large room furnished with spirits, lemons, and soda-water.

As he slowly extricated himself from the carriage, one if not two hearts began to beat more quickly than they had done a moment earlier. Pole, at all events, in a state of feverish uncertainty as to whether Countess Shimna might not be gone from him for ever, was utterly unprepared for being so soon and so suddenly left alone with her. Hitherto, as was natural, he had been seated with his back to the horses; and he at first remained where he was, though Lord Wargrave's place was vacant. But as they turned a corner, a gas-lamp threw a moment's illumination into the carriage, and that moment showed him Countess Shimna's eyes fixed on him. It showed him a vision of diamonds, silk, and swan's-down; and the eyes which had so lately laughed and sparkled to the world, still indeed shining, but not shining with laughter.

"Will you sit here?" she said. And she moved her cloak to make room for him. In another moment he was by her side.

"Well," he began, almost coldly, "and how do you like the world—the London world? Do you feel unfit for it— out of tune with it?"

"Shall I tell you," she answered, "what I think? Of all the men I have seen in it I think you are the best. You are in it; you belong to it; you ornament it; but you rise out of it. Of all the men there to-night the only man was you."

"No one to-night," he said, "would have suspected you of that opinion."

"Do you take me," she murmured, "for a *bourgeoise* that I should show what I feel in public? You are very clever, but you don't understand much. If you cared to hear, I could tell you in two words what I mean."

"Tell me," he said, dizzy with a mad prescience of what was coming.

All her silks whispered with an abrupt movement of her body, and her lips, close to his ear, articulated, "*Je t'aime, je t'aime.*"

So far as words went, he gave her no immediate answer;

but she was answered none the less. Then without any warning, she struggled as though to draw away from him. "Ah," she said, "let me go! Do not touch me. I am tire. I am not like your women of England. Reginald—make me leave you."

"Answer me, then," he said. "Will you be mine? Will you marry me?"

She shrank back at the words, but did not wholly disengage herself. "Oh!" she exclaimed, "I beg you, don't speak of that yet. How can I tell? I can give you as yet no answer."

"Well," said Pole, "listen. In another week I shall have another occasion to exert myself in the House of Commons. You will then be able to judge better of me as a public man. And a day, or a day or two, later will be the ball at Dulverton House. There you again will meet the world. I will wait till after the ball before I repeat the question; but remember, I will do so then. Will this arrangement satisfy you?"

"Yes," she said, "yes! How good you are! You may ask me then." Her supple form once more surrendered itself to the arm that held it, but a moment later, when they arrived at their own door, her voice was light and laughing, as though all life were a toy; and she was saying, "Mr. Pole, will you please to get out first. You are lucky in having so much less of yourself to collect."

Next morning at breakfast, for the first time since he had known her, Pole found her pensive, in the presence of a third person. Her cheeks had no colour but a hint of the most pale geranium, and under her eyes were streaks of transparent violet. In the course of the morning she at once surprised and delighted him by asking him if he would come with her when she went to see her child. He assented eagerly. She took him into the drawing-room of the lodging-house, and had the child brought down to her.

"Look at its little lips," she said, "they are coral; and at its little ears, they are shells; and all its soul and heart are playing hide-and-seek between its eye-lashes. Do you like my little daughter?" she asked presently. "Put your hand on her cheek. How cool, how soft, and yet how firm it is! *Mon ami,*" she went on, "wait a little, and be patient with me. I cannot yet bear the question which you asked

last night. Wait for a week, as you said. Then things may
be different. And now ring the bell. My daughter goes out
at twelve; and as for me—you must take me for a little fresh
air in the Park."

They went together in pale autumnal glimmer that gave
something of gold to the grass and the hazy trees. Except
for a ragged tramp or two the walks were prolonged solitudes.
Pole and Countess Shimna talked in low intimate tones, not
attempting to approach any serious topic, but sharing those
bubbles of thought which bead the mind's surface, and to
give expression to which is the rarest form of confidence.

The kind of relation between them established during
this quiet walk, remained, on the surface at least, unchanged
during the week that followed. Much of his time, as heretofore, was occupied by his official work; and she for her
part became very soon excited by the prospect of the advent
to London of one of her oldest girl friends—Mdlle. Thérèse
de Pontorson, a sister of the young *Attaché*. This piece of
news was to Pole doubly welcome, as not only promising a
pleasure to Countess Shimna, but also as explaining her
interest in her friend's brother.

There was only one other incident of any definite kind
which intervened between their walk in the park and his
impending speech in Parliament. This was a visit which
his mother, Countess Shimna, and he, made to Mrs. Steinberg for one Saturday night, Lord Wargrave having left
London to dine with the Corporation of Manchester.

"I think," said Miss de Souza to Pole, just before the
visit ended, they being at last alone together for a few
moments—"I think she is the most beautiful woman I ever
saw in my life. And her wit, her vivacity, her good humour
—there is no English word for them. They hardly exist in
England. If I were a man," she continued, "I am certain
she could do anything with me. I can see her with your .
eyes. But there is one thing—may I say this to you?—
that I don't think about her. I don't think she is half good
enough for you."

Her observation, though it confused and annoyed him at
the moment, yet left behind it a certain residuum of satisfaction. Not only were his vanity and his gratitude both
alike touched by the high value which it seemed that Miss
de Souza set upon himself, but her failure to see the entire

merits of Countess Shimna gave a new force, and even
piquancy, to his own belief in them, as though they belonged
to him doubly in virtue of his being their sole discoverer.
He was, however, hurt by finding that Countess Shimna's
admiration of Miss de Souza was even more qualified than
Miss de Souza's had been of her, though she indicated her
own views in a manner that was less direct. Having praised
Miss de Souza with a good deal of intelligent appreciation,
she proceeded to express her surprise at the sort of social
position which appeared in England to be occupied by the
rich *bourgeoise*. To this, Pole replied somewhat coldly, that
the position of the Steinbergs and the De Souzas had been in
Paris even better than it was in England. "Well," said
Countess Shimna, laughing, "I suppose I ought not to talk,
since I, in my own country, can't even go to Court. As for
you," she added, "I have not the least doubt that you've
quarterings enough for a Canon of Strasbourg. But whatever you have, you have one thing—the certainty of being a
great man. I see it in the way in which every one looks at
and speaks to you."

Ever since the Duke's dinner-party, Pole had been in-
creasingly conscious of the interest which Countess Shimna
took in his worldly prospects, and of the fact that this was
accentuated by the interest in him felt by others. Instead
of wounding his vanity, the discovery flattered and stimulated it. Just as some women would rather be loved for
their beauty than for themselves, so some men would rather
be loved for their success than for themselves. Pole's condition was not precisely this, but he felt a desire to be loved
for his success, not indeed rather than for himself, but as
well as for himself. It appeared to him to be in the fitness
of things that Countess Shimna's lover should be brilliant.
He felt the same shame at the thought of not being, in her
eyes, distinguished, that he would have felt at appearing
with her in public dirty, ragged, or unshaven; and for the
first time in his life he began, under her influence, to understand fully what worldly ambition means.

Under these circumstances it seemed to him as if his
whole nature were changing, and his mind and muscles
being invigorated with a new energy. Though he had never
allowed himself to succumb to the unnerving influences of
sorrow, yet the incidents of his life had, during the past four

years, secretly isolated him from the normal consolations of society, and burdened him in his loneliness with many bitter anxieties. The result had been that, though he bore his burden bravely, and though a passion as intense as it was unfortunate, had brought to him its hidden compensations, he had come to look upon life as a thing to be endured, rather than enjoyed; and its very pleasures and beauties had pierced him with a sad solemnity. But now his feet as he walked beat hopefully upon the ground, and the music of life had changed from an elegy to an inspiriting march.

In due time the night of the great debate arrived, in which he was to take such a prominent, and he hoped, such a successful part; but with it came the first disappoinment which he had known for many days. It so happened that he, Countess Shimna, and Mrs. Pole, had been invited for that very night to a dance at a Catholic house. The party was to be quite a small one, the company being almost entirely recruited from a circle of old Catholic families, who had lost their health and complexions by generations of inter-marriages, and who, whenever they met, celebrated their consanguinity, by Christian names, and nick-names, and much cousinly laughter. Countess Shimna, it had been well understood, was to forego this temperate festival, in order to be an auditor of Pole's oratory, and a spectator of the results produced by it. But at breakfast that morning she made the unexpected announcement that her friend, Thérèse de Pontorson, who had just reached London, and whom she had not seen for years, was to go to this very dance under the care of an old French aunt, and was specially anxious that Countess Shimna should go with them.

"I am," she said, "more than sorry, but I cannot dis-appoint them. And then," she added, "I shall see Mr. Pole's triumph in the papers; but I must see Thérèse with my eyes, or I shall not see her at all."

Pole was not only disappointed, but a little puzzled by her conduct. He treated it, however, as he had treated many crosses previously. He made it a motive to fresh effort on his own part, having learned by experience that effort is one of the best antidotes to pain: and he went down to the House more determined than ever to impress his per-sonality, not on the House only, but on the nation.

The result was beyond his hopes. He came home to bed

with applause echoing in his ears, not a vainer man, not a prouder man, but a man matured and calmed by an inward consciousness of his strength, elevated by a perception of new reasons for his self-respect, and at the same time troubled and restless with the growing vitality of his hopes.

CHAPTER XXXIV.

ALTHOUGH Countess Shimna had not witnessed his triumph, he felt, as he dressed next morning. that she would perhaps be even more affected by it than if she had; since she would, when she read of it in the papers, regret the spectacle she had missed. His spirits accordingly were damped, in some small degree, when he learned, on going down to breakfast, that she was tired and suffering from a headache, and in all probability would not appear till luncheon.

As her dance of last night, in fact, as well as in name, had been not only small but early, he could not help wondering how so sober a taste of dissipation could have proved too much for one who was so well accustomed to the world. But when the hour for lunch approached, and he found her, on entering the drawing-room, lying on one of the sofas, her head languid against a cushion, he saw that her indisposition was more than a girl's fancy.

"I wish," she said, "I could have heard your speech last night. They tell me that the papers are full of you; but I have been able to read nothing."

He asked her if she were suffering.

"No," she said, "I am only tired. I shouldn't have been tired if I had gone to hear your speech, instead of sitting with Thérèse, and watching that dance. Do you know," she went on abruptly, "what you had better do? I think you had better take me back again to Glenlynn."

"Will you let me?" he began; but then abruptly checked himself. "No," he went on. "I am going to keep my word. I will not ask you till to-night's ball is over. It happens, however, that I shall be going to Glenlynn myself to-morrow—only for a day or two. I have to go there on business, and I will take your answer with me."

To his surprise she raised herself. She appeared to be full of interest; but it was an interest he could not fathom.

"You are really," she said, "going to Glenlynn to-morrow? And for how long? For how many days? Tell me."

"For two days—perhaps three. I had a letter this morning from my builder."

"Hadn't you better," she said, "stay with me here in London? And yet no—no—no."

"You won't come with me, then?" he asked, half seriously.

She smiled and shook her head, and fell back on the cushions.

"I'm sure, my dear," said Mrs Pole, who at this moment entered, "that you ought not to think of going to the ball to-night."

"Nonsense, Augusta," grunted Lord Wargrave's voice behind her. "What tires young ladies like her is not dissipation, but the want of it. What is it?" he said, bustling over to the sofa. Feverishness? Here, let me feel your pulse. Stop there and rest. You want nothing but that. You must go to-night, if I have to carry you in my arms."

Much to Lord Wargrave's delight, this discussion about herself had the effect of rousing the invalid somewhat; for her eyes, as they met his, shone with a sort of mischievous determination.

"Yes," she said, "let me be quiet. That is all I ask. You shall find me to-night as ready to go as you are. I will stay now where I am; and my friend Thérèse is coming to spend the afternoon with me."

This last piece of news Pole heard with mortification; for it showed him that till to-night Countess Shimna would be inaccessible: and the few words that had just passed between them left him disturbed with a sense that even yet he did but half understand her. After luncheon, however, he betook himself to the Carlton Club, where he had the satisfaction of discovering, by the demeanour of many slight acquaintances, that he was more famous than he had imagined he was; and this had the effect of driving his mortification from him. As he was about to leave the building, an incident took place which was calculated to encourage his self-confidence further, and, by a singularly illogical process, to drive his doubts away from him. In the hall he encountered the Prime Minister, who, instead of acknowledging his services, as he very often did those of his most influential supporters, with the economical payment of a half-absent nod and smile, caught him by the arm, and said, with confidential civility : " Ah, Mr. Pole, I was wanting to have a word with you." They sat down and talked. " These points," said the Prime Minister, " are most important. If you are not better engaged, will you do me a great favour, and dine to-night with me, when we shall have leisure for discussing them. It's a man's dinner. My family are dining out, and going on to the ball, as I dare say you are also." And he mentioned the names of the other expected guests—three in number, and all members of the Cabinet. For a moment Pole hesitated. His thoughts were of Countess Shimna going to the ball without him, under Lord Wargrave's wing, and perhaps engaged by others before he could get near her. But he thrust these thoughts aside, and accepted the invitation.

When he reached Brook Street, he found Countess Shimna in the drawing-room. She wore a certain tea-gown, which was very far from being unknown to him. The lace of its floating sleeves had lain on his own arms, when her lips had been close to his, between the hearth and the chessboard at Glenlynn. For a second or two at the sight of her, his resolution failed him. He thought of sending an excuse to the Prime Minister, and remaining where he was, so that she might cling to him, as they went to dinner. But almost before this thought had completely shaped itself, his mind was impressed by her singularly rapid recovery; and the spirit of pique whispered to him that if she could rouse herself so readily for the ball, she might have done so after luncheon, for an hour of his own society; whilst when he heard that she had been actually out with her young French friend, he had a positive satisfaction in informing her that it was necessary for him to dine elsewhere.

" Where ? " she asked half petulantly. And he saw, or thought he saw, when he told her, a tribute of respect in her eyes to the political importance that was being attached to him.

The distinguished party which he had the honour of joining pursued its discussions till long after eleven o'clock ;

and his thoughts had impatiently preceded him to Dulverton House for a good half-hour before the statesmen separated.

"I suppose," said the Prime Minister, with a martyr's resignation in his eyes, "I should be doing the civil thing if I went myself with you, for a moment. Let us have a four-wheel cab, and go to this ball together."

If Dulverton House had been brilliant on the night of the dinner-party, it was doubly brilliant now, and its brilliance showed externally. The street was alive with carriage-lamps, and dark with a line of carriages, which was quite sufficiently long to indicate to an experienced eye that the entertainment within was large, and yet not promiscuous. Sounds of music spasmodically found their way to the open air, and the first-floor windows, glowing through half-drawn curtains, showed glimpses of gilded ceilings and the heads of dancers moving.

As the Prime Minister emerged from his humble vehicle, the spectators about the portico recognized him, and raised a cheer. Pole was conscious also of hearing his own name mentioned, and he followed his leader into the hall, with a future unveiled before him, in which hopes glittered so fast, that their features were indistinguishable.

Most of the company, it was evident, had arrived already; for the hall and the broad staircase were empty, except for servants. The life of the night began with the opening of the tall doors which flanked the marble landing; and suddenly through the aperture came the twinkle of countless candles, the colour of women's skirts, and the hoarse murmur of conversation. The new-comers found themselves in an ante-room, out of which the ball-room opened; and here the hostess and the more sober of her guests were enjoying themselves in comparative quiet. The ball-room, moreover, was emptying itself, a dance having just ended: but Pole, as his name was announced together with the Prime Minister's, felt that many glances were turned on him, full of a lively interest. Men shook him by the hand with the familiar and intimate friendliness which the civilized human heart reserves for success alone, and which flatters most of its recipients so much more than affection. Magnificent dowagers, peering over ramparts of brocade and jewelry, arrested him with benignant smiles, and talked to him with that animated tenacity by which women show pride, as well as pleasure, in a person whom they publicly monopolize; whilst, as for him, he had presently, with a certain air of distraction, begun to look about him for some one he could not see, and to send unquiet glances into the ball-room, now half-depopulated.

At last, as he was trying to escape from the elderly great ladies, he came across one belonging to his own county—a lady rarely in London, and present to-night only because she was a cousin of the Duchess's, and had a grand-daughter staying with her.

"It's so long," she said to Pole, "since I've been in a scene like this, that I feel as shy as I did when I first came out. I am really afraid to look at all these smart people, for I can hardly believe that any of them will remember me." And then they talked of the news of the West country, including some letters in one of the local papers, from Mr. Godolphin, about super-altars in English chancels. These topics exhausted, they came back to the ball. "They tell me," said the elderly lady, "that the great sensation of the evening is some wonderful new beauty. I can't remember her name, and as yet I have not even seen her."

"Who is she? Where is she?" said Pole, feeling his face on fire.

"I told you," answered his companion, smiling, "that I have not seen her myself. The Prince," she said—and she named the same Royal Personage who had shown himself so susceptible to Countess Shimna's charms at the dinner-party—"the Prince, they tell me, has been dancing with her all the evening; and no doubt they are having tea together in one of those rooms beyond the ball-room. When I have been in them they have generally been very quiet places indeed."

Pole could not doubt that the beauty alluded to was Countess Shimna; and he was pleased to think that if she were to be engrossed at all, she should fall to the lot of an admirer so distinguished, and of whom he entertained so little serious jealousy. Still he was annoyed with the thought that his chances of conversation with her were almost destroyed for the evening—almost, though not quite; and an irritable longing filled him to discover her, and to see how she was occupied. He was thinking how, without abruptness, he might free himself from his present companion, when the process of his liberation was simplified by a man with a star and ribbon, who broke, on seeing him, into an exclamation of surprise and pleasure. This *deus ex machinâ* was a Viceroy, lately returned from India. Though much older than Pole, he had once been his intimate friend; and his memory evidently had not been dimmed by years.

"My dear fellow," he said, "let us get out of this crowd. I would give my kingdom for a cigar. Let us see if there's not a smoking-room."

This suggestion Pole accepted with alacrity. His own object was to penetrate beyond the ball-room, and let Countess Shimna at least see that he was there. He and the Viceroy strolled across the empty parquet, the band meantime having again begun to play, and soon saw life and motion beyond one of the farther doors. They were about to pass through it, when a hurried and rustling movement was seen to take place amongst a medley of skirts and coats, as though every one was trying to become as small as possible: and a second later, the Royal guest of the evening emerged sedately into the ball-room with Countess Shimna on his arm. She was looking brilliant; but neither in her face nor bearing was there any sign that she felt herself to be enjoying any special honour. On the contrary, she seemed somewhat absent. As soon, however, as she caught sight of Pole, her expression changed suddenly. What the change meant it was not possible to tell, except that some thought had startled her, disturbing her bright placidity; but one or two male spectators, experienced in the ways of women, at once connected it with Pole, and drawing their own conclusions from it, began to regard him with a respectful, yet somewhat envious, curiosity. At the same moment the Prince, with a gracious smile, stopped and shook hands with somebody. Pole looked and saw that this was none other than the Prime Minister, who was leaning against the wall, as if to avoid the company, like a stick washed against a bank by the lappings of an agitated pond. From the Prime Minister the Prince turned to the Viceroy; and then recognized Pole, with whose face he was less familiar, and greeted him in a way which would have satisfied the most sensitive to Royal favour. Pole felt that Countess Shima would be watching this little incident keenly, and when again he caught her eye as the Prince was moving away with her, there was laughter between her lashes and a flush of gratification upon her cheeks.

"For God's sake, my dear fellow," said the Viceroy, "tell me who that is!" And taking Pole's arm he dragged him out of the ball-room, and down a gallery lined with whispering couples, which brought them to a library, consecrated for that night to tobacco.

"At last!" exclaimed the Viceroy, with a sigh of impassioned gratitude, as he brought out his cigar case, and offered its treasures to Pole. "Who," he continued, "did you say that was? Or perhaps you said nothing."

Pole told him Countess Shimna's name.

"You don't say so!" exclaimed the Viceroy. "I wonder if she's any relation to a beautiful Countess Stephanie O'Keefe, whose curious story I heard the other day in Vienna? If so, the O'Keefes must be a remarkably handsome family."

"I happen to know," said Pole, "that she is a cousin of the lady you mention. As for her—as for Countess Ste hanie—I heard her story myself. There was something about it very original."

"It's a curious thing," said the Viceroy, incidentally, "that some families, with birth, money, beauty, refinement—everything—not only can never be moral—we don't ask that—but never even respectable. Most of these lovely O'Keefes, they tell me, have been like that."

"This one," said Pole, annoyed by these last observations, "I assure you, is quite different; though I confess that, in her immediate relations, she is not perhaps very fortunate. But tell me," he said, anxious to change the conversation, "tell me about Countess Stephanie. Is she married, as I heard she was? and what has happened to her lover—the young man whom it was said she would not allow to do the right thing by her?"

"I did not hear," said the Viceroy, "that she was married to any one else; but if she is, that exceedingly rare visitant, Poetic Justice, has overtaken her, for I'm told the despised young man has inherited an immense fortune in Poland—a castle, family jewels, a territory alive with wolves, and also one of the finest hotels in Paris. Several of his relations were credited with Nihilistic sympathies, but the young man himself has made his peace with the Czar. I heard all this last week from my old friend, Count O'Keefe, who is not very proud of the larger part of his kindred. But he told me one thing, which the young lady we saw just now makes quite intelligible to me. He said that these charming cousins of his managed to lose their reputation as demurely and as daintily as other and wiser women keep theirs. It's a curious thing," he continued, leaning back in his chair, " the relation in women between the matter and the manner of their behaviour." And he rambled off into a discussion of the feminine nature, in which Pole joined, not without wandering thoughts.

At last, in the gallery outside, a sound of voices developed itself; and the Viceroy, rising, exclaimed: " Listen ! the Prince is coming. Let us escape while there is time. I'm too tired to-night to be a courtier." He had barely finished speaking before he had vanished through a side door; and Pole, full of the thought that Countess Shimna would now be free, was about to follow, when the voice of the Prince detained him. "Ah, Mr. Pole," he said, " I've been wanting to have a word with you." And Pole, putting on the matter the best face possible, was held there in honourable captivity till the half-hour was over, required for the consumption of a long Royal cigar.

When he found himself a free man again, he hurried back to the ball-room, and slowly made his way round it, skirting as he did so, a long dado of mothers, some of whom, by their drooping heads, announced the lateness of the hour. He noticed all the dancers, the number of which was much diminished; but Countess Shimna was not one of them. He then walked through rooms full of chairs and sofas, where many couples were murmuring under the chaperonage of a modest twilight; but nowhere was there a skirt, or a shoe, or a fan, like Countess Shimna's. The Viceroy's observations about the women of the O'Keefe family, had intensified his desire for this one—for this wild hawk who for him should be tame and tender as a dove. Finally, he betook himself to the supper-room, which was situated on the ground-floor. At the door was Lord Wargrave, talking to three Ambassadors and finishing a sandwich, which he had carried away with him from the supper-table. On seeing Pole, he darted forward and accosted him. "I've been looking for you everywhere," he said; "Where is our young

Countess ? It's an early ball, every one will be going soon ;
and I want to get her away before there is any rush and
crush. She was," continued Lord Wargrave, "on the stairs
half an hour ago, and then she went off with some friend
of that young monkey, Jacques de Pontorson's. They may
be at supper by this time. I wish you would go and fetch
her out of whatever corner you find her in."

Without any further waiting, Pole peered into the supper-
room, where the crowd of small tables still had numerous
patrons. As he did so, he heard Lord Wargrave's voice
mention Countess Shimna's name to one of the three diplo-
matists ; and he caught the tone of the reply which seemed
full of recognition and interest. He scanned each feasting
group, which was dawdling over quails and cutlets; and
passed, through smells of soup, to the far end of the room ;
but he failed to see her anywhere. As he looked about him,
he noticed a small door, opening into a conservatory, which
was full of lamplight and palm-trees, but desolately empty
of audible sound or movement.

From his former acquaintance with the house, he knew
that at one end of this was a stair which would lead him
back to the room in which the dancers rested themselves.
He accordingly took his way through the aisle of exotic
foliage, lingering there in the quiet to pacify the restless
thoughts, which were now buzzing like bees round the image
of the woman whom he was seeking; and a longing filled
his mind to woo her from the ball and ball-room, and make
her confess herself his own in the solitude of this mimic
summer, where sounds of music came stealing through the
palm-fronds faintly, and the stillness was freshened by the
crisp whispering of a fountain.

He saw the door before him that led back to the world,
and he approached it, shrinking inwardly from the possibility of some new disappointment. As he was on the point
of entering, something caught his eye, and forced him to
glance at a nook embowered in foliage, through whose roof
the lamplight sifted itself, and filled it with a flickering
dimness. Here was a seat covered with crimson cushions,
and on these cushions two figures were seated. One of them
was a man whose face was vague with shadow; the other
was a woman, with a shoulder leaning towards the man's.
Her face was close to his; her eyes were absorbed and flashing ;

U

and a fan, hiding her lips, palpitated slowly there like the wings of a butterfly on a flower. Whoever the man may have been, Pole did not recognize him; but about the woman, his eyes spoke to him with such scathing clearness that he could not at first believe them. The woman was Countess Shimna.

For every reason a few seconds of the spectacle were enough for him. Hurrying through the house, he made his way back to the hall, where Lord Wargrave was more loqua-cious and more fussy than ever.

"She's in the conservatory," said Pole, "talking to an old acquaintance. If you would not mind extracting her, I will get the carriage meanwhile. I intend to walk home myself, but I will wait here till you come back with her."

CHAPTER XXXV.

Except as she appeared clinging to Lord Wargrave's arm, and making her way through the crowd that had now gathered about the front door, Pole did not that night again see Countess Shimna. Having told Lord Wargrave that his carriage would be the next, he stepped outside, and heavily walked homewards. He hardly knew what had happened to him. All that night, through fantastic and restless hours, his eyes and thoughts were fixed on that single scene in the conservatory. Countess Shimna's remembered attitude, and even her slightest movements, he studied again and again as he tossed on his restless mattress. They all recalled the steps by which she had drawn him towards herself—those naïve audacities of a temperament whose seductions were made almost virginal, alike by their delicacy and the air they had of being for one man only. And now this child of the spirit, perfumed with the subtlest essence of the senses, who had filled the desert of his future with the glades of an enchanted garden, was suddenly changed into the likeness of—he dared not think what. His idea on waking was to take the first train to Lyncombe, and so to avoid, if possible, seeing her before he went. But he presently told himself that, after all, he had perhaps misjudged her; and anger, hope, and anxiety entered into an odd alliance, and forced him to put his departure off till the evening, and confront her at breakfast as though nothing whatever had been wrong.

Countess Shimna was down before him, and when he entered the dining-room she was just giving his mother her customary morning kiss. The difficulty of the part he had chosen became for the first time clear to him. He wished to behave to her as he had always done till now, but he now found that he had forgotten what his former behaviour was. The very smile he was preparing he felt to be frozen and unnatural. The utmost dissimulation in his power appeared to be a crude civility. But the moment she turned to speak to him his whole programme of deportment was disarranged. She showed no signs of fatigue as she had done the day before, but her whole aspect was in some vague way softened; and Pole, who, with an inconsistency not altogether unnatural, had been meaning to take her hand in the most careless way possible, was suddenly disarmed by finding how it clung to his, and how her eyes appealed to him with a sort of caressing welcome.

After breakfast they were left alone in the dining-room.

" I didn t," he said, " see much of you last night."

" I am very sorry," she answered. " For a long time the Prince kept me."

" I saw you," said Pole dryly, " in the enjoyment of that honour."

" Honour! " she repeated, looking at him. " I was merely a new plaything. I have been one too often to be either pleased or broken."

" The Prince," said Pole, " was talking to me, too. By the time he let me go you were dancing with some one else, I suppose."

" No," she replied, frankly; " I hardly danced at all. I met a friend—a man whom I knew when I was a girl, and I spent most of my time in giving him—you will know what I mean—some plausible account of myself. You see you know much that he does not."

This simple allusion to the complete confidence she had placed in him suddenly pushed out of his consciousness every bitter suspicion of her; but before he had time to reply she had anticipated what he was on the point of saying.

" And now listen," she went on; "are you really going to Glenlynn to-day?"

" To-night," he said; " at nine o'clock."

" And," she asked, almost eagerly, "how long do you stay there?"

He told her for about three days.

" Well, then," she said quickly, "when you come back to London I shall be able to answer a question which you have more than once put to me—if," she added, looking at him, " you have not forgotten all about it. Come, don't protest. This afternoon I must go out with Thérèse; but I shall see you at dinner before you go; and, would you like this morning to walk with me as far as my little girl's lodging? You mustn't come in, for I hear she is not quite well."

Pole hesitated. Pleasure and annoyance made a see-saw in his mind. There was something that piqued him in her announcement that she would leave him at her child's door. He was piqued still more by her intention of deserting him for the remainder of the day. Pique outweighed pleasure. " I am very sorry," he said. " I could have come with you in the afternoon, but all the morning I am engaged. I will ask you no questions now. I will wait, as you bid me, till I come back again."

She fixed her eyes full on him, and made a slight gesture with her lips. "Would you like," she said, "to show me that you are not angry? Because "—and here there was a momentary mischief in her expression—" I shall not be in even at luncheon."

He stooped and kissed her with a gravity of which he was hardly conscious, and slowly left the room, casting no look behind him. The next time he met her was at dinner —a dinner which took place early in order to allow of his catching the night mail.

It was not till he found himself isolated from all his late surroundings, and face to face with himself in the dim solitude of the railway-carriage, that he realized the full meaning of the doubts into which he was now plunged. At intervals he managed to persuade himself that these doubts were idle fancies, which would soon vanish like shadows, in the light of some simple explanation; but in the bottom of his heart was an unacknowledged conviction that this was not so.

At an early hour in the morning, when the darkness was beginning to have grey in it, he found himself deposited on the chilly platform of the junction, where for nearly an hour he would have, as "Bradshaw" told him, to wait for the local train which was to carry him on his further journey. Except for two porters, some luggage, and a commercial traveller in a fur cap, who stared at him with drowsy curiosity, the platform was quite deserted; but a dim glimmer was apparent in one of the waiting-rooms, and on looking through the window he saw a man in a black cloak, who was trying his eyesight by writing at the bare table.

He pushed the door open, and entered. The man gave a start, so violent that Pole felt inclined to beg his pardon for intruding on him. Then scrutinizing his face he saw that it was Dr. Clitheroe. "My dear Doctor!" he exclaimed, in accents of such unmistakable cordiality, that the Doctor, for it was indeed he, started again, but with pleasure now, not nervousness. Hastily stuffing his writing materials into a bag—one of the patent conveniences of which the Doctor was such a great collector—he trotted up to Pole, wreathed in welcoming smiles, and began to ply him with compliments and friendly greetings, at such a rate that it was impossible to acknowledge or answer them.

"And what place," asked Pole, "may you happen to be bound for now?"

"What place—now—what place?" said the Doctor, hesitating. "Well, to say the truth, for all sorts of places. I am going at this moment to a little village in Dorsetshire —I expect you never heard the name; and then for a week or two I am going to shut myself up—I shall not tell even my most intimate friends where—and get through my arrears of work. They are a positive mountain, I assure you. But you," he said, peering into Pole's face, kindly—"you are looking cold. I sincerely hope you have not taken a chill."

"Till you mentioned it," replied Pole, "I had not thought of the matter. But they certainly did forget to give me my warm rug in London; or my servant, who went down before me, has been clever enough to take it with my luggage."

"Look here," said the Doctor, "you must allow me to lend you mine. My cloak is so thick that, I assure you, I'm like a hot potato. You will do me," he went on, "a real favour by taking it."

Pole was much touched by the offer, but would not hear of accepting it. The Doctor received his refusal in a sort of undecided silence; and then, looking up at him, said almost timidly, "Well, since you won't have my rug, I am reminded of something which I have long been wishing to offer you. Perhaps you will take it now, and save me the trouble of sending it."

He seated himself again at the table, and began grubbing in his bag, turning his back to Pole, so that what he did should be hidden. Presently Pole's ear caught the sounds of a scratching pen, then of paper being blotted and folded up; and the Doctor, turning round, put into Pole's hands an envelope. "It is a little something," he said, "which I have desired to give you for your building fund. But it is so little," he added, "that until I am out of the way, you must not put me out of countenance by looking to see what it is. Hark! there is your train. I know the ways of this station at these early hours well." And taking his rug and bag with him, he accompanied Pole to the carriage.

"I hope," he said, in his demure, clerical voice, as he walked along the platform, "I hope—for human life, as we know, has many changes—that you will always remember and believe in the sincerity of the good-will I have borne you. It will be always a comfort to me to think that you do that."

"I am sure," said Pole grasping the Doctor's hand, "I am not likely either to forget or doubt it. This is my carriage, I suppose. Well, good-bye—good-bye."

The Doctor stayed by the window chattering, till the train began to move. Then, inserting his head as if to utter a last farewell, he contrived, by an adroit movement, to throw in the railway-rug. "You'll be warm now," he exclaimed, in triumphant accents, as Pole, embarrassed with gratitude, was swept out of reach and hearing of him. "At least," he said to himself, "I have one friend in the world— one unselfish friend—that little man—and," he added, "another—Ethel De Souza."

With some curiosity he opened the Doctor's envelope, and examined the contents by the flicker of the oil-lamp in the roof. What he found was a cheque for two hundred pounds, and the following words, in a tremulous hand-writing, accompanying it: "I could not explain this at the station; but use the enclosed in any way you like. Our investment has prospered beyond my most sanguine hopes. This is really a little bonus, morally, if not legally, due to you." Pole felt it would be difficult to accept this generosity; but the Doctor's kindness, coming to him in his present unhappy condition, filled him with a sense of gratitude of which he hardly imagined himself capable.

He found, when he reached Glenlynn, that his presence was indeed necessary, and that he would certainly have to stay there for two, or perhaps for three, nights. But though each day had its hours of urgent business, these hours were not many; and all the rest of the time he was left in a solitary idleness, that was infested with mordant memories of a mocking and miserable past. His eye, in fact, hardly lit upon anything which did not awake some painful thought or feeling. The house, except for his own bedroom and the breakfast-parlour, was, for the first time within the last sixty years unoccupied; and the furniture, covered with sheets was like ruins lost in snow. A dream and a glory had gone from the roseless garden; whilst hardly a path, a flower-bed, or noticeable view of the sea failed to remind him of the hours when it had been bewitched by Countess Shimna's admiration of it, and to madden him with sadness, as a thing which was his own no longer.

But his lowest depth of unhappiness was not reached till the last morning of his stay. When he had finished his business, he went up to his bedroom to look for a novel he had brought with him. It happened to have fallen on the ground; and, as he stooped to pick it up, he saw under a wardrobe a fragment of torn paper. He drew it out from its hiding-place. It was an envelope directed to himself; and the direction, covered with dust, was in the writing of Pansy Masters. He stared at it sadly; and presently, by the dates upon the post-marks, he realized that this scrap of paper had enclosed the cruelest of her letters; and yet, a moment later, he raised it tenderly to his lips. "Why did I leave you," he said, " no matter what you did to me ? "

For a little while he stood, staring blankly at the carpet; and suddenly all the impulses out of which religion is fashioned welled up in his heart like an unsealed fountain, troubling him with their unchannelled waters. Floating upon their surface came memories of his own childhood, interlocked with which was a sense of profound sorrow: and presently he performed an action which to many might have seemed meaningless and ridiculous. He approached the bed, and sank down beside it on his knees. His thoughts shaped themselves into nothing that if written would suggest a prayer; but at last they broke out in words. "My son!" he said, "my little boy — my son!" Then recollections flashed on him of his recent public life, and he compared the bewildered action of his mind and his will now with their action in the House of Commons. He rose to his feet, with a laugh at his own weakness. "I don't know how to think," he said. "I can reason about things only that do not concern myself."

He travelled back to London, as he had come from it, by night; and reached Brook Street at four o'clock in the morning. On the hall table was lying a pair of gloves, which he recognized as Countess Shimna's; and by them a packet, directed in her handwriting to his mother. At the sight of these objects her image again shone before him; and her influence tingled in his veins, as his one escape from misery. The packet, for a moment, was a puzzle to him. Why should it be there unopened? But he explained it to himself as some present made by her to his mother, and left there overnight, that his mother might be surprised by it next morning.

CHAPTER XXXVI.

"My dear Reginald," said Mrs. Pole, when they met at breakfast, "I've some very sad news to tell you. At least I feel it sad; and I think you will also. Shimna has been telegraphed for by her mother, and left last night for Paris. I don't know the reason, but the little girl is to go too; and they all, so I believe, are to winter together in the South of France. Poor child, she left this scent-bottle as a parting gift. I only had it given me when I came downstairs; and there was such a pretty little note accompanying it."

Pole received the shock of this intelligence with an absolute and apparently stolid calm, as a man sometimes

b ars a fall before he understands what it has done to him.
He asked if Countess Shimna had had bad news while he
was away—if her mother's summons had discomposed or
alarmed her — and other questions of the same obvious
nature. But beyond telling him that Countess Shimna, for
the last day or two, had seen a good deal of her French
friend, Thérèse, and had, after walking with her, sometimes
come in preoccupied, Mrs. Pole could give her son no information whatsoever. But he soon received some from a more
authoritative quarter A note reached him that evening,
bearing the Calais post-mark, and containing the following
few lines from Countess Shimna herself :—

"I was sorry not to have seen you, and said Good-bye ;
and yet to say it would have been difficult, because it would
have meant so much. You know my hesitation when you
asked me a certain question. I did not hesitate from any
light caprice. I have told you much about myself, which
nobody else knows ; but there was something I did not tell
you, because I was not myself sure about it. There was an
earlier tie which bound me, so long as it was not broken by
certain circumstances; and I did not know, when I was at
Glenlynn, whether it were so broken or no. I thought it
was ; but I had to wait; and it has not been broken. It
binds me still. Its links are made of honour, of promises, of
early association—of everything, in short, except the things
that I gave to you. Do not forget those things ; and burn
this letter which mentions them. When you hear that I am
married—for I had better speak plainly—remember that my
marriage was made for me by events which took place long
before we ever met."

Though Pole's apprehensive fancy had prepared him for
some news like this, yet so sudden and complete a fulfilment
of his worst, and indeed his wildest conjectures, was a
heavier, not a lighter, blow to him, because he was half
prepared for it. He had no immediate leisure, however, for
considering how it affected him. His most pressing care,
for the time, was not to understand what he suffered, but to
hide it—to hide it from his mother, and still more from Lord
Wargrave. Countess Shimna's letter had arrived just before
dinner; and as it happened, for a wonder, that Lord Wargrave was to dine at home, Pole summoned all his powers,
so as to meet him with an untroubled bearing.

He found that this task was rendered unexpectedly easy by the fact of Lord Wargrave himself being in a state of great perturbation on account of his young lady's disappearance, and taking no trouble to hide it. Lord Wargrave, like Pole, had been absent the night before, and the news affected him like some personal injury to himself. It was years since he had enjoyed any parties so much as the two at Dulverton House. Countess Shimna had supplied him with a new *raison d'être* in a ball-room; and he had been planning two dinners and an evening party in her honour. "And now," he said to himself as he drove down after dinner to his club, "this foolish flighty child has left for a mere whim the best society in Europe; and is going to ruin her prospects by associating with that painted disreputable old mother of hers."

He found reason, however, in his club to modify this last opinion. Having peeped into the smoking-room, with his hat lowering over his eyes, and with a severe stare at the members, as though they had all affronted him, his expression relaxed a little at the sight of a distinguished-looking man, whose white beard and moustache had something foreign in their well-trimmed neatness. This was one of the Ambassadors to whom he had been speaking at the recent ball; and dropping into a chair close to him, Lord Wargrave confided to him his annoyance.

"Ha!" exclaimed the Ambassador, with eyebrows mounting into his forehead, and all the rest of his face becoming puckered with wrinkles of intelligence. "You speak of that charming young Countess belonging to the O'Keefe family? I thought when I saw her at the ball I should find—. But tell me—she is a relation of yours—is she?"

"Nothing of the kind," grunted Lord Wargrave, with vehemence. "She's a distant cousin of a cousin of mine—that's all. What do you know? I should like very much to hear."

"Well," replied the Ambassador, "she has—as you can hardly wonder—been much admired in other places besides London—by men, you understand: for somehow, owing to her mother, she was never—if I have your permission to say so—very well received amongst women. Well, one of her great admirers was a certain young man, whom she favoured but refused to marry; and he tried one day to shoot himself at her doorstep in Warsaw. I need hardly tell you he was very poor at the time. Rich young men don't shoot themselves. Women don't drive them to do so. This young man, however, has lately inherited a vast fortune—ah, but vast! But tell me—the young lady, you call her Countess Shimna—is not that so? I ask because in her own country she was always called Countess Stephanie. She has both names, you comprehend, but it is Stephanie that is the first."

"God bless my soul!" exclaimed Lord Wargrave. "God bless my soul, you don't say so! And the young man—this delightful young suicide—who is he? What is he? Where is he?"

"You ask where he is," said the Ambassador. "Ah—that I cannot tell you. But as for where he was—why the other night he was in London, at the Duchess's charming ball. He was half the evening with Countess Stephanie, delighted to be still alive. My young friend Jacques de Pontorson, who is related to this young man, and whose sister is his bosom friend—told me, by the way, that he has just gone back to Paris."

"A very interesting story," said Lord Wargrave, getting up from his chair. "Countess Shimna, or Countess Stephanie, has just gone to Paris also." Lord Wargrave's annoyance with Countess Shimna had, for the moment at all events, been converted into an additional interest in her—not unmixed with respect. A beautiful woman with a history, especially if she were well-born, had always had a singular fascination for him. "By the way," he said, sitting down again, and leaning over to the Ambassador so as to speak to him in a confidential whisper, "the old yellow-haired Countess—this young lady's mother—she, too, is a curious social specimen. There is some mysterious baby in which she takes an interest, and which she left in England under the care of her charming daughter. I cannot help thinking there must be some mystery about that."

An odd expression played about the Ambassador's lips. He took his *pince-nez* from his nose, and began to wipe the glasses. Then, turning to Lord Wargrave, and speaking in a low tone also, "I hardly," he said, "know if I ought to tell you what I have happened to hear. Have you met our new first secretary? He has told me the whole story.

Countess Stephanie," he continued, seeing encouragement
in Lord Wargrave's face—"I dare say you don't know this
—was married to a Russian General, whose wife was supp sed
to be dead, but who proved subsequently to be alive.   The
old Countess arranged the marriage, in great haste, so it
appears ; and the husband had to leave the bride at the
church door for Petersburg.   The marriage was annulled,
and he never saw her again.   That is the version of the
affair given by the old Countess.   Whether it is true or not
I have really no means of knowing ; but the belief was——
However, that's nothing to you or me.   We hear these
things, and we must use our own judgment about believing
them."

"My dear Count," said Lord Wargrave, with a certain
gravity, " we are both of us men who have seen a good deal
of the world, and I am not talking to you now in the spirit
of idle gossip.   If I understand you rightly about this very
curious story, the mysterious baby is mysteri us for one
reason only.   The mother, I gather, is a delightful young
friend of my own, whose company I have just lost; and the
only doubt is whether its father was a Russian General, or a
certain poor young man who has since become a very rich
one.   I can only say," he went on, having once more risen,
and stooping as he spoke to mumble into his companion's
ear, " that whatever father this mysterious child may have,
it has at all events a most delightful and fascinating
mother."

As he went home that night Lord Wargrave had much
to think of.   From certain points of view Countess Shimna
had so risen in his estimation that he was prouder of her
than he had ever been, and more sorry to have lost her.
She seemed to him like Lady Thyrza O'Keefe come to life
again, with enlarged experiences ; and much as he regretted
her, his original irritation had disappeared.   He began to
feel that he should like to correspond with a woman who so
early had seen so much ; and he thought in what an interesting way their letters would figure in his " Memoirs."   He,
moreover, experienced no inconsiderable satisfaction in reflecting how cleverly he had judged her character from the
beginning.   " I always thought it," he mumbled to himself ;
" I always thought it."   And he recalled and repeated what
he had said about her to Pole.   " She is quite incapable of

doing anything that she thinks wrong, because she never would think wrong anything she might want to do. Before she tried to judge it she would have tied it up into a nosegay." But the thoughts with regard to the matter, which really were annoying to him, were thoughts as to how her conduct would affect Pole. Selfish though Lord Wargrave, in some ways, was, he was a man of profound kindliness; and he was at once pained by the thought that Pole might be deeply wounded, and also by the apprehension that he would be gloomy company in consequence He resolved nevertheless that at the earliest opportunity next morning he would inform him at all events of one of the facts which he had learnt—namely, that Countess Shimna was identical with Countess Stephanie : and this revelation, he argued, would include, or prepare the way, for the others.

He found, however, next day, when he began to approach the subject, that no diplomacy, and indeed no delicacy, was needed; for Pole, to his surprise, was as calm as on the previous evening. He joined in Lord Wargrave's praise of Countess Shimna's charms, and his regret at her departure, with so complete a freedom from embarrassment, that Lord Wargrave was forced to admire him as one of those happy men who can enjoy the pleasure of making love without suffering the inconvenience of feeling it. The two, therefore, compared notes with regard to the curious story, treating Countess Shimna with a chivalrous, and perhaps even a cynical, indulgence; and finally, Pole astonished Lord Wargrave, and, slightly to his annoyance, threw his discoveries into the shade by saying, "I have had a letter from Countess Shimna herself, in which she tells me that she is shortly going to be married. She does not mention the name of the elect-bridegroom, but she says he is an old and very intimate friend. And here," he went on, drawing a photograph from his pocket, "is a picture of what I presume to be the bridegroom's château in Poland. It was found in Countess Shimna's room, fallen behind the clock on the chimney-piece."

CHAPTER XXXVII.

LORD WARGRAVE, however, though he had, after his first state
of irritation, recovered the philosophic calm of a student of
human nature, began very soon to relapse into his former
malady. Countess Shimna's departure, though highly exciting
to his imagination, he found had rendered London most
provokingly flat and savourless; and for the first time in
his life the dirt of his house in Brook Street struck his eye
as something that was sordid and very nearly disgusting.

"My dear Augusta," he said to Mrs. Pole that evening,
"our faithless young lady has completely spoilt our season."
And gradually going on from one complaint to another, he
at last enunciated the view that there was no season at all;
that, except the two parties at Dulverton House, there had
been actually nothing worth the trouble of going to; that
Mrs. Pole would be happier at Glenlynn; that he himself
would be much happier visiting; and that Pole, while the
session lasted, would be much happier in a lodging.

Nothing could have been to Pole more welcome than
these words. He knew that without Countess Shimna, his
mother would be happier at home; and he felt for his own
part that life would be hardly endurable unless he could
escape from Lord Wargrave's restless scrutiny. From the
society of his colleagues in work he felt, indeed, no shrinking; but apart from this, what he wished for now was
solitude. He was, therefore, pleased to find that Lord
Wargrave's words had made on his mother quite as much
impression as on himself; and, luckily, a day or two later, a
letter arrived from Miss Drake, which at once brought
matters to a pleasant and happy issue. Miss Drake's house
in Lyncombe, to which she had now retired, appeard to be
suffering from a severe derangement of its drains; and
while these were being restored to health, she had proposed
to betake herself to a lodging. Mrs. Pole at once wrote to
her, begging for her companionship at Glenlynn; and on
the invitation being accepted with gratitude, joined her
there a few days later. As for Lord Wargrave, it appeared
that his dissatisfaction with London was not only due to the
events of his life there, but also to the rival attractions of

certain gaieties which had been offered him in the country. He was the gratified possessor of invitations to five consecutive shooting-parties, at which he foresaw himself, week after happy week, the oracle of libraries and drawing-rooms, whilst his rivals were with guns and loaders. He soon vanished accordingly into the region of parks and partridges, and Pole was left to the solitude he had so much desired.

The future of each of us is proverbially uncertain, and it is of course assumed that the main reason of its uncertainty is its dependence on causes not under our own control. But vulgar opinion converts this truism into a falsehood, by expressly excluding from these causes one of the most important—namely, the actions, not of other people. but of our own temperaments and consciences. The course of a sorrow is often as incalculable as the course of a disease.

This, to his own surprise, was discovered by Pole now. The thought of Countess Shimna's desertion still, indeed, beset and bewildered him. The rose-garden of the imagination and of the senses which she had caused to blossom in his breast, was now black with frost, and was beaten down by storm; and he was filled at times with a helpless and unhealthy craving for her, which was really wounded vanity longing for its own revenge—longing to enslave again a tributary that had broken free. But little by little he realized, with a half-incredulous wonder, that his sorrow for Countess Shimna by no means came up to his expectations. It grew, like a dissolving cloud, slowly less and less; but then, if he wished for sorrow, it came to him in an unforeseen shape. As one cloud dissolved, another, and a darker shaped itself; and this was his memory of the woman whom Countess Shimna had assisted him to forget. It came back to him now, but with a new and unfamiliar aspect. Whatever might have been blamable in his connection with this woman, and whatever misery might have resulted from it, her image had been once a symbol for him of something to which he had been, at all costs, true. He had suffered much for her sake; he had also suffered much at her hands. He had suffered so much that at moments he had been moved to hate her. But he had got the better of such temptations; he had made all sorts of excuses for her; and his love for her had been deepened and chastened by each act of forbearance. But now he began to tell himself that he had been true to nothing. A serious devotion which had cost him so many self-denials, became in his eyes degraded to the level of a vulgar adultery. For a part of each day, his political work distracted him, and, indeed, supported him with a sense that he was acting worthily; but he went to bed each night with a gathering impulse in his heart to do again what he had done by his bedside the other day at Glenlynn —to sink on his knees and confess himself to some Divine Power, if only such a Power existed, who cared to, or who would, listen to him. Foolish defenders of religion fancy they can confute the atheist by finding in Reason a God who is necessitated by the physical universe. A God, demanded by physics, may answer the riddles of the physicist; but if natural religion gives us a God at all, a God who can comfort the heart must be a God whom the heart fashions. As Pole, however, was shut out from any sight of this supreme comfort, his thoughts turned to another, which was neither more nor less than the human sympathy of Miss De Souza.

One morning as he lay in bed, after a late night in the House of Commons, thinking of the ease with which he could talk to her upon every subject, and the way in which her thoughts would run out to meet his own, he was surprised at receiving what appeared to be a literal illustration of this quality in them—that is to say, a letter in Miss De Souza's own handwriting. Its contents, however, showed her to be deficient, at times, in the kind of clairvoyance which he imputed to her.

"My aunt," said the letter, "has just written to your mother to ask if she would bring Countess Shimna again to luncheon. You know how beautiful I thought her. She has quite fascinated my aunt. You must not think me uncharitable, if I say that she did so unintentionally. If they come, I hope you will come, too. I have read your speeches with, I cannot tell you how much, attention."

He wrote back, "Will your aunt have me by myself? My mother has gone back to Glenlynn; and the young lady whom you flattered me by regarding as not half good enough for me, thinks herself quite good enough for a charming young foreign prince, whom she has known for years, who has just come into a fortune, and whom, at a moment's notice, she left us last week to marry. She was good enough to write me the news as a secret, the moment she had gone;

but she has now, so my mother tells me, announced the event to her; so I may, I suppose, announce it in turn to you."

Miss De Souza, when this reached her, was not in her usual spirits. Far from robust in health, and prone to over-exert herself, she was suffering from a form of nervous exhaustion, which confined her often, and confined her now, to her sofa. She was free from positive pain; indeed, so far as her mere bodily sensations went, her exhaustion showed itself chiefly in rendering rest a luxury; and, as she lay in her own sitting-room, with a table of books beside her, with a fire flickering on the pile of a crimson carpet and playing in ruddy lines of the gilded mouldings on the walls, and with a mountain of silken cushions, assisting each other to support her back, she seemed like one of the women whom a certain profound philosophy describes as the pos-sessors "of everything that can make them happy."

Miss De Souza, however, did not think this of herself. Her physical weakness had done what it often had done before. Instead of paining her body, it had produced a sadness in her mind. Thoughts of the lover to whom so long ago she had given her heart—and who valued the gift so lightly—were rising up from her memory, like mists from an evening meadow; and she was reflecting on the way in which this episode had affected her life, and on the difference between her nature before its occurrence and after it. Did she still retain for that man anything that could be called love? Sadly, but without hesitation, she answered to this question "No." And yet the recollection of him often produced in her poignant suffering. Could it be, she asked herself, that her experience had made her cynical, and that, still believing affection to be the most valuable thing in life, she had come to regard it as being also the rarest—so rare, indeed, as to be in most cases an illusion? No, she again answered, her suffering did not come from this. What it did come from was something far more personal. It was not from any disbelief in human affection generally, but from a vivid recollection of the pain which she herself suffered in con-nection with it, and a belief that she not only had failed to inspire it in a certain person, but that, for some reason or other, she was unfit to inspire it in anybody.

She said all this to herself with an almost tragic modesty;

x

and yet vanity, as she did so, forced from her a faint,
protesting sigh. Amongst the books that were on the table
at her side, lay a little hand looking-glass. Beautiful as
was her general appearance, and perfect as was the symmetry
of her figure, there were yet in her face certain defects and
irregularities; and taking the glass up, she began to examine
and consider them. "What," she reflected, "what man in
his senses would ever care for a woman, with this fault, and
with this fault, and with that fault?" And she was about
to lay down the glass with an abrupt movement of petulance,
when with a gentle dignity and a self-control that was
characteristic of her, she puffed away the impatient impulse,
as if it had been a piece of thistledown, laughing at herself
and it. Her laugh, however, did not dispel her gravity, but
only gave it a slightly different character. "Yes," she
thought, "I may have friends—I have them; but a man
who will love me, for my own sake, or love me at all, never;
and even if a man were to make me believe he loved me, if
he made himself believe it too, and tempted me, no matter
how much, to offer him some return, I would never again
do so—never—never. I will never run the chance of suffering as I suffered once. This may be selfish; but it is the
selfishness of self-protection. My peace—for I am at peace—
is now in my own hands. I will never again commit it to
another's keeping."

Then her thoughts wandered away to Pole, who had
known her intimately ever since she had left the schoolroom,
who had always talked to her with an openness rare even
between lovers, but had never attempted to breathe to her
a single word of love. There was rest for her in the thought
of him. She had always recognized and always admired his
talents, long before he had given any public proof of them;
and she was deeply interested now in his successes, which
were justifying her judgment. But what of late had
interested her even more, had been the kind of unhappiness
which she had detected in him, and of which she felt the
nature, though she had no knowledge of the causes. Her
mind, indeed, had constantly recurred to the conversation
they had had together in the boat under the willows.
When, however, she last had seen him, on the occasion of
Countess Shimna's visit, she had divined in him what had
seemed like the dawn of a new happiness; and she had

often felt a wish to see Countess Shimna again, so as to
reconsider what influence she was likely to have upon him.
This wish had now shaped itself once more in her mind,
when a servant entered with a tray, and on the tray was
a letter. This letter was Pole's, which announced to her
that Countess Shimna had departed, not only from London,
but also out of the writer's life.

She sank back in her chair, when she had read it, and
thought with increased sadness of one who she fancied would
be suffering somewhat as she had once suffered herself.
She was roused from her reverie by the vigorous entrance
of her aunt, whose mind and whose talkative mouth were
always stocked with sympathy.

Miss De Souza handed to her Pole's letter. Mrs. Steinberg read it, and immediately broke out into a sound which
was partly an exclamation of surprise, partly an exclamation
of disappointment, and partly a prolonged coo of com-
miseration for somebody on account of something.

"Dear, dear me!" she said, at last arriving at words.
"And so she's gone! This charming young lady's gone!
I declare I thought when she was here that she was setting
her cap at Mr. Pole. And he, poor man, is left all alone in
London, for I know Lord Wargrave's away—I saw it in the
Morning Post. Dear Mr. Pole—let us ask him down here,
and tell him to stop, if he likes, till this autumn session is
over. He can get from here by train to Westminster in
half an hour. Shall I write this evening? I'm sure we
should both of us like to have him."

A letter was accordingly written, and met with a prompt
reply, in which Pole accepted Mrs. Steinberg's hospitality
with gratitude, and agreed to arrive on the evening of the
day following, which was Saturday.

When he entered the drawing-room at Thames Wickham
he was not a happy man. Indeed, had there been much
light, Miss De Souza would have detected in his face a
sorrow deeper than any which her sympathetic fancy had
attributed to him; but when he saw the way in which they
both rose to meet him, when he heard their voices, warm
with the friendship of many years, the tension of his sorrow
was, for the first time during many days, relaxed; and he
felt as though a breath of spring had come blowing into the
heart of winter.

"My dear friend," exclaimed Mrs. Steinberg, when the lamps and candles of the dinner-table enabled her to observe her visitor's face more narrowly, "I'm sorry to see you're not looking the thing. I'll tell you what it is—you've been working too hard. You're very naughty," she continued, shaking her finger at him. "So much in the country depends upon you now, you've positively no business to be wearing yourself out like this. And it's not only politics, Mr. Pole—ah!—I know all about it. Even in the autumn there are plenty of charming ladies in London—old ladies and young ladies—ready to engross so important a person as yourself. It's for the good of the country that we're keeping you quiet here. And now, since we're talking of young ladies, do tell me all about that beautiful foreign cousin of yours. I know that at Dulverton House every one was admiring and talking about her. I hope it's not true, as Ethel tells me, that she's going to marry a foreigner."

Pole saw out of the corner of his eyes, whilst these last observations were being addressed to him, that Miss De Souza's face wore an expression of distress, and that she was doing her utmost to check her aunt's volubility. He knew the reason at once; and whatever may have been his own feelings, he could hardly help laughing at the incident. He knew that Miss De Souza had divined, on the occasion of his last visit, some relation between Countess Shimna and himself that was beyond ordinary friendship; and he knew her to be now fearful lest an allusion to it should wound his feelings. He wished to convince her that all such fears were needless. He accordingly called to his aid the same candid manner by which he had so successfully concealed the truth from Lord Wargrave; and he talked of Countess Shimna, her marriage, and her future husband, with all the animation of an interested and appreciative indifference. Miss De Souza looked at him with a suspicion that soon turned into pleasure; and his conversation brightening as the meal went on, ended by almost convincing her that he was suffering from nothing but overwork. Pole did not himself feel as though he were, in any way, recovering from his malady; but he felt as though his sufferings were being soothed by two kind, though unconscious, nurses.

The week that followed was a busy one for him in the House of Commons, and official work every day took him early to London. At first this prevented Miss De Souza from having any long and confidential conversation with him; but as she read his speeches in the paper, together with the frequent comments on them, and realized his calm vigour and his almost cynical lucidity as a statesman, her desire increased to penetrate to that other part of his nature which moved her by the pathos of its contrast to the qualities shown by him to the public.

CHAPTER XXXVIII.

AT last, at the end of the week, her opportunity came. Mrs. Steinberg, who was suffering in consequence of a genial indiscretion in her diet, from an attack of indigestion, which she delicately called neuralgia, retired to her bed, and some medicine-bottles, almost immediately after dinner, and left Pole and Miss De Souza alone together for a long evening. The night previous he had signalized himself in the House of Commons by an unusually brilliant answer to a question which it was expected would embarrass him. Miss De Souza, as they sat by the fire together, alluded to this incident, and then went on to speak of the satisfaction which public work, such as his, must bring him in many ways.

"I don't merely mean," she said, "that it flatters your ambition or your vanity; for all men who are worth anything *are* vain, just like all women."

"Yes," he replied, laughing; "there I quite agree with you. Vanity is the mother of all the graces of life, just as affection is of all the virtues. Of course," he continued, as though he was shy of a certain seriousness in her manner and was anxious to keep the conversation playing on the surface of things, "of course, male vanity should be of a very sober kind. I don't know, for instance, which I despise most—a man who leads fashion, or a man who does not follow it."

"I told you," she said, "I wasn't thinking of vanity. What I mean is, that whilst your own vanity is being flattered you must have the satisfaction of feeling that you

are doing good to others. A right career must help a man
as much as a true faith.

He hesitated before replying. She saw she had gained
the day. Against his will, he was going to speak to her
seriously about himself. "I will," he at last said, "put to
you a very selfish question. What should it profit a man if
he saved the whole world and lost his own soul? If you
want to hear a confession, I feel that I have lost mine. My
dear friend," he continued, "I see that you look shocked.
Let me express my meaning in a less alarming way. You
have alluded to my success in politics. It is nothing very
great as yet; but it has been great, no doubt, compared with
my expectations; and although I am not rich, yet, compared
with my expectations, I am a Crœsus. But unexpected
wealth, unexpected success in politics—yes, and even the
feeling that my work has been for the general good—none
of these things even tend to make me happy. I grant that,
had I happiness to begin with, these things would multiply
it; but the largest multiplier .if it multiplies nothing, will
yield nothing. External success is the casket, not the jewel;
and the fact of my finding my own casket empty, has, at all
events, made me an authority with regard to this piece of
wisdom."

She looked into the fire, meditating. "I wonder," she
said presently, "if I may ask you one question? You tell
me of your casket being empty. Have you lost from it—
well, what shall I say—any pearl or diamond lately?"

He laughed softly as he answered her. "I always told
you," he said, "that you are clairvoyant; and I am going to
show you that I have my moments of insight too. I know
what you are thinking of. You are thinking of Countess
Shimna O'Keefe. Well—I like to be open with you. I tried
the other day to speak as though she had been nothing to
me; but the truth is that I actually asked her to marry me;
and she for a time was debating whether she would not do
so. She was charming! She was delightful! You didn't
half do her justice. But it is not the loss of her that has
made my casket empty, though her charms, for a time, did
conceal its emptiness from me; and though she has
incidentally helped me to destroy the one poor treasure
there was remaining in it. But I am ashamed to be talking
in this oracular way to you, about things so unimportant as

these little private details. Let us talk about two things—thin s suggested by what you said just now—which are of real and general interest."

" Tell me," she said, " what things ? "

" Why," he answered, " should work for others—such work as mine at all events, which could only at its best minister to their material prosperity—bring me happiness as it were at second hand, when my own material prosperity brings me so very little at first hand ? People in these days tell us about the service of Man. They talk of Man as some great, almost immortal Entity. But Man does not exist. Man is a mere delusion—one of the Universals of an exploded philosophy. Man is nothing but a name for a countless number of men, who are always dying like insects, and have no greatness and no immortality, except such as they possess or do not possess as individuals. And yet, in spite of all this, I do work—I work on and on : but such str ng h as I get to do so, other than what ambition gives ı e, springs from something deeper than any thought of men's material welfare—and something, perhaps, more unreal."

" What do you mean ? " she asked.

" I mean," he said, " some faith, broken and confused by the blows of modern thought, but still not dead, in the value of the individual soul—in fidelity, and in affection—in the feelings that spring into light like electric sparks, between a mother and her little child, a husband and a wife, a faithful lover and his mistress. You see, this faith we must each of us find in our own hearts. We must light it on the altar, burning there—at a flame which is fed by experience, when not extinguished by it ; and, as for me—shall I tell you my history still more plainly than I have d ne ?—Other hands, not mine, have raked the fire on my altar out ; and the utmost I can do is to stand by it and chafe the embers. I hope you will excuse me. I did not mean to inflict all this on you. I am not given, I hope, to being the hero of my own anxieties."

" Don't be afraid," she said. " You are naturally the most reserved person I know."

" Well, then," he went on, " I will confide to you a certain fact. There is one man in the world who has done me a really great and unselfish kindness—a little, squat-figured, grateful clergyman ; but, otherwise, I doubt if I

have experienced from any man I can recollect anything
better than civilities; and as to women, of those whom I
have most deeply valued, you, my friend, with the exception
of my own mother, are the only one who has failed to repay
me with an unflinching selfishness. If you will think over
what that means, my condition will not be a puzzle to you.
You mentioned just now a young lady who is going to be
married. I have nothing to reproach her with, but I have
to reproach myself; for I have made my wretchedness worse
by making an attempt—which you witnessed—to escape
from it. And now, if you will bear with me, I am going to
say one thing more; but about this thing don't answer me.
My position is such that I feel I can never console myself.
I am married—not to the living cause of my sorrow, that
can never be—but to the mental results of that cause. I
feel that I have for ever lost all right to those affections
which can alone give value to the successes which I certainly
do not despise."

"I will do as you bid me," said Miss De Souza. "I will
make no comment on your confession; but, to-morrow, if it
will be of any help to you, I will make you one of my
own."

To-morrow was Sunday. Mrs. Steinberg was so far
recovered as to be able to sit during the morning before
the drawing-room fire, with a Bible and a prayer-book beside
her, adorned with golden clasps; but her constitution,
though the church almost touched her grounds, was scarcely
equal to the agitations of public worship.

"I wonder," said Miss De Souza to Pole, "if you would
care to come with me. I always feel," she said, dropping
her voice, so as not to wound Mrs. Steinberg's robust and
prosperous orthodoxy, "that church helps me to think, even
when it does not help me to pray."

"Dear Mr. Pole," said Mrs. Steinberg, "do go with her;
and see that nobody comes into our sittings. I declare I
sometimes expect that Tom, Dick, and Harry will some day
or other be writing their names in our prayer-books. And
here, Mr. Pole, put this sovereign for me into the collection
plate."

He assented willingly. "The morning is fine," said Miss
De Souza. "Shall we start early and have a little walk
first ? If you will, I will get ready at once."

"I will wait for you in the hall," he replied; and presently they were going out together.

As they went down the steps, she softly touched his arm. "Hold my prayer-book," she said, "while I am putting on my gloves."

"I would hold anything for you," he answered; "and, if necessary, bear anything."

"Let us go into the garden," she said. "We have a quarter of an hour before us. I told you last night that I would tell you something. I should like to do so now; and you can think it over in church. You have let me know something about yourself; and if you will listen to me, I am very anxious to advise you; but I want to show you first that I am in a position to do so. I, too—do you know, I have never spoken of this to any one except to you—I, too—if I may express myself in very unsentimental language—have had an experience not dissimilar to what I gather to have been your own. I once was going—or thought I was going—to be married. I had always felt that, for myself, marriage would have to include everything—confidence—affection—passion—all. You will understand, then, how I must have felt and acted, and what I must have looked forward to, whilst my engagement lasted. Well, as you see, I am Miss De Souza still. My free-will offering was no sooner completely given than it lost its value for the recipient; and it was at last thrown back upon me. There is history for history. All mine is contained in that."

"I am more and more touched by your kindness," he said, "every hour I am with you."

"Will you, then," she replied, "let me tell you where, I think, your error lies? We shall have to be going into church in another minute, and I don't think what I want to say to you will be a bad preparation for the service. You are pained, I gather, by two different sets of things—things which have been done to you, and certain things perhaps which you regret having done yourself. Well, I think even repentance for our own errors can be carried too far. Surely repentance, if we mean by it any cloistral sorrowing over sin, is valuable only as the chrysalis of healthy and of energetic amendment. Though we may kneel for a while, we ought not to grovel always. But what I am thinking of principally, is not what we have done ourselves, but certain things done

to us by others—the wounding of our personal vanities, the
breaking to pieces of our hopes, the dilapidation of our faith
in one we loved and trusted. I know," she continued,
speaking with more vehemence, "that our first instinct is
to sit by the melancholy graves where the things that we
prize lie buried, and to think that we shall insult the dead
by being ever again cheerful. But do believe me—for I am
sure of it—that this feeling is wrong and morbid. Try to be
happy, instead of fearing happiness. Open the windows of
every chamber in your heart, and let the fresh air into it,
and cleanse all stains, even if your heart's blood made them.
Whatever the past has been, the future is still before you.
If a few people have injured you, you can confer benefits on
many; and if the affection of one person has failed you, do
not lose faith in the fact that true affection is attainable—
by you, at all events, if you will only look for it. Look at
me," she said. "Let me be an example to you. I have
forgiven and yet not forgotten the person who wounded me;
but the thought of him would not prevent me from being
married to-morrow, if only the 'impossible he,' demanded by
my exacting principles, were to ask me."

These last words of hers brought them to the church
door; and for the next hour or so Pole had leisure to reflect
on them, in an air that was murmuring with devotion, or
shaken by the rolling organ.

Her advice to him was not without its effect. It seemed
to him indeed as though she had entered his heart herself,
and opened the windows of those stifling and dusty chambers,
where old faiths and hopes were lying shattered as they had
fallen. Her influence was all the greater over him on account
of the way in which finally she had spoken of herself as an
example. The words she had made use of, if spoken by some
other woman, would have seemed like an adroit, or a mal-
adroit, suggestion, that she might herself console him. But
Miss De Souza had uttered them with an air of such complete detachment from any thought of the kind, that he felt
as though they had lifted her into some superior region,
where sorrow and disappointment might exist, but no other
form of weakness.

"I hope," he said to her abruptly, when they walked
home, "that in talking as I have done to you, and in feeling
what I have admitted I feel, I have not shown myself to you

as a very weak and morbid person. Even the greatest of men in some ways can suffer as keenly as the weakest. In that sense the deeper affections make all of us equal."

"Don't be afraid," she said, "I guessed the truth only because I have known you so well and so long. No one, I assure you, could wear a more decent mask than you do; and you mustn't be angry with me because I happen to know that the heart's mask is made out of the heart's substance."

CHAPTER XXXIX.

THIS conversation had an effect on Pole, greater than he at the time anticipated, and also of a different kind. It did not, indeed, surprise him to find himself, after Miss De Souza's counsel, talking and even thinking with slightly improved spirits. The burden which he bore she had lightened, though not removed. But gradually he detected in himself a more serious change than this.

When Miss De Souza had spoken of the theoretical possibility of her marriage, if only the "impossible he" would be good enough to make his appearance, there was, as he had noticed, no trace in her manner of consciousness, although she was speaking to a man for whom she professed a most close affection. Her eyes and her manner were as frank as though she had been speaking to a sister. But by-and-by, Pole hardly knew how himself, an idea, gradual as the first colours of morning, began to show itself like a flush along the desolate horizon of his mind. It was the idea that he might find in Miss De Souza what he had sought for and failed to find in Countess Shimna—that he might even find something that he had found, and lost and sorrowed for in another who was still sacred to him. On his first perceiving clearly that this idea was actually present in him, it struck him as a mere vagrant fancy, not worth consideration. Then when it again presented itself, and forced him to give some heed to it, he laughed, for it seemed to him invested with a certain dismal humour.

He saw himself like a character in a farce, attaching

himself to three women in succession, coming to each like a
pedlar, with a pack full of sentiments and sorrows; and as
soon as all his wares had been finally rejected by one cus-
tomer, folding them up and again undoing them for another.
The very word "love" would at such times seem ridiculous
to him; and even the child over whom his thoughts hovered,
and Countess Shimna's mysterious daughter, would appear
to him with their respective mothers like the absurdly
balanced characters in a burlesque.

But the passions of a man's heart are stronger than his
sense of humour; and nothing is so difficult to laugh down
or resist as the craving felt for help and for near companionship in hearts which the conduct of others has reduced to
desert islands.   The heart is a country which not even a
Roman conqueror would venture to call peace, because it
had been made a solitude.   In the present case, moreover,
Pole's natural desire for sympathy had been reinforced by
Miss De Souza's philosophic counsels, which urged him to
seek in happiness, instead of turning his back on it, the
means of keeping his strength strong and his sympathies
active.   Such was indeed the gospel which she continued
quietly to preach to him; and the efficacy of her preaching
was reinforced in a way unexpected by herself.   Without
her being aware of it, her unselfish and sisterly solicitude
began, so it seemed to Pole, to suffer a gradual change, and
to take the semblance and perhaps the substance of a different
and less tranquil feeling.   He saw this change revealing
itself in all kinds of elusive signs—in the confidence with
which she assumed his companionship in all idle hours as a
certainty, and which expressed itself in such phrases as
"What shall we do to-morrow?" and in the tone of her
voice, and the lingering look which she fixed on him when
he said good night to her, and she halted for some last word
in the doorway.

At last an evening came when, having achieved in the
House of Commons a success more solid and important than
any of his previous ones, he returned to Thames Wickham
by a train which would bring him there by about half-past
ten.   A sense of elation, as he leant back in the railway-
carriage, went through him like physical warmth.   He
could no longer doubt it—he was a strong man amongst the
strongest.   "How pleasant," he said to himself, "would all

this be, were there only—were there only—some one to share my pleasure!"

When he reached the house Mrs. Steinberg had gone to bed, but he learned to his surprise that Miss De Souza still was in the drawing-room. He hastened in to her, with an expression of pleasure in his eyes that had long become unusual in them. She understood it, and yet for a moment she looked at him half incredulously; and then an answering expression lit up her own face, whilst the firelight, or her own pulses, tinged her with a faint flush.

"I had no notion," she said, "you would be coming back so soon. Sit down and tell me all that has happened."

He took a chair close to her, and leaning over its arm towards her, he poured into her ear a history of the whole evening, and then handed her a letter which he had received from an East End working-man. It was an artless tribute of admiration. She read it slowly and carefully. As she did so he heard her breathe hard with interest, and her dark eyes, when she gave it back to him, were shining like a night of stars. He had never seen such an expression in her face before. It seemed for a moment that she was on the point of saying something with reference to what she had just read; but instead of doing so she rose up abruptly from her chair, and said in a strange voice, "It is late, I must go to bed. Good night, Mr. Pole." And she began moving towards the door. He followed her and prepared to open it. Then they halted and faced each other. "Good night," she said again, and she held her hand out to him. He took it and raised it to his lips; and, still detaining it, looked her once more in the eyes. Hers, too, dwelt upon his, and a tremor of irresolution appeared to agitate her for a second or so. Then, shaking her head and smiling slightly, she escaped through the door, which she had already herself half opened. With a rapid rustling he heard her ascend the stairs, and he, for his part, moved back to the fireside, meditating.

He sat there for some time with his head resting on his hand, and at last roused himself with an apparently irrelevant exclamation: "Yes, I will try once more; I will write to-night, though by now she most likely knows." He went over to a writing-table, and the letter which he wrote was this:—

"DEAR LADY MASTERS,—As I have heard nothing from you since I answered your last letter and told you what the Line was to which the steamer belonged, I presume that you have all the information that you require. But in case you should not be aware of the facts, I wish to tell you that, having called this afternoon at the offices of the company, at Charing Cross, I learn that the boat in question leaves New York this day week for Milford, and your husband's name is telegraphed as being amongst the passengers. Have you quite forgotten—I think you have—that there is a person who never forgets you—such a person as R. POLE?'

There was a pillar-box outside Mrs. Steinberg's front gates, and going out, he posted the letter himsel·. "I shall see," he said, when he had done so. "Before long I shall see. I shall surely get an answer from her of some sort."

It was expected that the session would end in about a week, and his duties meanwhile happened to have become so pressing that he was, for the next three days, obliged to remain in London. He felt that his absence from Thames Wickham would in any case have been imperative for a time. At last, at his club, where he was sitting in the deserted reading-room, the letter reached him for which he had watched and waited. It was this:—

"DEAR MR. POLE,—Ever so many thanks for yours. Had found out all about steamer. Sorry you troubled about it, but thousand thanks all same.—Yours, P. M."

Having read this twice over he gripped the paper in his hands, and tearing the sheet in two, tossed the fragments into the fire. "My God," he said to himself, "and so there is an end of that!"

He looked at the clock, and then at some memoranda in a pocket-book. "I am not," he thought, "after all, wanted at the House to-night," and throwing himself into a chair, gave himself up to thought. At length he roused himself; he rose, and seated himself before some pens and paper, and began a letter, which though, in a certain sense, an answer to what he had just received, was nevertheless not even addressed to the person who had written it.

"I believe you," it was thus he wrote, "when you profess
a sincere friendship for me. I never can tell you the extent
to which I trust you; and I want you to believe that I, in
the way of friendship, give to you in return the best—the
utmost, of which I am capable. Will you think that I am
employing insincere and exaggerated language when I tell
you that lately you have been walking with me through
the valley of the shadow of death? You have asked me to
be candid with you. May I say to you one thing more? In
a certain sense we, both of us—you and I—stand alone. Do
you think it would be impossible for us to act together on
the advice which you yourself have given me, and to look
for happiness each with the other's help? If this suggestion commends itself to you at all, you will entertain it and
consider it, without any further rhetoric on my part. There
—I have said it! I must now abide the consequence. But
do not write me any direct answer to this, unless I have
offended you so far by what I have said, that you would be
annoyed by my returning to Thames Wickham. In that
case, indeed, I will ask you to let me know, and I will send
my servant down to fetch away my things. Otherwise, no
matter what your decision may be, I would sooner you let
me know it by word of mouth. Meanwhile, I shall have a
little time of hope—a kind of hope the light of which I
thought never to see again; and if, finally, the news should
be bad, I know that you will break it gently to me. Unless,
therefore, I get a telegram from you to the contrary, I will
be back to-morrow evening, when your hospitable aunt is
expecting me."

By lunch time next day, the following telegram reached
him: "Altogether surprised; but will explain when you
arrive.—E. DE SOUZA."

He did not reach Thames Wickham till nearly eight
o'clock, and he saw no one till he descended into the drawing-room. There, on the hearthrug, was Mrs. Steinberg,
with the firelight shaking amongst her satins, who welcomed
him with a motherly gladness, and very nearly embraced
him; and then, in the midst of this welcome, gliding with
a noiseless footstep, Miss De Souza entered, tranquil but
with her eyes shining. He had no opportunity that evening
of any conversation in private with her; but the way in

which she hung upon every word he uttered, the watchful
quickness and delicacy with which she seized his meaning,
and a certain buoyancy of spirits which he could not help
thinking he detected in her, sent him to rest with a certain
warmth and glow, as though a fire had been relit in his life,
on a hearth that had been long frozen.

He had told her, as he said good night to her, that he
would, the following morning, be obliged to go back to
London by about eleven o'clock. When the morning came,
she was down more punctually than usual; and, moreover,
she had her hat on, which was more unusual still.

"My dear," exclaimed Mrs. Steinberg, "you look
extremely active."

"I have," said Miss De Souza, "some one to see in the
village, and I thought I would walk with Mr. Pole part of
the way towards the station—that is to say, if he has no
objection to my company."

"I will start," said Pole, looking at her, "at any moment
you like; we can have, if you are willing, a stroll first in
the garden."

She gave a nod of assent, accompanied by a faint smile;
and they presently emerged into a morning scented with
slight frost.

"I suppose," she began, not waiting for him to speak,
and yet speaking herself with a certain sensitive hesitation,
"I need hardly tell you what an absolute surprise your letter
was. I want to tell you—if, indeed, it is necessary for me
to tell you—that—that you estimate me far too highly in
thinking that I could help you. You are deceiving yourself
by a little dream, of which you make me the heroine. I own
—I ought to confess this, for I want to be quite truthful—
that I have been selfishly pleased—I have been quite thrown
off my balance—by the way in which you flatter me; and
yet—yet—I must say—I regret it; for I am afraid it may
interfere, not with my friendship for you—not with that,
but with yours for me."

"It would interfere with it," said Pole, "in one way only
—by changing it into something better."

"Oh, no—no," she exclaimed, shaking her head and
laughing a little. "You don't know to whom you are talking. Dear Mr. Pole, I beg you to forget all this—and I will
remember only the uninvited compliment you have paid me."

They were both silent for a little. Then she spoke abruptly, and not without evident difficulty. "Will you," she said, "promise me one thing? I beseech you to do that. Supposing for a moment that you have been serious in all that you have said, promise me that whatever happens, you will never withdraw your friendship from me. I could not bear that."

"Yes, yes," he replied, "I will promise, though there is no need to do so. And now listen—on your part, you must do something also. Don't answer me now. Don't answer me for two days. I have hard work to do to-day. I have hard work to-morrow. Let me have hope to keep me company through all these hours. It is alive still. It has sunlight glittering on its wings. Let it live for at least two days, even if you kill it then; and meanwhile your behaviour to me will gradually prepare me for what is to come. But we will not recur to the subject till the day after to-morrow; and till then we will walk and talk together as we have done. Will you consent to this arrangement?"

"If you wish it," she said, "yes."

Presently their paths parted. He took the way to the station; and she, as she strolled on slowly in another direction, sighed with some ambiguous feeling, which was not entirely dissatisfaction.

When he returned that evening, Miss De Souza was as good as her word. She received him without embarrassment, and never had their intercourse been more animated, and more happy. The second day came, and its history was precisely similar; and Pole, on the third morning began to say to himself with confidence, "When I speak again to-night to her, it must be that she will answer 'Yes.'" That day he was back from London early, and he found Miss De Souza in the drawing-room alone, and bending over the tea-table.

"I was lunching," he said to her, "with the Prime Minister. I have any number of things to tell you. He has actually suggested that I—— But I hear your aunt in the hall. She is coming. One word first. To-night we are going to talk again together—and till then, I shall hope."

The door was ajar, and Mrs. Steinberg pushed it open and entered, accompanied by a bevy of female visitors, to whom she had been showing the many glories of her mansion, and to whom now, with even greater pride, she introduced her distinguished visitor.

"Look," said Pole by-and-by laughingly to Miss De Souza, when, on going upstairs to dress, he saw a few letters for him in the hall. "Whose writing is that?" And he held an envelope out to her. "It's from some one you know, and from some one you admire immensely. Take it, and study the direction while your maid brushes your hair; and tell me at dinner who, or what sort of person, the writer is."

Entering into the spirit of this challenge to her judgment, she took the letter from him; and when they met again at dinner, she said: "You have completely puzzled me. All I can tell from the handwriting is that it certainly is a man's; and if writing tells me anything, it is the writing of a man with strong character—but a character I should not like." She, and her aunt also, then made an unsuccessful guess or two; and Pole, having tantalized them long enough, said, "Well, it's Canon Bulman. I shall be curious to see what he can have to say for himself."

"Oh," said Miss De Souza, "I've left it, I'm afraid, upstairs; but when we go into the drawing-room, I'll tell my maid to fetch it for you."

She did not forget her promise; and when he was left alone with his cigarette, the letter was duly presented to him, in company with his cup of coffee.

Some twenty minutes later, when he rejoined his hostesses in the drawing-room, Mrs. Steinberg greeted him with a series of effusive congratulations on a couple of articles she had been reading about him in the evening paper; but he answered her so absently, that she looked up in his face, and was struck by a curious, though indefinite, change that had come over it.

"Dear Mr. Pole," she exclaimed, "are you ill? You look as if you had got a headache. I told you, Ethel, that the dining-room was too hot. I never saw any one so stupid as our servants are about the fires."

"Oh,' said Mr. Pole, "it is nothing. It is a little headache, as you say."

"Sit down," said Mrs. Steinberg, "and remain in the chair quite quiet. I shall not disturb you, for I'm going to write my letters."

He did as she recommended; but as soon as she left the

room. he rose from his seat, and moved about restlessly, Miss De Souza's eyes following him in perplexed anxiety.

" Tell me," she said at last, " what is it ? "

" Ah," he replied, coming near her, " that is just what I cannot tell you. I wanted to-night to have asked you—you know what question. I can't do so now. Let us both be silent about it a little longer. I have heard news which disturbs me, not because it affects myself, but because it affects another person; and I must do something in the matter, and as yet I don't know what."

"I won't ask," she said. "I can see in your face how troubled you are. Sit down a little by me, and I will be quiet and not disturb you. And that other matter—we will speak of it at some other time."

He seated himself in a chair close to her. "I am sure," she said, " that your head aches." And with the pitying kindness of a mother, a sister, or a nurse, and perhaps with a thrill of some other sort of kindness added to it, she laid her hand on his forehead, and just lifted his hair. "Oh," she exclaimed, " you are burning—positively burning! Is there nothing, nothing that we can do for you ? "

" Thank you," he exclaimed, " thank you ! But indeed you can do nothing. You can do nothing. I shall know better about all this to-morrow. I will, if you will let me, go up to my room, and think about it."

As soon as he was alone, he pulled out the Canon's letter, and read it again, with a frown of miserable attention.

CHAPTER XL.

" MY DEAR REGINALD POLE," wrote the Canon, " I am compelled to communicate with you, about a very serious matter. I would to God that this letter was to anybody rather than to yourself. You know the position which I—and how can any Christian act otherwise?—have always taken up with regard to certain abominable sins. You know also the movement of which I am, under Christ, the head. I mean the League of clean-living men, whose object in banding themselves together is to give stern and practical effect to the

horror—ay, the horror—which one special kind of sin, more
than any other, rouses in the heart of every decent, every
upright man. I speak of the sin against moral purity; and
as I mention it to *you*, I declare all the blood rushes into my
cheeks. Well—I and my colleagues have, as you will have
heard, pledged ourselves, at all costs, so far as in us lies, to
prevent not only the entry into Parliament, but the continuance in Parliament, of any man who has thus broken
God's law, and deliberately bespattered with beastliness his
own humanity. And now, I am compelled to put to you
this solemn question. Can it be, then, that you—you, mv
old pupil, who, I had hoped, till I met you at Glenlynn, still
cherished every feeling that I had implanted in you—that
you should be the first person against whom I should be
necessitated to proceed? If I am wrong—if I, residing here
in Windsor—have been misinformed, then all this will be
gibberish to you. Otherwise, it will be but too clear. I
will ask you a leading question. Do you remember our last
meeting? Carry back your thoughts to that; and whatever
is true or not true, come, if you value your own future, and
see me without delay; or others, less cautious than myself,
may soon be busy with your name, and not with yours alone.
Telegraph to mention the earliest hour when I may expect
you. In the meanwhile, I am, yours truly, RANDAL BULMAN."

Pole had felt when he first read this, and he felt again
now, as a man might feel who, after a day or two of
physical uneasiness, suddenly realizes that he is the victim
of some horrible and ill-famed disease. He could have no
doubt as to what the letter, in a general way, referred to;
but as to the question of what detailed facts might be implied in it, he was altogether in bewilderment. He knew
not of what evidence against him the Canon might possibly
be in possession; nor, thinking of the speech made by the
Canon at Thames Wickham, could he see any limits, in
honour or common sense, to the uses which the Canon might
make of it. With regard to his own conduct, Pole, instead
of being struck with shame for it, felt all his being indignant
with self-defence; but nevertheless did he see, with sicken-
ing prescience, his own private life being dragged igno-
miniously before the public; and, worst of all, before all, and
through all, he saw the same fate menacing, and perhaps
falling on, another. His whole life, indeed, seemed to be

turning topsy-turvy. His image confronted him, distorted in a new public opinion of him; and for many wakeful hours he became hardly recognizable to himself.

The morning restored him once more to his self-possession; though cool reflection tended to aggravate his anxiety. He summoned his servant before eight o'clock, who, of course, at that precise moment, when he happened to be most wanted, was doing what he called, "getting his breakfast;" and despatched him with a note to the Canon :—

"DEAR CANON BULMAN,

"What can have prompted you to write your extraordinary letter I am at a loss to conjecture. Had you been anybody but yourself, I should not be writing now to say what I am about to say—namely, that I will, as you suggest, come and see you this morning—at eleven, if that suits you.

"Sincerely yours,

"R. POLE."

As he went in the train to Windsor an hour or two later, the Canon's Thames Wickham speech was constantly echoing in his ears; and the more he thought of it the more did it bring home to him how dangerous, in affairs such as the present, a man like the Canon was—a man who was gifted with a fanaticism that was hardly sane, in odd combination with a considerable aptitude for affairs, and an almost puerile blindness to the contingent consequences of his conduct. Pole, therefore, resolved to treat him, not with diplomacy only, but with forbearance; and he felt his temper, when he rang at the Canon's door, so well under control that coldness would be the only sign of it.

The door was opened by Sophie, the Canon's ornamental parlour-maid, who was supposed by her master to be re-learning the beauty of virtue—a piece of wisdom which, if she had acquired it, she was too timid to show. Her eyes had the brown moisture that glimmers on a slug's back; and her large mouth smiled recognition at Pole, with a mixture of familiarity and demure professional respect. The house, as he entered, struck him as having undergone several changes. Sophie, to begin with, was arrayed in a feminine livery, which did complete justice to her figure, and which the

Canon had copied from the establishment of a guardsman's
grass widow in the neighbourhood. Again, the walls of the
hall, formerly distempered, were now covered with the richest
of flock papers, which consecrated its own costliness by
ecclesiastical fleur-de-lys in gold. There was a new marble
table, on which were a terra-cotta statue of a football player;
and a silver trophy, composed of cricket-bats, with an inscription on it. But there was not, as on a former occasion, any
study door thrown open, or any sound of the Canon's voice,
breezy with athletic welcome. On the contrary, Pole was
shown into the empty drawing-room; and the maid, tripping
out of the door, said that she would announce his arrival.

He was not in a mood to be much taken up with trifles,
but the Canon's drawing-room, nevertheless, commanded
his attention. He remembered how formal it was when he
had seen it first; and how its awkward and self-conscious
gentilities had been like those of a dentist's parlour. But
the Canon, meanwhile, had evidently lived and learnt, and
had been carefully copying the surroundings of his more
eligible friends. He had got rid of his extraordinary super-
fluity of little mats; he had banished the rose-wood chairs,
which he had probably inherited from his mother; he had
introduced others, upholstered in brocade and velvet; on the
chimney-piece was an overwhelming clock, which had been
sold him as old French; he had even started a table littered
with silver knickknacks; and here and there, disposed with
much anxious judgment, were various Travels in Palestine,
and some books about Christian Socialism. The Canon, so
Pole thought, was evidently living up to the means that
had come to him during the past year from the Doctor's
Australian mines. Whilst such reflections were mechanically
passing through his mind, the door opened, and the Canon
stood in the door-way. His chin was in the air; he was
solemn, even severe; and, without offering to shake hands
with his visitor, he made a gesture with his head, and said,
"Will you come with me?" like a schoolmaster summoning
a schoolboy to undergo the sacrament of a whipping.

"Will you kindly take a seat?" he said, when they were
closeted in his study.

He himself, as he spoke, sank into a morocco chair, one
freckled hand, adorned with a heavy ring, stretching itself
nervously upon his writing-table. He was evidently much

embarrassed; the blood was mounting to his face; and Pole, partly out of pity for him, partly out of a wish to come to the point at once, upset the Canon's calculations by beginning the interview himself.

"Look here, Canon Bulman," he said, rising and leaning his back against the chimney-piece. "I have come here, as a very old friend of yours, to ask for the meaning of a letter, which, had it come from any one else, I should have committed at once either to the wastepaper basket or my solicitor. You must not be angry because I say this; and if you see any anger in myself, you ought, till you know me guilty, to hail it as the indignation of innocence."

The Canon was silent for a moment or two. His mouth worked, and he scowled askance at a piece of blotting-paper. Then, suddenly raising his eyes to Pole, he said: "Do you mean to tell me, as you stand there in the presence of God, that you have no sin on your conscience which condemns you even before I do?"

"My dear Canon Bulman," said Pole, "there is no need for your adjurations. If I am ever in the presence of God at all, I am as much in his presence everywhere as I am upon your hearthrug; so I answer you precisely as I should on any other occasion. Sins—you say! Indeed I have. Yes, we have all sinned; but I have not come to Windsor to make a general confession to a priest. Be good enough to tell me what particular sin you mean—the place, the circumstances, the nature of the act or acts. But stay. Since you find some difficulty in doing what you are surely bound to do, will you let me help you? You alluded to our last meeting. The last time I met you in any other than an accidental manner, was here at your own house. Since then you came across me in a lane not far from this, when I had just said good-bye to a friend of mine and her little boy. When you spoke of our last meeting were you referring to that occasion?"

"I was," said the Canon, bringing his fist down upon his writing-table.

"Very well, then," said Pole, speaking with more sharpness; "may I ask if you insinuate anything to the detriment of that friend—that old and valued friend of mine? Should you find it embarrassing to say yes, I shall fully understand you, if you only nod your head."

As he said these last words, his voice suddenly softened, and betrayed so much consideration that the Canon instinctively recognized it, and surprised himself by saying, "Thank you," which he did with a gulp, and added the expected nod.

"And now," said Pole, with the sharpness returning to his voice, yet still with a note in it not altogether unkindly, "will you tell me, since we have broken the ice, what is the precise connection which you presume, or suspect, to have existed between this lady and myself?"

"I will," said the Canon, with the flush on his face darkening. "The link which, according to report—according to evidence—bound you to this person in question, was the link—for I will not mince matters—of unclean and of filthy living—and that practised in the very constituency which you represent in a Christian Parliament."

Pole resumed his seat, and, speaking with great quietness, said—

"Canon Bulman, before we discuss this further, let me ask you one question. What is the precise purpose with which you tell me all this? What is it which you expect me to say or do?"

"If you are innocent," said the Canon, "if only appearances are against you—and, alas, they are against you—my hope is that you will here, in this room, relieve me by giving me a categorical denial of the charge, and commission me to deny it to those who are working with me. On the other hand, if you cannot deny it—if you have really been so unhappy as to have bestialized yourself in the way imputed to you—then we—that is to say, the League—should ask you if you could satisfy us privately that you had repented of your uncleanness, and were resolved to live differently in the future. But if you refused to do this, or did not do it to our satisfaction, we should immediately take such steps as would either compel you to resign your seat at once, or, at all events, make it difficult for you to be elected again anywhere."

"I have," said Pole, "just one more thing to ask, and then you shall have my answer. Have you any knowledge of the character, the name, the social position, of the person with which your charge associates me?"

The Canon hesitated, and then, in a reluctant voice, he answered—

"I may say we have."

"Very well, then," said Pole, again rising from his chair, "I will now make you an answer, and it will take the form of an explanation why I did not make it sooner. Had the charge which you make against me affected myself only, or a woman with no reputation to lose, I should simply have declined to discuss the matter at all with you. I should have begged you and your friends to believe, if you liked to do so, I had twenty mistresses, and make the best or worst of it that you could. I would no more have stooped to explain a charge of this kind, than I would to explain an illegible passage in a letter of mine to some scoundrel who had stolen and read it." The Canon, at these words, turned his head aside, and rested his forehead on his hand, so as almost to hide his face. "But," Pole continued, "the actual case is different. There is a person concerned who, as you say you know, is of unblemished reputation; and her life would be practically ruined were your implied charge against her established. And now, Canon Bulman, I will beg you to consider this. When you ask me if I am innocent or guilty, and express a hope that I shall be able to inform you of my innocence, you are implying that were I guilty you would expect me to acknowledge, I do not say my own guilt, but that of another person, to a self-constituted inquisition of gossiping and prurient vestrymen. My own conduct, as mine, I have told you I won't discuss; but, for argument's sake, assume me guilty. In that case, a woman of previously unsullied character has put all she has in my hands, in order to give me pleasure; and you, who are a gentleman—what do you ask me to do? To betray this woman, who has done so much for me, merely for the sake of retaining a seat in Parliament for myself. Did you ever hear the saying of an American judge, that a man who would not perjure himself to shield a woman in the Divorce Court ought not to be believed on his oath as to any other subject whatever? So help me God, I am of that judge's opinion. However," Pole continued, changing his tone suddenly, "miserably misguided as you are, I will treat you as a misguided gentleman, and as a friend—an old friend of my own: and to you I will condescend to say that I am innocent of the charge you bring against me. I absolutely decline, however, to make any such statement to your

colleagues, because in asking them to accept from me any
assertion of my innocence, I should be announcing myself as
a scoundrel, who, if guilty, would admit his guilt. What I
will do is this. I will here, privately and confidentially, ask
you, not as authorized by me, but as acting on your own
judgment, to inform your colleagues that they are absolutely
mistaken in this matter, and to restrain them from a course
of action of which the necessary results would be to inflict
incalculable pain on an innocent woman and her family, to
make themselves amenable to the heaviest penalties of the
law, and also to cover their own career with ridicule."

Pole ended, and there was silence. The Canon betrayed
an embarrassment greater even than Pole could have anticipated. At last he spoke.

"You mistake," he said—"unfortunately you mistake—
the nature of the situation. I am indeed the originator of
this great national scrutiny into the morals of those who
offer themselves as the public servants of the nation; and I
have personally organized our Vigilance Committee in this
constituency. But the principal evidence against you was
not discovered by myself, and is not even in my possession;
though my meeting you near Laburnum Lawn affords a
fearful corroboration of it. The landlord of that house—
now mark me, I am not answerable for his conduct—he is,
however, a man of rigidly pure life, and an active member
of our committee—discovered, some weeks after his tenant's
departure, a certain letter under her dressing-table. That
letter," continued the Canon, growing more and more embarrassed as he proceeded—"now observe, in this particular
I do not defend him—he read; and at the end of the
letter—shall I tell you what he found?—he found your
signature."

"Ah!" exclaimed Pole, with an ironical laugh. "I
thought so! And you and he, and all the grocers in
Windsor, put your heads together, and read it over again,
and communicated its contents to all the grocers' wives."

"That is not so, sir," cried the Canon, striking his
writing-desk with his fist, and seizing the opportunity of
encouraging himself by a fit of anger. "Have the goodness
to be silent and hear me a little further. I have not read
the letter. I have not even had it in my hand; but
certain passages of it were read privately at one of our

official meetings, and till they had been read, I did not know
where they came from. Not till the end, was I told they
were from a letter of yours. Well, having heard them, there
seemed to me a possibility that they might not indicate the
actual extreme of guilt—I say a possibility—a chance
Nobody else thought so; but I insisted; and I will now
explain what has been done. A copy of that letter—the
original is retained by the finder—has been placed officially
in my hands, in order that I might see you privately, and
give you the chance of making a satisfactory explanation."

As he spoke he took from a drawer a long sealed envelope, and handing it to Pole, said, "You can assure
yourself that I have not read it."

Pole took it with a hand that was scarcely steady, and
extracting the contents, recognized his own words, engrossed
on a sheet of foolscap, in the handwriting of a lawyer's
clerk. It was a letter which he had written two years ago;
and in the middle of his anxiety a thrill of pleasure went
through him at the thought that its recipient should have
cared for him enough to keep it. As for its tone, that
doubtless was most unfortunate. The letter was one indeed
which might have been written by a mere friend, were the
circumstances such as would account for an intimate friendship; but it hardly could have seemed cold, regarded as the
composition of a lover; whilst one or two phrases, actually
written in innocence, were capable of being tortured into a
compromising double meaning. Pole, however, was sufficiently master of himself to read the document through as
coolly as if it had been a newspaper; and at last, putting it
into his pocket, he quietly addressed the Canon.

"I will," he said, "give no further expression to what I
think of the conduct of those who have made this interview
necessary; but I will tell you frankly that the facts you
have just disclosed to me make me see the situation in a
somewhat different light. The lady to whom I wrote this
letter is an old and valued friend of mine, whom I helped
when she was in great distress; and my expressions of
friendship for her, no matter how innocent, might be so used
by your friends as to torture her and even ruin her life.
Suppose some one had shown me some of the letters of your
late wife"—Canon Bulman started in his chair—"letters,"
continued Pole, "in which she poured out such complaints

against you, as I happen to know she confided to a sympathetic friend; and suppose I were blackguard enough to read these letters, and to show them—or to print them, say, in the Windsor papers."

A moment ago the Canon had been leaning forward in his chair. He was now leaning back in it, his hand masking his eyes. "I have no wish," continued Pole, "to wound you. I only want to show you that the best of people may be pained by unwarranted attacks against them: and to save the lady now in question the smallest pain on my account, there is nothing I would not do. Let me have a day or two to think the matter over. What you ought to do is to insist on my own letter being restored to me, and find some means of reducing those colleagues of yours to silence. But in case, during the next few days you should be unable to do that, I will think meanwhile of some means by which I may be able to satisfy them myself."

"Good," said the Canon, sitting up again, but having lost much of his confidence, and apparently glad to arrive at some temporary conclusion at all events; "you shall have a week. We will take no steps till then. I shall indeed," he continued, with a sudden pomposity in his voice, "be away for several days, on an important engagement in the country. I wish," he added, with an awkward look at the carpet, "your reply to this odious charge could have been more straightforward and whole-hearted."

Pole meanwhile had possessed himself of his hat and stick, and was already standing at the door.

"For the present, then," he said, "I can do nothing more except wish you good morning. I can find my way out. Pray neither come nor ring." And before the Canon could decide how far inquisitorial chastity, which had been browbeaten on its own judgment-seat, ought or ought not to speed the going guest, the guest had left the library, and had slammed the front door behind him.

CHAPTER XLI.

TILL the interview with the Canon was over, and he found himself in the road alone, Pole had hardly realized the full seriousness of the situation. It seemed to him, however, at all events, that if the worst came to the worst, he could protect the name of the woman which was now threatened, by yielding to the Canon's League, and renouncing public life. He had not gone many paces before he was considering this course as possible ; and by a single effort he had shifted the whole scenery of his future. "How little," he thought, " it costs us to give up anything! " He would not, however, succumb without a struggle; and questions thronged on his mind as to what he should do now.

Putting his hand in his pocket, he happened to feel a letter which he had received that morning, and which till this moment he had forgotten. It was a short line in the illegible hand of the Duke of Dulverton; and Pole remembered that it mentioned the word "luncheon." A new train of ideas had been started suddenly in his mind. He took out the letter and re-read it. It contained but a few words, dated the previous night. " Will you lunch with me to-morrow at 1.30 ? In the afternoon I am going down to Dulverton. I am giving a little shooting to my sniveller and some others. You have better sport, shooting folly as it flies, in the House of Commons. The birds there act as their own beaters."

He took out his watch. It was twenty minutes to twelve. He had gone already part of the way to the station. There was a train in ten minutes which would bring him before one to London. An idea had illuminated his mind. He had just now been thinking of taking the advice of a solicitor. His new idea was to consult the Duke of Dulverton. The Duke, he said to himself, in a question of the present kind, would understand a difficulty without any but the most general description of it; and would be able to give him the coolest and the most shrewd advice.

It was accordingly little after one o'clock when Pole, in clothes and in a hat which had never been designed for London, was descending from a hansom under the Duke's portico, and being received by the stout porter with a smile of decorous recognition.

"Is there any party for luncheon ? " he asked. " I want to speak first to His Grace on business."

" No party, sir," said the porter. " But His Grace was expecting you."

The bare, stone hall had now a very different aspect to that which it wore on the night of the celebrated ball. The sole signs of occupation were a few old overcoats and battered wideawake hats, on the bare marble tables. As soon as Pole entered, the porter rang a bell; and an elderly valet, who shuffled like the Duke, his master, appeared, and introduced Pole, after several knocks at a door, to an exceedingly dark room that opened out of the hall. This was the Duke's dressing-room, lighted from a dingy court; and the Duke, who sent forth a voice of sonorous welcome through the twilight, was completing his toilette by the act of brushing his teeth.

Pole began by explaining that he had special business to talk about—"business," he said, "in which, I am sure, your advice could help me. You have heard," he continued, " of your friend Canon Bulman's League ? "

A broad smile extended itself, like an equator, across the Duke's face.

"Oho ! " he said. "Yes, that Canon is a shocking fellow. Do you know what he's going to do ? I'll bet you you can't tell me. Eh ? Well, it's this. He's coming to-morrow to me at Dulverton to shoot my pheasants."

"Is he ? " said Pole. "I now understand about his engagement. He is, however, preparing to do something else besides. The long and short of it is, that this wonderful League of his are preparing to begin their operations by an attack against myself."

The Duke put his hand to his ear, so as not to lose a word.

".There was a lady," Pole continued, "a very old friend of mine, to whom I wrote often, using occasionally expressions which were, perhaps, open to misconstruction. One of these letters has, it seems, got into the hands of one of the Canon's henchmen; and he and his League at Windsor—you know they are all Radicals—are planning an attack on me by concocting some sort of scandal, which will inevitably drag this lady's name before the public. I need hardly tell you that the whole charge——"

"That the whole charge is a fiction," interrupted the Duke, sharply. "No—no—no—of course, you need not tell me. I know it is a fiction, or else you would not have mentioned it. Well," he continued, washing out his toothbrush in a tumbler, "and what do you gather that these gentlemen really intend to do ?"

Pole explained as well as he could the kind of action that might be anticipated. The Duke, whose operations were by this time finished, had settled himself to listen on a pile of his own old coats. At last he exclaimed, with one of his hollow chuckles—

"Leave the fellow to me; I'll manage him. I won't myself say a single word to him on the subject; and nobody shall mention you; and yet all the same I'll engage this, that before luncheon to-morrow the Canon's mouth shall be muzzled. You shall have a letter from me explaining by what means. My father was attacked once in precisely the same way. And now, I think, we'll come in and have our luncheon."

The confidence with which the Duke had spoken was an instant relief to Pole; though the grounds of such confidence remained a complete mystery to him. He was accordingly able during that day and the next to attend to his official duties with a comparatively tranquil mind ; and Miss De Souza, who, as he was conscious, watched him anxiously, clearly saw that the strain on his mind was lightened : but meanwhile, for reasons which she was not able to fathom, he treated her with an uneasy and evidently unwilling reserve.

In due time, however, the Duke's letter arrived, and the news in it more than justified the sanguine promises of the writer.

"I think," he began, "we've done him; and I will tell you how. One of my guests is Sir Gideon Fleece, the great criminal lawyer. I told him last night, in a general way, what the intentions of Canon Bulman were, and I begged him at breakfast or luncheon to draw the Canon out, and to terrify him with the legal dangers of the course he appeared to contemplate. Sir Gideon, who is a vulgar fellow, but has a bit of humour in him, said that in acting on my suggestion he would no only be doing a piece of professional work for nothing, but depriving himself probably of any number of future clients. 'Still,' he said, 'in return for the pleasure of destroying your Grace's game, I shall be happy to increase my sport by destroying the Canon's also.' Well, Sir Gideon has just told me that he's been as good as his word. If ever the law frightened any one, our good friend the Canon is a thoroughly frightened man; and he'll go back to Windsor, his head buzzing with thoughts of libel actions, of damages, of public disgrace, of imprisonment, in fact, every jewel in the crown of the modern reformer's martyrdom. You need fear nothing more from him. Write to him at once, and tell him to get your letter returned to you. He goes back in two days' time."

Acting on this last hint, Pole wrote to the Canon, saying that he had thought fit to seek legal advice. "The result," he continued, "is that I can enter into no further explanation with you; and with regard to your League, I cannot even recognize its existence. Indeed, unless you can secure for me my stolen letter, as soon as you return to Windsor, I may be compelled reluctantly to institute proceedings against yourself."

The answer to this came back with such promptitude that the Canon must have written it within half an hour of his arrival.

"Though, as I must say with grief," so his letter ran, "you have not convinced me of your innocence—rather the contrary—I am bound to admit that I cannot consider your guilt as certain; and technical difficulties would, I am advised, in the present case, embarrass our cause rather than aid it, supposing we took action. Mr. Snagg, the possessor of your original letter, is, I find, away from home to-day; but the document shall be returned promptly to you if it has not been destroyed. Remember that for the future there will be vigilant eyes on you. Go, sin no more, lest a worse thing come unto thee."

. The final relief which this letter brought to Pole gave him for a day or two a semblance of good spirits. He informed Miss De Souza that the difficulty which had made him so anxious was over; and the pleasure which she exhibited at the announcement restored him to his sense of intimacy with her, which his doubts and his apprehensions had for the past few days frozen.

"And now," he said to her, "I am going to ask you a favour. To-day I have a holiday. Let us spend our hours just as we have done hitherto. I will not repeat the question I have already put to you till the evening; and so, at all events, I shall have my hope till then."

"It shall be as you wish," she said, fixing her dark eyes on his. He just touched her cheek with a hesitating, slight caress; and he felt her, for a single moment, leaning her cheek against his hand; and he went out into the garden with her, bewildered by a host of thoughts, which filled his head like children playing in a spring meadow.

It is true that by this time he knew the world and himself well enough to know that a passion such as he had already experienced never repeats itself, and that the sorrow which had come to him from it might indeed be temporarily forgotten in the charm of such a woman as Countess Shimna, but could only be healed by a woman of a far rarer kind. As for Countess Shimna herself, he thought of her without the least bitterness. In a certain sense he admired her as much as ever; but she had ceased to represent to him, so far as her individuality was concerned, anything better than a super-refined distillation of that common and facile philtre which is everywhere being bought and sold; and to which, if Miss De Souza should throw him back on his solitude, he might, in common with many lonely and sensitive men, be driven to betake himself for its disturbing and sullying consolation. But no, he told himself; this certainly could not be. The woman by his side, who professed such profound regard for him, would never leave him to drown when a touch of her hand could save him.

One incident only disturbed him while in this happy mood, and it was not an incident which he allowed to trouble him for long. It was the arrival of a letter for him at luncheon time in a totally strange hand-writing. He feared at first it might be from a member of Canon Bulman's League, and contain some new threat against him. But his fears on this score were quieted by the sight of the Plymouth post-mark. This letter, when he came to read it, certainly lay outside anything which his most nervous or ingenious apprehensions could have suggested to him. It was from a complete stranger—a certain R. Mercer, and ran thus:—

z

"Sir,—Being aware that the Rev. Dr. Clitheroe, during
his visits to the West of England, was a frequent guest either
of yourself, or of your family, at Glenlynn, I venture to write
to you as a friend, in case you should have committed to him
any money for investment. I myself and several others in
this town have done so. Should you have acted similarly,
I advise you strongly to withdraw any sums that may be
in question without loss of time. Dr. Clitheroe's affairs
appear to be in a most unsatisfactory state, and it will be
well to recover from him whilst it is possible to recover
anything. I have demanded the repayment of my own
money, and, in justice to him, I am bound to say that I
received it. It is not for me to enter into particulars, but
I should advise any one who was financially connected with
him to examine carefully into the real nature of the business
in which he has employed their capital."

Pole's first feeling on reading this was one of vague
alarm; but as Mrs. Steinberg took in a number of financial
papers, he soon found an article which dealt with Australian
mines; and he presently saw that the position of those in
which he was interested fully bore out what the Doctor
had—as he now remembered—told him at the railway
junction; and that, beyond any reasonable doubt, they were
more prosperous than ever. He accordingly put the matter
out of his head almost immediately. It left nothing behind
it but a deposit of quite undistinguishable uneasiness.

Thus the hours wore on, and his hopes continued rising;
and finally, at the close of the evening, when Mrs. Steinberg
rose from her chair and said, with extended hands, "Dear
Mr. Pole, good night," Miss De Souza cast at him a
momentary half-serious look, which showed her remembrance
that for them there was something yet to come. She
followed her aunt to the door, and went with her into the
hall outside. Pole could hear the vague murmur of their
conversation, which now and then was varied with a little
burst of laughter. At last these sounds ceased. The dark
mahogany door, which had been but half closed, again
quietly opened, and Miss De Souza, tall and noiseless,
reappeared.

"You see I have come," she said, as she slowly advanced
towards him. "I have done as you wished. But listen—I

mustn't stop very long talking to you; and it "—she continued with hesitation, "I fear—oh, I fear I shall make you hate me. Mr. Pole—will you let me speak? It will be easier if I speak first. I want," she went on—but her voice faltered, and she struggled to command it with an effort that was like a sob.

"Sit down," said Pole, gently. "Whatever you want to say, I think I shall understand it, from merely the slightest hint."

"I want first," she resumed, "to repeat what I have said—at least I think I have said before—that I feel moved and honoured—even absurdly honoured—by your asking me what you have asked; and yet sorry. For indeed——"

"Yes," said Pole. "For what?"

"For indeed," she exclaimed hurriedly, "it can never, never be. If I were not sure that you were too kind to be making fun of me, I could hardly believe you serious"

"Why not?" he asked.

She gave him a long mournful look.

"Why not?" she repeated. "Can't you see why? We, neither of us—and you surely know it—have for each other what I, at least, require in marriage; and what you, I am sure, have yourself longed and looked for. You know that we could neither of us give that to the other."

"I am," replied Pole after a pause, "very glad of one thing—that you have told me of your own past, and that you divine enough of mine. I neither dishonour mine nor forget anything in it, when I speak to you as I am doing now. We cannot play at being boy and girl, offering each other a treasure unprofaned by experience. I do not even attempt the language which would, in that case, have been natural to me. But if we lived together I think you would grow fond of me—not perhaps because I could do much for you, but because you would find how much you could do for me. I could tell you everything. I could tell you my weaknesses—for we all have weaknesses; and you could strengthen me. Supposing you to be my sincere friend, as you think you are, would not this be worth doing, even if one flower—the rose scented with dreams—had not again blossomed for us? And perhaps with God's blessing that might arise also."

"No," she murmured abstractedly, "no, no. I couldn't!"

"Then, after all," he exclaimed, almost harshly, ".you don't really care anything about me, or about my welfare ? "

His tone roused her. She looked him in the eyes; she held her hand out to him and answered—

"Oh yes—I care a great deal for you. But oh—you overrate me. I should fail. I should break down. You would tire of me. I know it all so well—and that is a misery which I have not the courage to face."

Then abruptly she raised his hand to her lips. She dropped it as abruptly, and throwing back her head with a gesture almost tragic, exclaimed—

"No—no—this is nonsense! It is true you have attracted me. Why did you make me show it? I hardly knew it myself. I should have hidden it, for I cannot marry you."

This exhibition of feeling quite took Pole aback. He was seized with a sharp sorrow for her, and a desire to put her at her ease.

"You speak to me very kindly," he said. "Let me just add a few words more. I never will ask you, for your friendship's sake, to do anything against your will, nor will I attribute an unfair meaning to expressions which you have used out of kindness. I will only ask you, if you have really a little liking for me, to think this liking over, and see if it is not enough, joined with mine, to provision us for a voyage together. Don't answer me now; just say good night to me and go. I must, to-morrow, again be in London early."

"Good night," she said. "You treat me with great forbearance."

CHAPTER XLII.

AT breakfast next morning he was supplied with a subject of conversation which kept both his thoughts and Miss De Souza's from the things that had occurred last night. He received a letter from his mother which enclosed one from Countess Shimna, this last being accompanied by a photograph of the writer, and containing the prettiest allusions to her happy memories of Glenlynn, and also an account of her forthcoming wedding to the friend who, she said naïvely, had. been her boy *fiancé* when she was in the schoolroom. Mrs. Steinberg was immensely excited by all this interesting intelligence; and when Pole rose in order to catch his train, he left the photograph on the table, that his hostesses might examine it at their leisure.

Hope, of all passions, is probably the most illogical. In the course of the morning he got through some official business of a difficult kind with so much promptitude and success that he went to his club for luncheon, touched with the delightful feeling that in another matter far nearer to him he would at last be equally successful. Miss De Souza's very denials had last night had some promise in them; and he felt it a further good omen that the porter, when he entered the hall, handed him a letter in Mr. Godolphin's writing. He kept it till the end of his luncheon, and then opened it for a dessert. As he did so there fell from it a short cutting out of a newspaper.

"My dear Reginald," ran the letter, "I am writing to you about a matter which has so suprised, startled, and perplexed me, that all yesterday I could think about nothing else. I still trust it may refer to some other person of the same name—I mean the enclosed paragraph. Can you tell me what it means? I should be much relieved if you could explain it."

Pole turned to the printed paragraph, which consisted of a few lines only. It was headed, "Extraordinary Charge against a Clergyman of the Church of England," and proceeded thus:—"A warrant was issued yesterday for the arrest of the Rev. T. Clitheroe, on a charge of obtaining money under false pretences. It is expected that the case will cause considerable sensation, alike on account of the magnitude of the sums involved, and the position of the reverend gentleman, who is reported to occupy some important post under Government."

When Pole read this he felt for the first moment or two as if the floor of the dining-room was actually giving way under his feet. Before reading this paragraph he would almost as soon have imputed the possibility of fraudulent conduct to his mother as to Dr. Clitheroe; and even now, when he thought of the Doctor's face, his little kindly clerical voice, his devotion at family prayers, and his little patent inventions, the words of the newspaper ceased to convey to him any picturable meaning. All the same, with the prompt, half-cynical courage which generally characterized him in the common business of life, he had begun to calculate carefully, as he finished his pint of Burgundy, what his position would be, supposing that the worst was true, and his whole fortune had disappeared under the Doctor's spiriting.

He did not, however, waste much time in reflection. Before ten minutes were over he was seated in a hansom cab, and was driving to the office of a well-known firm of solicitors, with whose senior partner he had some private acquaintance. Pole had not been at the office for some years, and when he reached the broad, but dingy street in which it was situated, he found that he had forgotten the number. He dismissed the cab, therefore, at a corner and began to walk, examining the brass plates on the dirty doors as he went. Whilst doing this, his attention was suddenly diverted by a man walking rapidly, who passed without seeing him. The man was tall, and dressed in a long black coat. His face, thought Pole, was flushed, and' there was a certain excitement in his gait. Pole turned round and looked after him, noticing his long coat tails and the nape of a pink neck that glimmered above a clerical collar. He saw who it was; it was Canon Bulman.

A moment later he had found the house he sought; and, the senior partner being at home, Pole was soon explaining his business. He began, however, in a very guarded way, merely stating that a relation of his had entrusted Dr. Clitheroe with some money; but he had not had time to proceed beyond a few particulars, when the lawyer interrupted him with a curious smile, and said, "Mr. Pole, I think we know the story already. I presume you have something to tell me about certain Australian mines."

"You are perfectly right," Pole answered, with some surprise.

"I have already," said the lawyer, "been consulted about it by another client of mine, whose interests are involved— very deeply involved, indeed. Mr. Pole, have a glass of sherry. I gave one to this gentleman—a clergyman—a distinguished clergyman. His agitation was painful to witness. I'm afraid this may mean ruin for him. Well"—the lawyer continued—" were I you, I should get your relative to write, or else do it yourself, to Dr. Clitheroe, and ask that the money should be refunded. If applied to at once, he may still be in a position to do so. Then, if you wish to act on your relative's behalf, come and see me in a day or two, and I may be able to advise you further. You will probably get Dr. Clitheroe's address from his solicitors—a firm of very good standing. I will write the name down for you. If they decline to give you his address, they will, at all events, send on your letter."

Pole, acting on this suggestion, drove off to the solicitors who had been named to him, thinking, as he went, about the case with a half compassionate contempt, which did much to interrupt his anxiety with regard to his own welfare. On reaching his destination he was shown into a dim back parlour, and requested to take a seat on an old dining-room chair, close to the circumference of an overgrown round table, on which sticky American leather reflected the glimmerings of the window. In a few minutes a pale-faced young man entered, who spoke in demure accents, and smiled with a prepossessing secrecy.

"I am anxious" Pole said, "to write to a client of yours —Dr. Clitheroe; and have called to ask if you could give me his present address, or else forward to him a letter which, with your permission, I would write here."

The young man bowed, and a prim smile played over his lips. "I fear," he said, "we are not able to oblige you. His address is not in our possession. In fact, Dr. Clitheroe is a client of ours no longer."

"Indeed!" exclaimed Pole, "I have only just now been referred to you."

"Will you take a seat?" said the young man, performing the same act himself, and leaning towards Pole across the table. "May I ask," he continued, "if the communication you desire to send to Dr. Clitheroe has any connection with the unpleasant business that is being talked about?"

"It has," said Pole. "I know Dr. Clitheroe well. He has constantly stayed with my family. Let me give you my card, which I ought to have done before. I am anxious to discover what the truth of this strange business is. I always entertained the very greatest regard for him."

"So, Mr. Pole," said the young man, who, it appeared, was a son of one of the partners, "so did my father—in fact, everybody did who knew him. If a good character were a

kind of asset that could be capitalized, Dr. Clitheroe, ten
days ago, might have made himself a rich man. My father
says that in the whole course of his experience he has never
met with a case to come up to this. The Doctor came to
us about it; but we absolutely refused to touch it. Oh, it's
a bad business—very, very bad."

"I," said Pole, "know nothing. Were these mines in
Australia, then, not what he believed or represented them?"

"There never, Mr. Pole," replied the young man, "were
any mines in the case at all. The mines are well enough;
but the whole story of his own connection was absolutely
and entirely a fabrication of his own. What he did with
the money was to gamble with it on the Stock Exchange,
in alliance with an outside broker, who has managed to
escape from the country. He seems to have begun speculating many years ago, but in a very small way; and then to
have been led on by a few unfortunate successes. At one
time it appears that he made really some very large sums,
and this demoralized him. Since then, we gather, he has
made a systematic practice of using his character and
position to obtain money, by means of his deliberate and
ingenious fiction, from people who knew too little, or who
trusted him too much, to doubt it; and whenever he was in
difficulties about paying his promised interest he bled some
new victim."

"Upon my word," exclaimed Pole, "you astonish me!"

"I assure you," said the young man, "you cannot be
more astonished than ourselves. I can give you, should you
desire it, the name of the solicitors who are acting for him
—theirs is a line of business rather different from our own
—and should you wish to write at once, I can give you pen
and paper."

Pole accepted the offer, and wrote these few lines to the
Doctor.

"DEAR DR. CLITHEROE—

"Considering your good will towards myself, which
nothing will ever persuade me was other than genuine, I
should be greatly obliged to you if you would explain to me
what the real grounds are of the incredible rumours which
are being circulated with regard to your investments. If
you are in any serious difficulties, I have no desire to add to

them; but in justice, not to me only, but to yourself, I must earnestly beg you to write at once to me and explain matters. I have not cashed your cheque for £200. Under the circumstances, I am glad I have not done so; but I possibly understand more clearly than before the kindness towards myself personally which so suddenly instigated you to offer it."

This done, Pole walked to the House of Commons, reflecting anew on Dr. Clitheroe's story. His memory now went back to the Doctor's departure from Glenlynn, which struck him at the time as having something oddly furtive in it. Then he thought of the waiting-room in the dim railway-station—the Doctor's start, his nervousness, his cheque, and the little man's conduct about his railway-rug. "I am certain," Pole thought to himself, "that he wished me well even if he acted ill." And then his mind was filled with a sense of the absurdity of the incident; and the iniquities of the Doctor—a man who had lived so long gravely and demurely respectable—tickled his fancy like the naughtiness of some mischievous and incalculable child. This lightness of mind was fostered by something that occurred at Westminster. In the House there was nothing to detain him; but, before he left the precincts, he encountered his chief, Lord Henderson, who, taking his arm with an air of consequential friendliness, said to him, "My dear Mr. Pole, I have been wanting very much to see you;" and he proceeded to hint at the possibility of a post, with a substantial salary, being offered to Pole's acceptance at the beginning of the following year. "Well," thought Pole, as he set his face towards Thames Wickham, "if the Doctor has managed to make away with everything, I shall still be as well off as I expected to be when my aunt died."

When he approached Mrs. Steinberg's house, however, his thoughts wandered from Dr. Clitheroe, and recurred to his conversation of the night before with Miss De Souza. Endeavouring to read her nature by his knowledge of women generally, he became more and more convinced that she entertained some feeling for him, in addition to her sincere friendship, and of a different and a warmer character; but he also believed that this feeling was but partly understood by herself, and that its existence, at the present moment, troubled and even distressed her. Such being the case, he was very anxious to make her see that he was incapable of taking advantage of any unguarded expression of hers, and to put her at her ease by showing her that, whatever happened, nothing would disturb their old and agreeable intimacy.

Accordingly, during the hour before dinner, which was the only time when they were alone together, he at once diverted her thoughts from any embarrassing topics by giving her a description of Dr. Clitheroe and his doings, omitting, however, any mention of his own possible losses, and forbearing even to implicate Canon Bulman. Miss De Souza listened, at once shocked and interested; and the case, after dinner, formed, with Mrs. Steinberg's assistance, the subject of an animated discussion till they all three retired. The two ladies were surprised at the leniency of Pole's judgment of the Doctor. "I assure you," said Miss De Souza, "you are a great deal too charitable."

"If you, dear Mr. Pole," said Mrs. Steinberg, "had lost your own money through his machinations, I'm very much afraid you would not be so forgiving."

"I declare," said Pole, "if I had, I should think of him just as I do now. The poor little fellow may have been reckless, but he had not a touch of malice in him."

The first effects of a blow, however, are not always felt immediately; and in the watches of the night, as he lay awake thinking, the consequences of the Doctor's conduct, and the conduct itself, showed themselves to Pole under a graver aspect. Whatever official salary might possibly be in store for him, he would be far poorer than he had by this time grown accustomed to consider himself. It might well turn out that he would be altogether dependent on his mother; and in any case his expenditure on his charitable enterprise and his savings for another purpose would be curtailed. But these were not the considerations by which he found himself moved most deeply. What depressed him most was the thought, which finally took possession of him, that of the two sole friends, whose disinterested friendship he had believed in, one had not scrupled to treat him with selfish, though perhaps not malignant rascality, and would, it was more than probable, end his days a convict.

So deeply next day did Pole's face and manner betray

the melancholy produced by these reflections that Miss De Souza asked him if he was suffering from any new trouble. He had been always accustomed to answer her with perfect candour, and the question took him entirely off his guard.

"I told you," he answered, "the other day, that I had found during my life only two disinterested friends. You were one; and the other—even now I can't be angry with him—but I have discovered that when he walked by me, seeming to be so grateful, he was really picking my pocket. That friend was Dr. Clitheroe."

"What!" exclaimed Miss De Souza; "do you mean that he got money out of you?"

Pole saw that he had betrayed himself; and some subtle mental impetus prevented his attempting a retreat. "As far as I can tell," he replied, "he has taken everything that I had."

CHAPTER XLIII.

FOR some time the papers had no more news of the Doctor; but a letter from him reached Pole in a day or two, couched in the following terms :—

"DEAR MR. POLE,

"Until I am in a position to make a complete statement, I beg you will do me the justice to entirely suspend your judgment. I write to assure you that my embarrassments are purely temporary, and their nature has been entirely misrepresented by certain disappointed persons. If it were not for technical reasons, into which I need not enter, I would return the sum which I hold for you by this very post. Do not doubt, that it shall reach you within a few weeks at furthest, and meanwhile believe me,

"Yours sincerely,
"T. CLITHEROE."

This letter, which bore neither address nor date, Pole forwarded to his own solicitor, whom he asked to inform him of any farther developments of the case.

Canon Bulman meanwhile had received, two days earlier, a letter identical in purport, and indeed in wording. He was very far, however, from partaking of Pole's temper, and the last thing he thought of was to sit down and await events. The formation of his League, to tell the simple truth, had thus far attracted very little general notice; but various accounts of it had made their appearance in the newspapers; and it so happened, that shortly after his first meeting, he had been waited on by the head of a certain private inquiry office, who offered him the services of his firm at certain reduced rates, "in consideration," this gentleman said, "of the excellence and the sacredness of the objects which the League aimed at." The Canon and his committee had as yet made no alliance with him, the League being at present richer in zeal than funds; but the Canon now in his own private capacity, perceived a case for him, and silently thanked Providence for having thrown such an assistant in his way. It was indeed to him that he was hurrying off, when he had swung past Pole in the street near the solicitor's office.

The Canon's new friend had certainly proved a comfort to him. He had at once laid it down as his opinion that a man like Dr. Clitheroe was sure to have put by a considerable amount of money somewhere, which would enable him to escape, and settle in South America, in case his more ambitious projects should be ruined by some catastrophe. "The Reverend Gentleman," he had continued, "is at present in hiding somewhere, waiting to see the turn which affairs will take. You, Canon Bulman, are probably his chief creditor."

"Well," the Canon had said, with a sort of dogged reluctance, "I was imprudent enough last June to entrust him with ten thousand; and six weeks ago, with ten thousand more."

"I should think," his adviser had answered, "he would have at his command a far larger sum than that; and if by refunding it to you, he could convert the chief witness against him into a witness in his favour, he would jump at the opportunity of performing so politic a piece of honesty. Write him a letter here, and ask for your money back; but don't even hint a suspicion that there has been anything irregular in his conduct. Above all, don't hint that if you are paid, you will not prosecute. I am certain you never would wish to compound a felony. We will manage that the letter shall reach him somehow; and meanwhile, my dear sir, I would beg you not to worry yourself."

After some further conversation of this kind, the Canon had returned to Windsor, not indeed free from anxiety, but no longer in a state of distraction. Hope with him was an athlete, which forced its way through doubts, and prevented them from mobbing him, though it could not frighten them out of sight. The Canon was thus in a position to seek, during the period of suspense, for relief in pursuing, with more vigour than usual, his usual occupations, and usual train of thought. He had an engagement to preach in a fashionable church in London; and he threw himself into his sermon with an almost frenzied vigour. He took for his subject the question of Metropolitan poverty during the winter, which he attributed altogether to the comfort of the callous rich. He denounced their luxuries, their dresses, their horses, their carriages, their servants; and he threatened them all with the terrors of an immediate revolution, if they did not in the cold weather discharge half their establishments, in order to diminish the number of the unemployed. Then for his own edification he pursued the same train of thought when, in the absence of any fashionable friend to entertain him at luncheon, after the service he refreshed himself at a club which was decorously, though not fashionably, liberal. The iniquities with which he had been taxing the rich classes in general, "the possessors," as he expressed it, "of the unearned increment," all seemed to him now to be concentrated in Dr. Clitheroe; and the Canon felt that if he saved his fortune from this devourer— from this man who was such a scandal both to humanity and to his sacred calling—he would be doing to the cause of righteousness almost as great a service as to himself.

His Christian socialism, however, did not monopolize his energies. His quarrel with vice was even more bitter than ever, and he was constantly lashing himself into fresh fits of indignation against the "bestial sensualism," as he called it, which according to his view of life, was the essence of every link, and even of every sentiment, uniting the two sexes, but not leading to banns or licence. And more than ever, his thoughts were engrossed by Pole. Pole, whose guilt he had never really doubted, not only now represented for him aristocratic vice in general, just as Dr. Clitheroe represented the iniquities of speculation and capital, but he represented vice which was provokingly flouting virtue, and escaping like a bird from the net of practicable proof. He had, more-over, contrived to put the Canon personally in the wrong, and that when the Canon was actually sitting on the judg-ment seat. This fact still smarted in the Canon's memory, and inflamed him with something even stronger than right-eous anger, though he himself was unable to tell the difference.

He did not, nevertheless, by any means lose his head, or forget the sobering lesson he had learned during his visit to the Duke. On the contrary, he endeavoured to impress these lessons on his colleagues ; and actuated partly by a genuine sense of honour, and partly by a desire to show Pole he possessed it, he contrived to extract from the landlord of Laburnum Lawn the original of the incriminating letter, with a view to restoring it to the writer.

"I declare," said Mr. Snagg, as with some reluctance he handed it over, well thumbed, to the Canon, "when our servant girl gave it to me, and I read it, not knowing what it was, you might have knocked me down with a feather. When I think sometimes of the things that must have hap-pened within the walls of my house—when I dwell on them, Canon Bulman, so to speak—my cheeks get so hot that I have to go out and cool myself. And these are the people," he continued, with more clearness of thought than language, "that ride in carriages, and call themselves the friend of the working man. I'd work the men, if I had my own way, who support him! But mark my words, sir, we'll have our gentle-man yet. All the same, I entirely hold with you, that we shan't be doing the Lord's business by getting into hot water ourselves. It's they want boiling, saving your presence, Canon Bulman, not we."

The prophecy of this excellent man, that Pole would not escape them for long, though founded on nothing more defi-nite than faith and hope, appeared, the very next day, to be on the point of actually fulfilling itself. He wrote the Canon, begging him to keep Pole's letter, as other important evidence had just been put before him. It appeared that the servant girl who had found the letter and handed it to

him, had witnessed the visits of Pole to Laburnum Lawn,
and had spoken of several facts, which would confirm the
evidence of the letter—"kissing, embracing, and all that,"
said the writer, delicately. "I questioned the girl, to tell
the truth, and all came out as I expected. I have," he continued, "to be away for two nights, but the moment I come
back I will bring you the whole in writing; but I beg you,
sir, not on any account to let that letter go until we meet."

The Canon was delighted at the receipt of this inspiriting news; but the further retention of the letter worried his
sense of honour. He accordingly compromised with his
scruples by writing to Pole what was, as will be seen, accurate so far as it went, and enabled the Canon to think of
himself as a very straightforward man.

"Dear Mr. Pole," he wrote, "I have to inform you that
I have seen and spoken with the person who found your
letter, and I requested him to give it up to me in order that
I might restore it to yourself. But matters, meanwhile, I
must tell you, have assumed a very different aspect. Other
evidence has been tendered to us, which, together with the
letter in question, can leave little doubt in my mind that
your protestations of innocence to myself were so many
deliberate and shameless falsehoods. I shall write in a day
or two and ask you for another interview, which, however
painful to both of us, will be desirable for your own welfare,
and that of another, who you are good enough to say is
dear to you."

An hour or two after the Canon had despatched this he
received a letter himself, which, by some curious theological
process, made him feel that divine providence was taking
him at his own valuation, and managing his worldly matters
for him, in accordance with this satisfactory estimate. It
was from the head of the private inquiry office. The writer
reported himself as being now in direct communication with
the Doctor, whose present place of seclusion had been discovered with little difficulty; and he informed the Canon
that one of the agents of the office would, most probably, in
the course of a few days more, secure from the Doctor a
cheque, payable to the Canon's order, for very nearly the
whole of the sum which had been so rashly jeopardized.
"We are inclined to think," the letter continued, "that the
reverend gentleman's position is by no means so bad as has

been represented." The Canon's heart leapt with joy, like a football, his own letter meanwhile speeding on its way to Pole.

It happened that this was the last day of the session, and the last day also of Pole's visit to Mrs. Steinberg; and to Pole it was full of importance, as being the vigil of a crisis in his history. He had said nothing further to Miss De Souza with regard to the question which he had put to her. He had resolved to postpone doing so till he had finally left Thames Wickham, and he had resolved then to appeal to her in a carefully written letter.

Meanwhile, his hope of success had been growing day by day. Had he studied every possible way by which to strengthen his position with her, he could not have discovered a more powerful one than that on which he stumbled by accident, when he told her in an unguarded moment of his probable loss of fortune; and this was a way which intentionally he would never have so much as thought of. From that moment he had felt that Miss De Souza's manner to him had acquired a tenderer and more unreserved solicitude. He was oftener conscious of her eyes following his movements, and her smiles greeted him like her hand when she said "Good night" to him, or "Good morning." During the last few days the fine weather had ended, rain had fallen often, and the wind had become violent, so their hours together were passed at the fireside, not amongst the garden-walks; and often, as Pole listened to the noise of the weather against the windows, and then looked at the fire-light on the folds of Miss De Souza's dress, whilst her thoughts came to him embodied in her soothing syllables, he thought of the noble peace—though not perhaps of the happiness—which he might, with her assistance, attain to and win in life, and compared it with the roofless desolation which threatened him were he left solitary.

To-day, having been in London in the morning, he had returned earlier than he had expected, and Miss De Souza, not knowing he was in the house, was busy in her own sitting-room. She was not busy, however, with any visible occupation. Her work lay entirely amongst her sympathies, her thoughts, and her resolutions. Her sole visible action was to take up a photograph now and then, that was lying by her on a table, and to examine it very carefully. This

photograph was the portrait of Countess Shimna, which Pole
had left with her, and which hitherto she had forgotten to
return to him. Each time she looked at it she examined
some fresh detail, noticing the perfection of lip, and head
and instep, the clear contour of the cheek, and the dim
seduction of the eyelashes. "Yes," she said, with a sigh,
"he admires this, and this; and, tried by his pampered
memories, I, if ever I belonged to him—I know it well—
well—well—should first discontent, then weary, and at last
disgust him." For she, like Pole, remembered that a crisis
in their acquaintanceship was approaching, which might
perhaps end in her losing her friend of so many years, unless
she could nerve herself to retain him upon other terms; and
just as he was now thinking of her, so was she balancing her
conflicting thoughts of him.

She knew, and she blushed as at intervals she faced the
knowledge, that she not only regarded him as an admired
and sympathetic friend, but felt for him, at moments, that
tumultuous warming of the heart, and relenting, of the
nerves, which in some cases lead to, and in some, follow,
another feeling. And then through this reflection came
others, piercing it, adding to its power, and touching her far
more nearly. For in spite of her own diffidence, and her
almost morbid modesty, she had of late been growing
gradually to believe that, in one respect, Pole was right;
and that it might be in her power to do more for him than
she had, since a memorable experience, been able to believe
she ever could do for any man. She had always known as a
mere intellectual truth, that the lives neither of men or
women consist in the abundance of the things they possess;
but men's lives in this way were different, she had thought,
from women's. She had lately been led to see what hitherto
she had only known—that a man may be well born, possessed
of sufficient wealth, be caressed and befriended by all that is
brilliant in society, and advancing with rare rapidity on the
road to success and power, and yet may find—as she could
well have imagined a woman finding—that all these pleasures
and advantages were a jewelled and enamelled nutshell,
which might hold as well as not, darkness and bitterness for
its kernel; and Pole, as she studied him, had shown her this
all the more clearly because, whilst showing her how little
could be done for him by the world alone, he was far from

2 A

undervaluing such things as it gave him, still less had he
any quarrel with it. Though by no means a dandy either in
his dress or habits, she knew that under the surface he was
full of social fastidiousness; and she saw that though his
recent successes failed to make him happy, they acted on
him like a tonic, which saved him from complete dejection.
That such a man—one who valued the world thus—should
feel that the world, without other things added to it, was
nothing, taught her more of the actual needs of the nobler
amongst male natures than all the aspirations of a dozen
gauche recluses. She began to think of him as a swimmer,
drowning in icy water, whom a friendly hand might help;
and then when her thoughts returned to his probable losses,
the prospect of which he had borne with such kindly and
cool philosophy, her heart pleaded with her to go to him
with her own abundance.

But this chain of thoughts and feelings, as they circled
irregularly through her consciousness, always brought back
to her some which were stronger and clearer to her than the
rest, and pierced her mental ear with more poignant voices.
These were the thoughts supplied to her by her study of
Countess Shimna's photograph and those suggested to her
by her own past experience. She missed in Pole the note of
eager passion which had touched her in her former lover.
She bethought her that Pole did not even attempt it; and
whilst respecting him for his honesty, she missed all the
more the thing which he would not feign. Then, by the
light of what she had once suffered already, she pictured
with a self-torturing ingenuity, the gradual cooling of that
affection for her which she did believe him to possess. She
fancied his confidence in her becoming less spontaneous; she
saw him, having once possessed her, outgrowing his pre-ent
need of her; and herself, wounded every hour of the day in
an affection for him which, would she permit it, was ready to
spring up now. She shuddered at the thought. What she
knew of her own nature led her to a fatal certitude, that if
her affection grew she would be wholly unable to disguise
it; and her firm belief was that, in the present case, the
more it showed itself the slighter, so soon as her husband's
feelings for her cooled, would its effect upon him be; the
more terribly would each look and each wasted caress of
hers recoil on herself, converted into unbearable pain and

humiliation. "Never!" she exclaimed; "never!" And at the image of her own pain she leaned back in her chair, drawing a deep breath, and pressing her hands with convulsive energy across her eyes.

Presently a servant informed her that tea was in the drawing-room.

"Is Mrs. Steinberg there?" she asked.

"No, miss," he answered, "but Mr. Pole is."

She shrank from facing him, though at the very moment she was longing for his company. When she met him, her last resolve was again in danger of being shaken.

Pole, on reaching Thames Wickham, had found a letter awaiting him; and when Miss De Souza entered the drawing-room, he was standing by the fire, having just finished reading it. It was the threatening letter of Canon Bulman. Knowing how soon she would have definitely to answer him, she had meant to have prepared him for the event by a certain reserve of manner, from which anything that was more than friendship should imperceptibly have evaporated; but as soon as she saw his face her resolution melted. She came quietly towards him; she laid her hand on his arm.

"Tell me," she said, "is anything new annoying you?"

He looked at her with a gratitude which filled her with self-reproach; but he shook his head, trying to laugh cheerfully.

"Perhaps it is," he said, "that I want some tea. Will you give me some? Do you know that your kettle has been singing for you for twenty minutes?"

They went together to the tea-table, attempting to talk as usual, but the effort soon failed; and at last Pole said, "You are right. Something does trouble me. It is something that makes me anxious for the sake of another person, and may also have—though I can bear up against that—results that are unfortunate on myself. And now, my friend, since I have spoken about one serious matter, let me just allude to another. You know I told you that when my visit drew to an end, I would repeat my question to you. I had thought of doing so to-night. But with your permission I will say nothing till I leave you. I go the first thing to-morrow. I will write to you at once from London. If you are going to say No, you can write it more easily than say it, whilst Yes can be said with equal ease either way. I will not risk another disappointment before I go, or show to your aunt a gloomier face than I can help, on this last evening of a visit which I shall not forget."

"Thank you," said Miss De Souza with a lump in her throat. "I wish—I do wish," she stammered, but suddenly checked herself, murmuring, "Here's my aunt!" and in another moment Mrs. Steinberg was standing by them, blossoming with the newest of bonnets which she had been wearing on a round of visits, swelling in the richest of velvets, and submerging the remains of their tête-à-tête in a torrent of new gossip and of random expressions of benevolence.

CHAPTER XLIV.

TRUE to his word, by next morning Pole was gone. He did not, however, wait till he was in London before writing to Miss De Souza. He wrote to her over-night; and, starting from the house before breakfast, he left his letter to be taken up to her with her tea. What he had written to her was this :—

"You know me so well, and you know human nature so well, that I think you must know also, far better than I can explain to you, how much a woman like you—and that means you yourself, for there is no woman quite like you—might do for a man like me. But before I write more, I must make one request of you, which I am quite sure you will grant. As you read what I am now going to say, remember that I say it with a reservation, which I will force upon your notice at the end.

"I think—perhaps I am a coxcomb for thinking—but I am too weary to entertain exaggerated scruples, and what I think I had better say out plainly—I think that were you sure I could offer you what a husband ought to offer, your generosity would soften your heart, and you would stoop down and marry me. I am not flattering you, for you *would* stoop.

"I told you once before that I do not mean to protest. If you do not believe already in the reality and the sufficiency of what I feel, whole quires of note-paper would not make you; and yet even on this point I will say something presently. But my great appeal—I must tell you candidly —is to your generosity. The loss, or the probable loss, of my money makes it more difficult for me to speak; for I am not thinking of generosity in regard to money. I know that if you cared to take me, you would be glad if your money helped me, and would not impute to me mercenary motives. But for the matter of that, if the worst comes to the worst, I shall not be a pauper; or if your fortune were in any way to assist me, I believe I could settle Glenlynn on you, and so balance our obligation. Forgive these bald phrases. I am ashamed even to mention this subject. Were I a beggar, you would forget my beggary. No; when I talk of generosity, it is generosity of another kind. At present you enjoy— after a past experience of pain—a happy quiet, troubled only by the pleasurable agitations of sedulous and emulous friend- ships; and I ask you to share the lot of one who is bruised and battered, and whose body aches with wounds. I ask you to help me as one half buried in a snow-storm might ask, if he had voice to do so, one in a warm house, to venture for a moment into the cold, and lead him to the warmth within. Will you never know what you could do? I cannot protest even here. You would be a fire to a man freezing, a hand to a man drowning. Can't you understand this? Well, if you can't, I can never teach you.

"I am not going to write you a long letter. I have done with that part. I think, as I said at first, you would respond to what I have just said, did you only believe that I should prove myself worthy, throughout life, of so much goodness. But you doubt me. You think, as regards yourself, I have not the requisite disposition—that I lack the one thing needful. I must answer that thought in some way; and yet not, as I have said, by the protestations of ordinary lovers. I will not even make use of the word 'love,' stained as it is for me with the blood of many sorrows. I will only say—and this is quite true—that if I knew how to pray, and if I were married to you, I could kneel down with you by your bed, and, without any false shame or embarrassment, say 'Our Father' with you. From a disposition such as this, a new flower might rise, not the same as that which has blossomed for us both formerly; but yet not unworthy to succeed it.

"I have but one thing more to add. It was you yourself who preached to me that I should not turn my back on happiness—that it was the wise, the right, the manly, the sane thing, to seek it; and will you not now help me to carry out your own counsels? Do you think there is risk for your own peace in doing so? If you will not consent to save a soul alive, for fear that in the process you might have to sigh yourself, I have no right to urge you to risk anything for my sake. But I don't think I should make you sigh. Else I would not ask you.

"And now I come to the reservation of which I spoke. It is quite possible that something may occur shortly—but I think not—which will prejudice me in the world's eyes, and perhaps in yours. I shall know very shortly. Should such a thing occur, I will put the whole situation before you quite candidly. I do not believe that in your decision it would make any difference; but I mention it, in order to tell you that should you say Yes to me now, I should consider you free to withdraw the Yes, should the contingency I allude to arise, and make you wish to withdraw it. Will you do me one favour—will you write to me to-day, directing to me at my club in London?"

He had not long to wait before receiving an assurance that to one of his wishes at least Miss De Souza had assented. A letter from her reached him at his club by three in the afternoon. He opened it without hesitation, determined at once to know either the best or worst, and full of a faith in her, which bravely weathered his doubts.

"My dear Mr. Pole," she wrote. "Ever since I got yours at half-past eight this morning, I have been thinking of nothing else. I have been more moved by it than I have ever been by anything else that has ever been said or written to me. Every word you say goes home to me. Yes; we all want help, even the strongest of us; and the great men who can stand wholly alone—if any such are—are able to do so because in some ways they are not great. And you say I could help you. At first, I could not believe you; but you made me believe you afterwards. Perhaps I could, if you would only let me—let me be true to you, let me be close to you; but not in the exact way you wish. If only it might be in any way but that!

"I must speak plainly, though I have hardly courage to do so. I said to you long ago that I should never marry, and to this decision I adhere. I must nerve myself also to tell you the reason, even though you should despise me for it. You think too highly of me. You do not know the depths of my selfishness. A burnt child dreads fire; and what you propose and wish would mean for me, I know, pain which I could not face. You don't think so; but I know it.

"Let me explain, though it is going over old ground. Genuine as I believe the feelings which you express for myself to be, there is one feeling which you do not possess, and which you are too honourable to feign; and I know from experience that without that I should be miserable. A man without that, would not be what my nature looks for in a husband; and he could not be, however much he tried. But all this, too, is partly owing to deficiencies in myself. You fail to possess certain things that I require, because I have defects of charm—of—of—never mind what all the things are—of things that you require, and have before now found. We should both discover that this was so, if we tried the experiment you suggest; and a future like that I have not the courage to face. Why did you ever ask me to be more than a friend? The thrill of pleasure that I confess you sent through me by doing so, is lost in the sorrow—you will not believe me how deep—at having to say a final, an irrevocable, No.

"Yours very faithfully and sadly,
"ETHEL DE SOUZA."

Having read this he consigned it quietly to his pocket, put on his hat and coat, and slowly walked out of doors. The afternoon was dim and chilly, and the wind was flapping at the street corners. It suited his mood. He was no sooner alone than Miss De Souza's letter for a time sank beneath the surface of his consciousness, and its place in his thoughts was taken by his relations with Canon Bulman, and by all that might be involved in them for another and for himself. One reflection, however, came back to him, fraught with comfort. Whatever new proofs against him the Canon and his friends might have, he would be able to avert their action by yielding to their demands and resigning his seat in Parliament. He did not believe even now that these boasted proofs would come to much; but they might be sufficient to urge ignorant men into action, which would threaten the name of a woman by associating it fatally with his own; and he resolved that sooner than let even a shadow of trouble touch her, his own career should be sacrificed to whatever extent might be requisite.

Steered unconsciously by his thoughts his steps had led him towards Westminster, and looking up, he saw the towers and pinnacles of the Palace, endowed by smoke and vapour, with an aspect of majestic mystery. He had often looked at it before under similar atmospheric conditions. But for him it was now transformed: it stared at him like a new phenomenon. It was now a phantasmal mausoleum of his own dead hopes and vanities, whose value for himself he realized' for the first time, when he realized that they were no longer his.

He wandered about the streets till darkness had long gathered in them; and having settled with himself what should be his own conduct, his thoughts had once again centred themselves on Miss De Souza. He was amazed, he was astonished, when he thought about her; but he was not doubtful. The news that she would not marry him, he accepted with resignation; but what he rebelled against and resented was the reason of her refusal. The more he thought over the matter the more clear did it become to him that she had described herself with pitiless accuracy when she spoke of her own selfishness. It was, in a certain sense, not a low or vulgar selfishness. It was spiritual, it was refined, but for that very reason it appeared to him the more intense. Here was a woman who was tortured by the passing pains of others, who would imperil her strength, who would spend herself and be spent to relieve them, but who would not, to save the life of the oldest friend she had, risk any ruffling of the rose-leaves on which her life had settled itself. She would cry, on her rose-leaves, for her friend's sake, but she would not leave them for it.

This discovery with regard to Miss De Souza shook him far more deeply than Countess Shimna's inconstant levity.

What he rebelled against and resented was not Miss De Souza's refusal to marry him, but the way in which she desecrated by doing so the high ideal which he had worshipped in her. " Is all human nature like this ? " he said. " Putting my mother aside, I told myself that I had only two friends; but that these were true and unselfish, and would really risk a little to do good to me. And of these, the one has robbed me of every penny that I possess; and the other will let me go to the devil, sooner than turn round on her feather bed."

Similar thoughts kept him company as he dined at his club alone. Then he sat himself down to write an answer to Miss De Souza.

" I can never forget," he wrote, " your talents, and your abnormal sympathy. Nobody could understand me, and nobody could feel for me as you have done; and since, even in your eyes, I am not worth the remote chance of a single sorrow or anxiety, I have not much, I suppose, to expect from human nature. And yet I can explain to myself your conduct. I say you feel for me, and so you do. But you see me through plate-glass, as you see the frost and rain. Morally and physically you have lain cradled in eider-down. Every word, every act of yours, has been met with admiring and grateful glances. You have had your Miss Cremers to adore as superhuman heroism every self-denial on your part, every common act of humanity. Your virtues have been like flowers round which circumstance has built a hot-house, and they wither the moment they are brought into the open air."

He paused abruptly in his writing and tore the letter up. " God forgive me," he said. " Who am I, to find fault with anybody ! I will, at all events, not find fault with you—you are but human. It was my fault, for madly expecting you to be more."

He took up a newspaper and vainly tried to read; and then at last he sank into a half doze. From this he abruptly roused himself. An image, as if at random, had floated across his mind, and with it an address in London. He rose, put his hat and coat on, and went out into the streets. He walked rapidly, and evidently with a set purpose. The same image and address were still present in his mind. The image was the image of a woman, young, dainty, and tender.

Her eyes were modest in their almost timid abandonment. There was in her syllables a dainty and furtive music. It was the image of the girl who had walked with him through the quiet moonlight of Piccadilly, and her name and address for the first time since that night recurred to him. He reached the street where she lived—a street of stucco and balconies, where pink blinds in the daytime showed themselves like half-closed eyelids; but he had some difficulty in finding the right number. The numbers did not run regularly, being broken by two side streets. Before he had discovered what he looked for he reached again the corner, where the street that he was in led off from a main thoroughfare. At this corner he stood still for a moment, and turning his face westward walked back solitary to his lodgings. The thoughts which occupied him as he did so, and thus sent him back without having fulfilled his purpose, proved their intensity by still remaining with him when he slept, and reproducing themselves in a dream, in another and yet more vivid form.

He fancied that he was in a lonely road, he could not tell in what country. The fields looked bare and melancholy, and the gates and hedges were neglected. As he went along this he suddenly became conscious that he was not alone, but that he was leading a little boy. For a time he felt pleased by the sense of companionship thus given him; but gradually something told him that he ought to be quickening his pace, and the child, whose hand clung to him, he began to feel was an impediment. "I can't," he said, not unkindly, "take you any further with me." And letting its hand go he began to walk a little faster. For half a minute or so the little thing trotted after him, stamping and laughing as though this were some new game. Then Pole walked quicker still, and he no longer heard any footsteps by him. But presently he heard a cry, and turning round he saw the little boy trying to run after him, and then fall forwards on its helpless little hands and knees. Then his eyes were opened. The little boy was his own. In his dream he turned. He rushed towards it with open arms. "Oh, my child," he exclaimed, "oh, my little one—come to me—rest yourself on my breast—I am your father and your mother both." But the child receded as he advanced towards it, pitiful in its amazed loneliness, and with a cry on his lips, his eyes wet with tears, and with his heart palpitating, Pole woke.

The dream went, but the passion that was at the heart of it remained. His excited mind clutched at words in which o express itself; but what words could be full enough to express the passion that was shaking him? They must be sacred words—they could not be too sacred. "I will arise," he said, "and go to my son."

CHAPTER XLV.

HE roused himself next morning, full of a new idea—a new purpose—which he found had drifted into his mind on the tides of his troubled dream. Hitherto it had never occurred to him to speak of the proceedings of Canon Bulman to the woman whom they threatened, and whom his one aim was to shield. He was suddenly now convinced that it would be better, and even necessary for him to do so. He remembered the long letter which he had written to her from Glenlynn in August, and reflected that this, at all events, ought to be at once destroyed. He wished also to make sure that the letter which had been stolen by the Windsor landlord was the only letter that had been mislaid by her during her occupation of Laburnum Lawn. He determined therefore that he would instantly go down to Wales to see her, and explain to her as much of the situation as he could do without alarming her; and further, since he had not as yet heard again from the Canon, that he would instantly write to him demanding the return of his letter, together with a candid statement of the alleged fresh evidence against him.

"Dear Canon Bulman," he wrote, "I have been daily expecting some further communication from you. I have, as you are aware, discussed this matter at all with you, only for the sake of shielding another person from unmerited and wanton annoyance; and it is solely in the interests of this person that I write again. Whatever other evidence you may have become possessed of, you are by your position as a gentleman, bound to return my letter. I wonder that you can sully your honour by keeping it for a single moment.

I shall be out of London to-night, and to-morrow also; but the day following I will call on you in the morning, should that suit you, and receive it personally at your hand. I will also hear what further you have to say. I send this by my servant, who will wait while you write your answer; and if I have started before his return, he will send it on to me in the country. I shall thus, at furthest, receive it to-morrow night."

Having despatched his servant with this by the next train to Windsor, he turned to the advertisements of Welsh hotels in *Bradshaw*. One of them informed him that, in the little town that was nearest to St. Owen's Castle, though many miles distant from it, there was "an old-established family and commercial hotel," the landlord of which undertook "posting in all its branches." The time-table informed him that if he left London at four—by which hour he hoped his servant might have returned—he would reach his destination about half-past ten that night. He accordingly went out and telegraphed to the hotel for rooms, he himself packed up the little luggage he would require, and he beguiled the hours before starting in the best way he might.

His mind was agitated painfully, and yet he hardly knew how. Thoughts of Miss De Souza, of the Canon, of the shipwreck of his own career in Parliament, thoughts of his financial losses, and of the miserably fraudulent little Doctor, collided against him like wreckage colliding against an open boat; but somehow their blows and shocks hardly claimed more of his attention than was required by the endeavour to avoid them. What mainly occupied him was the thought of the faces he was about to see—two faces far off in Wales. They had drifted away from him into the company of impossible visions; and now, in a few hours, he would actually once more see them. At this thought his heart leapt and palpitated; then again it would sink or stand still with doubt as he asked himself what expression one face would wear for him. He would not inquire beforehand. He would soon know by experience.

The time approached when he ought to be starting for the station; but his servant had not returned. He had a cab at the door ten minutes sooner than was necessary, for, whatever happened, he was resolved not to miss his train. Five of these minutes he waited anxiously on the door-step, thinking that the man might arrive at the last moment. But he did not; and Pole drove off. The Canon's letter would reach him by to-morrow night at farthest.

Some eight hours later, he was sitting down to a supper consisting of a couple of chops, which were flanked by two bottles of pickles, and guarded farther off by a Gibraltar of towering cheese. The walls surrounding him glimmered with varnished paper, blotched here and there by an engraving of some county magnate. Here was a Wynne, here was a Talbot, or a Williams; and on one lower margin, exceptionally stained and fly-blown, Pole detected the name of a Pryce Masters. As a broad and dingy waiter opened and shut the door, he saw in the background the bottles and the tumblers of a bar; and at such moments there would come to him a breath as of beer and stables.

He had not announced his coming to the woman he was about to see, for fear that, if he did so, she might telegraph that she would not receive him; and the object of his visit he naturally shrank from committing to paper. But he arranged with the landlord of the hotel, before going to bed, to send over a mounted messenger who would reach the castle about lunch-time, and would carry a note containing these words merely—

"I want to speak to you a moment about some urgent business, and I shall arrive very soon after these lines reach you.—Sincerely yours,

"R. POLE."

He had also ascertained that Lady Masters was at home —that she had been, in fact, in the town the day before yesterday.

He woke the following morning, anxious, before all else, to see whether a letter had been forwarded to him from Canon Bulman. There was none. When he learnt the fact, he found that it was almost a relief to him. It would enable him to tell her himself that his apprehensions were altogether vague, and might, in the end, prove to be without foundation. It was also a relief to him, expectant and impatient as he was, to feel that he had in front of him a morning for solitary reflection. He had three hours, he found, when he had finished his breakfast, before it would be necessary for him to start for St. Owen's Castle. He wandered out, therefore, and sauntered through the little town, trying to rest his mind by diverting it from the ordeal awaiting him. Like most other people placed in similar situations, he found that the unnatural and painful vacancy of his mind rendered it susceptible of the most extravagant interest in trifles. At one moment the state of the streets, sloppy after a wet night, filled him with wonder at the remissness of the local authorities. Then he studied, in succession, objects in the various shops—buns, tin coffee-pots, coal-scuttles, and Brussels carpets; and, when he had done with all these, he started at a brisker pace, to look at some dwelling-houses with gardens, to which one of the streets led. The houses, when he reached them, he saw were mere road-side villas, having a strip of grass and some bushes between them and the public footpath. Then he came to a turn, beyond which was open country. A little way off a baker's cart was standing, and farther on still, a shabby-looking carriage of some sort—also standing, and empty, except for a slouching coachman. Neither object was very exciting in itself; but still, each was an object, so he strolled on towards them.

The air was raw; the hedges were black and leafless; and the crevices in the bark of the bare road-side trees seemed to have winter clinging in them. He passed the carriage, a sort of clumsy phaeton, and leaned over a gate beyond it. Before him was a path, which led over some ploughed fields, and so far as he could see, would take him back to the town. He idly settled on returning by it. At the end of the second field was a little wicket-gate, leading into a transverse path, bordered by thick thorn hedges. He was speculating, being still in the field, which direction he should take, when behind the thorn hedges he heard a pattering noise; and a very small creature emerged through the gate running. He started and stared at it. Between a red pelisse and cap was a little face with a pair of large dark eyes in it, bright at the present moment with the busy happiness of childhood, and yet touched with a melancholy of which their possessor did not know the meaning. Pole could hardly believe that he was not again dreaming. This little thing was his own.

" My little boy ! " he exclaimed.

The child stood still, and looked at him. It was startled at first, then frightened, and then for a moment it seemed on the point of crying. Pole spoke again, in a softer and more caressing tone; and finally called it by all of the pet names it was accustomed to. "Don't you know me?" he said. "Does the little boy not know me?" The child's mouth relaxed. In each of its cheeks came a dimple, and a laugh of recognition in its eyes; and running to Pole with all its helpless speed, allowed his arms to enfold it, and put up its face to his.

Close to the gate was a heap of rough stones, collected as materials for some piece of rustic masonry. Pole sat down upon this, and placing the child on his knee, he began to caress and talk to it, with more quietness indeed than a mother would have displayed, but with a passionate affection which no mother could have surpassed. "And who is my little boy with?" he asked a moment later. "How does he come here?" He was in the middle of this question, when something caught his eye. He was not conscious what, till it had caused him to look up; and his question was answered, for the child's mother was before him. She was standing there motionless with surprise. Pole stared at her, almost fearing that she would call the child away, or else break out into an audible reproof or anger. Instead of detecting any signs in her that would justify such apprehensions, he saw a face whose expression was very nearly as childish as the child's. At first it revealed nothing but surprise of the most naïve intensity, which expressed itself verbally in an "Oh," that was long drawn out. Then the surprise melted like snow in sunshine, and the "Oh" was followed by just such a ripple of laughter as a little girl might give at the news of a half-holiday. After this came more coherent speech. "How did you come here? How?" she exclaimed, with a deep gasp. He held his hand out to her. She seized it, clung to it, gripped it.

All his preconceived ideas of the various possibilities of this meeting were upset so completely by what was actually taking place as to make him feel that either the present, or else the past was a dream. Could this be the woman who had treated him with such heartless cruelty? Or was she cruel still under an April mask of smiles? This last doubt could find no harbour in his mind. He was still perplexed, but his perplexity melted into happiness—a happiness which he had long since felt certain he should never taste again.

"Pansy," he said to her softly—and these were his first words to her—"tell me, are you glad to see me?" The grey blue of her eyes looked at him with rain in it and dancing sunshine. "Yes, Reggie," she whispered, "very glad." Then she went on, "You must tell me how you came here. Are you staying here? Of course, Reggie, you were coming to see me. I will drive you back to luncheon. Our carriage is over there, waiting for us. It is so old and shabby. Come," she said, pointing to the little boy, "take his hand, and we will go to it."

Had he died and come to life again in some happier world, he felt that he could have known no radiance like that of this leafless day, roofed with bitter clouds and floored with these sodden furrows.

"I meant," he said presently, "to have driven to your castle in an hour or so. I have a fly at the hotel ordered for me at one o'clock. I am staying there. I came last night."

"But why?" she asked. "What brought you—so suddenly—without writing?"

"I will tell you," he said, "by-and-by. Will you take me back to the inn, and I will countermand the carriage; and then, if you will, you shall drive me out with you."

She assented, and he ordered that the fly should come for him at four o'clock. He then took his seat beside her, with the little boy between them; and they set off through the lanes in her old-fashioned lumbering vehicle.

"What I want to speak about," he said, "is a little piece of business. But that will keep. You must now tell me about all this country."

So they went. She told him the names of the villages, and something now and then about some old church or ruin; and only once or twice this sort of conversation was interrupted, when she said to him, "Reggie, you are such a great man now;" and when he said to her, "You are looking younger than ever—more than ever like a little girl."

At length before them they saw a line of woods; and then some swelling masses of oak-trees and ragged evergreens; and then, between dips in these, the waters of a leaden sea; and then two towers, like black ears, above the foliage.

"There," she said, "is the castle! Oh, how you will like it!"

A painful but momentary change passed over his face, as he answered her, " D-ar, shall I ? "

"Don't," she whispered, shuddering at a something which she detected in his face. "I can't help living here. Do be interested in it. See, we are coming to the gates."

He looked at her with restored composure; and the carriage, out of the dark approach, passed rumbling through the two gate-houses, into a small court or yard, where it halted amongst the huddled buildings. The place was so curious, and it attracted him himself so strongly, that he could hardly wonder at her life taking root so naturally in it. Whilst waiting for luncheon, she took him through some of the rooms and galleries, repaired by the late owner in the worst and most trumpery taste. He only once interrupted their talk upon architecture and antiquity by saying to her, very gently, "Why have you never written to me ? "

"I could," she said, hesitating, "have written to you more if I had wanted to write less. I couldn't have written what I wanted to. But I thought of you. One night I woke up in my room, which is quite by itself, Reggie, in that tower there, and I heard a little noise. It was early morning, and light; and I saw there was a mouse on my pillow. You creep into my thoughts, like a mouse, at all moments. But you frighten me sometimes, and I make you go away—but only behind the wainscot. I know you are still close by."

Then luncheon came; and as the meal proceeded, Pole's spirits sank when he thought of the explanation that was to follow. "You must remember," he said, when they got up from the table, "the little business about which I have come to speak to you. It is that," he added in a lower tone, "which has brought me here at a moment's notice."

"Come," she said, with the beginnings of anxiety in her face, "come into another room. I thought we would have gone outside; but it is blowing so hard, and it rains too. Well, dear, what is it ? " she said, as she closed the door of the room to which she had taken him—a musty and ragged library, whose windows were rattling in the gale.

Before beginning his explanation he looked at her with a half-humorous smile, " I know the dimensions of this room," he said. "Its length is just forty feet." Then his smile, faded. "Let me tell you," he continued, "about the business. I don't think it is much," he said. "But the landlord of your house at Windsor, who is a friend of my old tutor, Canon Bulman's, found an old letter of mine to you, which you had lost and left behind you. There was not much in the letter, but still it might be made to mean things which I certainly was not thinking of when I wrote it; and the idea of Mr. Snagg, who is opposed to me politically, was to make a scandal of the matter, so as to get me to resign my seat. But don't be alarmed about that. The Canon has spoken seriously to him—the Canon who is the head of the League to which this man belongs—and I am going to-morrow to see him, and get it back. But I want to know if you have any other letters of mine, and still more, if you think it possible that you have lost any."

He had certainly put the case to her in the mildest way he could; but she listened to him with a self-possession which, even considering this, surprised him. She at all events showed nothing that appeared either consternation or confusion. On the contrary, she began with a slight puckering of her forehead, to answer the question which he had asked her, in its direct and literal meaning.

"I knew," she said presently, "that there was one letter which I had lost, but I am sure there was no other. Most of your letters I have kept. I should not like anybody to see them; but except in one or two—and those I burnt— there was never a word which an enemy could have taken hold of. The reason was, dear, the way in which you have always thought of me. Reggie—Reggie, that speaks very well for you." And she leaned across the table, stretching out her hand to him.

He rose and went round to her. At the action she slightly started. "Don't be afraid," he said; "I am going to do one thing only. I am going to stoop down and kiss you once lightly upon your forehead. I am going to kiss you as a brother might. Perhaps it would have been better had I never been anything but that. And yet, Pansy, though I say this, I cannot bring myself to feel it." She pressed his hand to her lips, returning him his sole caress. Then he left her side and went back to his seat.

"Well," he said, "this is the reason why I came down to see you. I thought it right to tell you. I shall go back relieved. Yes, Pansy, and more than relieved. I believe you like me still; and as for me, I know—I lately have had many means of knowing—that you are the dearest thing I possess in the whole world."

"Ah!" she exclaimed, half crying, half smiling, "you mustn't tell me that you like me better than—— "

"I don't know," he said. "I think bettter even—— But we three are all one. I wish we could live together. And now," he went on, "come and show me your castle. I must go back at four, and this evening I return to London."

"To London!" she ejaculated, as if the idea had never before struck her. "And I shan't see you again! Can't you stop and dine, and be for a day or two at the hotel? 1 shall be quite alone for at least two days longer."

"I am going," he said, "to-morrow morning to get the letter back from the Canon. The other things he has said are nothing—they are mere talk; but if a day or two later you would like me to come down, I will come for a night or two nights. You shall telegraph and tell me if you would like it. Come, dear, and I will be happy with you for an hour amongst your own battlements."

She took his arm for a moment, and they moved together towards the door; and then, both pensive, they started on their tour of sight-seeing.

By the time he left the castle the early dusk had fallen, and the wind was more wild than ever. All the breath of the Atlantic was bellowing up the Bristol Channel. The fly-driver, blinded by the rain, was compelled to go very slowly; and the fly, on one windy eminence, was caught by a gush so strong that it actually was blown over against a hedge, and only pushed back with difficulty. Pole's first question at the hotel was about the evening post from London. He was informed that it had just arrived, and the waiter handed a letter to him. It was the one he expected, and he retired upstairs to read it.

"DEAR MR. POLE." thus the Canon wrote, "I was on the point of communicating with you when I received your letter. The additional evidence of which I spoke has been just forwarded to me in writ·ng. It is the circumstantial evidence of a servant at Laburuum Lawn, who is prepared to swear to having seen conduct on your part, which I need not particularize, as you will be able to do so for yourself; and which, taken in conjunction with your letter, would suffice to prove your guilt before any jury in the world.

"My wish is, however, to temper justice with mercy; and I may inform you that I have persuaded my colleagues to leave the matter entirely in my own hands, they having given their word that they will be guided implicitly by me. The specific object of our League is to purify public life, and not primarily to inflict punishment on offenders. I herewith inform you, therefore, on the League's behalf and my own, that we, without requiring of you any protestation of innocence, any admission of guilt, or any promise of amendment, will agree to take no further cognizance of your past conduct, if you on your part will undertake to fulfil one condition. This condition is that before Parliament reassembles you apply for the Stewardship of the Chiltern Hundreds, and engage not to offer yourself, for the next seven years, as a parliamentary candidate in any constituency whatsoever.

"If you are in earnest in your wish to save a sinful woman's reputation, you will not hesitate in accepting these lenient terms; and if you accept them, I must say I am convinced that you will keep to them. I know you to be a liar and an adulterer, but I still believe you to be a gentleman.

"I trust that what it still remains for me to say may not really be necessary. In the event of your refusing my mediation, on the terms just mentioned, one of my colleagues, at all events—even if we should not act as a body—will communicate with the lady's husband as soon as ever he returns from America; and I leave you to yourself to conjecture the probable consequences. My hope is that I shall see you the day after to-morrow at eleven o'clock; when, on receiving the required promise from you, I will hand you back your letter.—Yours truly,

"RANDAL BULMAN."

To this, without a moment's hesitation, Pole wrote the following answer :—

"DEAR CANON BULMAN—
"I will return you the sole compliment which your conscience allows you to pay me. I believe you to be,

according to your lights, a gentleman, even though you have failed in your original promise about my letter; and as such I must ask you to interpret my answer to your proposal. My letter, which, innocent as it is, involves the reputation of another person, practically represents to me that other person taken captive by brigands; and you ask me, on the brigands' behalf, to give up my whole career as a ransom. I assent to your demands. You shall have your ransom in full; and I will call to-morrow and receive my letter at your hands. Considering that I am in your eyes what you call a ' bestial sensualist,' I will ask you to do human nature the justice to notice that such bestiality does not incapacitate a man from sacrificing himself to the interests of another, who, I fully believed, when you first approached me in this matter, cared for him so little that she would not have shed a tear for him if he were dead. You mentioned eleven o'clock as the hour at which you would expect me. It will be simpler for me to sleep to-night at Reading; so I will call and get the business over as soon after your breakfast as possible.—Faithfully yours,

"R. POLE."

This he posted in the mail train by which he travelled, knowing that it would be delivered at the Canon's house next morning an hour or two before his own arrival. That it would not by that time reach the Canon himself was a possibility he had not considered; yet, owing to peculiar reasons, such happened to be the case.

CHAPTER XLVI.

AT the very moment that Pole was driving in the gale to the railway station from his hotel, the Canon was sitting himself down before a tureen of thick ox-tail soup; and his two parlour-maids, with noiseless and soft dexterity, were busying themselves, one at the sideboard cutting him a square of bread, the other holding the tureen-cover, while he made use of the ladle. For some time past the Canon had been eating little. His financial anxiety had tugged so hard at his heart-strings that, even when it relaxed on his hearing more hopeful news. his system remained disordered; and even his sermons and the work of his League, instead of making him hungry, killed his appetite by excitement. But to-day both his mind and body were recovering their normal tone. A highly satisfactory letter in the morning had reached him with regard to Dr. Clitheroe, and he confidently expected that that evening, or the following morning, his capital, in some form or other, would be brought to him by a special messenger. The preceding day, however, had also brought its triumph—not, indeed, a triumph of finance, but a triumph for the cause of righteousness, which had been accomplished by his own diplomacy, and a record of which had been duly sent forth in the shape of the ultimatum just received by Pole. Pole, he felt, had now been completely conquered by the League, and conquered in a manner so adroit that even worldlings could not cavil at it.

The Canon reflected on this as he drew up his soup between his teeth, and experienced a sensation which had by this time become strange to him—the grateful sensation of hunger being assuaged by food. His soup and his consciousness of conquest together made him generous. "It is true," he said mentally, "that the man has made a beast of himself, and yet, according to his own distorted lights, he has acted like a gentleman. He shall see that I can be as good a gentleman as he." The Canon in his speeches was always denouncing gentlemen. It was curious how he clung to the thought that he was himself the accursed thing.

As he drank no wine, he did not sit long over his meals When he began to peel his apple he turned to his maid Sophie, who was always unobtrusively hovering about his chair, and, touching her arm kindly, said, "Poke up the fire in the library. Go now—that's a good girl. I'm coming in directly."

Amongst his many growing gentilities he had never introduced a manservant. He was a man who in his own house felt more at ease among women.

He found the girl in his library still busy at the fire. "That's right," he said. "That is a famous blaze. I had a touch before dinner of my old enemy, the toothache. It's all right now; but a cold room brings it on again." The girl departed, and the Canon seated himself in the glow. He looked about him with a feeling of unutterable relief. Even if he should have lost something by Dr. Clitheroe, the bulk of his fortune, he reflected, at all events, would be saved. His chairs, his expensive bookcases, his books, and his walls became his own again. They lately had acquired a habit of becoming, as it were, transparent, and he had been chilled by seeing through them a ghastly void beyond.

Presently the door opened, and Sophie reappeared smiling, and bearing a letter just come by the evening post. The Canon almost snatched at it. He knew by the tint of the envelope that further news had come about Dr. Clitheroe; and this letter would, in all probability, announce the important messenger as due on the following morning. But before he opened the envelope the Canon began suddenly to reflect that the amount refunded to him might prove less than he had been anticipating. In addition to the ten thousand pounds, which the Doctor had spoken of to Pole, the Canon subsequently, by mortgaging everything he could —even his own clerical income—had contrived, as he had told his agent, to raise a second ten thousand, which he had committed to the Doctor's care only two months ago. He had been calculating that out of twenty thousand pounds he would get back seventeen, or at least sixteen, or at the very least fifteen. But now he said to himself, "Suppose it were even less than that!"

He put the letter down by him, fearing a disappointment; and sat for ten minutes or so, fencing his apprehensions with his hopes. At last he opened the envelope and proceeded to read as follows:—

"Reverend Sir,

"We find—though for certain reasons we much regret the discovery—that we had done Dr. Clitheroe a serious injustice. Our information as to the matter is exact, as one of our men has just returned from Boulogne, where he has interviewed a head clerk of the brother with whom Dr. Clitheroe did business; and we know the whole details of the very last of his operations. Whatever may have been Dr. C.'s delinquencies, he evidently believed so completely up to the last moment in the success of his own speculations, that instead of putting aside any of the large sums, which, as we lately advised you, we knew him to have received lately, he has not only thrown the whole of this good money after bad, but he has, in a last effort to make good his losses, contrived to ruin his mother—a very old lady—whose purse he previously had spared, and to whose income he had even contributed: for, strange as it may seem, he appears to have been constitutionally generous. We think it as well to save you needless anxiety, by saying that Dr. C.'s assets cannot possibly exceed four hundred and fifty pounds. His arrest, as you will see in to-morrow's papers, was effected early this morning. There can be no reasonable doubt that his fate will be penal servitude; but this will, we fear, be but poor comfort to his creditors, who will be fortunate if they receive so much as a farthing in the pound. We may mention that we also shall be very considerable losers, as the out-of-pocket expenses, which were all that we agreed to charge for, in the event of our recovering nothing for you, will only partially cover the actual expenditure we have incurred."

When the Canon had got half through this, he rose trembling from his chair; and he leaned stupidly, as he read on, against the chimney-piece. His face meanwhile had turned to an ashy white; and when he had finished, the letter fell fluttering from his hand. A cold sweat broke out all over him. He stared at the cornice of the room—a cornice with a deep gold beading; but he stared blankly. Nor did he think. His mind was passive; but his mind, though not his eyes, saw. It was, in fact, all eyes; but eyes bewildered like those of a drunken man. And what they saw was a series of portentous visions that came tumbling together, like scenery drawn across a lurid stage, without any order, and sometimes upside down. He saw his house, like a castle of cards, fallen about his ears; he saw his bankruptcy made the heading of paragraphs in newspapers. He saw that all his desirable friends were hidden from him by fragments of his ruin. Then presently he saw things more appalling yet. He saw a Brocken-phantom of himself, enlarged and distorted odiously. He saw himself—himself, the self-chosen champion of labour against capital and against the rich, caricatured as a man who had run recklessly into debt, in order to surround himself with a rich man's luxuries, and exposed to derision—him, who had called all interest robbery, as a man who had beggared himself in an attempt, at once childish and underhand, to secure for himself on his own capital interest at fourteen per cent. In this particular matter he had up to now justified himself, by arguing that wages were exceptionally high in Australia; and that unlike the slave-drivers of Europe, the employers of Australian labour enriched their labourers instead of defrauding them. He had also told himself that the right to the enjoyment of interest depended on who enjoyed it; and on the life which it was used to nourish. But these poor pleadings he now could not even remember.

After a time he tottered a little as if he were dizzy: and for a moment there gleamed before him a sunny mirage of cricket-fields, in which he had struggled to train young men to healthy exercise. Then he pressed his hand to his eyes, glared at the furniture, and sank heavily into a chair. Here he lay in a sort of semi-stupor, from which at last he was roused by a miserable sense of sickness. Close beside him was a bell. He pulled it with spasmodic effort, and presently Sophie entered with a smile of inquiring willingness. She had always been singularly attentive to him. Her smile was some faint comfort.

"I am rather ill," he said, making a faint endeavour to raise himself. "Be quick, and bring me up a small bottle of Burgundy. And Sophie—stay—just see if that is shut."

"What, sir?" said the maid, who was now standing close to him. As if too feeble to speak, he took hold of her wrist, and pulled her past him towards the window.

"It's shut, is it?" he said. "Thank you. I fancied there was a draught, which begins to bring back my tooth-ache. And now the wine. Be quick, please."

The bottle was brought, together with a large wine-glass. At the sight the Canon raised himself, and eagerly helped the maid in her struggle with the cork and corkscrew. The purple fluid came jerking itself into the glass slowly. The fume of the vineyard rose from it to the Canon's nostrils. He swallowed it greedily, and sank back as if refreshed. The maid left him with the bottle and the glass beside him. His eye followed her figure till the closing door hid it.

The Canon for the last twelve years had rigidly abstained from alcohol, with the exception of the sip of sherry he had taken in the lawyer's office. The effect of the wine was in consequence all the stronger on him. It was like a rousing hand laid suddenly on his shoulders. It gave him a better heart for facing the facts of his situation; or was it, he asked himself, actually helping him to forget them?

He drained a second glass. He rose from his chair and warmed himself. The thoughts which had been so lately overwhelming him were still close at hand. He could see them in the obscurity that surrounded the confines of his consciousness, like wild beasts or savages in a midnight forest; but something like a ring of fire seemed to be holding them back. They might attack him again to-morrow. They were not attacking him now. He took from a box one of his best cigars, and smoked it with an epicurean pleasure in every whiff of flavour. A quarter of a glass still remained in his bottle. He drank this at a gulp; and closing his eyes to circumstances he began, as he smoked, to consider what was afoot within him, just as though he had been listening to a singing in his own ears. He still was conscious of his life having been shrouded in sudden darkness, but his sense grew stronger of that fire, half golden, half rosy, which immediately surrounded himself, and which the darkness did but beautify. It did not fall from heaven; it came glowing up out of the ground. There seemed to him to be warmth in it—a dancing and companionable madness. He rang the bell again, with a brisker movement than before. "Sophie," he said to the maid, "another bottle of that wine. I shall be better presently, Sophie."

She looked at him over her shoulder as she went out of the door. Her glance became part of the vague kindliness that seemed to be thickening round him, and was almost turning into exhilaration. "When will she come back?" he thought. "She is a very long time." And he welcomed the sound of the door handle, when he heard it touched by her, as though he were a wounded man in the desert, who was feeling that his friends had abandoned him.

"That's right," he exclaimed, when she entered bearing the bottle, which, as the wine was old, she handled with great care. In this case, also, the cork, when she tugged at it, proved refractory. "Dear me," said the Canon, "don't you try. Give it to me, Sophie. Those little hands of yours can hold a plate or a dish, and they can dust my books nicely; but they were never made to uncork bottles of

Burgundy. Give me your hand. Do you see—you should hold the corkscrew so, and here we are—out at last! Did you ever taste Burgundy? Would you like to try a little? Here—take a sip."

The girl's eyes were at once good-natured and impudent. She did as the Canon told her; and meanwhile she half seated herself on the arm of the chair from which he had risen. His eyes wandered from her, and looked round the room. A little while ago all the furniture had been transparent—had been but a shadow interposed between him and desolation. Now it was once more solid, with the warm firelight playing on it. All the friendly physical relations of life were coming nearer to him to shelter him, and were offering him—so it seemed to him—a sister's cheek. He looked again on the girl; and his thoughts with a sudden speeed, were wheeling round with spangles on them, like riders and horses in a circus.

"Now, sir," she said, "for you," and held the glass out. to him. Her eyes had grown brighter than they had been but a few minutes ago. Her consciousness was being invaded with various visions and images. Amongst these was a vision of increased wages—a vision which glowed before her like the crucible of a mediæval alchemist. She also liked the Canon, who had been always kind to her; and at this crisis of his life she understood him better than, till some minutes later, he understood himself. Self-understanding came to him soon enough, when she had rushed from the room crying, and left him in his library alone.

He stood on the hearthrug, rigid as if he had been turned to ice. He no longer knew himself. It is said that a man with his arm between a lion's teeth feels at the time no pain. He only wonders when the pain will begin. The Canon had fought with his own nature for years, more savagely than Paul fought with beasts at Ephesus; and suddenly his footing had betrayed him, and his body had been in the beast's jaws. Presently he moved from his place with the rickety gait of an automaton, and threw himself forwards into one of his armchairs kneeling, and battering his forehead with a mad vehemence into the cushions. He drew in his breath as if in extreme pain; and a sound like the Englishman's convenient monosyllabic oath came through his teeth as an involuntary hiss of pain. The

unhappy man started as though he had shocked himself by
some atrocious blasphemy; and, clasping his hands together,
and stretching out his arms, he exclaimed, "Oh God, I have
sinned, and I know not what to do with myself. Forgive
me my trespasses," his voice went on almost automatically.
But then he stopped. He had risen by this time from the
chair, and a rush of thoughts, sharp and clear as steel, cut
their way into his convictions. They were not selfish
thoughts, though it might seem that he had every temptation to selfishness. The moments that followed, indeed,
were amongst the best and the noblest of his life. His
thoughts were of his attack on Pole, of the stolen letter, of
those indirect threats against a woman, and Pole's own
readiness to sacrifice anything in order to shield that woman
against a possibly undeserved menace. "And if it were
deserved!" thought the Canon. "My God—what then?"
His contemplation of his own situation had thrown him off
his balance. His glance at the situation of another had
restored him, for the time at least, to his normal vigour.
The proposed proceedings of his committee filled him with
a kind of moral nausea. He longed, if he could, to wash
his committee and himself clean.

He seated himself at his writing-desk, and wrote a short
letter, without hesitating for a word, to the landlord of
Laburnum Lawn.

"DEAR SIR," he wrote, "some days may elapse before I
can again meet you. I write, therefore, to say that I have
considered with the most intense care the case we have had
under consideration; and I have come to the conclusion that
we must allow it to drop altogether, as we have no sufficient
justification; or else the consequences to ourselves may be
such as we should rue to our dying day. I shall therefore
restore the letter in question to its owner, whom I shall see
to-morrow morning. Taken by themselves, the allegations
of your female servant are not worth the paper on which
they are written, and I frankly confess I do not believe a
word of them."

He put this into its envelope, directed it, and fixed the
stamp on with a bang. But how should he post it? There

was a pillar-box on the opposite side of the road, but he was shy of going out of the room. He was afraid of his own hall. The window, however, was near the ground. He could easily get out of that. He threw up one of the sashes. The night was clear, but a gale was careering through it, and nobody would hear his movements. He had his foot on the window-sill, when suddenly he saw that a policeman was standing in the penumbra of a gas-lamp, not far off. He whistled to the man, who rapidly approached the window. "Will you," said the Canon, "put this in the letter box?" The man touched his helmet, and said, "With the greatest pleasure, sir." And the Canon watched him, and saw him commit the letter to the post.

He pulled the sash down, shutting himself up again in an air heavy with calamity. But his thoughts were still clear, and the conviction now burst on him that he never could have the courage to face Pole next morning. He would enclose the letter in an envelope, accompanied by a few lines from himself, and this should be given to him when he called.

He proceeded to his work. The strokes of his pen had an almost vindictive firmness in them.

"MY DEAR REGINALD," he wrote. "I cannot see you to-morrow. Come not near me, nor ask why. This shall be given you at the door, or, if you do not call, posted to you. I enclose your letter. Need I say I have not read it? I return it freely. We ask nothing of you—no promises—no conditions. Go on and prosper in your career according to your conscience. No one will molest you, for there is now no shadow of evidence. I dare say there was never more than a shadow. But if any member of the League should attempt—though no one will—any molestation, show them this—the acknowledgment of my own shame. I am fit to throw a stone at nobody. May God have mercy on all sinners —all vile, hateful, damnable, polluted sinners—of whom I am chief.

"RANDAL BULMAN.

"P.S.—I shall post this to you in London, not leave it to be given you. I might be weak and take it back. I am going to post it now—now, at midnight, whilst I am still mad with fortitude."

This, with Pole's own letter, he put into a thick envelope, which he stamped and carefully sealed. And now, how should he post it? Outside in the road were some drunken men quarrelling. Whilst they were there he could not get out of the window. Should he go out through the door? He must do so sooner or later, and by this time all his household would have retired. He took the letter up, he approached the door, and opened it a little way, stealthily. He had no sooner done so than he heard a loud sob. The gas in the hall was turned down very low, but he fancied the sob to come from somebody sitting on the stairs. He was not equal to detecting a certain something that was artificial in it. The sound horrified him, but not so much as another sound which he had heard almost simultaneously. This was the sound of some other human beings disappearing into a passage behind the dining-room, with a quick rush of petticoats.

He closed the door sharply. He suddenly felt all over as if he had been drenched with icy water, and his scalp seemed to be telling him that his hair was standing straight on end. He had been watched, then, all the time! This was the thought that came now on him like a thunderclap. By that time to-morrow his shame would be public property—or, at all events, he would be at his servants' mercy. Not only self-contempt, not only sorry for her he thought his victim, not only financial ruin, but a public disgrace, compared to which financial ruin was nothing, was showing its face like a monster, gibing at him and preparing to bound upon him. He mentally looked round him, with the quickness of a hunted animal, to see if there was no escape. He could see none; but just then an accidental relief came to him. This was a sharp, an almost agonizing twinge of toothache, doubtless brought on by his exposing himself at the open window; and this, at any rate, prevented his thinking clearly. He dropped his letter to Pole helplessly on his writing-table, and paced up and down the room, pressing his hand against his cheek. At last he took from the chimney-piece some medicine, which he had used that morning, and with some success, to assuage the pain. But he hesitated whether to use it now. He felt that pain was a species of protection to him. Then he touched his gum, feeling for the tender place, meanwhile mechanically reading the directions on the label. He knew them very well. There seemed only one choice before him—the choice between pain and his thoughts. His thoughts for the present were congested, they were inert and da.k; but he felt them to be like gunpowder. If once his consciousness touched them they would ignite, explode and annihilate him. Yet he still fidgeted with his gum, and his eyes still fixed themselves on the label. The liquid was to be applied with a small camel's-hair brush. He determined at last to take it, but to take it in a different way—a way which would affect him he neither knew how nor cared to know. He applied the bottle to his mouth and emptied it at a single swallow. Its contents, so taken, were calculated to soothe other pains besides toothache.

CHAPTER XLVII.

FROM an early hour next morning—a bright morning, such as succeeds stormy weather—the brass bell-pull at the Canon's front door was busy. A doctor arrived, and various other persons. The house was pervaded by a sort of subdued bustle, when, shortly before ten, a station cab drove up, and a youngish man, with a grave and rather sad face, emerged from it, and added yet another pull to those that already had been received by the burnished handle.

In answer to the summons, with an aspect of genuine consternation, one of the parlour-maids — not Sophie — appeared.

"Is Canon Bulman at home?" said the caller.

"If—you—please – sir, Canon Bulman," replied the maid in gasping accents, "Canon Bulman—there has been an accident—Canon Bulman died last night."

"Died!" echoed the other.

"He was suffering, sir," said the maid, "terrible bad from toothache. Sophie took some wine to him, and she came out half hysterical to see him suffer so bad. He had some stuff—some laudanum, and by accident took too much of it. I think, sir, you're Mr. Pole. There was a letter left for you on his desk, stamped, ready to be posted to you. I'll give it to you if you'll please to step inside."

"No," said Pole. "I will wait here." And a moment later the large thick envelope was handed to him, which bore the writing of a hand that would never hold pen again. He asked the servant a few ordinary questions, and then told the cabman to drive back to the station. From the feel of the envelope, as well as from its being sealed so carefully, he felt convinced that his own letter was in it, returned to him; but it was not till he was in the London train that he found himself in a mood to open it. When he had read it, he drew a long breath of relief. He was like a man who, struggling with the sea, should suddenly find himself on land. Before long, however, he began to think with wonder—a pitying wonder which had no malice or triumph in it—of what could be the shame or sin to which the Canon alluded. His first conjecture was not very wide of the mark; and yet for some reason he refused to believe it true. Then he bethought him of Dr. Clitheroe, about whom for some days he had himself heard nothing. Then he leaped to the conclusion that some bad news had reached the Canon; and that the shame with which he taxed himself was that of having taken part with the usurers, seeing that usury had betrayed him. A vague suspicion, too, that his death might not have been wholly accidental, crossed Pole's mind, though he did not give it harbour.

But the news of the day were not by any means yet exhausted for him. Having reached Paddington, he was following a porter to a cab, when a hand, amongst the crowd, was laid unexpectedly on his arm, and somebody was saying to him, "My dear Reginald, how are you?" He turned and looked, and close to him was a white knitted comforter, and a tall silk hat, very much the worse for wear, and between the two were the eyes and nose of Lord Wargrave.

"Where are you going, and how?" he said. "Have you any luggage?"

Pole named the address and said that he had two small bags.

"Humph!" said Lord Wargrave. "In that case I'll come with you."

As they went to the hansom Pole mentioned what he had learned that morning. Lord Wargrave's first feeling—though it lasted for a moment only—was the wish that he himself had been the first to hear of so shocking and so sensational an event. Though his own life was unclerical, he had always liked the clergy, especially any scandal connected with them. But, all the same, no part of his personality was more easily moved than his kindness, and the Canon's death touched him like a real tragedy. He had not been in the cab five minutes before he had several times exclaimed, in a tone audible to Pole above the rattling of the doors, "God bless my soul—God bless my soul—how shocking!" adding at last, with a grimace which he could not repress, "When I met him last, at your house, I felt certain he was made to be a bishop." Then, with a change of tone, and something more of his usual manner, "But this," he said, "is nothing to your other friend, Dr. Clitheroe. He, I consider, is really a very remarkable man. I wish I had had an opportunity of becoming more intimately acquainted with him. If you've got his autograph, my dear Reginald, I'll ask you to give it to me, to put in my book of criminals."

"I," replied Pole, "have heard nothing of the case lately. During the last two days I have hardly seen a paper."

"The man," said Lord Wargrave, "was a genius. Of course you know he is in prison. They wouldn't accept bail. Invalid ladies, to whom he administered the sacraments, were his principal clients. No one else, that I know, has managed 'to live of the Gospel' in precisely the same way. He is known to have got possession of ninety thousand pounds at least—and every penny is gone."

Pole, being prepared for the worst, received this news stoically. Indeed, his chief feeling was a certain renewal of the amusement which had already been excited in him by the incongruous criminality of this genial, respectable, and hard-working little mouse of a man. Presently he mentioned to Lord Wargrave that he had been in South Wales yesterday. To this Lord Wargrave responded by grunting, "Much damage there?"

"How do you mean?" asked Pole, perplexed by this cabalistic question.

"How do I mean?" repeated Lord Wargrave. "Why, trees—trees—trees. Every single elm in my best avenue is down. I've just been to look at it. It's ruined my place completely. In the north whole woods have gone. Wales must have suffered too. Haven't you seen that a South

Wales collier has collided with an Atlantic liner ?—that is, at least, the telegram; and a Dover packet has run into Calais pier. Hi!" exclaimed Lord Wargrave, throwing up the door in the roof, and transferring to the driver some of his indignation against the storm. "Brook Street! Brook Street! Which way are you going ?"

During the rest of his drive with his companion, Pole was absolutely silent. Having deposited Lord Wargrave at his door—the well-known door round which a memory of Countess Shimna clung like stale scent to a handkerchief— he drove to his own lodgings, where he found a letter from his mother. He read it while he changed his clothes. "Who would have thought," it began, "that that poor little man could have been so wicked ? But, dearest Reginald, to you it shall make no difference. All that I have is yours and mine. Indeed it is yours a great deal more than mine. Miss Drake had hysterics when she saw about the Doctor in the newspaper; and for the first time since I have known her, I saw her front detach itself from her forehead. It is lucky he didn't get her little all also. And yet I can't help being sorry for him; and I would send him if I could, some of his own patent soups in his prison."

It was a considerable relief to him that his mother took the matter thus. He dressed quickly and hurried off to his club, eager to see the papers and latest telegrams, and also to get letters which he felt sure would be awaiting him there. But the porter, as he entered, handed him two only. One was from his lawyer; the other from Miss De Souza. He looked at both with a certain kind of indifference, and at Miss De Souza's with a feeling not far from shame. He tore it open; but the first words he saw touched him immediately, and he went into an empty writing-room in order to read it quietly.

"DEAR MR. POLE," it ran, "I write to you very humbly, for perhaps you will think that any sympathy from me is a mockery. Indeed I am sure you must despise me, or else I think I should have had a line from you. I feel how wrong I was—I don't mean in refusing you—but in giving you grounds to think—and I see now that I did that—to think that I would do anything else. Try for the sake of all our old happy friendship, to believe in me enough to believe how profoundly sorry I am to learn that the friend who was entrusted with so much belonging to you has really betrayed his trust. I think I feel about it far more than you do. Yours, asking your forgiveness,

"E. De S."

Before doing anything else—before even glancing at a paper—he felt himself constrained to make some reply to this.

"I did," he wrote, "begin an answer to you, the moment I got your first letter; but I thought it was not a fair answer, and I therefore tore it up. At first I thought of you as one who had great possessions, and who would do any kindness except the last—that of selling them and giving to the poor. But I feel now that I have nothing for which to blame you. I know myself better than I did some days since. It is not that I did not mean all that I said to you. But you were correct. I did not mean, and could not mean, all that you had a right to ask. You never pained me but once, and that was when, in my time of sorrow, you taught me this piece of wisdom. It was I who was selfish, trying to snatch at a happiness which, for many reasons, I ought not even to have tried for. I am much touched by the way in which you allude to my losses. I have hardly had time to think of them; but I accept your sympathy gratefully as an earnest of its continuance. Your old friend,

"R. P."

He had just finished writing when he heard behind him a waiter's footstep. "Post this, will you?" he said, turning round to the man. The waiter took the letter, and at the same time tendered to Pole another. When he looked at it, he was aware that something was happening to his cheeks, but whether they were getting pale or red he knew not. As he opened this letter his hands trembled visibly. The direction was scrawled and blotted. It was, indeed, hardly legible. But one thing was plain to him. It was the writing of Pansy Masters. The contents were written in a manner no less disordered. They were as follows—

"Of course you have heard of the collision. I have had a telegram from Milford. A hundred people saved but no names. Is there not a place called Lloyd's, where they know everything? Could you go when you get this, and inquire and then send me telegram? You will know that I must be—it could not be otherwise—anxious. It seems all so dreadful. Be kind and go; and telegraph to your friend P."

Without losing a second's time he obeyed her; various feelings and impulses gave wings to his movements. He did not even attempt to realize what they were. He wished no evil to anybody. How could he wish death? He happened to know at Lloyd's one of the principal people, and learned from him all that up to the moment there was to learn. "Of course," said his friend to him, "there may be other survivors, but here are the names of those that were picked up in the boat." Pole read it through carefully; and then telegraphed thus: "Information as yet very imperfect, but name not amongst those who are known positively to have been saved. Will inquire again here to-morrow, before starting for Glenlynn." A few hours later an answer to this reached him: "Please do not trouble further. Have had telegram sayin; it is known that he was not saved. Will write to you at Glenlynn, but not for few days."

CHAPTER XLVIII.

MOST of the trees round the house at Glenlynn were evergreen; and except for the want of flowers, a bright winter's morning showed through the windows a prospect not unlike summer. The silver on the breakfast-table was twinkling like a summer sea; and the ivory-handled tap of the old Georgian urn was awaiting the mittened fingers of Miss Drake, who had not yet descended.

"My dear Reginald," said Mrs. Pole, to her son, who had come down the night before, "what a pleasure it is to have you back again. I hope you are not troubled about Dr. Clitheroe's mischief. One comfort is that it was your aunt's doing, not yours; and you could not—so far as I see—have withdrawn the money, had you wished to. Besides, I shall always say this — if one wasn't to trust a man like the Doctor, whom could one trust ? "

Pole smiled, and put his hand on his mother's shoulder.

"Look," she continued, pointing to a local paper, at which she had been glancing before her son appeared, "there is a long account of poor Canon Bulman's funeral. He was always an ambitious man—at least so I thought him. I am sure he would be pleased, could he read of all those wreaths and carriages. And to think that so short a time ago they were both at this breakfast-table, and that the Doctor was pattering with his little black legs in the garden ! By the way," she went on, with a faint laugh in her eyes, as she touched a certain thin volume, which lay on the table like a large piece of sticking-plaster, "who is to read prayers? Will you ? I think you ought to. Miss Drake used to do so in Miss Pole's time, when there was no clergyman here."

"Then by all means," said Pole, "let her do so still. It will make me feel that the old life here has never been broken. I will efface myself in the library till she comes and has well begun, or else perhaps she will force me to take the Levite's place."

Glenlynn from his earliest days had seemed an abode of peace to him; until during the three months that he had spent there after Miss Pole's death, all the sorrows of life had, as it seemed, assailed him there; and its unreal solaces been offered to him, and its rewards dropped into his life, whilst the sorrows, as he knew now, had remained with him all the time. But now everything was changed. The pain at his heart—the perpetual secret aching—this at last was ended. His eyes roamed along the shelves, with their faded and gilded volumes; and from them a spirit was exhaled on him as though from souls at rest. He heard through the door, that was ajar, the waddle of Miss Drake's footsteps. A moment later the murmur of prayers began. Then he followed her, and knelt before one of the mahogany chairs, his heart full of a thankfulness which, though it hardly followed exactly in the steps of Miss Drake's orisons, he felt, whatever its nature, it was necessary to express, kneeling.

His peace, however, had yet enough of trouble in it to show him that it was not a dream, but belonged to the world of fact. He had to consider, in consultation with his mother, how far the loss of his own private means would affect the completion of his buildings, and the work that was to be carried on in them. With regard to this matter Mr. Godolphin's advice was sought, and the details of Dr. Clitheroe's dealings with Miss Pole and her great-nephew were for the first time confided to his astonished ears. No human being could have been more deeply moved than he was by the thought, thus brought home afresh to him, of a brother's fall; and yet Mrs. Pole, whose sense of humour was keen, was unable to help smiling to herself at the solemn magnificence of his grief, which made him, with his beard, as she said to her son afterwards, look something like the Deity, in an old picture, creating Eve, or contemplating the fall of Adam. Of the genuineness of Mr. Godolphin's character Mrs. Pole and her son had, of all people, least reason to doubt. "For a little property of my own," he said, "not far from London, I have just been offered by a builder a rent which, I confess, astounds me. Allow me to consecrate this piece of unearned increment by applying to your good work the first year's rent at all events. Come, Mrs. Pole and Reginald," he continued, as he laid his hand on his heart, and showed the glitter of his large Apostolic ring, "I have never yet asked a favour of you, though you have shown me so many kindnesses. Do not refuse this. To this small extent let me be a humble sharer in your benevolence."

. It was impossible to refuse such an offer. The day after it was made a letter arrived for Pole, deeply edged with black. "I know," it said, "you will forgive me for not having written to you before. It was not that I did not want to. But this has been so sad—so terrible. It has frightened me—you know. I dare say you will be kind, by-and-by, and find some means to come and see me, for I have nobody to ask advice of. The children—and especially my darling little boy—have been suffering these last few days. This house is so cold now, and there are draughts everywhere, and I cannot keep him warm enough. I think in a day or two we shall have to go to Tenby, which is not very far off, and take some lodgings. I don't fancy that we shall be at all rich. It would be easy for you to come there, for there are hotels."

That day at luncheon Pole said to his mother, " Did I ever mention to you a friend of mine whom I knew in Germany ? She was Mrs. Price Masters then. She is Lady Price Masters now."

" I think you did," said Mrs. Pole; "that is five years ago. You said, if I remember, that she was a very nice pleasant woman."

" I mention her," said Pole, "for this reason. She has lost her husband. He went down in the *Arctic*. It was a very unhappy marriage, so we need not pity her for her loss. But I had a letter from her this morning, and she tells me that her children are ill. Her home is over there in Wales, in an odd old ruinous castle, and she talks of taking them to Tenby, so as to give them a warm lodging. I thought if you liked the idea we might ask her to bring them here."

The idea of the children touched Mrs. Pole at once; and after some discussion of the matter between her and her son, it was agreed that she should herself write to Lady Masters, and ask her to share at Glenlynn the warmth and the shelter of a house in which many little children had thriven in years gone by, and which was now too quiet to jar on the most recent sorrow. Pole also wrote himself, adding his own plea.

Each letter duly received its answer—answers whose artless wording was tremulous with shyness and acceptance. " For my children's sake," said the writer to Mrs. Pole, " I cannot refuse your kindness. Your son once was very kind to me when I was in very great difficulties; and for your own kindness, I believe I shall thank you best by believing that you mean it. I am very grateful. I hope you will not dislike me. My little boy is so ailing. Would you let us come on Friday, and we would not trespass on your goodness for very long ? "

" I am sure, my dear Reginald," said Mrs. Pole, when she read this, "that your friend must be a nice woman. I shall like her better than Shimna, though she, as you know, quite captivated me. But she—I can't help thinking now —was more or less of a little minx. Friday—— " she continued. " Lady Masters says Friday. Mr. and Mrs.

Godolphin dine with us that evening. Do you think that she would mind meeting them? At all events, I will tell her that a clergyman and his wife are coming; so if she likes it, she can put off her arrival till Saturday."

Lady Masters, however, expressed no such wish. She arrived on Friday as she had proposed, and Po'e met her and her party at the Lyncombe station. It was dark when the train arrived, and during the long drive the moorland grew wild with moonlight, showing through the windows of the carriage its headlands and tracts of wilderness. Lady Masters, who had a young step-daughter opposite to her, could say little to Pole, her other companion, except to exclaim at the aspect of the strange country they were traversing; and when they began to descend the zig-zag carriage-drive to Glenlynn, the step-daughter and she, both of them, yielded to the same excitement. "To-morrow," said Pole to the girl, "I will take you for a walk in the woods, and will lend you Grimm's Tales, which will tell you about the dwarfs who live in them."

Till they reached the house and entered the lighted hall, where a peat fire glimmered on the busts and china, and filled the air with a subtle smell of the moorland, Pole had not had an opportunity of seeing his friend clearly, and he could hardly restrain some expression of admiration when he saw her black-gloved hands lifting her black veil, and the rose of her face became visible, soft and fresh and tender, with its fringe of curling hair ruffled childishly by her journey. Just at this minute Mrs. Pole came downstairs quickly; and Pole saw her start, touched by its unexpected beauty. He had never heard his mother's voice more musical than it was when she greeted the young and half-shrinking widow. Then presently came a small cry from somewhere, and a little boy was seen clinging to his mother's dress, and asking her with his eyes where he was and what had happened to him. "You beautiful little boy!" exclaimed Mrs. Pole, with enthusiasm, and, stooping down, took him up in her arms, which had not forgotten the skill taught to them by her own son.

An hour and a half later the front-door bell jangled, and the old butler was announcing Mr. and Mrs. Godolphin, whom Pole had intercepted in the hall, in order to tell them that they were about to meet the widow of one of the victims of the last collision in the Atlantic, and that it would be well for them to avoid, if possible, the subject of accidents at sea. The result of this caution was not exactly what Pole intended; for though it had the effect of keeping them from the forbidden subject, it made Mr. Godolphin say, "How do you do?" to Lady Masters with an intonation precisely similar to that which he would have used had he been breaking to her the news of her husband's death; and his wife also endeavoured with conscientious care to render her accents lachrymose with unworded sympathy. Of all results this was the last that Pole desired. He accordingly did more than he would have thought of doing otherwise to give the conversation a light and cheerful tone; and in this at last he succeeded. Mr. and Mrs. Godolphin had both of them a fountain of gaiety, the source of which lay deep in their guileless consciences, and was always ready to well up and display itself whenever they felt themselves in a sufficiently intimate circle. Their humour was possibly not in the best of taste, but for this very reason it was calculated to excite in others a deeper sense of amusement than even its own merits justified. Dinner had accordingly not proceeded very far before Mrs. Godolphin, having discarded her tearful accents, was informing Mrs. Pole that her husband slept not infrequently in his chair, by announcing that "dear Sunderland owed her five pairs of gloves;" and she intimated that her son was approaching marriageable age by declaring that very soon "he would be looking out for Mrs. Suitable;" whilst Mr. Godolphin, despite the majesty of his decorum, showed that his consort's humour was by no means uncongenial to his own. Lady Masters, whose hilarity was naturally not remarkable, could not forbear smiling at some of these simple sallies; and Mr. Godolphin, as he drove home with his wife, declared her to be "even more fascinating than the beautiful Countess Shimna." He had indeed at parting been successful with a witticism of his own. Lady Masters had accompanied Mrs. Pole and her son to the front door when the two guests were departing, so as to see the wonderful brilliance of the moonlight that was to light them home — an attention which Mr. Godolphin had artfully encouraged them to bestow on him, in order that Lady Masters might be impressed with the beauty of his horses. "This one," he said to Mrs. Pole, "does all the work up hill.

Mrs. Godolphin declares that the off-horse is much too fat.
Do you know, Lady Masters," he said, turning to her, "what
we call them?   We call them Flesh and Spirit.   Good night
—good night.   Now, wife, you must get in, please."   And
out of the depths of the carriage had come Mrs. Godolphin's
voice, exclaiming, "I tell dear Sunderland that he's growing
dreadfully naughty."

"Pansy," said Pole, next day, "I have many things to
tell you, but I will tell them to you by-and-by.   To-day let
us take the children and wander about the gardens—gardens
which even now are as much yours as mine; and to-morrow
morning we will go to Mr. Godolphin's church."

He was too full of the new life that was dawning for him
to do more than glance at the newspapers, which generally
he read with care.   Had he done so, he would have known,
as he went along the roseless walks, which now for him had
roses brighter than those of any visible garden—as he went
along the walks with the one woman by his side who had
made him feel that life without her was nothing, and as
he watched the delighted movements of the little boy who
accompanied them, he would have known that the day
previous had been the day of the trial of Dr. Clitheroe, and
that the sentence pronounced on him had been seven years'
penal servitude.   Mr. Godolphin knew this.   He had read
the trial at breakfast; and throughout all the rest of the
day tears, which were not unmanly and not idly sentimental,
had been taking the liberty, at intervals, of mounting to his
sacerdotal eyes.

The results of his sorrowful meditations showed themselves the following day, when he mounted his pulpit, a d
with an audible tremor in his voice, not unlike that which
had distinguished it during his sermon after Miss Pole's
death, he chose for his text the parable of the Pharisee and
the Publican, and warned his hearers against judging others
hardly.   In his arguments and his language there was
nothing that could be called original, except one thing only;
and that was the manner in which they were uttered.   There
was a passion, an unconscious pathos, in them, which carried
them to h.s hearers' hearts; and amongst his hearers not
the least moved was Pole, when he heard the sermon conclude with a certain memorable saying which he himself had
once quoted to Canon Bulman.

"I will not," said Mr. Godolphin, with an amount of logical perspicuity which is frequently wanting in exhortations on the same subject, "I will not ask you to tell yourselves, when you witness a brother's fall, that had you been subject to his temptation you would necessarily have fallen likewise, for that would be fatalism and a denial of man's free will; but I will ask you first to remember that in your sinful brother's life there may be many secret virtues of which you yourselves know nothing—gentleness and forbearance, acts of kindness and self-denial, or devotion, perhaps, to some one near and dear to him; and that these will plead for him before the throne of God and before the Lamb; secondly, I will ask you to examine your own hearts, whether you cannot find some weakness there which may well suggest to you that you might—had you been tried equally—have fallen lower even than your brother fell; and, lastly, I will ask you, should your hearts tell you that this is impossible, to attribute such confidence solely to a Power above yourselves, and to say, as was said about a criminal by the author of 'The Pilgrim's Progress,' 'if it had not been for the mercy of God, I might myself be where that man is.'"

Whilst Mr. Godolphin was engaged in giving the blessing, and was stalking back to his vestry to the sound of an elaborate voluntary, Pole's thoughts strayed from Dr. Clitheroe, to Canon Bulman, and the scorn with which he had rejected so abject a view of the human character; and a suspicion recurred to his mind, which had more than once suggested itself, that the Canon's sin and shame were connected not with money matters exclusively, and that his death was of the very kind which, on the platform at Thames Wickham, he had denounced as an impossible thing for any but the most brutalized or the most degraded.

Mrs. Pole that day had been kept indoors by a cold. He and Lady Masters had gone to the church alone together.

"I want to ask you," he said to her, as they were driving home, "to do for me what Mr. Godolphin has informed us a generous-minded Higher Power——"

But she interrupted him, laying her hand upon his arm. "Oh," she said, "please don't laugh. Don't put it like that."

"I am not laughing," he answered her. "I am speaking to you very seriously. I want to tell you that I have many sins to confess to you—not now, but by-and-by; and it was, I dare say, no merit of mine that I did not bring into your life real and great disaster. And all that time, when I thought you were hard and cruel, and had quite cut me adrift, I did my best to cut myself adrift from you. But through all this I have still remained devoted to you. I think you must see that now; and when you know all, as you shall, let this fact plead for me."

She laid her hand upon his, and tried in vain to answer him. But presently she found her voice, and said to him with a dawning smile: "And was I very hard and cruel? Do you mean because I would not write to you? The reason was that I really did not dare. Had I done so at all, I should have been tempted to say too much. I thought you would understand. But," she went on, "I want to tell you this: your only rival was the old simplicity of my life. I feared that, if I went to you or saw you, I should never recover that."

A man who is accustomed to philosophic reflections will sometimes find philosophy intruding itself amongst his deepest feelings. Pole, for a moment, was silent, whilst the following thoughts flashed across him. "How little women know of the pain they are capable of inflicting! Physical pain they understand, and will give up their own health to watch by a sick man's bed; but they are almost as selfish in seeking their own spiritual welfare as men are in seeking their material comfort." There was no bitterness in the thought as applied to the woman at his side. The selfishness he imputed to her seemed to him merely like a form of weakness, hardly to be distinguished from the single-hearted simplicity of a child.

"Never mind," he said presently. "At last I have recovered *you*." Then in his mind another thought shaped itself, which it was on his lips to utter, but he hesitated and did not do so. "We must not forget that our reunion is not of our own making, and that the new simplicity of our lives springs from an accidental grave."

But the feminine nature is less given to reflection. His philosophy was interrupted by a sudden question on her part, which she put to him with eyes shining with tears and eagerness. "Who put that money in the bank? Did you? Oh, Reggie—did you?"

"Yes," he answered; "I did so, Pansy. I can tell you now."

She moved close to him, and for a moment leaned her head against his shoulder. Then almost humbly, she said to him, "I want you to tell me, dear, what happened about Canon Bulman. What would you have done, Reggie, supposing he had not died?"

"He and his friends," Pole answered, "could have proved nothing against me; but they might have caused you great trouble, and dragged your name before the public; so I had arranged to buy their silence at the price they asked for it—to give up Parliament for—I think it was—seven years. I would have given it up for life in order to save you pain."

A little to his surprise she received these words in silence. Presently he looked and saw that she was looking straight before her, with all her features rigid. Then her hands moved nervously about her jacket, and snatching her pocket-handkerchief, she buried her face in it and sobbed.

In the afternoon she said to him, "I want to be by myself for a time. I have so much—so much to think over."

He respected her wish, and did not see her again till he went to dress for dinner, and passed, on his way, what now was the child's nursery. She had heard his footstep; she stood waiting for him in the doorway, and putting her finger on her lips beckoned him to come in. "There is no one else here," she whispered. "He is going to say his prayers. I want you to listen." She lifted the little child upon her lap, and supported him there, as he knelt with his diminutive hands folded, and half like an angel, half like a talking toy, he faltered, as best he could, his miniature Lord's Prayer.

When the little sound was ended, Pole bent down and kissed the mother on her forehead, and the child on his shining hair. "Do you think," he said to her, "that he knows what the words mean?"

"Perhaps not," she answered; "but he feels it."

"And so do I," said Pole. "Which of us can say more? Let us, at all events, do our best for his sake; and we perhaps—or his generation—shall one day again know."

THE END.

THE NEWEST FICTION.

DR. IZARD.

By ANNA KATHARINE GREEN, author of "The Leavenworth Case," "The Doctor, His Wife, and the Clock," etc., etc. With frontispiece. 16°, paper 50 cents ; cloth $1 00

MASTER WILBERFORCE.

The Study of a boy. By "RITA," author of "A Gender in Satin," etc. 12° $1 00

SENTIMENTAL STUDIES

and a Set of Village Tales. By HUBERT CRACKANTHORPE, author of "Wreckage." 12°.

CAUSE AND EFFECT.

By ELLINOR MEIRION. Uniform with "A Literary Courtship." Copyright American edition. 18°. . . . . . 75 cents

GOD FORSAKEN.

A novel by FREDERIC BRETON, author of "A Heroine in Homespun," etc. 12°.

CHERRYFIELD HALL.

An episode in the career of an adventuress. By FREDERIC HENRY BALFOUR (ROSS GEORGE DERING), author of "Dr. Mirabel's Theory," "Giraldi," etc., etc. 12°.

THE HONOUR OF THE FLAG.

By W. CLARK RUSSELL, author of "The Wreck of the Grosvenor," etc. No. 4 in the Autonym Library. Oblong 24° . 50 cents

THE HEART OF LIFE.

By W. H. MALLOCK, author of "A Romance of the Nineteenth Century," etc., etc. 12°.

ELIZABETH'S PRETENDERS.

By HAMILTON AÏDÉ, author of "Poet and Peer," etc. 12°.

WATER TRAMPS

or the Cruise of "The Sea Bird." By GEORGE HERBERT BARTLETT. Uniform with "A Literary Courtship." Frontispiece. 16°, $1 00

YALE YARNS.

By JOHN SEYMOUR WOOD. Uniform with "Harvard Stories." Illustrated. 12°. $1 00

G. P. PUTNAM'S SONS, PUBLISHERS,

NEW YORK AND LONDON.

RECENT FICTION

DR. IZARD.—By Anna Katharine Green, author of " The Leavenworth Case," " The Doctor, His Wife, and the Clock," etc., etc. With Frontispiece. 16mo, paper 50 cents ; cloth $1 00

AN ALTAR OF EARTH.—By " Thymol Monk." Uniform with " A Literary Courtship." 16mo $1 00

SHIPS THAT PASS IN THE NIGHT.—A Novel. By Beatrice Harraden. 16mo, paper 50 cents ; cloth . $1 00

IN VARYING MOODS.—By Beatrice Harraden. 16mo, paper 50 cents ; cloth $1 00

THE STORY OF MARGRÉDEL.—By David Storar Meldrum. 16mo, paper 50 cents ; cloth .   .   . $1 00

A CONFLICT OF EVIDENCE.—By R. Ottolengui, author of " An Artist in Crime," etc. 16mo, paper 50 cents ; cloth $1 00

A MODERN WIZARD.—By R. Ottolengui. 16mo, paper 50 cents ; cloth $1 00

RED CAP AND BLUE JACKET.—A Story of the Times of the French Revolution. By George Dunn. 16mo . $1 00

PRATT PORTRAITS : Sketched in a New England Suburb.—By Anna Fuller. 16mo, paper 50 cents ; cloth $1 00

A LITERARY COURTSHIP : Under the Auspices of Pike's Peak.—By Anna Fuller. 16mo, illustrated . $1 00

PEAK AND PRAIRIE. From a Colorado Sketch-Book.—By Anna Fuller. Uniform with " A Literary Courtship." With Frontispiece. 16mo, cloth $1 00

HARVARD STORIES. Studies of the Undergraduate.—By W. K. Post. 12mo, paper 50 cents ; cloth .   .   . $1 00

YALE YARNS. By John Seymour Wood. Uniform with " Harvard Stories." Illustrated. 12mo, cloth .   . $1 00

G. P. PUTNAM'S SONS, New York and London.

Lightning Source UK Ltd.
Milton Keynes UK
UKHW012232110219
337137UK00006B/1153/P